LOVE
MADE WELL

LOVE
MADE WELL

CLAUDETTE KING-WELCOME

ARPress
ILLUMINATING IDEAS
EMPOWERING VOICES

ARPress
45 Dan Road Suite 5
Canton, MA 02021

Hotline: 1(888) 821-0229
Fax: 1(508) 545-7580

Ordering Information:
Quantity sales. Special discounts are available on quantity purchases by corporations,associations, and others. For details, contact the publisher at the address above.

Printed in the United States of America.

ISBN-13:   Softcover   979-8-89356-574-4
                    eBook   979-8-89356-575-1
                    Hardback   979-8-89356-576-8

Library of Congress Control Number: 2024903162

TABLE OF CONTENTS

DEDICATION

Ingrid, Danielle, Gavin
Your dreams are my first thoughts

ACKNOWLEDGEMENT

To my Sweetie, Charles, I love you.
-A world of thanks…to my family, friends and supporters.

CHAPTER ONE

Less than a year after the death of her father, Marlene became totally withdrawn from the spotlight, and her lifestyle favoring aristocracy, quickly became a blur. In their circle of friends and associates, she and her husband, Barchas, were dubbed the "power couple;" and the weight of their presence spanned pretty much the entire city of Watertown. But those days were long gone.

Except for the patience and understanding of one of her good friends, she used her anger to disengage all communications with her other friends and well-wishers. No more dinner parties were allowed at their home. But as hard as she tried, she couldn't prevent Barchas from continuing to socialize with his main group of friends. As District Attorney, he knew he had to keep up with making appearances if he wanted to maintain the respect and support from his people.

Anyway, Marlene was soon to pick-up on the imminent breakdown in their marriage. She tried convincing her husband to join her for weekly marriage counseling, and he reluctantly agreed to the arrangement. He was deeply concerned about casting any doubts about his prominence in town; and most importantly, the impression he gave, was that life at home couldn't be better.

In keeping with his concerns, Barchas kept telling his wife that he was not to be blamed for the breakdown in their union. However, because he was truly aware of his wife's difficulties with accepting the loss of her father, he tried to be compassionate as best as he could.

However, the very lengthy ordeals of trying to cope, as well as changing Marlene's mind about blaming her sister for their father's death … simply devoured Barchas' patience.

Then, after realizing the animosity towards her step mother, Carolyn, his frustrations grew even deeper. She argued that her step-mother was partially responsible for her father's depression leading up to his tragic end.

Barchas knew better than to believe his wife's argument about Carolyn being responsible for her husband's sick mind. He knew darn well that his wife was carrying a heavy grudge for her stepmother, not because of her father's depression, but because of how quickly she had shut down her idea of making her the new president of the very successful, "Tate Corporation."

"Over my dead body, my dear," A bit harsh on his wife, Barchas would admit; but knowing Carolyn and the grit she embodied, he was not a bit surprised about the way she denounced her bright idea about taking over the company. Barchas still recalled the moment when Carolyn responded to Marlene's suggestion of becoming the new president of Tate Corporation. He was sitting right next to them at the kitchen table in Bluefield Heights. He tried not to get involved, but it was quite a show of the survival of the "survivors." Of course, he dared not remind her of the incident. He was well aware that it would take even far less than that to sink his wife deeper into her depression.

From Marlene's point of view, however, she argued that their marital breakdown grew out of her husband's lack of support, and she accused him of being self centered and disrespectful. Not only was she struggling with finding ways to cope with the loss of her beloved father, but also the loss of Gracie Mae, her grandmother ,whom she had adored completely.

Though was she was never hesitant in admitting guilt for being dissocial and quite often spiteful towards her husband's romantic desires; profanity and name calling from h_m, were indeed unacceptable to her. For years, she had trouble with trying to keep her insecurities behind her, because during one of their arguments, he swung back and told her that he was embarrassed about the woman she had become.

She was deeply wounded by that remark and it pushed her farther away from the public life that she once enjoyed, but it was her doubts about his fidelity that ultimately made her an inmate of her perception. Many nights, in his absence, she would lock herself away in one of the bedrooms and grieve about her miserable life… while her children listened from the outside and wept.

Her demands for apologies continued falling on deaf ears which kept pushing her further away from the thought of rekindling their diminishing sex life; hence the onset of their miseries.

Several months of the marriage counseling continued, but without any progress. Barchas was very clear in telling his wife, that he wanted to drop the sessions as he felt that his participation was pointless. However, he tried persuading her to seek counseling alone, and he conveniently dropped the name of a well known psychiatrist in town. She became furious with his idea and insisted that they needed to spend a bit more time together if he was interested in saving their marriage, which was rapidly going downhill.   Barchas refused to comply with her demands and held his grounds until she gave in and promised that she would consider his suggestion.

Their daughter, Bethany, who was around twelve years old at the time, and their son Monk… about fourteen, agonized deeply from the loss of their grandfather. And things worsened for them six months later, they lost their great-grandmother. Although it appeared that their seven months of private counseling had pulled them through, having to overhear the constant bickering and fighting of their parents kept their progress at a standstill. However, as much as they adored their dad, they sided more with their mother and they wished that they could help to get her back on track.

After realizing the damaging effect to their children, Marlene conceded to her husband's demands of seeking help elsewhere. She would do anything to protect the well being of their children and to see them happy again.

***

Within a few months, or so, Barchas started to see some small, but positive changes in his wife's demeanor. One day, after not seeing her inside the den which was her favorite place for plopping on her chaise, he became a tad bit concerned. Though he thought it was pointless in looking out the back window, he did look; and he saw her sitting next to the pool reading one of her favorite magazines.

She wasn't wearing her bathing suit which would probably shock him into drooling after her sexy body. He'd almost forgotten what his wife looked like in a bathing suit and better yet, her birthday suit. He went and pulled up a chair next to her because he felt the need to compliment her on her improvements since her weekly visits for treatment. He was under the impression that she was being treated by Dr. Freeman, who was the psychiatrist he had wanted her to see; but that was not the case. However, in his ignorance he proudly moved to take full credit for pointing her into the right direction, and he encouraged her to stick with Dr. Freeman. As if he hadn't said a whole mouthful already, he took the risk and hinted that nothing would make him happier than hearing her say, she no longer blamed her sister for the killing their father.

Going by the look she gave her husband as soon as his wish for Chrissy escaped his mouth, he suspected that she was nowhere close to letting her sister off the hook; and he realized that he had just pissed her off…majorly. So before she could start crying and saying negative things that could possibly create a setback in her progress, or maybe start an argument, he jumped back in and comforted her by saying he had not seen her looking so vibrant and beautiful in a very, very long time.

His face lit up as he experienced the immediate change that captured her countenance. Her eyes widened and were bursting with sparkles while her skin glowed around her soft and tender smile. He kept his eyes on her and saw the slight tremors in her lips when suddenly they parted even more and exposed a much broader and captivating grin …one he had not seen in years. It was at that moment when he realized how long it had been since he had touched his wife, or kissed her goodnight, or good-morning, or goodbye. He remained quiet looking at her, but deep within, his guilty conscience was ripping him apart because he knew he was not to be held harmless in the situation.

Of course she sensed that he was doing his best to let peace abide, but for a split second a faded shadow of doubt had clouded her mind about his behavior. However, because of the unexpected compliment and thrilling effect that followed, she became more relaxed and was enjoying the much needed attention her husband gave.

It was at that time it behooved her to thank him for pushing her to giving him the preference of the doubt. And, it was from the same emotion she developed the need to let him know that she had been going to an out of town psychologist, and not the well known Dr.

Freeman that he had recommended. She felt it was best to come clean and let him know the truth.

Undoubtedly, Barchas was taken by surprise after hearing that his wife had not followed through exactly as he anticipated. But in order for him to show what was most important, he smiled and told her that it was quite alright as long as she continued to make progress.

Although a tender moment was starting to develop between them, Barchas was taken aback from hearing the truth after such a very long time; and he became a bit wary of what else she could be hiding from him. He could not help wondering if his wife had found out that Dr. Freeman was also Carolyn's psychiatrist for at least a year after the death of her husband. And if that were the case, he reckoned that she would want to stay clear of the Doctor and any other associates of her stepmother's. Anyway, Marlene knew nothing of the sort. She only sought counseling out of town, because she felt more comfortable with keeping her condition a secret.

That, tender moment which grew out of the little time spent together, soon slipped away, but only in the mind of Barchas'. He did not appreciate not knowing everything about his wife, and at the same time he did not want to badger her about *"stuff"*—knowing how fragile she was. So, with his confidence shaken and in limbo, he quickly excused himself to get a drink.

At the same time, going by her feelings, Marlene assumed that things were looking up for them. Even though they had not made love in over a year, she was confident that it would happen *any- day- now*. She immediately closed her eyes and slid off the *scrunchy* that was holding her hair in a bun. And with her fingers spread apart, she loosened her hair while it fell softly on her shoulders. That loving feeling had not crossed her mind in a very long time and she started seeing herself back in the passionate arms of her husband, again.

While her eyes were still closed, she kept working her fingers through her hair and stopping every now and then to carefully untangle a knot. But to her it felt as if she had drifted off into his caress with his fingers massaging her scalp and smoothing her hair, which was always an arousal for him and foreplay for her.

That dream came to a sudden halt after she heard him hollering to her from the kitchen. He wanted to know if she preferred cranberry juice or grape. Upon that request, she felt even more confident about their relationship because it had been a while since he had tried offering her anything; and she was just as bad.

In keeping with the idea of trying to make amends, she yelled back and told him she's having what he's having. Her mind drifted again, and she contemplated whether she should wait… or, should she make the first move to try to start over with a kiss.

Within seconds of her heightening imagination, Barchas returned with two glasses of grape juice. She thanked him and she took a small sip and placed the glass on top of the magazine that was resting on the floor. He quickly pulled up one of the small tables close by and politely placed both glasses on the magazine.

He said nothing to her because he was still slightly perturbed that she had withheld the truth about seeing a different psychiatrist. So in trying to fill some of the void between them, he picked up the magazine and pretended to browse.

Meanwhile, she remained quiet and wondered if she should be the one to make the first move. Her idea was to …just throw caution to the wind and pounce on him. But her insecurities about herself instantly became flushed in her mind and she panicked. And Marlene could not muster up the extra push needed to get her *"pounce off the ground"*

She sighed and tried slowing down her thoughts; she took a closer look at him while he was still flipping through the pages. She had not realized that he had been *working out* to that extent, and she became aroused after seeing the size of his muscles along with the tautness and overall tone of her husband's physique.

An even deeper shot of insecurity quickly severed her idea of revealing more of her body to him.   She immediately tried pulling on the robe she was wearing in order to cover more of herself. She then crossed her legs and she clammed up again. Her concerns laid heavily on her weight gain and she could not help wondering if he had noticed the difference in her size.

She tried distracting herself from her immediate letdown and she asked him if he could be home for dinner with her and the kids, for a change. He apologized and told her that he had a very important business matter to attend. However, he promised he would do his best to make it home on time. He finished the drink, handed the magazine to her and remarked that she had not touched her drink. She forced a smile and told him she had all afternoon to finish it. It was at that point when he walked away from her without acknowledging her loosened hair that she recalled as his fetish and was always very irresistible to touch.

After getting all worked up for nothing, she lost her appetite for the drink. Without saying another word, she found herself staring at the glass of juice and watching the ice cubes disappearing ...just like her dreams of winning back her husband.

She became concerned about the situation because she was not able to ignore the sudden bout of insecurity that came over her. She then raised her arms and shook them to see if they were giggly, but they were not, really. Her weight gain was mostly in her stomach, thighs and her backside. She then pulled up her robe halfway above her knees and stared angrily at her thighs and started poking around on them. She spread her legs a little more apart to look on her inner thighs. She noticed that she had developed a few tiny lumps and dimples — something she was noticing for the first time. She immediately started pressing hard on her thighs as if she was trying to bring them back in to perfection. But after realizing that she was stuck with the developing cellulites… at least for a while, she vowed to start trimming down and getting her appearance back on track.

Within fifteen minutes after Barchas left to go back inside, she was ready to do the same. However, she wanted to be certain that he had left the house. Quite frankly she had no desire of bumping into her husband, so she stayed back and listened until she heard his car pulled out of the garage.

But, all wasn't lost. As soon as he was gone, she heard what sounded like another engine rolling in. And going by the sound of it, she could tell it was Allora, the maid, coming home with the kids.

Marlene quickly rose to her feet, and vowed to start losing some weight. She angrily kicked over the table with the glass of juice into the pool, and she continued walking around to meeting up with her children.

Allora said nothing, but Marlene noticed that she had taken a second look at her when she walked up. However, her children appeared surprised when they saw their mother walking towards them. Monk was the first to laugh out loudly followed by Bethany placing her hands over her mouth. But her wide opened eyes told them that she was very pleased. They were very proud to tell their mother how beautiful she looked with her hair down… and they begged her to wear it like that more often. That was the perfect timing for that extra boost she needed to pull herself together and take her power back.

Her gut feeling told her that her husband would be calling her in a few hours to tell her to go ahead with dinner without him. So, in fighting to protect her pride, she immediately called her husband and told him to take a rain check for dinner, because the children had talked her into taking them out to a nice restaurant. He commented that he was happy to hear that she was getting out. She thanked him for the comment, but she did not believe a word of it. She assumed that he was relieved that she let him off the hook, and she was happy hearing him hanging up the phone. She could not wait to hear the telephone hanging up, so that she could call Lexa and invite her and the kids for dinner at the Long Ranches Steakhouse.

Except for that one time when Barchas complimented her on her progress, her main boost and source of encouragement came from her children and her best friend Lexanna Mignott. It was Lexanna whom she called, *Lexa*, for short who was always there for her.

Whenever she felt like going to the mall for *"shoe therapy,"* even though she never wore them; it was always Lexa that she could count on to keep up with her and the all day event. Certainly, Lexa was very proud to help Marlene to stay focused on losing the weight and take better care of herself

CHAPTER TWO

Another year flew by and Marlene was mostly back to her old self. She eventually stopped the therapy sessions and was completely weaned off her medication. She looked the picture of health and she was able to find happiness again.

Life at home with the family was wonderful and Barchas regained his status as the perfect husband something he enjoyed hearing very much.

Monk excelled in sports as a swimmer. Aside from winning a scholarship, he also won several trophies that year. He was a terrific kid and his parents were very proud to send him off to College. He wanted to follow in his parents footsteps in becoming an attorney. Bethany, who was the apple of her father's eyes and quite a pretty a girl, took her mother's advice to try out as a contestant to become the next *"Miss Teen* Watertown." This pageantry meant everything to Marlene and if it weren't for her dreadful breakdown, she would have pushed her daughter into the competition from the previous year. Naturally, because of her previous involvement with the organization and helping other young girls, she would never trust anyone besides her best friend Lexa, to serve as her daughter's chaperone. And the only reason why she would do that was because Lexa was also a "Miss Teen Watertown" several years ago. Anyway, because of Lexa's busy schedule as an actress, she was only available to chip in every now and then. That being said, Marlene was always very happy having her daughter all to herself for coaching.

So with Monk away from home and Barchas very busy with at work, Marlene, for the most part thrust all her energies behind her daughter's agenda. Although it appeared that she stayed constantly busy by catering to her daughter's needs, taking her to ballet and helping out with homework left her with too much time being idle.

Marlene spent the next few weeks thinking of ways to do something worthwhile with her spare time.

She thought of returning to her career, as an attorney. But after being out of the field for so many years working for Carolyn and her father, she wasn't too excited about showing up as a *peon* around town, especially, with her husband's important position as District Attorney.

Anyway, with the ambition of making something more of herself, Marlene carefully measured her options. She was certain that at all costs she must keep her three year battle with depression from getting exposed. She was aware of the damages that could follow should it become public knowledge– especially where her husband was concerned. She contemplated getting back into oil painting which would have been her *calling* if she had not taken her dad's advice to become an attorney. It's still hard to believe that outside of the family and a couple of her closest friends, no one was aware of her artistic talent. The massive and outstanding artwork hanging in her house and her husband's office down town, still remain a sight for sore eyes.

Anyway, with her fixation on seeing her daughter beating out all the other girls to becoming the next Miss Teen Watertown, Marlene had very little time to shop around for the perfect spot where she would love to set up as her studio for her artworks. Once she was able to locate this special place, her intention was to let it remain her private escape, where she could explore all of her talents until she was confident enough to show off her *true colors* to the world.

She would have preferred to let Bell Inez who was a realtor and an old friend of the family, take care of business for her, but, in her quest to keep her plans private, she reckoned that it would be safer to handle her searches alone.

After a few months of searching through the real estate section of the Sunday newspapers, Marlene found only a few possibilities. However, there was none of which really that suited her fancy. The idea of finding a place on her own had her thinking that she had failed miserably, so after seriously considering her limitations, she reckoned that it was time to give Bell Inez a phone call

It had been several years since they had seen or spoken to each other. Although Bell Inez wasn't one of those friends that Marlene had deliberately cut off, her unfortunate situation forced her to keep friends like Bell Inez at arm's length. Anyway, going by her old vibes about Bell Inez, she assumed that calling her would be like old times and she would not have to explain too much about the *in- between- years.*

One day, while returning home from getting a regular check up at the doctor, Marlene switched routes. She took the longer way home and drove along Gladstone Drive. It was on that same day she was scheduled to stop by Bell Inez's office to surprise her with a visit and an opportunity to locate the perfect place for her dream studio.

After just over five miles driving along Gladstone Drive, she noticed a *"For Sale,"* sign that was posted on the same side of the street she was traveling. Although she had already given up and was prepared to let Bell Inez take over from her, presence of mind told her to stop and look anyway. And with one hand on the steering wheel, she immediately started digging inside her handbag for pen and paper while she stayed focused on the sign ahead of her. As soon as she came up to the gate where the sign was posted, something inside of her clicked with a deep excitement.

The painted phone numbers were barely visible on the weathered beaten metal signage. She had to bring the car to a complete stop to take a closer look at what was written there.

After that, she stood at the bottom of the hill and stared at the little old house with its front door swinging in and out from what appeared to be a broken hinge. Her curiosity swelled and she was fully charged and ready to go and take a look inside. She anxiously went back inside her car and slowly drove up the sandy hill to park in front of the house. She looked around and wondered if it was safe to go inside. But without any further reservation, she immediately dismissed all concerns and found herself stepping up.... one, two, and then the third red brick steps. Finally, she was standing on the little front porch with her neck stretched to the *max.* And with bulging eyes, Marlene sneaked a peek inside.

Except for the shattered wooden floors, the pale, gray walls and the tiny brick fireplace, there was nothing to attract the naked eyes. But while she stood there with her eyes roving around the space, her vision exploded and it filled her mind with endless possibilities.

At first, she pictured herself spending most of her time there alone in the quaint, little, three room cottage, where she could produce and hang masterpieces, after masterpieces of her paintings. But as her imagination continued to emerge while still peeking inside, it took an even, deeper dive into her psyche. Her strong connection with the space has transported her to a place where she was soon to be possessed with the spirits and the souls of the gifted that have been waiting for someone like her to come along and finish from where they had left off– so they can rest.

Though a stranger to the scene, to her it felt just like one of them as she entered into their world. She brought gifts of many palettes that were loaded with her oils, rich in pigment and vibrant with her favorite colors. And while they stood aside and watched her loading her brush and stroking effortlessly across their canvases, they moved closer and were enchanted by the outpouring of her creativity.

While her mind was still full and overflowing with her dreams, Marlene immediately pulled her head back from peering through the broken front door and waited for her senses to comeback around to face what was really there. She was fearful about stepping inside. The shattered wooden floors were enough to warn her *"do not enter."* So, she left, but with a compelling urgency of returning to minding her pursuits.

As she walked back to her car, she pondered the idea of owning instead of leasing, which was the only daunting aspect with regards to her initial plans. Anyway, going by the appearance of the place she figured that owning it could be just as conservative as paying rent. And after comparing the property with everything else that she had previously looked at, Marlene couldn't shake, that *"gotta have it"* feeling about the place.

As soon as Marlene was back inside her car, she picked up the paper with the phone number and immediately called.

The feeble sounding but welcoming voice of a man answered. She introduced herself to him… but only as Marlene. She was careful about stating neither of her last names because of the weight they carried in town. The surnames of Tate and Sander, in Watertown, came with pride, wealth and power.

"Well, howdy ma'am, Miss Marlene! What time will you be here?"

"Here; what do you mean by that, sir?"

"Oh, I'm so sorry ma'am…I thought you were the new nurse they're sending out to see me. So what is the purpose of your call, madam?"

"Well, I'm calling about your property for sale on Gladstone Drive."

"Oh, Okay…I see. So, tell me, madam. Are you looking for yourself, or, are you a realtor?"

"No Sir, I'm not a realtor. Well, sir, are you the person in charge of selling the property?"

"Yes ma'am, you're talking the right person. Would you like to take a look at it? It's quite a charm."

Yes sir, I can see that. And with whom am I speaking, sir?

"Chase, Barnswell Chase. My wife and I lived there well over fifty three years. But after she relocated to make heaven her home, I had to move away. For several years, many investors have called me about it. But, I won't let them have it, so they could flatten it and put up some fancy office building or big box restaurant."

"Oh, I see. Well I'm most definitely not an investor, Mr. Chase. And as I've already told you, I'm not a realtor."

"Huh-huh. So, what's your intention towards the place, Miss Marlene?"

Sighs followed before Marlene responded to Mr. Chase.

"Well, let's just say it would be my home away from home. How much is it, anyway?"

"Tell me more, Miss Marlene. Kindly explain what you mean by home away from home. Are you from out of town?"

"No sir; I'm a local. It's been several months since I've been looking around for a place to work out of as an artist….but without any luck. So, when I came upon the sale sign, I decided to stop and take a closer look. It's perfect for what I've got in mind. So tearing it down would totally destroy my dream, Mr. Chase. I love it just the way it is.

"Hah- ha- ha! Oh, Sweet Jesus! I like what I'm hearing so far. But I'm the kind of man who doesn't like doing business over the telephone, you see. I'm the kind of man who likes to see whom I'm dealing with before taking things to the next step. So, tell me Miss Marlene, when can we meet to further our discussion?"

"I can certainly appreciate your way of doing business, Mr. Chase. Just let me know when would be good for you and I'd be too happy to comply. However, if you'd prefer to take a couple of days to think about it, let's do so and then I'll check back with you, if that's okay"

"Good thinking, young lady. I like that. Very well, I'll wait for your call, Mr. Chase replied

As soon as Marlene was off the phone she turned the car around to take the normal route back home. She reckoned that after listening to Mr. Chase's drawbacks about realtors and investors, traveling along Gladstone Drive to surprise Bell Inez was no longer in the works. And with everything back to normal again, she wondered how long she could really keep her plans a secret.

Two days, later she called Mr. Chase to schedule the appointment. During their conversation she sensed that he was excited about the meeting, and she wondered if he also had picked up on her heightened interest. That same morning of the phone call they mutually agreed to meet at the property later that day.

However, Mr. Chase had a slight drawback about finding proper transportation to make the trip out to, Gladstone Drive   and without asking him where he was located, Marlene immediately offered to make it easier for him by meeting with him at his home.

Sadly, Mr. Chase was less than a minute in giving Marlene directions to his residence when something he said sprung a *bad taste* in her mouth. By the time he could direct her to take the "Gray Banks exit," a huge flutter and a thump came on and tightened her chest. She opened her mouth and took a deep breath to help herself better manage the shock.

***

It had been twenty seven years since her father moved them away to live in Bluefield Heights. She was happy when they left and she never wanted to look back. She was afraid of facing the memories she had left behind. And she still remembered running away from the bedroom window after watching her mother taking her last breath. She was angry that Chrissy had moved back into the house …one she thought she would never set foot in again. Also, by no means could she deny admitting that the lavish lifestyle she'd grown accustomed to…. helped with disconnecting her from her humble beginnings.

Just to be certain, she repeated the directions back to Mr. Chase and then she was on her way. While her thoughts ran dauntingly she wondered if the address given by Mr. Chase would land her anywhere close to her childhood home. But in order for her to forge ahead and remain focused on her current objective; she sort of brushed it off and told herself, it would be by a long shot. By this she was a bit more encouraged in taking the trip to Gray Banks so that she could quickly wrap things up… and *just get the hell back out of there.*

In less than an hour, she cleared the Gray Banks exit and she was careful in following the directions to finding Mr. Chase. In as much as she cared nothing about Gray Banks, it was impossible for her to keep her eyes only on the bit of paper on which the direction to finding Mr. Chase was written. As she drove along Main Street, her widened eyes kept roving from side to side to notice the huge difference from what she could remember about the place.

But, not everything was that different about Gray Banks. It took less than a few minutes more for her to realize that she was coming up to the "Tabernacle AME Church." That landmark reminded her that she was only a few more minutes away from, 1917 Amsterdam Lane... her dreaded birthplace. She immediately tried fighting off the guilty conscience that was gutting her as she forced herself to keep on going towards her planned destination. But she couldn't get pass the church...she knew her mother was buried there, and that was the closest she'd ever made it since the day she was laid to rest.

She slowed the vehicle and pulled off to the side. She remained seated with a blank stare, but just long enough to get choked up before the onset of the weeping. The insides of her stomach tensed from the bundles of nerves that felt as if they were twisting into knots. And without having Allora or Lexa around to call on, as she would normally do, she closed her eyes and dropped her head in agony. She sobbed woefully with her hands hugging her stomach and pushing against it as a way of hushing her pain. She kept, saying Mama, Mama I'm so sorry! And she kept repeating herself until she was soothed and back to a reasonable composure.

She then turned the car around and drove to the church. She quickly got out and started looking for her mother's grave, but she couldn't find it.

Although the church building remained the same, the graveyard behind it was much different   from what she remembered as a child. She recalled her mother's grave was never marked with a headstone. She sobbed and felt confused as she walked away from the unmarked graves, but she couldn't help wondering if, by chance, her mother's grave could be one of those covered with shrubs and wild flowers.

While she continued walking way, sobbing and feeling ashamed about abandoning her past, her keychain fell from her hands.   She immediately stooped to pick it up, when she suddenly realized that she was actually standing on her mother's grave.   The keys had fallen directly on top of the broken brick marker with her mother's name still etched in it. It was barely recognizable, but the caked in dirt that followed the lines of the etching helped with making it readable.

Her unbelievable discovery pushed her into an even deeper state of shock, grief, and guilt.

She fell to her knees and immediately she started to clear the weeds while leaving the wild flowers untouched. She tried dusting the broken brick footstone with her handkerchief from her handbag, but the result of her cleaning was without any noticeable difference.   However, she felt much better after making her own *"mark."* She then removed her lipstick from her purse and placed it on her mother's the grave, and then she walked away.

As Marlene continued walking back toward her car,   she noticed a difference about her. It was like; an extreme burden had been lifted off her shoulders. She reckoned it must have been way back , in her teenage years, since she had experienced anything so enlivening and surreal, all in the same breath.

She slowly drove away from the church and started looking for the address, according to Mr. Chase's direction.   However, he did not disclose to her that he resided at a retirement home. So after pulling up her car up to a retirement home, she wondered if she was in the right place. And she was.

As soon as she entered the office- like setting inside the huge, colonial design, retirement house, her eyes met with a woman that was sitting behind an old, mahogany desk. As Marlene came closer toward her, the woman appeared a bit uneasy and she immediately erected her posture with a straight face. Marlene then broke the tension with a smile while waving the bit of paper with the address and saying, "I think I've come to the wrong place. Tell me, I'm looking for Mr. Chase. Is this where he lives?"

She was quick to inform Marlene that Mr. Chase was resting.

"Oh, my goodness, I'm so sorry; I should have introduced myself. I'm Marlene and I've got an appointment to meet with him today. Could you please let him know that I'm here?" Marlene said.

The woman, who did not say her name, responded to Marlene, saying, "Mr. Chase had been waiting out on the front porch for several hours. And after not seeing you turn up, he started getting very tired and was asked to be taken back to his room feeling very upset.

Marlene came off as being very humble and apologetic. She explained to the woman that while on her way there she had to make an unexpected stop which caused her to be late. She politely asked if she could be so kind to explain her arrival to Mr. Chase. An about face from the woman told Marlene that she didn't mind letting Mr. Chase know that she had arrived.

Going by his low and feeble sounding voice on the phone, he looked nothing like what she had imagined…except that he was white. And that didn't count, because his diction was a dead giveaway.

Seeing the very tall and large frame, old man, with his shoulders slouched while being pushed in his wheel chair, immediately explained his concern about taking the long trip to Gladstone Drive, where his much sought-after property is located.

Marlene began walking moved toward him with an arm extended to shake his hand. She was smiling broadly and it was plain to see that he was dazzled undoubtedly by her beautiful smile. Although he was slow in raising his arm to welcome the handshake, it was quite obvious that he was trying his damndest to make it quick. However, after she heard him saying, *"ouch,"* Marlene realized that she might have been a bit overzealous in her approach and she quickly apologized for shaking his hand so hard.

She slowly released the clasp and helped him with placing his arm back on his lap while he kept his eyes on her face. She took a closer look at him, and when their eyes met, he smiled and told her that it's nice being in good hands. A chuckle followed his gesture and Marlene did likewise.

He politely turned to his Nurse and asked her to push him back to where he'd sat earlier while waiting for Marlene. Marlene remained quiet and followed behind them to a more private area on the far end of the front porch where they could conduct their meeting privately.

"I thought you'd forgotten about our little meeting this morning, Miss Marlene."

"Oh, no, Mr. Chase, I would never do any such thing. This meeting means everything to me

"So, did I give you good directions?"

"Couldn't be better; that was the best direction I've ever received from anyone"

"Ha, ha, that's what I like about you. You just have a way of making me come alive, Miss Marlene— congenial, beautiful and smart. What more can I ask for?"

Marlene thanked Mr. Chase for the compliment, but she was starting to get anxious about getting down to business. So right after she thanked him for the compliment, she cleared her throat without having anything else to say.

While both of them were paused for many seconds, Mr. Chase took the lead in beginning their meeting.

"Anyway, my lady, I know you didn't come all the way here to try and put a smile on my face. So, let's get down to business. Well, how much of the place did you see?   Did you go around the back and look around?"

"Actually, I did not. I only stood at the front door and looked inside. I imagine it has about two rooms and a bathroom with a small kitchen, but, I could be wrong." Marlene said.

"You're pretty close; except that it has a very large basement with another bathroom. It's just a wide open space, down there. It was left that way so my wife could have it to conduct her business. She was in the arts, you see. Yep, that was my *Winnie.* God...I miss her so."

"I'm so sorry about your loss, Mr. Chase. I know it must be hard not having her here with you.
So, you said she was in the arts; what kind of an artist was she, Marlene asked Mr. Chase, while thrills ran up her spine after hearing that his deceased wife was in the arts.

"Oh my goodness … she was a ballet instructor. She used to take in private students for tutoring. Believe it when I tell you…my wife was the best in the business. I can give you names of some famous dancers who were students of my wife.   Have you ever heard of the Winifred *Lambert School of Ballet?* If you're familiar with the city, it's the bright pink building at the corner of Colonial and *Bridgeport."*

"As a matter of fact, I do, Mr. Chase. My daughter is a student there, as we speak. Wow! How amazing that is, "Marlene said, while showing great excitement.

"Uh- huh, I'd say very amazing, young lady.   Well, fifty years ago that idea started in that same little house you're eyeing now.   And I will not be giving it up to some big investors who can't wait to throw sticks of dynamites in there so they can destroy my reason for being. No sir! Not by the hair of my, *chinny- chin- chin."*

Marlene, though not shocked about his adamancy, was taken aback by the way he came through and solidified his commitment with a fairy tale ending.

So as to acknowledge his strong feelings about keeping his memories alive, Marlene quickly reminded him that she wouldn't have had it any other way. So going by the look he gave her after she assured him of her word, she felt as if her response strengthened his confidence in her. She then tried adding the finishing touches by telling him that "The Three Little Pigs" was one of her favorite bedtime stories.

This was true, but it was her mother who used to read to her. And that flash of memory was quite pleasing to her and from that she was able to share a winning smile with Mr. Chase. And then it was back to business again for him.

"I find it most gratifying to hear that your daughter is getting her training at the school. I'm sure she's going to be a star before long… what a wonderful opportunity for a young girl to have."

"So, tell me a little more about yourself, what type of an artist, are you?"

"I'm into fine arts. I'm a painter. I haven't done much in the field for a number of years, but it's my passion and I'm ready to go all the way and make a full time business out of it."

"I really hope something can be worked out in my favor, Mr. Chase. I'm very anxious in finding out your asking price."

"Miss Marlene, before we start taking about the price, I'd suggest you go back to the property and take a second look at it. Walk around from side to side, and make sure you look at the basement. Then, when you come back to see me, I'd like you to make me an offer. If I like your offer, I'll be happy to let you have it…I give you my word."

Marlene, not expecting to hear Mr. Chase almost saying yes, blurted a loud, "wow" followed by laughing, and telling him thanks as if he were already handing over the keys to her.

He appeared quite relieved from her gestures. Deep within he was starting to find closure from believing that Marlene would keep her promise. However, in trying to show her who was still in charge, he forced himself to keep a straight face while hers was twisting with glee, as she spoke.

Oh, wow! This is awesome, Mr. Chase. I'm going to have to really do my homework here. You have no idea how great it feels knowing that I could be the one to save your dream. I'll be working tirelessly to come up with something favorable so that we both can have a great deal. Anyway, just to give me an idea, it would be very helpful if you could tell me the size of the lot.

"Oh, sure… it's just little more than half an acre. But when you clear the bushes from the back to the lake-view, it's going feel as if you're standing on miles and miles of a private island."

"Lake-view, oh wow, I didn't realize there was a lake back there" Marlene said while Mr. Chase watched her eyes popped with excitement.

"Uh- huh, oh, yes, my lady, that little house is backed up to a lake and the view is second to none. When you're looking out from the basement you see exactly what I mean; and that's why I'd prefer that you go back out there and take a second look."

"Oh, my goodness… it continues to get better, Mr. Chase. So when was the last time since you've been out there?"

"I'd say about year or so, ago. Due to my condition, I'm not able to walk more than a couple steps around my room; not to mention getting in and out of a vehicle. It's just too burdensome having people trying to push me in and then pulling me out. Lately I haven't been getting any calls about the property. So I said to myself, what's the use in trying to go out there. It's not like I'm in any hurry to get rid of it."

"The floors looked a little shaky though, Mr. Chase. I'm concerned about some of them falling apart with me while doing the walk through."

"Oh! Nonsense, young lady! My wife and I built that house from scratch! And we used only the best materials. The floors may look a little shoddy, but they aren't going anywhere. I'm sorry you've come all this way without making too much of a headway with your plans, Miss Marlene. But, I'm sure everything will work out."

"I'm sure they will, Mr. Chase. I'll start working on this right away; and I'll be calling as soon as possible to schedule another appointment with you.

Marlene then got out of the chair and she gently shook Mr. Chase's hands. She smiled and thanked him again, and she left.

***

As soon as she made it back to her car, she became even more hopeful about becoming the new owner of the property. Her hopes were banking on the idea that Mr. Chase believed she would make him happy by preserving the character it was built on.

Anyway, within a few minutes after getting pumped about seeing her vision coming alive, she came upon the church again. She slowed and looked over and said "don't worry mama, I'll be back."

The lipstick she left on her mother's grave was promise in itself that she would return; but not just only for a visit. She felt the need to go back and clear the weeds from the grave and erect a prominent headstone with pretty flowers around it.

As she sped along the highway towards home, she pondered whether she should follow through with her initial plans of not telling her husband about the property. She imagined that keeping it a secret from him with the intent of surprising him later once everything was in place would be a cool idea of showing off her full recovery. However, since she was no longer interested in renting, she became wary about the idea of making a purchase without her husband's input. She reckoned the undertaking, otherwise, could backfire and blow up in her face.

After waiting up more than half the night in bed for Barchas to come home so she could tell him about her big plans, she experienced a huge *let- down* from him. At first he laughed, because he thought that it had to be a joke.   But shortly after another round of laughter, he realized that she was not thrilled about his impish gestures. She painfully rolled her eyes at him while he slipped into his pajama and then climbed into their bed.

An instant silence from Marlene beckoned Barchas to pay attention. So in trying to keep a straight face and show some respect for what she was trying to accomplish, he began questioning her about her ideas previous to his mockeries.

"OK, Marlene, let's say that you're really serious about this *"painting thing"*, why not start from home? There's plenty of room around here for you to set up a studio.   What's wrong with the room downstairs; you still have got all your materials piled up in there, and I haven't seen you doing anything with that."

"That's not what I want, Barchas" Marlene replied.

"I wish if you'd tell me what you really want, Marlene. After all those years of never picking up a paint brush, and now all of a sudden you want to buy some shack across town so that you can start painting? I mean, honey, think about it. What's going on in that head of yours?" Barchas said.

"After everything I've been through, I thought you would be proud that I've come this far and trying to do something positive for myself. All that I'm asking for is your support. It's not like I'm asking you for the money, I'm only asking for your support, Barchas!" Marlene said.

After hearing Marlene's response and the way in which she said it, Barchas couldn't help an immediate softening towards her, but she was too worked up to sense it. Anyway he continued with his queries:

"Okay, okay; speaking of the money, how much is this guy asking anyway?"

Marlene was peeved by her husband's question and she fired back by saying:

"I, already told you what he said about making him an offer, Barchas. It's like you're not even paying any attention to what I've been saying. Look, if I can't get your blessing on this, then… just forget about it! I'll handle it myself."

She immediately rolled over in the bed and tried repositioning her pillows; and with her back turned to him she remained quiet and very disappointed.   Silence returned and lingered while Barchas thought about his wife's decision to get her way, with, or without his blessing.

A more sympathetic mood grabbed his attention followed by a streak of guilt. And with his eyes staring at the back of her head, he moved closer to her side of the bed and wrapped his arms around her. He felt her body tensing and somewhat motionless and he knew then that he'd hurt her feelings much deeper than he'd thought.   He kept his arm around her and tried rolling her back around to face him so he could apologize and start over the conversation on a more serious note.

"Look honey, I didn't mean to upset you and I'm sorry that you took it the wrong way."

"What do you mean I took it the wrong way? You think that I don't know what the hell I'm doing! Don't you, Barchas? You think taking this step of going outside to start something like this, is way out of my league! Tell me it *ain't* so, Barchas…and I'd call you a liar!" She retorted.

Oh, come on now, honey. I can see that you're very hurt and I'm sorry. But you shouldn't make it sound as if I don't want to support your ideas; I do. And I'm proud that you're finally trying to do something other than just being home and running back and forth with Bethany.

"All I'm saying is that I think it's a great idea for you to get back into painting; but from the privacy of your own home." Barchas said.

Marlene said:
"I would really like you to come with me tomorrow to see the place, Barchas. It feels as if you're trying to ruin my dream and it's driving me crazy.   I've never asked you for anything like this before; and this is something I want to call my own. This is serious business for me, Barchas"

He released his arms from around her and pulled up the sheet a little higher above his knees and remained quiet. She rolled back to the original position and pulled the sheet much higher to cover over her head. She remained quiet also, but needless to say her ears were cocked and waiting for him to give in and tell her something favorably.

A few minutes later she felt him twisting or turning in bed and then he started rubbing his feet against hers and he tried rolling her back around to face him, again. Then slowly he pulled down the sheet from her face and she put up no resistance, although she was still annoyed at him. She opened her eyes to look at him and he asked her to turn off the light. It was the lamp on her side of the night stand that he was referring to, but she did not budge to heed his request. So he climbed on top of her and reached over and turned it off. Her pain grew deeper and she closed her eyes again and she wished if he would just get off her, when suddenly she felt him breathing closely to her face. And then he kissed her face gently.

Marlene liked the attention her husband gave, but it was not enough to completely take her mind off her concerns. He kissed her again but from the first kiss on her cheek he realized that she had been crying because of moistness and saltiness on her skin. However, he pretended as if he didn't know. He ran his fingers through her hair and massaged her head lightly as if to adjust her emotions to a more comfortable state. He sensed that she was coming back around, because he could feel her body becoming more relaxed.   He was encouraged by the change and he continued his foreplay in hopes for an early arousal. And while he ran his fingers slowly down her spine, he gently sucked on her lips and licked about her face and neck as if she were a newborn pup to its mother. Her nipples plumped and sent shivers down his spine and his mouth watered with the taste of ecstasy.

He kept caressing his wife whom he had not touched that way in a very long time, and then he moved his lips closer to her ear and whispered to her "How badly do you want this place."

 "Really, really bad, she replied"

She immediately spread her legs and asked him "So, sweetheart, how badly do you want this?" and he replied "really, really bad." She smiled inwardly and responded with her special kinds of foreplay, the ones she knew would drive him crazy until he was brought to his knees. And then she really, really let him have it…badly.

Marlene and her husband had not made that kind love in years, and Barchas was quite pleased about his wife's romantic uprising. And as soon as he was able to catch his breath and come back around from her being so liberal, he was quick in declaring her the winner of the feud.

She rolled away from him and tried resting on her stomach. But in as much as she thoroughly enjoyed that well deserved lovemaking, it didn't take long for her personal goal to surface and rest upon her mind.   She remained quiet and wondered what would happen next, when suddenly she felt him drawing closer, placing his hand on her backside. She didn't make the slightest twitch while holding her breath and waiting for him to come out and say something positive about her plans.

"So, will tomorrow be soon enough for us to check out this place you're dreaming about?"

Although she was dying for him to have a change of heart, she never expected him to be so quick in coming around; and, in full circle.   She exhaled and was elated. Her gratitude was so huge, that she started sharing the story of how Mr. Chase and his wife built the house from scratch and beautiful years spent there with his wife, Winnie. However, while she continued rambling in her moment, it didn't not take long for her to realize that she was only talking to herself, because of her husband's dreadful snores

It had been a week since Marlene and Barchas had gone to see Mr. Chase's house. But before going inside, she was dying to see the lake that Mr., Chased had bragged about so broadly. Barchas followed behind his wife and helped her with parting the bushes with his hands and both were mesmerized by the tranquility and breathtaking view of the water.

He looked at her and she looked at him. She was smiling and barely able to contain herself while she tried *picking his brains.*

"So, what do you think so far, honey?" She asked her husband.

"I think it's terrific. No wonder those guys downtown have been after this place for so long."

Marlene became surprised about Barchas' response and she quick turned to him saying,

"Seriously… Barchas; You mean to tell me you knew about this place all along? How could you? She whined.

Barchas looked at his wife as if she appeared clueless and said, "Marlene, who doesn't know about this place. It didn't just fall out of the sky, it's been sitting there for ages.

Marlene gave a light chuckle while throwing her hands in the air followed by saying, Well my dear, I must have been living under a rock, because as you can tell; I had no idea.

Well, it's hard for me not to know because I drive past here at least twice a week. I'd never paid any attention to it. And, yes over the years I've heard on and off conversations about putting up a restaurant here. And now I can see why."

"Well, now it's going to be mine" Marlene said proudly.

"Wait a minute, Marlene. Let's not get ahead of over selves here. You realize it's going to be very expensive, given the lake view?" Barchas responded.

"Like, how much, you think?" Marlene asked her husband.

"Well, before saying anything further about money, why don't we take a look inside and see what's going on in there?"

Marlene agreed with Barchas' suggestion and they turned and walked around some more and tried entering the house from the back door, which was boarded up. So, while walking back around to enter from the front, they stopped to check out a huge oak tree which Barchas found to be intriguing. However, Marlene was more interested and very anxious about getting inside, so she tugged on his arm and told him to get going.

Although he found the outside to be more favorable, which was because of the lake, he failed to see what Marlene described as a diamond in the rust. He was mostly concerned about what it would cost to make it habitable. He tried as best he could to point out the splintered hard wood floors, the cracked walls, damaged ceilings and a broken water main in the basement.

She saw nothing major about his concerns, and she told him to shut up and to try tuning into the vibe of the place. He then stopped speaking and watched her moved around the rooms as if she were in conversation with the unseen. He asked her, " what the hell she was doing", and she told him that the place was speaking to her, and that was all that mattered.

At that point Barchas inwardly wondered if his wife was on the cusp on another breakdown.

In keeping with his concerns he tried laughing and remarked that he had never seen this side of her before and he asked her if she knew where it was coming from, but she only told him to "shush."

Then in trying to better understand what was going on with her, he changed the subject by telling her how exciting she was the night before when they had made love. She totally ignored the compliment and acted as if she was oblivious to his presence. He found her attitude a bit unnerving but tried his best to suppress his feelings. So he walked up behind her and tried slapping her rump and jokingly he told her that he *kinda* liked the new Marlene that was emerging. He muttered that the old Marlene was not as hot and sweet in bed. After saying that, he waited for her to respond because he was still thinking that something *screwy* was going on in her head.

Anyway, before too long, she turned to him and said "Honey, I am not going to let you steal my dream, nor my future, nor my peace of mind. I know you're thinking that I'm crazy, but this time you're wrong."

At that point he realized that she was adamant about making the purchase. So, in a more subdued tone, he advised that they should start looking around for an appraiser to help with making a good offer. She looked at him and smiled quite pleasingly about his change in attitude. However, because of her impatience she curiously asked him what he thought it was worth. He laughed out loudly and said…

"Look Marlene, I can see how badly you want this, but we're not going to spend a dime over, fifty thousand dollars."

"Come on now, Barchas. You've got to be kidding! That's less than half the price of your yacht."

Barchas thought Marlene's response was quite funny.

"Hah-hah-hah! Let's not start with talking about my yacht, honey. There's just no room for a conversation when you start comparing apples to lemons."

"Oh, by the way…since we're on the subject of the yacht, I've noticed that you haven't taken me out sailing anymore."

Hey, don't start up with that. You're the one who complains about nausea every time you get on board. That's why I don't bother pushing you to come out with me anymore. Anyway, speaking of comparing apples to lemons, let's get back to business; fifty thousand, or no deal.

"Wow, what a nice thing to say, Barchas! It's obvious you're not going to make it easy for me in getting this place."

"Wait a second, here, Marlene. God knows— the last thing I want is to get into a fight with you over something like this.   I'm sure the property appraiser will come up with a fair market value of the property.

So let's just hope he doesn't go any higher than the fifty grand," Barchas said to his wife with a cautionary undertone.

Marlene had no idea what to think about a fair market value, but deep within she reckoned fifty thousand was too much of a low ball, and her husband's warning fell on her ears like water on a duck's back. Anyway, in trying to keep the peace between them, she quickly backed off and told her husband that he was right about letting the appraiser handle the pricing.

Marlene kept wondering what was taking the appraiser so long in getting back with her. It had been almost a week since they met. If it weren't for Bethany's busy schedule with school, ballet and the pageantry, her mother would probably be sitting around and biting her nails from the impatience that was tearing her apart.

Barchas tried his best to steer clear of his wife's henpecking. She kept pushing him to call Joe Farnsworth to find out what was taking him so long, and Barchas was tired of telling her that Joe was the best appraiser in town; only that he was a little slow because of his age. Matter-of-factly, Barchas couldn't care any less if Joe had taken another month in getting back to his wife. But, that was it for her...she could not wait any longer and she decided to give Mr. Farnsworth a phone call.

According to Mr. Farnsworth, it was perfect timing when she contacted him because he had only one aspect of the appraisal left to work on. He was pleased to let her know that he would be following up with her no later than the same day. She queried about what aspect was left to handle and informed him that time was of the essence. Her tone during the conversation was clearly agitating to Joe, and he came back swinging with a ball park figure that dropped her jaw and left her speechless.

As soon as the shock of the news wore off, she asked him if he was sure about the quote. He gladly reminded her that it was only a ballpark figure and that was why he needed a little more time to work on making a few adjustments.

Although she was not thrilled about Joe's performance, she was somewhat relieved after ending the phone call.   She realized she had no choice but to wait for Joe to get back with her with much better news.

CHAPTER THREE

As soon as she was off the phone and about ready to start fuming about her setback, the telephone rang. It was Lexa calling to touch base after being out of town for a while. In as much as she would have preferred hearing from Joe in the moment; hearing from Lexa was a pleasant change of pace. Lexa was quick in picking up on a *"negative"* in Marlene's tone, and she queried if everything was okay. Marlene could hardly wait for her to finish inquiring about her wellbeing so that she could start updating her about her life while she was away making movies.

After carefully listening to Marlene and without getting a word in for at least seven minutes, Lexa finally snatched an opportunity to start talking again. She was anxious in complimenting her dearest friend Marlene on her accomplishments in such a short time. Bu most importantly, Lexa was very impressed that Marlene was able to make the first steps of meeting with Mr. Chase without the help of her husband *holding her hands.*

While Lexa continued with boosting Marlene's confidence, her thoughts raced back to Marlene's home and the stunning *masterpiece* that hung so beautifully in her entryway. She had not forgotten that outside of Marlene's family, she was one of the fortunate few to be apprised of her artistic talent. And out of sheer respect and appreciation, Lexa was quick in commissioning her on the first piece of work to come out of her new studio.

Marlene fell deep in elation by Lexa's kind gestures. She imagined the timing was right to show off to Lexa what was causing her to be so excited. So, she quickly offered to pick her up and to drive her across town to where the property was located. Lexa apologized and asked for a rain check because of a previous appointment to meet with her banker the same day. However, in trying not to appear to be a *killjoy*, she was quick in suggesting that the following day they could meet up for lunch and then go with her to check out the place. Marlene was appeased with the arrangement and she thanked Lexa for the call.

Upon rising the next morning, Bethany reminded her mother about their three- thirty appointment for dress rehearsal at the school of dance. She was glad her daughter reminded her and she promised that she would make it there on time. While Bethany was still sitting next to her mom at the kitchen table, and waiting to be served breakfast, Allora handed Marlene a note.

She immediately opened it and saw that it was from Joe Farnsworth. Her focus changed immediately and she took two sips of her coffee and then kissed her daughter goodbye. Although the note clearly stated that Joe Farnsworth asked to have his call returned, she ignored the request and drove straight to his office downtown.

Although a bit surprised, Mr. Farnsworth did not mind getting a visit from Marlene. He thanked her for coming and saving him the trip from going to her home to meet with her. That was what he had intended to do when he called and left her that message with Allora
Marlene gave a nervous laugh and assured Joe that she was more than happy to save him the trip. However, given the many years of experience, Joe was only too familiar with what to expect of clients such as Marlene. So as to ease her anxiety, Joe left and quickly returned with

the appraisal package along with a much smaller envelope with his bill enclosed

Marlene on the other hand, disregarded Joe's bill, by throwing it aside; as she was completely engrossed with opening the appraisal package. Joe became a little touchy about the way she disregarded his bill, but he remained quietly peeved and looked on as she tried opening the appraisal package.

While she struggled with peeling away the hardened glued package, her impatience deepened and to her it felt as if it was taking too long for her to get to the long, awaited information.. So, while she kept on trying to remove the gummy taped envelope, she looked up at Joe and gave a nervous smile, followed by saying, *"Just t tell me how much and put me out of my misery please Joe."*

Joe however, used her anxiety as an opportunity to gain her respect his respect; so he quickly told her the price was "one twenty nine."

When Marlene heard those *numbers,* the package fell from her hands and her eyes popped with fright.

"One twenty nine?" she asked him, with utter surprise.

"Yes madam, one twenty nine is my price," Joe said dryly, as if he were totally oblivious to her rising ire

Are you sure about this, Mr. Farnsworth? Do you realize that you are quoting a price higher than what you told me yesterday?

"No, Mrs. Sander; I'm certain we didn't discuss anything about my price."

It was then it occurred to her that Joe was referring to his fee for his service. She became uneasy from the sudden change in Joe's attitude toward her. Then presence of mind told her that he was only trying to regain his respect from her.

After realizing what taking place was, her eyes softened as she turned her head to acknowledge the bill that she had tossed aside. And as soon as Joe saw that she was finally paying attention to what was most important to him, he immediately cleared his throat as if to remind her of his objective. She immediately turned her head around and faced him with an apology.

Mr. Farnsworth, I'm so sorry. I didn't realize you were referring to your bill. Normally I'm not like this, but I've been so excited about purchasing the property, and at the same time very nervous about the price, that I've forgotten my manners. Will you please forgive me?

Joe, feeling a bit amused by her reaction, and trying not to let it show, was quite the hypocrite in offering his understanding of her behavior. She quickly wrote him a check in the amount of one hundred and seventy five dollars and told him that lunch was on her.

Joe was quite pleased about the tip. He quickly pulled up a chair and asked her to sit while he grabbed another for himself. She knew she had to be on her best behavior because she reckoned that she was back in Joe's good favor. He asked her to let him have the package back so he could go over the details with her. And then she became anxious again and was tempted to ask him to just let her have the numbers, but she knew better not to piss Joe off again. She tried faking a smile, but her smiles have never appeared to be anything but sincere, because they always came off so beautifully.

Joe looked at the check again and thanked her for her generosity. As if to punish her a bit more, even though that was not his intention, he slowly rose to his feet while she watched him painfully. He then removed an old black wallet from his back pocket and carefully placed the check in the one of the compartments. And then he seated himself again, while she watched painfully from the anxieties that were gutting her.

Finally, it was time to get down to business and Marlene was quite taken aback by Joe's suggested market value of one hundred thousand dollars. Going by the way she was looking at Joe when he pointed out the price to her, he informed her that the house was not taken into consideration, due to its dilapidated condition. So, Marlene reckoned she would be paying out that amount of money for just the plot of land.

Joe then moved to ask what she thought the property was worth. She confided in him that she had no idea, but that her husband was thinking along the lines of fifty thousand dollars. He quickly reminded her that the property was zoned commercial a few years ago which potentially hiked the value. He cautioned that the one hundred thousand was quite a conservative amount, if she were to take his advice and make a full offer. He then cautioned that old man Chase was in no hurry in getting rid of the property because of his emotional ties to it.

You, know Mr. Chase? Marlene asked Joe.

But of course! Who doesn't know Mr. Chase? Well, let me take that back....I should have known better. You're too young to remember Barnswell Chase. But I'm sure your daddy, did. Barnswell's wife, Winnie, became a huge success after she started up with the ballet business, several decades ago. But it was her husband who pushed her into doing it after watching his wife dancing for him time and time again while he played his piano.

Then he paused and looked to the side where a tall pile of filthy files and dusty paper work were located. But judging by his indirect look, it would be more appropriate to assume that he was looking way out into yonder.   He then shook his head from side to side and said "Wow... those were the good ole days. That, Barnswell Chase, was a *helluva* musician. Even, if I have to say so myself.

As if Marlene heard nothing else of what Joe had said, it behooved her to keep him focused on one aspect of the entire conversation…her father.

You, knew my father?

But of course! Who didn't know your father? Larry was a good guy and I still miss playing golf with him. I'm really sorry about your loss, Miss Tate.

So how did you know that he was my father, Mr. Farnsworth?

Oh, come on now, young lady…. word gets around in Watertown, you know. I may be eighty six years old, but I'm still alive and kicking. And, some of my good old friends are still around.

She panicked because she was thinking that her defenses were being threatened. And before finding out what else he might have known about her and her family, she thought it was wise to get going. Most importantly she wondered if he had had heard anything about her nervous breakdown, following the death of her father.

As much as she tried, she could not keep the tremors from showing in her fingers. But she had to do what she needed to… so that she could end the meeting quickly.   She smiled at Joe and told him that he wasn't the only one missing her father. She nervously gathered the documents and carefully placed them in the envelope. And with teary eyes she shook his hand and thanked him for everything and she walked out the door.

Before making it back to her car, Marlene was able to immediately squash the sorrowful feeling she developed after hearing Joe Farnsworth speaking so highly about her dad. She was proud of how quickly she managed to push aside the pain as if it were a slight bump to the head, and then moved on with business as usual. It was at time she had confirmation that she could handle anything, including running a business.

Although Marlene had no trouble coming up with the hundred thousand *grand,* to her, it sounded like a large amount to put out for that place. However, she was not prepared to let the sound of that amount deter her from moving forward with her plans. She immediately used her car phone to contact her husband with the news but, he was unavailable. She then called Lexa and reminded her of their lunch date and their visit out to see the property.

As always, Lexa was a stunning woman. And as her friend, Marlene had no qualms in complimenting her on every occasion. So, while she sat waiting for Lexa to join her inside the car, she began complimenting her on her gorgeous looks, as she strutted towards her.

Lexa, who was a little on the conceited side, and not liked by many, quickly returned the same compliments to Marlene. And as soon as she made it inside the car, Lexa suggested they had lunch at the "Vines" which was a fairly new restaurant downtown that Marlene had never heard of before.

Under normal conditions, Marlene would question Lexa whether she had tried their food, and what type they served, but she had more important things on her mind. Things, like finding her husband to tell him about the fifty thousand dollar difference in his offer. Things, like what he would say if she were to agree with Joe's point of view, and to call Mr. Chase with the full offer. So, while Lexa was retouching her lipstick and rambling about going to see her mother next week, Marlene was speeding and deep into thoughts of what's next.

As soon as they entered the restaurant, Marlene was quick in suppressing her concerns, so that she could properly appreciate the elegant entryway and interior design. Going by the genre paintings hanging on the walls and the background music of instrumentals, gut feelings told her they most likely would be having *French* for lunch. As they followed behind the Greeter to be seated, her eyes were still roving, but mostly at the paintings.   And, as soon as she turned her head to look across the other end of the hall, she saw her husband among a group of people having lunch. She instantly recognized Blossom Rigby, who was one of the several lady friends she had dropped, after shying away from the spotlight several years ago. She immediately became uncomfortable with the scene.

With the exception of her husband, she had never disclosed her insecurities to anyone, including her psychologist. But it was always in the back of her mind that her husband could be unfaithful. She pinned her doubts mostly on his unusual schedules which sometimes kept him out of town for a day or two. Those insecurities developed during the time of her depression. However, over time while she tried to get her life back on track, she was better able to suppress her doubts.

Anyway, after seeing Blossom Rigby sitting next to her husband while chomping on onion rings and sipping white wine, evoked contempt and a reversal of trust that she couldn't control. Her first thoughts from the jealousy she grew were… "I'm going to kill that bastard! I knew it! I knew he was cheating on me all along. But I won't let him get away with it!" Then in her mind's eyes, she saw herself kicking Blossom's ass to a pulp, and making her confess that she was right about her paranoia.

Although she was still shaking from the instant rage that clouded her judgment, she was still able to keep the peace while she nervously seated herself across from Lexa at their table. She tried to relax as best as she could, because she was too embarrassed to share her suspicions with Lexa.

So, in trying to keep things under wraps, she rose to her feet as if she was only trying to straighten her suit. Her real goal, however, was to try and stretch her neck out to the point of getting a quick scan of the others in her husband's group.

They were Frank Roulette, who was her husband's best friend since college, Jeptha Stoddard, Reign Fuller, and Martin Broach... all of whom were attorneys and close friends. Although she was not quite up to date with all the ins and outs of the politics in town, she recalled her husband saying that Frank was on his way on becoming a judge before the end of that year.

After seeing the guys and the serious look on their faces, Marlene assumed then, that it could be an important business luncheon. And presence of mind told her it was best to give her husband the benefit of the doubt. However, because of Blossom's presence which she thought was odd, made her question her husband's innocence. She sat down and contemplated going over there to say hello, and staying just long enough for brief pleasantries. But, by her doing so, was mostly to see how her husband and Blossom would react after being caught in what could be perceived to be the *"act."* However, after not seeing everyone for at least a couple of years, she reckoned that under the strained circumstance the outcome of her visit could result in leaving some adverse effects to her favorable character as a wife, and an advocate for women in politics. And so she decided against it.

Although Lexa was oblivious to Marlene's discovery, she was quick in picking up on the sudden change in her demeanor. And with nothing else to go on, she assumed that it could be something unfavorable about the restaurant. She became concerned and asked Marlene if she wasn't in approval of "Vines."   Marlene was taken by surprise from what she thought was a silly question and she tried appeasing Lexa with an about face.

Except for the internationally inspired salad bar, the food was undoubtedly French. Marlene was anxious in trying the "cottage salad" that Lexa's had been raving about… so they decided to go over and get started with the samplers. Upon arising from her chair, Marlene could not help stretching out her neck again to see if her husband and his group were still around, but they were gone. She was very relieved not seeing them; but still a bit edgy about Blossom's association with her husband.

As much as she tried, she wasn't able to keep Lexa out of her painful suspicions about her husband and Blossom.   And while they were still working their way around the elaborate salad bar, she came right out with it.

Upon listening to Marlene spilling her guts, Lexa became even more surprised. Her plate of salad fell instantly from her hands and went crashing onto the marble tile flooring. After seeing bits of veggies and raspberry salad dressing stuck to Lexa's shoes, Marlene quickly apologized for ruining the moment.   Lexa, however, appeared to be more interested in hearing more about what Marlene had to say, so she didn't mind wearing the salad on her shoes.

After standing around for a few minutes and watching the food losing their appeal, both ladies agreed that their appetites were no longer in favor of Vines, so they mutually agreed upon leaving the restaurant. While walking back to the car, Lexa suggested that they should grab a bite to eat somewhere along the way and spend some time together at her condo.

Although the ladies were very conscious about eating healthy, Marlene suggested that getting some food sounded like a good idea as long as a bucket of fried chicken and chips was on the menu. Lexa loved the idea and she suggested that a few bottles of wine would help even more with washing it down. Marlene quickly reminded her that she wasn't a drinker, and Lexa was quick in letting her know that was why she thought of getting only a few bottles.

Not much was talked about after they arrived at Lexa's condo, because Marlene was mindful about not upsetting her any further with her troubling suspicions.   It wasn't until after she started complaining to Lexa, when she recalled that those two never got along. That was back in the days when Marlene headed the "Women's League" of which all her friends including Lexa and Blossom were a part of.

After Marlene's inopportune resignation which was due to the onset of her depression, Blossom was voted in as the new President of the organization. Lexa was the youngest and one of the new comers to the organization, but she had been a long time friend of Marlene's. However, Lexa's membership only lasted a month after Marlene's resignation; but their friendship remained close. And, over time, Marlene kind–of severed all ties with all the other members in the group.

Marlene was never quite clear on the reason behind the animosity between Lexa and Blossom. She perceived however, that Lexa could be right about Blossom being jealous of her looks and her blooming career as an actress. Though that could be partly true, Blossom's deep-seated resentment towards Lexa went back several years while they were in college.

Back then, Lexa was a freshman while Blossom and her then boyfriend were both seniors at the same college. However, it wasn't long after she got there before Blossom's boyfriend, Granger, began hitting on her. Despite the fact that she was informed by her roommate that Granger was dating Blossom, Lexa could not be stopped because of her out of control attraction to him.

Blossom agonized and spent sleepless nights over losing Ranger to Lexa. And although neither of them ended up with the guy, both ladies ended up being enemies without any apparent chance of reconciling.

Except for a handful of the chips, Marlene did not touch the food. She became very concerned and took responsibility for upsetting her best friend to the point of where she consumed almost two bottles of wine in just a few hours. This had never happened before, Marlene pondered, and she wondered what could have pushed her friend to such limits.

After watching Lexa getting drunk and then falling soundly asleep on the couch, Marlene reckoned that her plan to show the property to Lexa would have to be postponed. So she left her a note saying that she had to leave be with her daughter for her three pm dress rehearsal.

***

CHAPTER FOUR

As nightfall settled in, Marlene patiently waited for her husband to come home. Though daunted by the idea of getting him to confess to what she surmised to be the truth, she was anxious in getting to the bottom of her pressing concerns. Suddenly, thereafter, she realized a change of heart was taking place inside of her. Her priority of getting back with Mr. Chase to close off on the deal was no longer as important to her as finding out if her husband was being unfaithful. She immediately left the bedroom to go to the den and she threw herself down on her favorite ....the chaise.

She kept looking at the clock which was showing past midnight. The painful doubts about her husband's fidelity swarmed her mind like locusts on succulents in an untended garden; and the hurt she endured plunged deep.   She immediately reached for the telephone and called Lexa, but there was no answer.   She didn't trying calling Lexa again because she assumed that she was still sleeping off the extra glasses of wine.   She then left the den and went into to the kitchen to start binging… which was something she had not done since her successful weight loss. While she sat at the kitchen table and shoved peanut brittles and chocolate ice-cream in her mouth, the telephone rang.

She immediately grabbed it while being hopeful it was her husband calling. But in the same breath she assumed that the call was more likely coming from Lexa. So she said "hello" in a much more relaxed tone. However, she was quickly taken aback after she heard her husband said "hey honey, it's me."

"Uh-huh" said, Marlene.

She would have liked to say a lot more to him than just the, *uh-huh*. But the blend of the chocolate ice-cream and peanut brittle that were swirling inside her mouth created a fumble in her response. Anyway, that was just long enough for her to finish enjoying the stimulus from the sugary duo that was allaying her pain. That lapse in time gave Barchas an opportunity to start redeeming himself.

"I should have called earlier to let you know that I'd be home a little late tonight. But things *kinda* have gotten out of hand. Don't worry honey…I'm okay, and I'll be home soon."

"It's after twelve and you're not home; since when after twelve is considered a little late? It's already *"tomorrow"* Barchas! And you're not home. So where are you?" Marlene blurted.

"Where else, honey? I'm still at the office working. I'm working on a very important file that I need for tomorrow."

"That so called very important file you're working on at this time of the night, Barchas, would it happen to be called, Blossom?"

Barchas was truly taken by surprise about his wife's question, and he couldn't help changing his tone to let it show.

"What? What's gotten into you, Marlene? And what kind of a weird question is that?"

"Just answer the question, Barchas! I need you to tell me what the hell is going on with you and Blossom Rigby! And, since when taking her out to lunch, is OK with me? You know how much that woman slandered my name all over town, when I was sick. And, after all that… you still have the nerve to disrespect me like this!

Barchas was shocked by the numerous and heart rending outbursts from his wife. Though he could not deny being out to lunch with Blossom, in public, which wasn't his first time, he was not prepared to fully defend himself of any wrong doing. He sighed and tried putting an end to the conversation.

"Look, I understand what you're saying but it's not like what you're thinking. Oh my God, honey, what kind of a husband do you think I am? I can't believe you would think so small of me, knowing how much I love you. You and I will talk more about this after I'm home. I'm so sorry, honey, but I have to go now.

Barchas hung up the phone, and Marlene was livid. An instant fear of divorce crossed her mind, and she wondered what her life would be like without her husband, whom she loved dearly. He was her first and only love, and life without him was unimaginable to her.

She returned to the den and plopped herself on the chaise again and tried calling Lexa. She was at a breaking point and she needed someone to talk to. The phone rang numerous times until the answering machine came on. And at that time Marlene left a message asking Lexa to callback as soon as possible,

She shook both her legs to get her slippers off her feet, and she tried curling her body with her knees almost touching her chin. She felt as if she needed someone to speak with right away, and she was nervous.

She tried calming down and reflected on some of the deep breathing exercises her therapist had taught her back in the days when she was unable to cope with her panic attacks. As soon as she was able to muster the courage of dropping her shoulders and inhaling from the pit of her stomach, her eyes popped. She remembered having a few sleeping pills left over from almost two years ago.

She immediately went to her bathroom and started rummaging through the drawers that were filled with cosmetics, and other toiletries. Some, over the counter the drugs and other outdated items were all mixed in, but the sleeping pills weren't among the rubble. Though unlikely, she checked inside the medicine cabinet, but without any luck.

She started sobbing and feeling overwhelmed and wished if she could find a way to relax. And while she fidgeted and wondered if she was nearing her wit's end, it suddenly came back to her that the pills could be in her night stand. She was right about her recollection; and it helped in making her feel that she was not as crazy as she feared.

She immediately uncapped the bottle and swallowed two of the pills, followed by a palm-full of water drawn from her bathroom faucet.

While Marlene was enjoying a restful night's sleep, her husband quietly entered the room at two forty five am. Without knowing exactly what his wife had up her sleeve, he was prepared to come back swinging with a great defense that would quickly put her grouse to rest. He knew he could not deny having lunch with Blossom, but his plan "A" was to have his wife prove how that made him disloyal.

Though he was okay about coming home to the unexpected "peace and quiet", he was nonetheless disappointed that she was not up and ready to attack. So, in order to get his way of clearing himself as quickly as possible, he tried shuffling around the bedroom room in hopes that she would wake up. However, under the circumstances, her deep sleep could run well past breakfast time.

Although he knew better than to assume that she would be interested in having him to touch her, he tried snuggling up next to her and started fondling her breasts. Stroking her nipples was always a 'given' that she would jump right out of her sleep…which of course, was purely his goal. But nothing happened and he became concerned and tried shaking her into waking up.

Within a few seconds of calling her name and pushing a bit hard on her shoulders a few times, Marlene opened her eyes followed by closing them again. Even though she appeared to be still sleeping, Barchas unintentionally found himself on the defensive, because he thought the arguing would be starting any minute then. However, because of her unconscious appearance, he also found himself wondering if she was under the influence of some kind of drug. He stepped away and left her to continue sleeping but not without thinking that he could be right about his hunch of her taking some kind of drugs.

In keeping with his hunch and trying to figure out what his wife could have done within the few hours of their last phone conversation, Barchas immediately started his own investigation. He intended to start checking in the bathroom and medicine cabinet, but of course, he found nothing alarming. He then went into the kitchen and nosed around and noticed the smeared ice-cream bowl and spoon that were left sitting on the table.

He left to check into the wine cellar, but knowing his wife, it would be very farfetched for her to drink alcohol….even if it were to help with sleeping off her cares. He immediately went back to the bedroom to check on her while thinking where else he could look. He then checked into her nightstand and came up with nothing. He jumped back into bed and tried shaking her but with very gentle movements. His efforts were not very successful, but while he was still there in bed with her, he felt something hard against his body. He immediately reached towards his thigh and came up with the little pill bottle. He sprang out of bed again and turned on the bathroom lights to see what was written on the on it on the bottle

He was not very surprised that they were sleeping pills, but he was worried about how many she had taken. According to the directions, half of the pill should be taken at bed-time when necessary, but a single dosage should not exceed more than one pill.

Barchas took the rest of the pills and hid them where he thought Marlene would not find them. But there was no comfort coming to him by hiding them because his main concern was how many she might have taken.

Presence of mind told him that she might have taken just the one, which would undoubtedly put her out for a while. But on second thought he wondered if her intention was anything other than just getting a good night's sleep. However, his second thoughts, quite frankly, sprang out of his guilty conscience as a cheating husband because he couldn't help wondering how much more she had found out about his secret life.

He nervously went back to the kitchen and poured himself a double scotch and then he tried relaxing in his recliner. While his mind boggled on what the heck would happen if his wife had really found out about his secret love affair… he started assuming the worst.

He finished drinking the liquor and quickly returned to the bedroom. He wondered if his wife intentionally overdosed on the pills which he assumed could be fatal.   He shook her body very hard and called her by her name, again. He heard her made a groan which sounded like good news to him because that was how she would normally respond. However, just to be on the safe side, he started talking to her and asked about her appointment with Joe Farnsworth. He watched her shrugged her body and tried repositioning herself in the bed while she changed sides. Then he asked her again about Joe, and in a very low tone he heard her mumbled that they could talk about Joe, tomorrow, because she was feeling very tired.

Finally, Barchas got the relief he so desperately needed. He quickly went to bed feeling confident that his wife's ranting about Blossom was just another one of her jealous episodes. And he assured himself that her accusations would be an easy fix over coffee the next morning.

Early next morning while Marlene was still asleep, Barchas got out of bed and left to chit chat with Bethany who was in the kitchen with Allora. As soon as he walked up to the breakfast table to kiss his daughter, she asked her dad where her mom was. He appeared surprise by the way she queried about her mother, but he acted as if he thought she was being funny. Anyway, before he could pay any further attention to her question, he signaled Allora to bring his coffee right away so that he could think clearly.

"What do you mean, where's your mom? Are you two going somewhere?"

"C'mon dad, just answer me, please. All I'm asking is if mom's in her room"

"But, of course, Honey, and she's still sleeping. Where else do you expect your mother to be when it's only eight- twenty in the morning?"

"I don't know, Dad. It's just that last night I thought I heard her on the phone and she sounded a little upset. So I was just wondering if everything is ok."

"Upset, like how, Bethany?"

"Dad, you know… I'm talking about the place that she's so nervous about. I sure hope she gets it, dad.   I've never seen my mother so excited about getting anything before."

"Oh! That. Don't worry about it, honey. I'll see to it that your mother gets the place. You know your daddy will do anything to see her happy"

Those reassuring words to Bethany from her dad came to her like water on a duck's back. Because, after she tried hugging him and telling him how proud she was that he agreed to the one hundred thousand dollar asking price that her mother was so concerned about, his attitude changed.

"Bethany, what one hundred thousand dollars are you talking about?"

"Dad, didn't mom tell you what, Joe, or whatever his name is, said about the price of the place?"

"Not exactly, dear"

"So, what exactly did Mom, tell you, dad? I thought you said you were going to get it for her."

"Look honey, why don't you leave this up to your mother and me? This isn't something for you to be concerned about."

The father and daughter conversation ended because Bethany left to go upstairs to kiss her mother goodbye before leaving for school. However, she was not surprised seeing her sitting on her chaise, in the den.

"Mom, I thought dad said you were still sleeping"

"I was honey, but I just got up and I overheard everything your father said"

"Did you really?"

"Uh-huh"

So, Mom did you get through with the place?"

"No honey. Not yet; but I plan on getting it today"

"You should see Dad's face, when I told him about the price. He looked like he'd seen a ghost, Mom."

"Uh-huh…your daddy has a lot more ghosts to see honey."

Bethany had no idea what was brewing in her mother's mind but she thought her mother's response was kind of cute. Anyway without furthering the conversation she kissed her mom and left for school.

Barchas was certain about hearing voices from the den. He assumed they could be none other than those of his wife and daughter. So, In order for him to be certain, he left the kitchen with a fresh cup of coffee and went to check. There he saw his wife leaving and heading back towards their bedroom. He walked up quickly behind her and asked if she was going back to bed. She ignored his question and continued walking until she was back in bed. Though he was not surprised that she needed more sleep, he pretended otherwise. He sat at the foot of the bed and he sensed that she was definitely not interested in speaking. But he wasn't interested in waiting any longer in feeling out her mind.

And so, the mind games began, and Barchas took the lead.

"Hello sleepy head? I brought you some coffee."

"No thanks, I'm fine."

"After I came home last night, I tried waking you up, but it seems that you were doped, or *something*. What was that all about? I've never seen you so out of it before…and I was very worried, about you."

"Doped huh? Well as you can see, I'm OK and definitely not doped. "

"Yeah…I can see that. But you really had me going crazy."

"So why were you trying to wake me up?"

"Hah, ah; good question.   I was hoping you could relax me from a long day's work and help put me to sleep. Making love to my wife is my best sleeping aid… you know that."

"Cute… very, very cute, Barchas.

"OK, so you don't feel like accepting the coffee that I brought up foryou? I can live with that, but, what's up with the attitude?

"What attitude?

"Ah, come on now, Marlene. You're acting as if I did something to anger you and I have no idea what that could be. So, what's really on your mind, honey?"

"Oh, I see where you're going with this one, Barchas. You're thinking that I have a memory lapse about last night's phone call. Or, maybe I should ask you if you're having one."

"No, I'm not thinking anything, sweetheart. And from what I recalled about last night, it was a simple phone call to let you know that I would be home a little late. Other than that, I have no idea what you're talking about. If you've got something to say, I wish you would and stop acting as if I'd done something that is causing you to be so grumpy."

"Ah, I like that word....grumpy. First, dope, then grumpy...can't wait for what's next. Well maybe if you just leave me alone and let me to go back to sleep so I can clear my head of all the cobwebs, that you think I've got floating around up there, then hopefully I'll wake up on my un-grumpy side, Marlene retorted with a heightened pitch to her voice, which put Barchas more on the defensive.

"Well, how much sleep do you need? This is not like you to be acting so childish. And, what cobwebs are you talking about?"

"What the hell do you want from me, Barchas? Can't you see that I'm tired and not in the mood to talk? Just get away from me and leave me alone.....please!"

"Look, woman, you know how I feel about stupidity. And you know how I feel about these little games that you play from time to time. They're annoying! And I don't have the time for this sort of crap, especially on a day like today!"

Barchas' response to his wife seemed to have awakened her fully and she was ready to for a fight.

"Before you start with picking apart my intelligence, Barchas, let me just share with you something my grandmother told me, a long time ago." *There's no darkness in the face of a woman where her unyielding courage of light cannot permeate.*

"So, you see Barchas, you know how I feel about stupidity, and you know how I feel about these little games that you play from time to time. Quite frankly honey, they're annoying! And I don't have time for this sort of crap, especially on a day like today!"

Right after that unexpected response coming from his wife, Barchas became a bit frazzled and wondered if she had noticed any difference in his demeanor that would make him appear guilty. Normally, he expected her to snap and to be crying and throwing figurines at him. But this new take on how she communicated her suspicions was keeping him on the edge. He wondered what could have changed since the night before when she made mention of, Blossom Rigby.

He got off the bed and pulled up a wing chair that was in the bedroom so that he could still sit closely to his wife. He was starting to feel a little jittery about things, but not enough for Marlene to pick up on. He lowered his voice and asked her what she meant by that statement.
He thought her response was vague and found it to be quite troubling.

"You can take it to mean anything you want, Barchas. I only wanted to share that little lesson that my Grandmother taught me a long time ago."

"Well, my dear, my apologies to your grandmother, if I'm wrong. And, may God rest her soul. But, knowing how much you like Chinese food, I would be very surprised if that little quote didn't come out of one of their damn cookies."

Marlene's eyes widened by her husband's response and she was infuriated.

"I will not sit here and allow you to disrespect a word of my Grandmother's! And, your idea of making fun of me under the circumstance is pathetic and meaningless. All things considered I think it's best if we just dropped the conversation", Marlene said

Barchas' comment about the Chinese cookies was a mere strategy in getting Marlene derailed and off her *high horse*. Her willpower, however, blocked his ridicule from ripping right through her as they normally would, whenever they were caught up in an argument. However, this time he failed miserably in his attempt to shatter the unexpected facade of confidence that his wife portrayed.

With nothing left for him to go on, and in trying to further analyze his wife's strange behavior, Barchas concluded that her actions were all signs of defeat. Presence of mind told him that she must have realized that she had no way of backing up her suspicions about him. So, in order for her to keep proving to herself that she was no longer *"the emotionally challenged"*, she wistfully conceded by suggesting that the conversation should be dropped.

In keeping with his summation and priding himself for being on top of his game, Barchas left his wife in bed to finish sleeping off the pills. He left with confidence and was enjoying the feeling that he was back in control over his wife's ignorance again. While his confidence swelled as he walked away, Marlene was deep in thought and was enjoying the rush of how she would capitalize on his arrogance. But, all in good-time.

***

While Marlene slept that morning, Barchas hurried and tried leaving the house as quickly as possible to start taking care of business as usual. As soon as he drove out, he called Blossom from his car phone to postpone a three o'clock meeting for the following day. It was not unusual for him to meet with Blossom once or twice a week. Although there was nothing sexual between them, Barchas could not deny having a very close relationship with Blossom. And despite the fact of his wife's disapproval of Blossom, Barchas had been using her for years as his eyes and ears around town.

However, in trying to keep things from getting ugly, Barchas continued to painfully deny himself the opportunity of taking their relationship to the next level. So, in order to keep her happy and at arm's length while she worked for him, he continued with paying her the big bucks. But, that did not stop Blossom from trying to enticing Barchas into her every now and then—all of which went unaccomplished.

Blossom was relieved about Barchas calling to reschedule the meeting. And while she still had Barchas on the telephone, she informed him of a leak. A leak… meant that she had gathered some more information on an impending case he was working on.

By mid-day, Marlene was up and out of bed. She spent a little time chit-chatting with Allora while she tried finishing her half of a grapefruit and two cups of black coffee. Normally, she would have had toast with butter or maybe an egg. But most importantly, coffee to her was no coffee without lots of cream and sugar with a dash of cinnamon. So, in trying to off-set the hundreds of calories from the chocolate ice cream and peanut brittle she had devoured the night before, she tried and forced down the grapefruit and black coffee.

As soon as she was done with the torture of breakfast, she called Mr. Chase to inform him that she was ready to make an offer on the property. He was delighted hearing from her and asked if she could come that day. She quickly said yes and told him that she would be there within a few hours.

With only a little time to spare, Marlene immediately called Lexa to chat a little and catch up on things. Lexa apologized for not returning her phone call from the night before. She explained that the food made her sick and that she stayed up most of the night throwing up. Marlene became a bit surprised after Lexa's response about the food, because she did not recall seeing her eating any of it.   She only remembered seeing her finishing two bottles of the wine before she passed out on the sofa. But, without trying to bother her about what exactly she had eaten, Marlene assumed quietly that her stomach ache could have resulted from too much drinking.

However, just to be certain of Lexa's wellbeing, Marlene asked about her feelings after passing through the night. Lexa replied that she was just about to ask her if she could accompany her to see the Doctor. Marlene was not expecting to hear Lexa say she needed to see her Doctor. But at the same time, she wasn't too surprised because of how she had perceived Lexa to be a bit of a hypochondriac, from a long time ago.

Without waiting for Marlene to say *"yes"* about going with her to the Doctor, Lexa took it upon herself that was what her response would be. In keeping with her expectation of getting her way with Marlene, Lexa immediately changed the subject and enquired about the way she handled her suspicions about her husband and Blossom. Marlene could hardly wait for Lexa to finish her inquiry, so she could start complaining.

"Would, you believe that my husband had the nerve to call me after midnight to tell me that he'd be home late?

"Really…. Did you ask him about Blossom? Lexa asked Marlene.

"Of course, really…Lexa! And when I tried confronting him about that bitch, he quickly got rid of me by saying that he was still at work. At work, my ass? What kind of an idiot does he really think I am?   I can't believe he'd think that I was just going to leave it at that!

"OK Marlene… I'm with you…but, what did you do or say, after he told you, that?"

"Well, I immediately tried calling him back as soon as he hung up the phone. And, of course, I wasn't surprised when the blasted answering machine came on! Look, Lexa, although I'm not able to prove anything, I know my husband is cheating on me and that hunch is gutting me so much deeper than you could ever imagine."

"Uh, you have no idea how pissed off I am right now! It really makes me mad seeing you going through something like this, Marlene. After everything that you've gone though already, you shouldn't have to put up with living without the surety of your husband's loyalty."

"Thanks Lexa, but don't worry girlfriend…..I'll be watching him like a hawk.

"What'd you mean… watching him like a hawk, Marlene. Are you thinking of getting a private investigator?"

"Girl, I don't even know yet. I just don't know how I'm going to do it. But I'm sure I'll come up with something good."

Lexa appeared pensive while Marlene stared at her in waiting for her to respond.

"Well, you know I'll help you with that. I don't think it's safe for you to be out there by yourself…. *you know what I mean?* Lexa said.

Marlene shook her head from side to said and said to Lexa, "Uh-uh, What do you mean?"

"C'mon Marlene, two heads are better than one.   I really think it's best if you'd let me come with you. At least you can drive, and I'll take pictures. Or, we could do it the other way around. And, you don't have to worry about the video camera. You can use mine."

"Hah! ha- ha. You must be thinking you're still in movie-land, Lexa" Marlene said.

An, about face, came over Lexa after Marlene's response. She immediately turned to Marlene and said:

"Oh, my God, you can't be serious! I don't take it lightly that Barchas is doing this to you, Marlene.   It really upsets me that Barchas is screwing around with that woman. Trust me on this one, Marlene I'm here for you and I'll do anything to help you getting that bitch out of your life!"

Although Marlene didn't have the courage to ask Lexa, she was somewhat concerned about how impassioned she had become since she broke the news to her in the restaurant.   But because of the longstanding grudge between Lexa and Blossom, Marlene conveniently chalked it up as an opportunity for Lexa to see Blossom getting kicked off her high horse. Also, and most importantly, she would definitely lose her position as President of the Women's League. However, on the other hand, Marlene struggled with the idea and wondered if Lexa who was her only best friend was acting purely out of concern about her wellbeing.   She reckoned that Lexa could be more focused on keeping her out of the doldrums that she had worked tirelessly to help her overcome. Then, a bit of guilt flared, and her thought process raced on that emotion.

"You know, Lexa, I feel so guilty about dragging you into all this mess. I should have known better not to say anything to you at Vines, yesterday. Oh, my God... I ruined a perfectly beautiful day for having lunch and maybe doing a little shopping which we haven't done in a while. I should have kept my big mouth shut!   It's not like I caught them kissing, or better yet, finding her on top of him. I'm only going on a hunch, right now. And I'm so sorry for making you so upset, my friend."

"C'mon …don't start with the apologies, Marlene. You don't owe me any. I'm glad that I was there for you when all this came about and you shouldn't have to hide anything from me. That's what friends are for. Which wife in her right mind is going to see her husband with another woman without feeling some kind of bias?"

"Uh-huh, that's so true, Lexa.   I don't know what I would do without you as my friend. I hope you know that I'm always here for you no matter what. Anyway, I think I need a little more time to think things through.

"What, kind of things? I hope you're not thinking of letting them get away with it. It's time for you to take control of your life, Marlene."

"Yeah…you're right about that. But I do have my children to think about, especially Bethany who is praying so hard to make it in the top three. And, I really don't want to make the mistake of exposing myself to anything that could jeopardize my business plans for the studio. So, before jumping the gun and making myself looking like an idiot, I think I'll sit on the fence for a while. You know what a mean?

"Uh-huh. But I'm just thinking about the nerve of them to be so blatant, Marlene."

"Uh-huh, and it really makes me mad. But, as I've said, it's not like I caught them in bed or alone together at Vines. It was just the fright of seeing them sitting next to each other and looking so chummy that got me so worked up. But now that I have thought things through, I'll have to give myself some time while I keep an eye on things.

"Yeah, I guess you're right. I think we should wait. But just in case you'd prefer taking the other route, I know a good private investigator who could work wonders for you. So, anyway, you haven't told me what happened after he came home last night. What did you say to him?

"That's another story, my dear. Frankly, I don't know what time he came home last night. I was so pissed off and stressed out that I could only focus on finding a way to calm my nerves. So, I looked around until I found some old sleeping pills, and they worked like a charm. Anyway, this morning he tried starting a conversation with me. I know that he was thinking he could worm his way into my head and take control of the situation as he always does. But I was not going to let that smart ass get away with thinking that I was the same old dummy whom he could twist around his little finger anyway he liked.

"That's what I like to hear! I'm so proud of you, Marlene, and I know we can figure out a way to handle Blossom." Lexa then looked away while taking a deep sigh; followed by saying to Marlene, Anyway, girlfriend, don't forget you're going with me to the doctor later today."

Lexa was disappointed after Marlene finally told her that she would not be accompanying her to the Doctor later that day. But after she explained about her appointment with Mr. Chase in Gray Banks, she changed back to be more understanding. However, Marlene promised that she would check back later with her to hear what the doctor had to say about her upset stomach.

CHAPTER FIVE

While Marlene hurried along the highway to meet up with Mr. Chase in Gray Banks, she thought long and hard about what she should do in making the deal happen. Although she felt that her husband was being slick about keeping her in the dark, she realized that she was becoming hardened enough to withstand the pressure. She had mentally assigned herself the rest of the week, or month, or whatever it was going to take for her to remain focused on getting Mr. Chase to sign off on the deal.

As soon as she cleared the exit to get onto Main Street, her thoughts about taking revenge and taking care of business were soon to be postponed. She was a lot more receptive and pleased about the idea of visiting her mother's graveside. Though she hadn't forgotten her plans to clear the area and erect a headstone, seeing it again in the shambles was just as comforting knowing that it was only for a matter of time.

There she stood and noticed that the lipstick was almost covered by dirt and if it weren't for the shiny casing, it would be a lot less visible. She took a deep sigh and reflected on her first visit which was less than a month prior. But without the need to cry and feeling ashamed like she did before, being there gave a new meaning to her life and a huge sense of pride. She then closed her eyes and tried speaking to her mom. Somehow, in her mind, she believed that her words were being transported by an echo or some other medium of getting her message through.

"Oh, Mama, I miss you more than you'll ever know. Mama, since daddy took it upon himself to end his life, mine has never been the same. Oh, Mama, I feel so lost without having him around, and I pray that he's with you in heaven. I still struggle with finding closure about my sister and the lies she told. So many times, I've tried to forgive what she had put us through. But how can I mama? how can I, ?when I know that our father was not capable of stealing a pin from any of his children. But Mama, as much as it hurt to say it, sometimes it makes me wonder if she could be telling the truth. Mama, I need to know the truth because it's so important to me now; and I'm so confused about everything. My life is just a mess and I wish if I could fix it and let go of the pain I so deeply embody. But I can't Mama, and I just don't know what to do."

Although Marlene started out with dry eyes when she tried communicating with her mother, she left overcome with tears of sorrow and joy. She pitied herself for not being able to being the person she was when her father was alive. She felt that he was the anchor that made her strong.

However, her tears of joy came from the power that was quietly feeding her spirit and building her up to find her own anchor within herself. The feeling to her was as surreal as painting a picture of herself speaking with her mother and father in a garden somewhere in heaven.

By the time she pulled in and looked for a close spot to park her car, she could see Mr. Chase patiently waiting. She assumed that he was anxious in speaking with her about what offers she had in mind. And while her confidence felt as if it were taller than her, she perceived that dealing with Barnswell Chase would be *just another cup of tea.*

Hello Mr. Chase! It's great seeing you again,   said Marlene, as she approached him sitting in his wheel chair on the front porch. She was smiling beautifully and Mr. Chase was enjoying the pull from the energy she brought with her.

Well, it's good to see you again young lady. For a minute I thought you had changed your mind. The way you sounded the last time you were here, I thought you would have been back before long. Anyway, so what have you got for me?

"I've got some good news for you sir, and I know you'll have some even better news for me before I leave today."

"Hah! Hah! Oh, Sweet Jesus. Young lady, you're such a delight to be around; no wonder I couldn't wait to see you come back. So, tell me about this good news you've got for me."

"OK. Well what I have here is an appraisal of the property in the amount of one hundred thousand dollars. I'm sure it could be worth even a little more than that… going by its prime locale. But after thinking long and hard about this, Mr. Chase, I'm comfortable with offering you seventy five thousand dollars cash. And, in return I promise to preserve the integrity and the history of the place. This way I'll carry your dreams with mine….you have my word.

Going by Mr. Chase's standards as a businessman, it was very surprising that he stayed the course listening to Marlene's presentation. Normally he would assume that she was not serious about getting down to business because she came to see him without a written offer. And, he would have had no qualms about asking her to leave right away. However, that was not the case.

Barnswell Chase was floored by the sincerity that spewed from Marlene when she spoke. And, he was overcome with emotion long before she was finished with stating her offer. Although he had turned down several offers of up to two hundred thousand dollars, when he responded to hers, it was clearly without prejudice and pride.

"Miss Marlene, you have no idea how uplifting it feels to hear you say that. It's like seeing my wife coming back to me in black leotards and pink slippers... and, she's dancing only for me. I don't expect you to understand what I'm trying to say, but there's a concert going on, and it's only taking place in my head. I have only you thank for this moment, because only you could put it there."

"I believe in your promise and I trust you with all my heart. Yes, I will accept your offer of the seventy five thousand dollars and it's so much more than I could ask. As soon as you can put it all in writing, I'll sign it and have my attorney to handle the rest for me. I give you my word."

Marlene was ecstatic about the outcome of the meeting. She jumped out of the chair and shook Mr. Chase's hand, gently, and kept thanking him, over and over again. He took a deep sigh as if a huge weight was lifted from his shoulders.

Marlene then sat down in the chair again so that she could gather her belongings to start heading back home. And out of curiosity, Mr. Chase asked her who her appraiser was. Though she felt as if nothing could steal her thunder in her monumental victory, for a second everything seemed to have stopped. But she told him any way.

"Actually, his name is Joe Farnsworth. He's has been around for a very long time and he's well respected in his field. Do you know him?

"Yes, ma'am, I do know, Joe. And you're right; he is the best in his line of work...if I may say so myself."

"Marlene immediately became a bit uncertain of what else to say, because Mr. Chase's tone and facial expression showed that he was not exactly thrilled about hearing Joe's name. So, in order to keeping things on the upside she smiled and told him that she was happy to have had the best in the business handled the appraisal for her.

Barnswell looked at Marlene and sensed that she was cautious about being caught in the middle of what could have been a century old duel between *them* two old men. But having found a good friend and confidant in Marlene, Barnswell came right out and shared the unsettled score between himself and Joe.

"So what did that old turkey tell you about me?"

"What do you mean by that, Mr. Chase? I only met with him once, and from I recalled he did mention that you're a good man."

"Yeah…It's nice to hear.   But he should have just come out with it and say I was the better man. He-he."

"Well, going by that little chuckle, I'm sure you're right. But, can you explain?" Marlene said to Mr. Chase.

"Of, course my lady. But this could take all night.   So, just to give you the long and short of it, let's just say we placed a bet on who would get Winnie to marry him first. But, I loved her more, you see… and I was a *helluva* lot better looking. My Winnie didn't care that Joe had money and I had none.   All she ever wanted was having me to play the music so that she could dance. The story of my life… Joe Farnsworth never forgave me for stealing my one true love from him. But Winnie wouldn't have it any other way and neither could I.

Marlene was happy to stay back and accommodate the stories Barnswell told about his life as a young musician. Aside from making a good living from that, his wife Winnie who kept her last name after they were married became a huge success. He claimed that she was such a perfect woman, that to change her last name to his, would undoubtedly flaw her innocence. So he begged her not to change it.

Marlene left Mr. Chase reminiscent and feeling good about sharing the wonderful stories about his life. But as much as she enjoyed listening to him, she had to quickly clear her thoughts to take on the challenges ahead in owning a business.

Before getting down to business, she used her car phone to call Lexa as she promised that she would. Lexa did not answer, so, she assumed that she was still out. Going by the distance from Gray Banks to where Lexa lived in Quail Run, Marlene figured that she could make it out there within an hour. She thought it would be nice to pay her a visit and land her with the fantastic news.

As she traveled along the highway, she thought of ways to approach her husband about her agreement to pay Mr. Chase the seventy five thousand dollars for the property. Though he was clear about not paying a dime over fifty thousand for what he thought was a dump, she had mentally prepared herself for the onslaught of his objection. And, so as to make sure that he didn't get his way of blocking the deal from going through, she thought it would be wiser to just move ahead without informing him of her verbal contract with Chase.

Since their twenty years of marriage, her most expensive single purchase never exceeded two thousand dollars. Her cars, gowns, coats, jewelry, furniture were hers for the choosing, but it was her husband who handled all the payments. All the monies that she earned from her Dad and Aunt Carolyn while she was their corporate attorney were never touched. Plus, she used to share in the dividends from the company's stocks.

Although she had close to a million dollars in savings, she wanted to prove to herself that she had the guts to make her husband pay for her property whether he wanted to, or not. A bit gusty and a far cry from the woman she used to be, but she was gradually building up herself to take on bigger challenges…. powered by her commitment for independence and success.

She finally came upon the exit and was less than ten minutes away from surprising Lexa with the good news. She reached for her handbag and dug around to find lipstick and comb to freshen her looks. Then her phone rang and it was husband, calling.

"Hello"

"Well, you sound a lot better, Honey. That extra sleep was what's missing this morning. Anyway where are you? I called the house and Allora said you went to a meeting"

"Uh-huh. I am feeling a lot better."

"So, what was your meeting about?"

"Oh, I took a ride out to meet with Mr. Chase"

"Oh…that's right. I'd almost forgotten about that. I thought you'd changed your mind."

"Whatever gave you that idea, Barchas?"

"Well, hasn't it been about a month since you've asked Joe to work up a price for you?

"Uh-huh"

"So, what happened, honey? I hope Joe talked you out of buying that lump of dump. Ha-ha-ha."

"What's so funny about me trying to do something for myself? You're starting to get on my last nerve, Barchas. Why don't you just get to the damn point and tell me why you're calling?"

"What the hell is the matter with you? What are you trying to say, Marlene? Come on now, honey… can't I call my wife anymore to say hello and to tell her that I love her?"

"You should have thought about that when you're out cheating on me!"

"God *dammed!* Here we go again. So, that's what's on your mind. You think I'm cheating on you, and it makes you mad that you can't prove it. Look baby, you're making yourself sick over nothing."

"What were you doing in Vines yesterday with Blossom Rigby"?

Barchas sighed and paused before answering his wife's question. And the dead air made her assume that he could have hung up on her. But soon after, he began speaking.

"Whoever's feeding you information about my whereabouts should have told you they didn't see me alone with her in Vines, yesterday. I'm very aware that you two are at odds, but I've got an obligation to perform on behalf of the people of Watertown. So, if every once in a while I'm seen in public with someone whom my wife despises, what am I supposed to do? I need you to tell me how to avoid that, knowing the importance of my work.   C'mon now, Marlene…You keep accusing me of these adulterous affairs, and you know damn well that I've never cheated on you! Haven't you put me through enough already?

"Uh-huh. Well, maybe if we were having this conversation last year, I would have ran off crying and feeling guilty for being a distrusting wife. But, thank God! I'm way over your ramblings, Barchas. And, your blah, blah, blahs didn't make it to first base, for me."

"I can't believe my ears! This is downright outrageous! Look, I don't know what's gotten into you lately, but you're really pushing my buttons, Marlene! You need to take some time and think about the way you've been treating me. Look, I'm on my way to an appointment, and I should be home by seven. As soon as I'm home I'd like to sit down with you so we can talk and try to get to the bottom of all this craziness!"

Barchas immediately hung up the phone after responding to his wife's unacceptable behavior. But other than the seven o'clock meeting that he mentioned, his argument about her attitude towards him left her carefree. She glanced at her watch and saw that it was three pm which would easily allow a few hours for her to relax and unwind with Lexa… and still be home in time for their meeting.

Their telephone conversation lasted well over the ten minutes it would normally take to get to Lexa's house, after clearing the Quail Run exit. However, because the argument between her and her husband was so heated, she immediately looked for parking as soon as she was inside Lexa's development. She was quite agitated and couldn't wait to stop the car so she could continue arguing without the distraction of traffic.

Having said that, after the phone call ended, she backed up the car and left to find parking closer to Lexa's building which was much further inside the development.

As she proceeded with backing up her car, she noticed… or, *kind of* noticed a car similar to her husband's, driving by. Though it was not unusual to see several of those silver colored Mercedes Benz in that neighborhood, the custom tint on the windows was what grabbed her attention when it drove by.

At first, she felt nothing. Then she began sensing an unexplainable rush coming over her. Her hands shook while she was still holding onto the steering wheel. Her head raised and her heart raced while she removed one hand from the steering wheel to cover her mouth in awe. Her thoughts were still fresh from the glimpse of the custom tint. And as they developed more into what she feared, her assumptions left her into an even deeper state of shock.

Marlene realized what was happening to her and she tried shaking te thought of being so insecure; she was on the verge of an anxiety attack. She immediately started her deep breathing exercises. With each exhalation she inwardly rebuked her *demons* as she tried taking control of her jealousy. Second thoughts chimed in and told her it was best to give her husband the preference of the doubt. But she was already too deep in curiosity and her thoughts remained focused on the car.

She gave herself another few seconds to pass and then with both eyes roving from side to side she continued driving towards Lexa's building. She only spotted four Mercedes Benzes of similar shades. None of them resembled what she thought she had seen, and that was only because of the significance of the custom tint. However, after she kept on going until she found parking next to Lexa's building; she noticed a similar car to her husband's, in the same area of where she usually parked.

She pulled up to take a closer look at the tag; and surely enough she was looking at her husband's car. She immediately stopped her car and she gasped from the shock of seeing her husband's car in the parking area of where her best friend lived. And while her jaw was still hanging from the sudden drop, she experienced a major jab hitting dead center of her breast bone. The gripping pain caused her to close her eyes while she leaned forward to rest her head on the steering wheel. She waited and prayed for the pain to subside and she nervously wondered if at that time she was having a heart attack. Her mouth watered and her palms became clammy while she prayed. The intensity of her calamity seemed to have deepened the pain throughout her flesh… and Marlene agonized all over.

While her head was still resting on the steering wheel, she heard a knocking against the window of her car. She slowly raised her head to look, and saw that it was one of the Security Officers inquiring why she had stopped there. She tried apologizing but it was too late for explanations because she appeared to be at a total loss for words. The security officer saw that she was in distress and asked if she'd like to call an ambulance, but she said no. He then asked if she'd like a drink of water. She shook her head to mean no, but to him; it appeared as if she wasn't sure of herself.

He kept his eyes on her and was about to call on his radio when suddenly he noticed a slight change, in her. She was no longer holding her stomach and she was sitting upright in her car. He then asked her name and queried about her presence in the complex.

Under those conditions, Marlene did not appreciate being asked to disclose her identity because she was fully aware of all the drama that would follow. So, in order for her to get out of that snag without appearing to be uncooperative, she started coughing and begged the officer to bring her the cup of water. As soon as he left to aid her request she immediately started the engine and quickly got the *hell* out of there.

On her way back to the highway, she tried telephoning Lexa, again, but there was no answer. Though she recognized that it could be nothing more than just being foolishly sentimental, she was left at a lost without having the crutch of Lexa's coaching.

Anyway, going by her own thoughts, presence of mind had her convinced that Blossom was also a resident in the same building as Lexa's. And, to her, that assumption easily solved the mystery of why her husband would go there.

Marlene was still shaking and very tearful from the frightening experience. And while she hurt as she drove and tried keeping a steady hand on the wheel, she used her car phone to call Dr. Fiji. He was their family physician for years and she was thankful that he was able to see her as soon as she could make it there.

After listening to her woes and watching her slipping into fragility, it didn't take but a few minutes for Dr. Fiji to recommend that Marlene should start seeing her psychologist again. He was deeply saddened by her dilemma and cautioned her not to drive home alone that afternoon. However, after hearing Dr. Fiji's recommendation about going to see her psychologist, she panicked and tried pulling herself together. She had vowed never to go back to be seen by a psychologist again.

However, she reluctantly took his orders about not driving home alone. He wrote a prescription for *Xanax,* and strongly advised her about scheduling a visit with her psychologist. She quickly left the room where she was seen by Dr. Fiji and promised him that she would contact her therapist. That response to Dr. Fiji, however, was just to get him off her back politely. She was determined never to let anything or anyone force her into that mindset again.

She asked the receptionist to call a limo to take her home, and while she waited, she tried taking control of her anxieties. She noticed that two of the the nurses kept coming around while she waited and she suspected that they were ordered to keep an eye on her. In keeping with her suspicions she remained mindful about controlling her anxieties and to show that she was by no means going crazy.

She was very relieved when she saw the limo driver walked in.   She immediately started digging into her handbag to find her sunglasses before leaving the doctor's office.   She was being careful about being seen in public, looking a mess, and quite the out of sorts.

Allora was just in time to see the limo pulled into the driveway with Marlene sitting inside.   She wondered if everything was ok with her boss. Going by the looks on her face and how roughed up she appeared, it would be difficult for Marlene to convince Allora that she was ok. But she told Allora that she was ok, anyway. So, Allora reluctantly left it at that.   It had been several years since she had seen her boss looking so distraught and disheveled.   And seeing her come home without her car had definitely heightened her concerns even more.

As they walked back together into the house, Marlene anxiously removed the prescription from her handbag and gave it to Allora.   But instead of going off to the drug store to get the medicine as she was asked, she stayed back knowing she could get her head and took the chance of getting her head bitten off by Marlene.

Though Marlene knew the goodness in Allora, and how protective she was about her wellbeing, she had no patience dealing with her concerns.   Marlene immediately became annoyed after watching Allora hanging around and being inquisitve about the whereabouts of the car and why she was looking so crazed.

And, by the time Marlene was through with getting her point across with aggression and ridicule towards Allora,   Allora bolted and left feeling unappreciated and like a headless chicken, while she scurried along to the drugstore.

With Allora out of the way and only an hour before seven o'clock pm, Marlene went to her bathroom and showered.   She fixed her hair and spattered her neck and arms with after body splash, followed by poking around her closet for something casual to slip into.   It didn't take but a few seconds to decide on her peach colored satin long dress with big pockets and a coordinating sash.   It was quite an attractive piece of garment and one of the many girly gifts exchange between her and Lexa.   She looked closely into the mirror and she wondered if her husband would notice her slightly swollen eyelids; or, if he would care that she had been crying. She checked the medicine cabinet and found and old bottle of eye drop from which she put in a few to help with clearing the red from her eyes. However, she wasn't completely satisfied with her appearance,   so she applied a feint tint of pink blush to her cheeks.   As she walked away from the mirror she folded her lips to catch the saliva from off her tongue, because her Chap Stick was left back in her car.

She heard the door pushed in, and her heart thumped. She wondered if it was Barchas coming home to keep their seven o'clock appointment. She waited a few seconds more and listened if the *honey-I'm-home* routine would be the next sound she heard.   But that was not the case. What she heard thereafter was the sound of rattling dishes and pans coming from the kitchen, which made her assumed that Allora had returned home with her Xanax. She was anxious in getting started with taking the medication, but before she could quite make it into the kitchen, she was welcome by the ever loving voice of her daughter.

"Hey Mom, where have you been all day? You were supposed to pick me up after, dance. I had to call Allora, and I hate having her pick me in that old station wagon

"Oh, Sweetie…your mommy had a rough day and it was crazy. I'm sorry that I had to put you through that."

"What do you mean, crazy, Ma?"

"Oh, you know…. I had a headache and my stomach hurt and all that stuff. So I had to go to the doctor to get a checkup."

"Sounds like you're coming down with the flu, Ma. But you don't look sick to me; you look very pretty, Ma."

"Oh, honey…You don't know how good it makes me feel hearing you say that.   That's medicine enough for me already. Don't worry honey; I'll be good as new within a few days."

Marlene noticed that her daughter was busy around the kitchen looking for something to eat. Though she was struggling with her issues, she was happy to fill in for Allora and help her daughter with finding some food. Bethany was amused to sit back and watched her mother puttering around like a stranger in her own kitchen. And while she was going back on forth in trying to decide on paper or cloth napkins, she casually informed Bethany why Allora was not home to serve dinner.

She carefully removed the cover from a mid- sized porcelain tureen that was left on top of the stove. She noticed that Allora had made stuffed cabbage which was a favorite of Barchas, but it was something that Bethany hated. She checked inside the fridge and the microwave but found nothing else… until Bethany suggested the oven. Bethany was even more tickled after her watching mother opened the oven and acted as if they had struck gold. "Wow, honey, I can't believe my eyes. She's got your favorite!" Bethany already knew that the lasagna was ready and waiting in the oven. But, she thought it was such great fun to pretend otherwise and allow her mom to get a little more familiar with things inside her kitchen.

While Bethany sat and watched her mother fixing dinner, she asked what time her dad would be home. And, the sharp and sudden response along with the grimace on her mother's face caused her to apologize to her mother for enquiring about her dad.

"Mom, are you and dad, fighting again?" Bethany asked her mom.

"No, Bethany. Your dad and I aren't fighting again. It's just that he makes me so mad, sometimes."

"Does he know that you have the flu?"

"Well, Dr. Fiji didn't say it was the flu. But, you could be right. Anyway, promise me that you won't tell your father that I went to see the doctor today. I don't want him to worry about me."

"Ma, you know I don't ever tell daddy anything."

"And I don't want you to tell your brother anything either. I don't want him to worry about me"

Bethany had no response to her mother's last request. She knew she was guilty of updating Monk about everything that took place in the family. She missed him terribly and she was dying for the Christmas holidays to come so that he could be around for her eighteen birthday party.

Marlene placed the food on the table and she turned her head slightly to look at the kitchen clock. It was seven twenty pm, and her husband was not yet home to keep his promise about their meeting. Although she was doing her best not to ruin the special mother and daughter moment, she was starting to feel worn-out from faking her way through it.

So, while Bethany kept her eyes closed in total enjoyment of every mouthful of the lasagna, she was silently wishing if her mother could cook like that. However, while her mother sat quietly next to her and showing a plastic smile, she was totally without an appetite for the food. So in order to keep her daughter distracted from what was *eating* her, she took a few sips of water and started a conversation about the pageantry, which was another six months away.

<> <>

They heard the rumble of the garage door. Marlene suspected that it was her husband coming home. However, she pretended as if she had not heard the garage, or that she even cared about him coming home. That was not the case, but due to her underlying circumstance while trying not to breakdown, she clammed up and took another sip of the water. However, Bethany was quick to respond to the sound.

"I believe that's him, Ma." Bethany chimed in.

"What are you talking about, sweetie? Marlene said.

"Who else Mommy, I think Daddy is home. I thought you'd heard the garage door opening."

"I'm sorry honey; I guess I wasn't paying attention. Well, I guess your dad's right, on time, to have dinner with us."

"Uh-huh. But not with me, I'm almost done and you haven't touched a leaf of your cabbage."

"So, aren't you having a little dessert?"

"Noooo mother, that's a no, no, for me; I've already cheated on my diet."

Marlene did her damndest to have her daughter keep her company while she continued with mustering to keep her wits about her. All along she was praying for strength to help her from falling apart. She knew she was totally pulled apart from the inside but she was hanging on to every bit of courage to keep it all in.

And then came the dreadful announcement from her husband, *"Honey, I'm home."*

Marlene glanced at the kitchen clock and saw that it was seven forty five pm. She took deep breaths with every step he made while walking towards the kitchen. She watched him loosen his tie and rolled up his sleeves. And she knew what was next to follow; she knew he was coming over to kiss her on the lips. Her body tensed and her insides quivered while she mentally prepared herself not to ever let him win.

When his lips touched hers, he quickly pulled back because of the way she tightened her lips against his. She didn't care about the stale smell of liquor on his breath, but she was deeply hurt because she assumed that he had been out drinking with his lover. An immediate pang emerged from her suspicions, and she wished if she could plaster his face with the plate of stuffed cabbage and then break the china over his head. But she knew she didn't have it in her to hurt her husband that way. And, even if she could, she realized that the game would be over long before it had begun. And, again, she would come out the biggest loser.

Barchas was not surprised by the non-responsive pout when he tried kissing his wife's lips. He had not forgotten that she had pissed him off earlier and he suspected that she was still in a bad mood. He left and went to the wine cellar to get something of his liking. And while he was on his way there, he articulated inwardly how best to start off the meeting without losing his temper. Coming home that evening to deal with an angry wife was not something he was up to handling. His visit to Quail Run had left him in a tail spin and he was quietly suffering and simmering in frustration.

Before Barchas could make it back to the kitchen, Allora had walked in with the medication. Marlene was anxious to get it from her before Barchas found out that she had gone to see Dr. Fiji. She thanked Allora and apologized for the way she had snapped at her. After many, many years working for Marlene, Allora had kind-of outgrown her once in a while *shake-ups;* but the apology was very much appreciated.

Marlene quickly swallowed one of the pills and slipped the small container with the rest of the medication into her pocket. She left and went directly upstairs to her bedroom. On her way up, she thought of different ways of communicating with her husband without losing the calm and control she thought she needed to successfully have things going her way. However, after carefully considering the blow to her already painful doubts, she was somewhat skeptical about maintaining the facade. But she was determined on giving it her all.

***

Marlene sat patiently on her bed and waited for her husband to turn up so that they could get the *ball- a- rolling.* She was shivering with anxiety and she hoped and prayed that the xanax would kick in and help with keeping her off the edge. Then, Barchas walked in and she noticed something different about him, but she simply chalked it up to one of his defense tactics. So, Marlene quietly ignored the glaze in her husband's eyes; and then she began talking.

"I thought you said you'd be home by seven"

"I'm sorry honey, but things got a little crazy at the office"

"Oh, it must be my mistake; I didn't realize that your appointment was at the office. I thought you said you were on your way to an appointment, and you'd come straight home from there. But you're right. That was my mistake."

Barchas became a little edgy after Marlene's comment, because he clearly recalled that was what he had told her. And so he inwardly wondered why she was being so lenient with him.

Marlene stared at him holding a glass of liquor in one hand and a huge bottle of two liters or more in the other. She had not recalled seeing a bottle of liquor of that kind around the house before. She wondered if someone had made a gift to him and she thought it was quite attractive because of the decorative wooden encasement halfway around it. However, she had no comments as she was more interested in their meeting.

He poured another drink and left the bottle sitting on the dresser. She watched him take large gulps of the liquor before responding to her last comment. And the more uncomfortable he appeared, was the more her confidence grew.   She already suspected that he was guilty, but her plan was to ensure she nailed him without any glitches.

"So, what's our meeting about, Barchas? I need to get going with it because I'm a little tired and would like to get some rest."

"Well, it's not like you're oblivious to anything I'm going to say to you, Marlene.   Things are getting a bit out of hand here – obviously. Don't get me wrong …I'm aware that you'll sometimes question my fidelity; but, that's okay. Quite frankly, I'm ok with that. However, I just don't understand why I should be held accountable every time you get fixated on what I could be doing while I'm out and with whom. After all these years of being married to you, you were never able to prove any of your suspicions.   But, that's just you, Marlene, and I realize that the only way I can fix your problem is to stay home with you, *twenty –four- seven*, and every day of the week. And, as you know, darling, I just can't do that. Anyway, the thing that bothers me the most is this change that I've noticed in your behavior— something that I've never seen before.   It's like; all of a sudden it feels as if I hardly know you."

"I don't think any of this is about, you not knowing me, Barchas. I think I'm the one who should be questioning who my husband is. You have a way of coming off with such innocence in your arrogance, and that's why your   selfishness has kept you from realizing the impact it has had on me.   Every time you do this to me, I get blindsided by your well thought out spiels.   It never occurred to me that my husband, my one and only true love, could be so cruel." Marlene said.

Barchas waited a few seconds in responding to his wife's remarks, because he realized he had to be extra savvy with her, because she could be in fact becoming a far cry from being the *old* Marlene.

"What's that supposed to mean, Marlene? Good God! After giving my all to you and your family since the day I married you, I never thought the day would come to hear my wife call me, cruel! If you really want to know the truth, woman, don't think that it hasn't crossed my mind that you could be the disloyal spouse. Quite frankly I think you've lost all perspective in being an understanding wife. And all this nonsense about buying a property and starting up a business is not you! What the hell has gotten into you lately? And how could you be so ungrateful and disrespectful after all that I've done for you!"

Marlene's eyes widened shockingly after her husband's response. And while she stared at him with searching eyes, she wondered if he had lost his mind.

"I think this conversation is over, Barchas! You must be drunk or something. The gall of you to stand there and tell me about what you've done for my family, makes me sick! Have you lost your mind! Have you already forgotten that, if it weren't for my father, you wouldn't be standing under this roof, free and clear? So, please, Barchas don't go there, trying to   tell me bulls about what you've done for my family! If you had to bust your ass to build a mansion, like this for me, you'd be a pauper, by now. So, don't you stand there and try telling me about what you've done for my family. Please don't!"

As the anger spewed from Marlene's eyes when she spoke, Barchas had trouble looking at her, so he kept his eyes looking up at the ceiling while she ripped through him with the truth.

Barchas was bitterly bruised by his wife's open revolt. His pride about being the *big man* of the house, coupled with the *well- to- do* lifestyle that he provided his family with ease, was instantly obliterated.   He'd almost forgotten that is was her father who had in fact paid every penny to build their stately house as their wedding present.   But, according to the circumstances around his suicide, it wouldn't be too farfetched to say that it was built from *"blood money."*

He then looked at his wife with utter disgust. And without her knowing the truth about his dilemma, her unfortunate choice of words simply pushed him over the edge, or so it seemed

The one thing he'd promised his wife never to do again was to call her names and use profanity.
But he couldn't help himself in the heat of the utter disgust her felt toward her.

Tempers flared and he began cursing at her and called her names of gutter level profanity while pointing his finger in her face and threatening to divorce her if she ever tried dishonoring him like that again. Looking at her husband's finger pointed right between her eyes, while looking on and off at the vengeance in his eyes as their eyes locked, had her spiraling out of control . She quickly rolled back her tongue and gathered enough saliva to spit on his finger and into his face. The fright of her actions shocked Barchas as the pulled back his hand from her face. She stepped back a few steps, and then she called him a drunken bastard and a loser.

The situation escalated even more, and the *loud- and- never-heard- before- screaming* from the bedroom, sent Bethany and Allora running to help save Marlene's life. They were just in time to witness Barchas adding more pressure around her throat and neck with both hands, but there were no more sounds left coming from Marlene by then.

Bethany's eyes widened and she placed her hands on top of her head from the shock of what she was looking at. She immediately began screaming at her father.

"Oh, my God, Daddy, what are you doing? Take your hands off my mother! Daddy, daddy, stop! Stop choking her; can't you see you're killing her; her eyes are popping out of her head!" Bethany lamented.

It appeared as if Bethany's pleas for mercy had fallen on deaf ears, or only deepened her father's wrath against his wife.

But while Bethany screamed helplessly, it was Allora who sidestepped her in fright and started clobbering Barchas over the back of his head with the huge bottle of whisky that was left sitting on the dresser.

After a few more pounding from Allora, Barchas' grip on Marlene loosened and then released. He turned his head to face Allora and while she was still holding the bottle she hit him hard in the face and he fell, hitting the back of his head on the floor. She kept pounding his face until the bottle was completely shattered in her hands.

Then Bethany screamed, "Allora, Allora please don't kill my father. You need to stop now, stop it!."

Allora immediately threw the neck of bottle aside and rushed to pull Bethany towards her until her face was centered between her breasts. She was trying to comfort her and hide her from the gruesomeness. But nothing could erase the image from her mind, and the *poor girl* was horrified.

Over the period of another five minutes, nothing happened. No one spoke, no one moved, and nothing happened. Everyone, but Barchas, appeared to be in a state of shock. Either he was beaten unconscious or was sleeping from being drunk.

A few minutes later, Allora broke the silence in the room by encouraging Bethany to go sit on the bed. She was bleeding profusely from the several gashes she'd received   while beating Barchas with the broken bottle. She then nervously went to the other side of the bed to where Marlene was left lying on the floor unresponsive. Both ladies were shaking terribly and the blood from Allora's hands pooled on Marlene's body as she tried to comfort her in her despair.

Her eyes were puffed up, she was bleeding heavily from the nose and her bottom lip was split open and bloody.   Allora agonized deeply over Marlene's body and she wondered if she was able to speak.

"Can you hear me, Miss Marlene?" Allora asked.

Marlene shook her head and Allora was relieved.

"What do you want me to do, ma'am?"

"Just hold me, Allora, and tell me that I'm not dead"

"Yes ma'am you're alive, I wasn't going to stand there and let him kill you"

"I owe you my life, Allora. I don't know how I'm ever going to repay you."

"You don't owe me anything, Ma'am. I was only doing my job."

"That's such a nice thing to say, and I can't thank you enough. I think we should call the police, now."

"Um, um, oh my God, Mrs. Sander, please don't call the police"

"Why, Allora?"

"Because I know they're going to put me in jail"

"You have nothing to worry about. You did nothing wrong. Just leave me here, Allora, and please call for help."

"When Marlene spoke to Allora, her voice was barely audible. There were several pauses between her words and it pained Allora to tears to see her suffer like that. She reckoned she needed to get herself together and do what Marlene had asked of her. But, because of the unrelenting fear of being hauled off to jail, it was still challenging for her to fully comprehend the urgency and the importance of Marlene's requests.

She reluctantly tried getting up from the floor to get to the telephone, but she was immediately forced to sit back down. She had almost forgotten about her wounds. She looked at her right hand and saw that the bleeding has slowed. The thick and wavy curdling of the blood followed along her palm and outwards to her fingers. But the pain was most severe in her wrist and thumb. However, after a few more attempts and with the help of her other arm, she was able get on her feet. She nervously walked to the other side of the bed where Bethany laid quivering and sobbing. She had not made any attempts to look at her mother's condition. She was deathly afraid to look because the horror inside the room was more than she could take. So while Allora's insecurities deepened, she selfishly ignored Bethany's state of shock and tried pressuring her to make the dreaded phone call.

While Bethany remained curled up in bed and unresponsive to Allora's request, the telephone rang. Allora, instantly looked towards the direction of the telephone, and she panicked.   The ringing telephone had worsened her phobia, and she was threatened by the idea of answering.   After the fourth or fifth ring, the answering machine came on and it helped with calming her when she heard Lexa's voice coming through with a message.

"Hey, Marlene, it's Lexa. Just calling to say hi and to see how your appointment in Gray Bank turned out. Anyway, it's almost ten o'clock, so I guess I'll hear from you tomorrow."

Listening to Lexa's messaging temporarily returned Allora to a sense of normalcy around the house, and it helped her to finally muster up the courage to dial zero, and the response was instantly.

"Operator" said she Operator.

Though she was unprepared for the quick response after dialing the zero, Allora did her best in fronting.

"Hello, Operator, Um… I need you to call the um… police and the ambulance, right now."

Allora was barely audible but her pitch had the telephone operator properly erected in his chair.

"Hold on a minute, please, said the Operator.   This is Officer Windahl, speaking. Ma'am I need you to slow down and repeat what you've just said. And I need you to try speaking up more clearly for me please. "

"Yes sir. Okay. I need someone to come out to the Sander's residence because there's been an accident out here."

What kind of accident, ma'am? Has anyone been shot?"

No, no. It's not like that, but they need to come right now!"

"Ma'am, please calm down and tell me if you're calling from the residence of Mr. and Mrs. Sander"

"Yes sir… and I am the maid."

"So, are you alone in the house?"

"No sir. Everybody is home and everybody is hurt. Can you please hurry?"

Within ten minutes of the phone call made by Allora, three police cars and two ambulances were parked in their driveway. She immediately opened the door and she pointed them upstairs to where they found Marlene and Barchas still lying on the floor. However Bethany was not to be found.

While the paramedics worked hard and fast on getting both husband and wife into the ambulance, the police officers and Allora were busy trying to find Bethany. The maddening and emotionally stirring household was more than Allora could take, and while she kept calling for Bethany to show herself, she fainted.

One police officer immediately started to perform CPR, but was quick to heed the suggestion of one of the paramedics who wanted to take over. After Allora was successfully resuscitated the paramedic who was paying very close attention to her noticed the deep gouge inside her right palm; as well as some other small slashes on her left hand. Although her condition was nowhere close in severity to Marlene's and Barchas' the paramedics thought it was best to have her treated in the hospital. But before she could be wheeled out on the stretcher, the policeman intervened to ask her a few questions about what took place and the possible where-about of Bethany.

She clearly understood the policeman's inquiries but because she was so deeply entangled in the confusion, it was difficult for her to respond coherently.

"I don't know what happened, and I don't know where Beth is. I left her crying in the bed because Mrs. Sander told me to call the ambulance. And now I can't find Beth."

"So, you said you're the maid?"

"Yes sir. I am the maid and I know he was going to kill her".

"Huh, uh…. and what did you say your name was?"

"He was going to strangle her and kill her, so I had to stop him. Um, Um and she said I saved her life and I can't get in any trouble. You can ask Beth; I swear that's the truth."

"Calm down and tell me your name, lady."

"She's my boss and her name is Miss Marlene and my mine's Allora…. and I don't know what happened to Beth. You people need to find her for me" Allora began crying.

With the exception of Bethany, everyone was on board and ready to be taken to the hospital. After trying to make sense of Allora's fast talking and jumbled statement, the policeman's notepad had but a couple lines to go on.

While the paramedic wheeled her to the ambulance, the police officer returned upstairs and looked around until he finally found Bethany. She was found cowering in Monk's bedroom closet.

The policeman whose name was Durand Singer was no stranger to the credentials attached to Barchas. Although he had never met the man personally, seeing him on TV time and time again, made his acquaintance almost real. So, without getting to the bottom of the situation, he concluded that he was in the midst of a *soon- to- be- high -profile case.* In fact that was the main reason for his patient and kind approach.

Bethany instantly turned her face to the darkest corner of the closet with her eyes slammed shut from the blinding glow of his flash light that was blaring down on her face. The officer knowing that the dimly lit room would overshadow his investigation, immediately turned off his flashlight.

He told her that he meant no harm. Bethany remained at a loss for words but the officer's kind gestures behooved her to turn her head back around to face him. Though he would have preferred to get a look at her face, he kept up with the polite approach and tried making do with the thin streaks of light from the hallway to where they were.

"Bethany, I'm Officer Singer. Allora is very worried about you and that's why I came upstairs to help her find you. I think it's best if you'd please come out of the closet so that she can see that you're okay. If you're hurt and need help getting downstairs, I can help you with that."

The officer waited and watched as Bethany slowly crawled halfway out of the closet. He stretched out his arm toward her, and without acknowledging his kindness, she mumbled:

"I can walk by myself. I don't need any help"

"Well that's great, Bethany, I can see you're doing a lot better that the others. Anyway I really would appreciate it if you would try coming out of the closet so that we can get back downstairs."

"Is my mother going to be okay?" Bethany asked the police officer while her eyes remained downcast toward the carpeted closet floor.

"Well, they're taking her off to the hospital right now. So, if you'd like to see her before she leaves, you'll have to hurry." The police office said the Bethany.

"But, you didn't answer me. I need to know if my mother is going to be okay." Bethany replied to the police officer.

"Bethany, the paramedics will be pulling out any minute now. They need to get your mother to the hospital so that she can be okay," the police officer said.

"Well, you people can't leave without me! Please don't let them take my mother out of here without me. She's all I've got left.

The Officer raised his eyebrows in surprise about Bethany's statement. He was curious why she said that her mother was all she had left. However in the moment, he conveniently let her off the hook, so they could to keep things on the *straight and narrow.*

He quickly stepped aside to allow Bethany to get out of the closet. And, as soon as she cleared the area, he was able to take a good look at her face. Her eyes were bulging with fear and tears. Her lips trembled and she was perspiring profusely. He followed behind her and waited outside her bedroom. Soon after, she came back out with slippers on her feet, and a robe over her nightgown.

While they hurried to get downstairs, Officer Singer failed to keep the suspense about what he thought was an eye-opening statement from Bethany.   So he made the move and asked what she meant by saying that *"her mother was all she had left."*

Bethany unexpectedly became indignant, and her tone pushed the officer into firing back at her with more authority.

"Why don't you leave me alone? I don't feel like talking to you or anyone right now. I just want to be with my mom. If you want to know why she's all I have got left, then you can ask my father, and let him tell you!"

"Look, young lady, I've been very patient with you. I need you to try and calm down so that we can keep things running smoothly. Do you understand?"

Bethany was quick on picking up on the drastic change in the Officer's tone and she reckoned that she could really piss him off *royally* if she kept up with the attitude. However, instead of trying to appease his command with a *"yes sir,"* she spitefully ignored him with silence.

The overwhelming imagery of her father's hands crushing her mother's windpipe was still very fresh and too raw for her to allow the Officer's agenda to take precedence over hers.

As soon as they stepped outside, she pulled up the massive front doors behind her while   from the corners of her eyes; she kept an eye on him. She watched the displeased officer take advantage of the outdoor lighting to make scribbles on his notepad. Going by the flaring tensions between them, she automatically suspected that he had put a bad mark against her name. But she was dauntless about the Officer's opinion of her, so without saying anything, she walked away and continued towards the ambulance.

"Not so fast young lady, I still have a few questions for you."

Bethany did not appreciate the Officer's tone neither being kept back from going to see her mother. However, she stopped and turned around to acknowledge his order, but not with the intention of making his job any easier.

"How old are you, Bethany?"

"I'm almost eighteen"

"So, in other words you're seventeen years old. Correct?"

"I'll be eighteen in a few months"

"I understand what you're trying to say, but it's not going to change the fact that you're still seventeen."

"Whatever! But I'm still old enough to take care of my mother, and you cannot change that!"

Officer Singer would have preferred to detain Bethany until he was through with all of his questions. But after realizing how terrified she had become from expressing her fears about her mother, he quietly surrendered his demands for the night. Without her knowing what was going through Officer Singer's mind, Bethany proceeded with walking towards the ambulance and he allowed her the free rein.

The paramedics were quick to open the doors to let her in so they could be on their way to the hospital. It tore her deeply to see her mother and father together lying in an ambulance. She immediately rushed to the side of her mother's stretcher and held her hand. And while she heeded the recommendation of the paramedic to fasten her seatbelt, she took a quick glance at her father looking almost dead.

CHAPTER SIX

While midnight passed over the throng of hungry Reporters, they remained hopeful in pursuit of the first sound- bite to come from the *"Barchas and Marlene" story*. There, with each man for himself, the main gateway to the *"Pastor and Finn Memorial Hospital"* became an overnight sensation from the buzzing crowd.

In relation to the other hospitals in Watertown, *Pastor and Finn* was the newest and undoubtedly the most innovative. The concept of a new hospital of its kind with the best state of the art equipment and medical associates was well received by the city and other charitable organizations. And, when Carolyn Tate got wind about the plans for the new hospital, she was pleased to show her support to the tune of One Million dollars.

The sound of sirens coming from a distance was an indication to the crew of Reporters that relief was coming their way. They waited and watched as the ambulances finished snaking their way around the bend leading up to the Emergency Entrance, while they followed behind.

Meritta Stockholm, Watertown's queen of gossip, was the last to get to the scene. However, by the time the ambulances were properly positioned; she had successfully swished her way in front of the crowd with her microphone in hand.

It was twelve thirty three am when the ambulance came to a dead stop and Bethany was first to get out. Her frightful and withdrawn appearance seemed to have placed a sympathetic grab on the hearts of the Reporters. But even on their best behavior she was not prepared to handle their concerns about her wellbeing.

She turned her face to look away from them but it was to no avail; she was completely surrounded. Thankfully there was ample security on site to help with protecting her from the Reporters and their slew of inquiries.

Everything went like clockwork. The entire family including Allora was quickly transferred inside the hospital. Other than what was caught on camera, the news crew ended up leaving the scene with many unanswered questions.

By the next day, Watertown was taken by surprise after reading about the incident in the morning newspaper. Other than what was gleaned from Allora, there was not much detail to report. However there was no mistake in the caption, *"Maid Clobbered District Attorney to Save Wife."*

Barchas' best friend and colleague, Frank Roulette, had just poured his morning coffee and stepped outside his front doors to pick up the morning paper.

Words, could not describe the looks on his face when he saw the headline on the front page of the newspaper. He took another sip of the coffee and hurried towards the den where his collection of cigars was displayed. His hands shook while he anxiously poked one inside his mouth and tried lighting it up. He then sat down and sucked deeply on the cigar as if he needed that fix to help him with digesting the news about Barchas and Marlene.

As soon as he was through reading the disturbing news, he immediately contacted the office where he and Barchas worked. He left strict orders that everyone there should remain tight lipped about the allegations, and especially to all News Reporters should they stop by scouting for information. He immediately contacted Blossom to find out if she had heard about the news. Blossom was still in bed when he called, but after hearing what he had called about, she immediately ran outside to pick up her issue of the paper. The shocking news had her grappling with confusion. She found it hard to believe that Barchas would ever lay a hand on his wife.

The short and sketchy but ever so shocking story ended quite like a cliffhanger. Blossom was flabbergasted and she immediately telephoned Frank to keep her posted. Her connection with him told her it was best to lay low for a while. However, without knowing much of anything, Frank's main objective was to get to the hospital as soon as possible to see how he could help with keeping his best friend and confidant from being ostracized.

Frank was the first visitor to turn up at the hospital that morning. He came out of his car wearing a dark blue suit and he leaned against it with his legs crossed. As if he were still in total disbelief about why he was there to face Barchas, he slowly removed a cigar from his coat to smoke it. He took deep, long puffs and tried relaxing with the newspaper tightly rolled up and under his left arm. And, if it weren't under such unpleasant circumstance, his stature and pose while exhaling the smoke would have made him a perfect snapshot for *"Ebony."*

He appeared confident when he entered through the main doors and was approached by the Greeter. He introduced himself as Mr. Roulette and informed the Greeter that he was there to see Mr. Sander. And with the news swirling all over town, she assumed that he was someone of high importance.   From that she was quick in pointing him to where the elevators were located, while telling him to get off on the third floor.

Frank's noticeable confidence did not take long to wear off and be replaced by shock. The nurse on the third floor who helped him with his questions about Barchas was captivated by his bold and his stylish looks. But in the same instance she pitied him after seeing the newspaper fall from his hand after she informed him that his best friend had suffered a massive stroke and was clinging to life in the intensive care unit.

Out of curiosity he asked the nurse how Marlene was handling the news about her husband's life threatening illness. Out of concern about her trying to protect her from the added stress the doctors ordered that she should not be told right away. So Frank was asked to be considerate and not say anything to her.

Without being able to hear Barchas' side of the story, Frank realized that it would be a huge challenge to help with defending him the way that he would have liked. So with nothing to come from his best friend, he half-heartedly left and went to visit Marlene who was being treated on a different floor.

After turning up and seeing her face and the bruises around her neck, Frank immediately stopped in awe. His mind raced back to what he had read in the newspaper. And although he was looking at Marlene and making connections with what he'd assumed to be rumor, he questioned if his friend was really capable of attempted murder. Besides the fact that he was terribly disappointed in what he was witnessing, he was dying to find out the truth behind such terrible acts of violence. So, without being able to hear Barchas' side of the story, his main focus relied heavily on whatever Marlene would have say.

He noticed that Bethany was asleep. She was sprawled out on a pale green leather arm chair which was next to her mother's bed; and she was covered from neck to toe with an off white blanket. Marlene's eyes were swollen and black and blue.   Her nose was broken, her top lip was split open and her face was puffy and an utter mess.

Frank stood quietly in the doorway and stared pitifully at both mother and daughter and he wondered if Marlene was also asleep. But she was not.   From the minute he walked in, she had sensed that someone other than her nurse or her doctor had entered the room.   The intoxicating mix of cologne and tobacco coming from Frank permeated the air and changed the feeling in her room.   And without being able to see, she conveniently assumed that it had to be another detective from the precinct downtown… fishing for a statement. However, just to be on the safe side, she forced through her pain and said: "who is there"

"Marlene, it's me, Frank. I'm sorry, I thought you were asleep. Jesus Christ, girl, I can't believe my eyes. How do you feel?"

"Could be worse" Marlene replied, followed by a groan from her that shook Barchas to the core.

"What do you mean by could be worse? Nothing could be worse than this, Marlene"

"Well, at least your buddy didn't get the chance to finish killing me." Marlene said.

"Wow! That sounds like some heinous shit when you say it like that. I'm still having trouble believing that my main man is capable of laying a hand on you. I mean— this is just not Barchas…it's just not like him, Marlene." Frank said.

"Oh, well, it's never too late for a shower of rain, as they say; I guess you could say your friend is innocent until proven guilty. I can see you defending him already."

"Oh, Lord, have mercy. C'mon now, Marlene, you're like my own sister, and Barchas is closer to me than my own brother. This is not about defending Barchas and what he did to you. It's just so damn hard to accept that he really tried to kill you. I'm still in shock. Anyway, we're going to have to treat this *thing* like family. Please Marlene, let me help you take care of this."

Marlene groaned even deeper as she was starting to become agitated by Frank's responses, and it pained her even more to keep him engaged on her husband's behalf.

"I don't need a lawyer, Frank."

"Well, I didn't mean it like that, Marlene. I'm just trying to say that I'm here for you"

"So, your buddy didn't give you his side of the story, I imagine."

"No. I haven't spoken to him as yet. But I'd like to hear your side of it."

"Is that so? How come, Frank? I thought he'd be the first person you'd want to go to help consoling, or did they put our District Attorney in jail for beating the hell out of his wife?"

After that comment from Marlene, Frank recalled that she was not aware of her husband's condition, and he did not want to be the first to inform her. So in order to keep things running smoothly he deceived her by saying that Barchas was sleeping and should not be disturbed.

The burden of Barchas' future weighed heavily on Frank's mind. He wished if he had, *"something,"* to go on, after speaking with Marlene. But her sarcasms told him that his quest for mediation was either too soon or a little too late. So with nothing left to go on, he kissed her hand and told her that he would be back.

***

It was on day two when Marlene was able to make short glimpses, but only from one eye. The other was still badly swollen. The doctors conferred and thought it was time to give her an update about her husband's condition.   Anyway, going by what they assumed her husband had put her through, they wondered if she would even care if he made it out alive. So, without knowing what to expect, Dr. Presley met with her during the absence of Bethany and he came straight to the point.

"Hello, Mrs. Sander; I'm Dr. Presley. I see you're coming along very nicely. Before long, I'm confident you'll be up and about again. Anyway, I'd like to update you on your husband's condition."

He's dead, isn't he, Doctor Presley? Marlene said, very dryly.

"Well Mrs. Sander, your husband is very lucky to be alive. Your husband has suffered a massive stroke.   We're going to have to keep him here for a few weeks, and after that he will be transferred to rehab."

"How long will he be in rehab, Doctor?"

"Well, no one knows for sure, but I would give it six months to a year."

"And what did my husband have to say about all of this?"

"I'm sorry Mrs. Sander, but your husband is not able to speak, and that is something we're going to have to really work on."

"So, he's not talking, eh?"

"No madam. I'm afraid not."

"Well now, that's just too bad. Just when I thought I would have my ever loving husband to stop by and sing to me, you come and tell me… he's not talking. That's not nice Dr. Presley"

Marlene's strange response left Dr. Presley with a raised eyebrow.

"I guess you're right, Mrs. Sander But we're doing the best we can to get your husband well again," Dr. Presley said.

"Take all the time you need, Doctor. There's absolutely no hurry on my part."

Her revealing moment of candor regarding her low opinion of her husband was not surprising to Dr. Presley. However, he was not interested in being her audience for sarcasms or what others would find to be amusing. Her last response was most disturbing and from that he instantly ended the conversation and excused himself out of her room.

Four days had gone by since the incident and it was time for Marlene, Allora and Bethany to be released from the hospital.   Allora could have been home from the first day, but Marlene insisted on keeping her back so that they all stuck together.   She was especially concerned about her daughter's emotional downturn, but nonetheless, she also realized that Allora's pain went much deeper than the thirty eight stitches in her wound.

While they sat together in the same room and waited for the nurse to come with the discharge papers for Marlene, Merrita Stockholm walked up and greeted her. Marlene was not appreciative about the visit, but she tried to keep an open mind.

Good morning, Mrs. Stockholm. What brought you by?

"I'm very sorry it's not under a more pleasant situation, Mrs. Sander. But I dropped by to see if you would agree to an interview."

"…Interview?" Marlene asked Meritta Stockholm.

"As one of Watertown's favorite families, the city was taken by surprise after reading about the unfortunate news in the newspaper. I realize it maybe be a bit too soon Mrs. Sander. But just in case you'd like to clear up the allegations and set the record straight, I'd appreciate the opportunity of an interview with you."

Marlene listened carefully to all Meritta had to say, and she was sure to adequately coin her words before responding.

"Tell me why I should be so kind to you, Meritta? After all the hell that you had put my sister through, Mrs. Stockholm, tell me why I should be so kind to you?"

"I take it that you're referring to Christina, someone whom I haven't seen or heard from in twelve years or, there about. So, I'm not sure I understand the question, Mrs. Sander. Would you be so kind to explain?

"Twelve years, or, there about, is not too long ago for me to forget what my sister and her then boyfriend, Dr. Wigginton, were put through. I'm talking about the day when her successful career as a journalist collapsed; and what our family was put through because of the action of a disgruntled camera-person." Marlene said.

"My God, I can't believe my ears. This is unbelievable! But since you brought it up, let me just say that I was only doing my job when I took those pictures.   That wasn't anything out of the ordinary coming from me… as a cameraperson.   Matter-of-factly, there was no way for me to know that the gentleman in the car was connected to your sister. And, going by the ethics in journalism, no one in this line of business would expect to see Miss Tate in the company of a drunk while having lunch. Mind you, Mrs. Sander, this incident took place in broad day light while on the grounds of the studio while your sister was still on the job. Wow! I find this meeting to be quite disturbing and disappointing…I might add. Meritta said.

"Oh, I didn't realize you knew that he was there to have lunch with my sister, Meritta. This sounds like someone was watching my sister's every move. I find that quite interesting."

"Well, I don't know about anyone watching your sister, Mrs. Sander. I only found out about it after all was said and done. Twelve years was a long time ago, and it's hard for me to remember details. Anyway, to put your sister and the rest of your family in the media spotlight and tabloids the way it happened is something I'm truly sorry about. I can't stress it enough when I tell you that I *was only doing my job.*"

Uh-huh.   I see. Well thanks for clearing that up for me, Mrs. Stockholm. I'm sure my sister will be pleased to know that you meant no harm. Anyway, I'll put some thought into your idea of an interview and I'll call you, if I'm interested.

"That would be lovely, Mrs. Sander. Here's my card, and I wish you and your family a speedy recovery."

The awkward parting between the two ladies indicated a mutual feeling of animosity.   Meritta left the hospital feeling that could be the last time she'd ever set foot in front of that family again. That major gaffe about Jax and Chrissy meeting for lunch in the parking lot that day was what would do her in, and that was a gut feeling Meritta wouldn't be able to digest anytime soon.

Though Marlene was not functioning at her fullest potential, Meritta was shocked that she was still sharp enough to catch her in a lie; one she thought was none of her business to begin with. The fact that Meritta was no longer a camera-person and that she had come a long way since then, was not enough to keep her from losing confidence within herself. She felt as if Marlene was trying to belittle her position as such… compared to that of her sister, back then. So, while she was losing grounds with Marlene, Meritta assumed that her chance of getting the most sought after interview would never come to pass.

Marlene coolly handed the business card to Bethany and told her to throw it in the garbage. Bethany, who was at a loss during the entire conversation, anxiously asked her mother what it was all about. Listening to her mother defend her Aunt Chrissy was like music to hear ears. Her last memories of being together with her only auntie went back to when she was five or six years old, and they were very precious memories…very near and dear to her heart. However, after she and her brother Monk, were caught in the middle of the split, they learned to keep quiet about missing their aunt Chrissy.

With her heart still bubbling with the private memories in reflection, Bethany crumpled the business card and threw it in the trash can while waiting to get an answer from her mother. But with so much going on, and so much to talk about, she promised her daughter that one day she would explain. Soon after, her nurse walked in and gave Marlene her discharge.
Standing next to her was a porter who would be taking them home in a private shuttle that was provided by the hospital.

***

It was not unusual for Monk to speak to with his family once or twice a day. However, when it came to his sister, it was more frequent than that. So, after not hearing from his family for at least three days, Monk suspected that something terrible had gone wrong at home.

He tried calling his dad's office, but on each occasion he was pacified by the soothing voice of the receptionist who acted as if everything was on the up and up. Anyway after leaving several messages without hearing back from his dad, he made the next best choice. Monk dialed zero and asked the Telephone Operator to assist him with getting through to Lexa. However, with every attempt, he would only end up with getting her answering machine. By the following day, Monk was on his way home from College to check up on his family.

While all three ladies were being transported home, Monk had already made it there. His first sign that he was right about his assumptions was after walking up and finding the front door unlocked. He instantly dropped his duffle bag in the foyer and walked directly to the kitchen while calling, Allora. A sudden rush of fear washed over him and he stopped at the entrance of the kitchen and he called his mother… Mom, Mom! Then, he called for Beth. He turned around and looked as if he was watching his back. He proceeded to go inside the kitchen and he frantically picked out the largest knife he could find in the knife drawer. His heart pounded heavily and his hand shook. Still holding the knife he looked from side to side and tiptoed to the wreck- room overlooking the pool. He peered through the blinds and scanned the area with suspicious eyes. Without seeing, hearing and smelling any signs of life other than his, raw instincts had him in the throes of a deadly encounter. While his thoughts developed and thinking the worse, Monk defensively went upstairs to his parents' bedroom.

Over his lifetime, falling and bruising his knees and getting cuts and scrapes here and there, those little drops of blood were nothing to be afraid of, or too much for his mother to heal with a band aid. Though

Monk was ready to take on and destroy whatever he had pictured in his mind's eyes, there was no way for him to fight back and protect himself from the power of his *sleeping offender*. After seeing the landscape of dried blood which covered most of the flooring, and turning his eyes to discovering large blobs here and there around his parents' bedroom, the knife fell helplessly from his hand.

Monk's devastation was left hanging as he did not know what to suspect and where to pin them. And after noticing the chards of broken glass scattered around the room, his visions of losing his family to death one by one, sent him screaming and calling out their names, one-by-one.

He fell to his knees while assuming the worse and he wept woefully. And while he mourned the loss of his parents he heard the front door slammed. He picked up the knife again and waited cautiously.

Bethany, who noticed that her brother's duffle bag was sitting in the foyer, immediately called him and asked where he was.

"I'm here Beth, I'm here! Are Mom and dad, with you?

"Where are you, Monk?"

"I'm up here. I just need to know if Mom and Dad are with you!"

"Come on down, Son, and give your mother a hug."

"Mom, how you scare me like, that? Do you guys know what I've been through; I've been calling for three days and couldn't find anyone to talk to. When I saw the big pool of blood, I thought everyone was killed or something! Oh, Mommy, I'm so glad that you're alive; you'd never understand what it feels like losing you"

Monk was still holding the knife while running downstairs to see his family and saying what was on his mind. He was shocked to see his mother's face, and without acknowledging his sister and Allora he screamed… "Mom, what happened to you? I knew it! I knew someone was trying to kill you!"

"Put that thing away, honey and give your mother a hug."

The knife fell effortlessly from Monk's hand and the instant it landed on the floor he had his mother all wrapped up in his embrace. She carefully rested her head on his chest but he did not kiss her as she asked.   He only patted her head and stroked her hair because he was painfully afraid of kissing his mother's wounded face. She then pulled back to look up at him while her eyes were brimming with tears.   He was the spitting image of his father. Same… half-caste looks, long neck, thick black wavy hair and light brown eyes.   And, he was the same age as his father….nineteen, when they fell in love.

She saw the questions in his eyes and she knew she couldn't hide the truth.

"Your father did this to me, son. I still find it hard to believe that he would try to kill me."

"Dad, did this to you? My father ..did this, to you, Mom?"

"Uh-huh. And if it weren't for Allora, I don't believe I'd make it out alive."

After paying close attention to everything his mother was saying, he immediately looked at Allora with a bit of shock and humility all in the same demeanor. It was as if he was trying to say, "Hold on, Allora, I'll get to you later to thank you for saving mom, but just give me a minute to finish holding on to her.

"So, Mom, where's dad? …No, let me guess…he's in jail." Monk said, angrily.

"Nope. He's still in the hospital, Son. Very sick, I'm told…. massive stroke."

"Stroke, what do you mean by massive stroke Mom, will you please just tell me what happened! You're killing me with suspense. And what's with all the blood upstairs?"

"I know. You're right, you shouldn't have to come home and be faced with all this.   I'm sorry for being so sketchy but I promise to tell you everything as soon as I feel a little stronger.   Let's just thank the Lord that we are alive.   Anyway, I'm really not feeling well, and now is not a good time. I'm sure your sister will fill you in, but I have to get some rest."

"Mom, you can't go into that bedroom…I don't want you to go up there!" Monk said.

"I know son, I understand. I was thinking of staying in the guestroom for the time being.

While Marlene walked away and left Monk in the company of Bethany and Allora, she ached deeply about the burden placed on her children.   Given her unfortunate series of events that followed her over the years and which were no fault of hers, she felt threatened about opening up and telling them the real reason behind her latest downfall. The fact that she has had trouble managing her suspicions, and was never able to prove that her husband was unfaithful, has left her with a guilty conscience about the emotional wellbeing of her children.

Hunches, she reckoned, would not be fair or near be enough for her to use as accusations against their father. And after seeing the damage and the toll it took on their lives, she feared that her weakness could turn her children against her over the long run. Having said all of that, it had never crossed her mind about forgiving her husband for attempting to end her life.

As miserable as she was, and wanted to throw herself across the bed to try sleeping off some of her worries, she sat at the edge and telephoned Lexa. She assumed Lexa had not yet gotten wind of the bad news. She recalled her saying something about leaving to spend some time with her mother. She was certain Lexa would come to visit her, had she not left town already. And after trying to call her a few times without getting an answer, Marlene presumed that she was right about Lexa leaving town.

By evening time, Frank was on Marlene's doorsteps and ringing her doorbell. It had been a few years since he had visited their home. Things used to be a lot more different before Marlene had lost her dad and became ill. When it came time for the big parties and a place sit back and unwind, Marlene's and Barchas' home was the place to go. Anyway, all wasn't lost for Barchas and Frank. Since the *"cease and desist"* order that was introduced and enforced by Marlene….both men along with some of their other colleagues have found other avenues of diversion.

Frank showed up unannounced because he assumed Marlene would not okay the visit if he had called ahead. The fact that she showed him no great appreciation for his concern about her safety and wellbeing was not going to stop him from still trying to help. And, given her past, he feared that her actions toward him could be nothing more than a sign of an imminent emotional shut down

It was quite a pleasant surprise for Monk to see his dad's best friend showed up. However, the shock of what he had come home to, still had him locked into an overprotective mode, and without any reasonable explanation he was hesitant about opening the door.

He stood quietly at the door with his eye socket fully engaged over the peephole. While nothing specific was going through his mind during his fixation on Frank's face, he heard the doorbell ringing again. The unexpected second ringing of the doorbell, spooked Monk and he immediately pulled back.   He tried regaining a reasonable composure and then he opened the door to face Frank.

Although Frank was not expecting the visit to be a pleasant one, he became lighthearted after seeing Monk standing in front of him. He immediately gave him a manly hug and patted his shoulders as a father would his son; he was genuinely pleased to see him. He asked him about college and he broke a wide smile after complimenting him on his athletic achievements that his dad constantly bragged about.

They stood in the foyer and chatted a little about the freshman years in law school. Frank encouraged Monk about staying the course on becoming a successful lawyer like his dad. After hearing Frank reminding him about how great his dad was, it instantly changed his mood to more of a *chill- out* and relaxed state of mind.   But as soon as Frank changed the subject to ask about his mother, Monk's anger flared and zapped his moment of the much needed pause.

While Frank followed behind Monk to the living room where they sat to talk, he was by no means surprised by his response.

"I'm very worried about my mother, Uncle Frank; I'm still shaking from the news. Mom told me dad had a terrible stroke which could take up to a year for him to recover. I don't want my mother to get sick again, like….you know what I, mean…. Uncle Frank?"

"Yes, I know exactly what you mean, Monk.   But your mother is a very strong lady, and I'm positive she's going to work her way through this; you and your sister have to believe that. I believe that she's going to be just fine.

"How can you say she's going to be fine Uncle Frank? Do you think she's ever going to forget that my own father tried to kill her?"

Frank gasped and sighed deeply before responding to Monk's distress.

"Listen to me, Monk… you're lucky to have two great parents. I know it's hard for you to hear me say this, but I have known your dad, long before he met your mother. I'm having a great deal of trouble with this tragedy, Monk. I find it hard to believe that your father is capable of killing anyone— especially your mother."

"So what do you think really happened, Uncle Frank? Do you think Allora and Beth made up the story even after they witnessed my dad strangling Mommy?"

"I know how upsetting this is for you and the others; and that's why I came out here to see how I could be of help.   I wish your dad could speak and tell us what really happened that horrible night." Frank said.

"So what are you trying to say, Uncle Frank? Are you saying that you would take his word over Mom's? I'm telling you, Uncle Frank, my father tried to kill my mother! Why are you having so much trouble with the truth? Is this what becoming a lawyer is all about?"

Frank cringed at Monk's line of questioning and it pained him to see the sorrow in the young boy's eyes.

"I'm sure you know that's not the case, Monk. I'm so sorry for what you're going through and I can certainly understand your frustration. Before we jump to any conclusions, I think it's best to allow a little more time to work things out. Anyway, Monk, if you don't mind, I'd really like to say hello to your mother and to see if I can help her in any way."

Monk was not satisfied with Frank's response and he blurted:

"No, Uncle Frank; please don't leave... I'm still talking to you. I'm not done; you've got to hear me out!"

Frank was most certainly taken aback by Monk's behavior and it made him more curious about what he wanted to say.

"I'm asking you, Uncle Frank. As lawyers, at what point does the truth start making sense to people like you and my dad?"

Frank sighed heavily while staring at Monk, and he searched himself for an answer to his question. Monk remained focused while looking eye to eye with Frank.

Frank then said to Monk:

"Attorneys, are like regular people too, Monk. Some truths can be so devastating that it could feel like a sinful act to believe it. Some truths are so scary that when it's in your face, Monk, you could be blinded by it. Some truths are so deadly to live with, that once it takes a hold of you, it never sets you free. And, that, young man... is the God's honest truth."

Monk's jaw dropped and he was speechless from Frank's response. He was simply at a loss for a comeback, as he tried making sense from what he had just heard. But, his concentration suddenly broke and it gave way to footsteps they both heard coming their way.

Monk turned around and looked and saw his mother. She was just in time to walk up and tune in to Frank lecturing her son. Going by the little that she'd overheard, she concluded that it would be an uphill battle in trying to change his mind about the way he felt about her husband.

Frank was very relieved about seeing her showed up. Monk, however, was not satisfied with Frank's response. But, without prolonging the conversation, he left the room so Frank and his mother could have some privacy to talk.

Marlene said:
"Hey Frank, when I heard the talking, I wondered who that could be. I'm not all that surprised that you came; but, what brought you by?"

"Well, I'd stopped by the hospital to check up on you and Barchas, and I was very glad to hear that you had been discharged. I take it that you're doing a lot better, Marlene, and it shows." Frank said to Marlene with a smile.

"Thanks Frank. So, with my husband out of the picture, what's new on your agenda, now that you're the top gun back at the office?"

"Marlene, I'm very concerned about what's going on between you and Barchas. The doctors aren't saying much to me because they said I'm not family. If you don't care to stay in touch with the doctors about Barchas, trust me… I understand. But, please Marlene, what I'm asking of you, is to authorize the doctors to communicate his progress with me."

"Oh, okay. So what I think you're saying, Frank, is, that you're not really here for me. You're here mostly because you need me to help you with working on my husband's behalf."

"I'm here for the both of you, Marlene. It's just damn hard for me not to want to help my friend knowing that he would want to do the same for me."

"Uh-huh, I understand. But I'm not going to be the one to help you with saving your friend. I can't wait for them to take him off life support and then drag is his ass off to jail." Marlene said.

"Jesus Christ!" Frank exclaimed, from the shock he felt from Marlene's response.

"What's your problem with, *Jesus Christ,* Frank? You heard what I've just said." Marlene blurted.

"Yeah, I heard you, alright. But…you know…..oh, wow. I agree you have a right to your feelings, but I'm sorry to say that you just shocked me with that statement."

"Uh-huh…well you better believe it, Frank. That son of a bitch deserves to rot in jail."

"Well, Marlene, as I've said, you have every right to your feelings and no one in his right mind can blame you for wanting to fight back. Forgive me if I come off a little out of touch here, but as you can see, I'm still having a great deal of trouble receiving this."

"Oh, wow! That's great! Even though you're looking at me, you're still having trouble believing that my husband is guilty of attempted murder; Is that what you're trying to tell me, Frank?"

"Oh for Christ's sake Marlene, that's not what I'm saying, and you know that. Look at you! I'm mortified seeing you this way, and I know you didn't do this to yourself. However, with all due respect, I can't help wondering what could have driven Barchas so far out of his mind to have caused him to snap like this?"

"Well, I don't think your temporary insanity plea on my husband's behalf is going to hold up in court… if I have anything to do with this. If that man makes it out alive, Frank, I'll see to it that I get my day in court."

Well, I can appreciate your anger, but I'm not about to give up on either of you. Since I don't know exactly what took place because you've totally clammed up on me, I guess it's best for me to leave it all up to time. God, oh, God, how I wish if he would just wake up out of that damn coma and tell me everything so that we could try and fix this *helluva mess.*" Frank lamented almost to tears while Marlene looked on.

Soon after, Marlene became choked up followed by an alarming breakdown in tears. Frank rushed to her and sat next to her on the sofa. She immediately turned her face away from him as if she was bashful about his attention. He tenderly placed his arm around her and gently pulled her around until her head was fully resting on his chest.

Without knowing what to do or what to expect from the unexpected turn of event, Frank found himself somewhat confused by Marlene's *about face.* However, he did his best to be supportive during her breakdown. But other than trying to console her by patting her shoulders and saying … *"Shhh take it easy Marlene,"* he was at an utter loss for words

The fact that he was very experienced in comforting other women who have bawled on his shoulders about affairs of the heart, he came off sounding nothing like the pro as he normally would. The thrust on his conscience after Marlene's chilling outbreak left him feeling a bit clumsy and quite markedly disingenuous.

"My husband has been cheating on me, Frank. I'd be surprise if you didn't know who she is. I don't expect you to admit the truth to me, anyway; as I know your loyalty to him takes precedence over everyone, including me.   But that's ok, Frank. Its ok…. really! And you know why I said that, Frank?

"No. Tell me why."

"I said it because after everything that I've been through, I've finally learned how to survive. If you really *wanna* know the truth, Frank, I've survived damned near everything and this one is going to be no different!"

Oh, Marlene! Now that's what I'm talking about.

What, what are you saying Frank?

You, don't know how glad and encouraged I am to hear you say that. You keep on believing in yourself this way and everything is going to be all right. But, you're *gonna* have to believe me, when I say this to you, Marlene.

I'm not going to promise anything, Frank….but go on.

"Look, I'm not surprised you'd assume that I know everything about Barchas. Not after all the years we've been friends, but if he's cheating on you I'm not aware of it. Please, Marlene, your husband is a very sick man. What's the point in contemplating situations that could only make things worse for you?"

"Well, if you'd really like to help, I'd appreciate you letting me have Blossom Rigby's address. Please, Frank."

"What? Blossom Rigby!! Don't even think about it, Marlene. I can tell you right now that you're way off— if you're seriously thinking that your husband has been sleeping with that woman."

As if Marlene heard nothing of what frank had said while her head was still plunged in his chest, she could literally feel his heart raced by her queries.

"Where does she live Frank? Or, are you not going to help me like you promised that you would?"

"Marlene, you're asking me to do something out of the ordinary. You could get into some serious shit, *pardon my expression*, and make things worse for yourself and your entire family. You have no idea how badly the press would love to follow you out there and watch you trying to making a fool of yourself. Trust me on this one, Marlene…don't even think about it."

"Okay Frank, I heard you. So, let me put it this way for you then. All I need is a simple answer to a simple question. Does Blossom live out by Quail Run?"

"Hold on a minute here, Marlene; I need to get this *straight* in my head. Whatever gave you the idea that Blossom lives in Quail Run? What's this all about?"

"Will you just answer the question for me, Frank? I have my reasons"

"No, Marlene. Blossom does not live in Quail Run; but I do."

Marlene's eyes popped and they stayed widened after hearing Frank's response. She immediately raised her head from off his chest, to face him. After their eyes met, he thought to himself that Marlene was giving him a wicked stare and he became uneasy being so close to her. However, he tried finishing response:

"I owned a condo out there; I bought it less than a year ago."

Marlene appeared as if she was pondering Frank's response for a moment, or so, and then she said , "do you really expect me to believe that, Frank?

Her question to Frank didn't come off sounding as if she was shocked or insecure about his unexpected answer.   It came off as if she wanted to give him the impression that she still had him on the hook. But her acting ability or lack thereof, had Frank thinking otherwise.

"Well, if it will make you feel better, Marlene, I'll take you there. I'm sorry, but I thought you knew about it. I'm still living in my older home, though.   Anyway, maybe it's just a guy thing… but every now and then I'd have my buddies to meet me at Quail Run so we could hang out and watch the games over a few drinks.

"Oh, really" Marlene said.

"Just say the word, Marlene, and I'll take you there; I think it's the only way for me to convince you that I'm telling the truth."

Frank had barely finished his response when Marlene started feeling embarrassed in his presence. And she quickly tried redeeming herself before things got worse.

"Oh, Lord, please forgive me, Frank. There's no need for you to do that; I believe you. It's just that things are so crazy right now that I can hardly focus on doing or saying the right thing. I just don't know what came over me, and I'm so very sorry for drilling down on you with such resentment. I hope you forgive me for taking out my frustrations on you. It's not right… but I just couldn't help it."

Frank felt pity towards Marlene and he tried calming her.

"Oh, Marlene, no offense was taken. It's not just you; things are hellish for all of us right now, and I haven't been myself either. But you have to try and continue taking care of yourself. I don't want you to worry about anything other than getting your life back on track and I hope you never lose sight of that."

Marlene remained quiet after Frank's response and he wondered if he had said too much, or if what he had to say, really mattered. Without making matters any worse he reckoned it would be best if he left. He then casually glanced at his watch and said…"I'm sorry; I shouldn't wear you out like this. I think I'm *gonna* have to leave now and let you get back to bed."

Marlene welcomed the idea of Frank's decision to leave. She immediately tried rising to her feet by pressing down on the arm of the sofa for support. Her intent was to walk with him back to the front door.

Frank noticed that she was a bit achy or somewhat fatigued but not to the point of where he'd want to stay back. He reckoned that she'd be ok as soon as she was back in bed, but most importantly as soon as he was out of there.

He politely excused himself by saying "Don't worry about getting up, Marlene; I'll see myself out. The only thing I'll beg of you is to promise to call me if you need help with anything. I'm sure you know that I'll always be there for you."

Frank's gestures *kind of* touched Marlene to the point of where her tone became a little subdued and agreeable. She thanked him for coming and again she apologized for her behavior. However, her attitude didn't quite show that she would gladly run to Frank if she needed any help. It was teetering more towards something like... *"Thanks for the offer, Frank...but, I think I'll pass."*

She politely accepted his hug and watched while he walked out of her living room and continued toward the front door. And, while she watched him walking away, his stately gait and his sexy swagger reminded her of the good-old days that came rushing back to her. While her eyes followed until he exited her front door, she stood still in bittersweet reflections.

With a shot glass brimming with cognac and a cigar in his hand, she recalled how Frank used to relax out back with her husband and some of their other colleagues. They never got tired of listening to him brag about having to hide from yet another amorous spinster who was on the prowl for a husband. But to her, Frank was nothing more than a handsome devil with a reputation of breaking beautiful women's hearts....both young and the not so young.

Frank left Marlene's home feeling unaccomplished and quite edgy about his visit. He recalled his heart pounding several times faster than its normal pace after she had quizzed him about "Quail Run."

Yes, he did tell the truth about purchasing a condo in the Quail Run development. And, yes, he and his colleagues including Barchas have palled around there from time to time...*shooting the breeze,* playing poker and what have, you. However, his accelerated heart rate emanated from keeping Barchas' secret very closely to his chest.

It was clear to Frank that Marlene had been doing some kind of checking up on her husband. However, he was quite shocked that a woman of her intelligence could be buried so deep in naivety, that her obvious threat had bypassed her without a questionable doubt. Instead, she chose to pin all her doubts on Blossom Rigby who was really a contender …but only in Blossom Rigby's mind and hers.

CHAPTER SEVEN

He contemplated driving out to Quail Run to try and catch up with Lexa. He was concerned about how she was handling the news about Barchas and Marlene. Also, he was very cagey of Marlene's suspicion about her husband having an affair with someone living in Lexa's *"neck of the woods."*

Anyway, in trying to help with covering Barchas' tracks which he thought would also help save Marlene from the dangers ahead, Frank threw caution to the wind and he drove straight to Quail Run to find Lexa.

Frank arrived just in time to see Lexa entering a limousine that was parked very closely to the main entrance of her building. The door -man was still loading luggage into the limo and Frank immediately assumed she was not just heading back to "movie land".... she could be skipping town.

He immediately pressed his horn to get her attention. She instantly turned around, looked in his direction and she stopped. He slowly pulled his car up close to her and said "I'm so glad I caught you, Lexa. Please give me a minute to park....I really would like to have a chat with you."

Lexa did not answer Frank about waiting.   But according to the way she stood, rolled her eyes at him and sighed, he could tell she was not thrilled about the untimely visit.   However, before she proceeded to get inside the car she finally gave him the *nod* that she would wait for him while he looked around for parking.

Frank felt relief.

Lexa was by no means surprised about seeing Frank turned up; she suspected that he would want to come and *feel-her-out.* But she wished she had left earlier and avoided what she perceived as additional stress to her dilemma.

Frank walked hurriedly from the parking area to meet with Lexa. He peered inside the limo and he saw her sitting with her head hung low with a gaunt-like profile.   He presumed that it was mostly likely the shocking news that had taken a toll on her.   He knocked on the window to get her full attention but she ignored him.   He then tried the door which was unlocked and he invited himself inside and he sat next to her.   She slowly raised her head to acknowledge his presence but her actions revealed that she was still very annoyed and not quite prepared to entertain his company.

Despite her gauntness and what might have been, Lexa came off sounding quite the persnickety and prissy woman he recalled about her. And even though they had not seen each other in a year, or there about, she peppered him with arguments about his presumptuousness.

"Frank, why are you here and sitting inside my limo? Don't tell me you've changed; I don't recall you as the type to sneak up on people and force them self into their space."

Although Frank wasn't the type for such biting remarks, he swallowed his pride so as to keep her ego on the rise.

So his response to Lexa was:

"My apologies; you're right, Lexa.   I know I should have called first; but I couldn't find your number and time is of the essence.   Matter-of-fact I don't even want to beat around the bush. So, if I may, I'd like to get straight to the point.

Lexa then turned to Frank and said:

"I' couldn't agree with you more, Frank. Time is of the essence. And, as you can see, I'm just about ready to get going... I have a plane to catch."

"Yes Lexa, I understand. And, I can appreciate your disapproval about the way I turned up.   But with so much going on over the past few days, I find it hard to believe that you're all that shocked about me wanting to come and see you.

"Okay," Lexa replied while staring at Frank with half-cast eyes.

Frank ignored the look and saw past what he presumed was a front behind her fears. He then lowered his tone and said to her:

Anyway my lady, how are you? Really, Lexa, how are you?"

When Frank asked Lexa how she was doing, she could not deny feeling his genuine concern. However, she was not about to show him that he mattered.

"I'm a big girl, Frank; I can take care of myself." You said you weren't going to beat around the bush. Don't tell me you came all this way to find out how I'm doing.   I hate to be rude, but will you just get to the point."   She retorted.

Frank's eyes widened at Lexa's response, but it didn't deter him from trying to wiggle his way to her good side.

"Oh, wow!" Frank said with his eyes still widened. "It has been a while since I've seen you. I can't begin to imagine what its' like for you, given the current event. However, I've got to let you know you're still as beautiful as can be."

"Thank you. Go on." Lexa said, in a cold and unappreciative tone, while Frank looked on and prepped himself for yet a better in.

"Let's just say I was hoping to catch you at home so we could talk privately. But if you insist, I'm sure here is just as good." Frank said.

"You're wasting my time, Frank. Will you spit it out, or just get out… so I can be on my way? Look, Mr. Frank Roulette, I'm already aware of Barchas and Marlene's demise… the news is already stale and has taken over the entire city. Is that your reason for trying to breaking your neck to catch up with me? And, if that's the case, why are you acting so pent up and nervous about it?

"Me … pent up? Frank responded amazingly.

Yes, you Frank, said Lexa with much aggression.

Then Frank, continued. "Well, I'm not sure if pent up is quite the word, my lady. But then again…. yeah… I guess you could say that. And, why shouldn't I be nervous or pent up as you described it? We are talking about my best friend who's in the hospital and fighting for his life."

"So, let me just ask you, this" Frank continued.

"Ask me what? " Lexa said to Frank while feeling a little roughed up despite his caring approach.

Is that why you're leaving town, Lexa; are you running away? Your best friend is in a lot a pain right now and I'm sure she could use your support; she's been through a lot since the incident, you know.

"How, arrogant of you to force yourself upon me like this and speak to me this way?   Chances are you think you can wrap me around your *pinkie* because you think you're some top notch lawyer! How dare you accuse me of not being there for Marlene?"

But, have you? Frank fired back at her.

"Shut up and let me finish, Frank!" Lexa blurted.

And, what the heck is that suppose to mean, huh? What do you mean by suggesting that I'm running away? And, running away from what, Frank? Whatever you've got up your sleeves, I think you should keep it there and get out of my car, right now! I will not tolerate your insinuations"

***

Frank immediately picked up on how badly Lexa's fingers were trembling. Her eyes were watery and his gut feeling was that she was very, very worried, to say the least. "She had to be," Frank said to himself.

So, in keeping with his mindset, Frank immediately changed his tone to a more comforting temperament. He reckoned the change would accommodate any further affronts coming from her without taking an offense. He suspected that she was only trying to rid herself of him so he could be kept out of her private business. However, Frank was not about to let her off the hook that easily….no matter what it was going to take.

"Look, Lexa, I know this is a bad time for you. And I didn't come all the way out here to make things worse; I only came to see if there's a way you could help me get to the bottom of this. Quite frankly it's killing me knowing that I'm not able to speak with Barchas so I could find out what really took place that night.   I'm having a great deal of trouble figuring out what could have driven him into doing something so outrageous. Damn it, Lexa! All of Watertown is accusing the man of attempted murder!   I just don't know who else I can turn to for help other than you."

Then Lexa said:

"So, what about Blossom Rigby; Why come to me and not, her? She's Barchas's confidante. Did you not think about that? I saw the way she was chummy, chummy with Barchas, at lunch the other day at Vines. She's the one you should be badgering for answers.   Not me!"

Frank was taken aback by Lexa's reveal. Having lunch at Vines with their colleagues along with Blossom was easily recalled. And he was certain Blossom's presence among the group was all about business for Barchas. However, he couldn't help zoning in on the fact that Lexa sounded like a jealous lover. So, he carefully committed that vital piece of info to memory.   He surmised it could come in very handy as he pursued his goal of getting to the bottom of Barchas' downfall.

While Frank's head swirled with false accusations from both Marlene and Lexa about Blossom, he tried holding back his tongue from defending her.   He was more interested in gathering any information he could, regardless. But, unlike his usual self… tactful and together, his wits got the better of him in his response to Lexa.

"Pardon me Lexa, but I don't see the sense in wasting our time talking about Ms. Rigby. You and I know that there's nothing going on with her and Barchas, other than business. And as you said, it's time for me to stop beating around the bush. Well my lady, I totally agree."

"So, let me just get straight to the point. I know that you're the only woman Barchas is involved with romantically other than his wife. And I've known this for years."

Lexa's eyes widened as she raised her head to face Frank directly after he addressed her love affair with Barchas, so casually. To her it felt uncomfortable and she wondered who else in their circle knew about them.   She tried interjecting to let Frank know that her relationship with Barchas wasn't something she was proud of.   Frank quickly raised his hand as a show that he was not done making his point. So while his hand was still in the upright position he politely asked her to let him finish.

She regressed and allowed him to proceed.

"That night of the incident, I'm fully aware that Barchas was with you before he went home. I recall him telling me over the telephone that he had just left your place. And, he sounded very upset. I asked him if everything was cool and he replied that it was the worst day of his life. I asked if there was anything I could do to help, but he said he and I would talk later that night, or, at the office next day. I know Barchas, and I've never heard him sounding so distraught since Larry Tate's suicide. That being said, is the reason why I came here to see if you could help me shed some light on what could have pushed him over the edge."

At the end of that statement, Frank remained quiet as if to respectfully turn over the floor to Lexa. He kept his eyes on her and waited for answers but she shyly looked away and she somewhat appeared at a loss for words. While several seconds elapsed with Frank hanging in suspense, Lexa finally turned to him with her twist to the story.

"I'm sorry Frank; I appreciate your concern, but I have to go now. There's absolutely no reason for me to stay back and wait for reporters to start hanging around here. Pretty soon my relationship with Barchas is going to come out; and I know it's going to be ugly. And regarding all that other stuff you are alluding to— I don't know what you're talking about.

"With all due respect, Lexa, I find that hard to believe."

"Are you calling me a liar, Frank?"

"No, Lexa; I wouldn't dare. All I'm saying is that I know Barchas well enough to tell that something terrible happened the last time he was with you."

"Well Frank, as I've told you, I don't know that you're talking about."

"C'mon now, Lexa, you've got to *cut me some slack* here. You know that I know Barchas more than anyone and that's not the Barchas I know. Look, I'm not here to judge you; you have my word. I wouldn't do anything to put you at risk. I know how Barchas feels about you and I have to respect that. I just want to help put the pieces together."

Lexa looked away in a somber state while Frank waited for anything she had to say. However, she slowly turned her head back around to face Frank and she said:

"So, what has Marlene got to say about this? Don't you think she of all people would have the missing pieces to your puzzle?"

Frank kept his eyes on her while hoping she wouldn't look away again. Then he said:

"Speaking of Marlene, Lexa,   Don't you think she's going to start wondering why you, of all people, haven't checked in on her? Good God, Lexa, you are her best friend! She's all you've got. And you, more than anyone knows how fragile she is.

Lexa's heart raced with anger while pointing her finger toward her chest as she tried defending her stance.

"So what about me, Frank; don't you think I've got feelings too? I've spent several years nurturing Marlene so that she could be on her feet again.   If it weren't for me, I hardly think she'd still be around for her children. And, now after all that I did for her, things are about to blow up in my face.

"Oh, Lexa, I don't think you've heard a word of what I just said, so let me repeat myself ...I am here for you. And, you don't have to explain.... I know how much you've helped Marlene. But, that's beside the point now.   Even I know how much she loves and cares for you. Everybody knows that!

That response from Frank seemed to have hit Lexa in a certain kind of way that he could tell he was getting through to her.

Then Lexa said:

"Well, this may sound odd after being in an affair with her husband for so many years. But in my own way I do love Marlene. However, I've got my own problems now and I've got no one to turn to while Barchas is laying half dead in the hospital. So, how do you think that makes me feel having no one to turn to? A little fragile too....you'd think?"

Frank marveled inwardly at Lexa's comment about loving Marlene, but he dared not ask her what she meant by saying that she loved her. So he kept the conversation taut in his response.

"Lexa, I empathize with you wholeheartedly. I'm sure there's a way I can help protect you. Quite frankly I don't think you'd want Marlene to find out about this; you know it would kill her."

Lexa found Frank's response to be offensive and she fired back at him saying:
"So why are you pushing me on her! Why are you doing this to me, Frank! Why don't you just drop it and let me be?"

Lexa broke down in tears and sobbed dreadfully while shaking her head from side to side. Frank pulled her closely to his chest and hugged her tightly as she wept and kept repeating herself:
"I'm still in shock, I'm still in shock, and it's all, my fault"!

Frank was surprised after hearing Lexa's chilling outburst about faulting herself. He raised her head off his chest to face her and he asked her what she meant by that statement. He waited for an answer while he wiped away her tears. She remained speechless. Then he gently raised her chin to get her to look him in the eyes while he waited for a response, but she simply closed her eyes while her lips and chin shook. And with her eyes still closed and brimming, she turned and looked away from him as if she were ashamed of herself.

Again he turned her face to have her looking at him, and he asked her why she was to be blamed.

At that point, she appeared a bit less uptight but somewhat pensive and doubtful all in one. However, he sensed that he was making headway. And in a much gentler tone he lowered his voice and stared at her with an earnestness that successfully nudged her into a *"tell- it- all -moment."*

"I'm pregnant, Frank!" Lexa blurted with streaming tears and agony flooding her face.

Franks eyes widened and continued popping from what he thought he'd heard Lexa said.

"Say What! Repeat that, what you just said" Frank said to Lexa with urgency in his voice and Lexa knew that he was quite shocked by the news.

"Yes, Frank, I'm pregnant…and Barchas fathered my child."

Lexa, broken down and frightened, sobbed quietly while keeping her eyes looking down on the floor of the limo.

Frank too was quiet and while they contemplated, moments passed over the emerging silence that would later sear Lexa's frustration.

"Say something, Frank. Aren't you going to say something? Or did you not hear me? I said I'm going to have Barchas's baby!"

After hearing Lexa's plea for a response, his immediate thought was "what the hell does she mean she's going to have Barchas' baby while looking at her dumbfounded.

Frank sat motionless while his hands fell to his side. He too was looking down at the flooring of the limousine …and he remained speechless. Then suddenly, Lexa turned around and started pounding him in the chest with her fist and ordering him to say something. He grabbed her hand to stop from adding another blow to his body, when suddenly their eyes met. She felt panic because while she kept her eyes looking straight into Frank's, she saw flares of anger .... *It was flashback time for her.*

"Let go of me" she said to Frank with her teeth clenched, and he too, saw flares of wrath coming from her; so he gently released his grip.

Frank then raised his hand and started pushing hard down on his head and pushing his hair back as if he felt they were standing on ends. He then rolled up his sleeves and covered his face with his hands, because he was deep in frustration and somewhat at a loss for words.

While Frank worked on regaining his composure, Lexa was wondering if she had made a mistake by blurting out what was truly driving her out of town. Then suddenly Frank removed his hands from his face and asked if Barchas was aware of her *"recent development."* Lexa was disturbed by his question and the way he came off so coldly. She felt that he was more interested in getting to the bottom of his mission of protecting Barchas, without showing her that her wellbeing also mattered.

She then fired back at him saying... "Oh wow, Frank, I'm surprised you haven't asked if I was positive that Barchas is the father!"

It was after that comment that Frank realized he was still in aftershock about the news. He apologized to Lexa and told her he meant no disrespect and how he was truly flabbergasted from the unexpected news.

From there on he tried focusing on measuring his words more carefully, because he clearly understood that their clashing emotions were at the tipping point of disaster.

"Lexa, now that you have told me this, I totally understand your dilemma. To be honest, if I were in your situation, I most likely would want to do the same thing. But please…just hear me out.

"Having said that,   I'm sure one more day wouldn't hurt if you'd stayed back so we could talk some more." Frank said in an effort to detain her to his advantage.

Deep sighs followed and Lexa appeared a bit more tolerant while her tone matched quite the same when she responded to Frank's suggestion.

"Well, since I've already missed my flight, it's just as well I stay back."

"Alright… sounds good" Frank said to Lexa, pleasingly. He then started rubbing his palms together and said to Lexa,

"Well, how do you feel a about getting something to eat? Would you be so kind and join me for dinner; I'm famished and I could take a large bite out of anything right now. So, what do you say?

Lexa then started shaking her head from side to side while thinking about the invitation and her response to Frank was:

"I'm sorry… I'm just not up to being out, right now"

"That's quite alright, I'm sure we could think of something else. And by the way, as you know, I've got a place here; my condo is just around the corner. I could order some take out and we could have dinner there." Frank said to Lexa.

"No, I don't think I'd like to do that; I hate to be so stubborn, Frank, but I'm just not in the mood for company,"

After Lexa made that comment, Frank became tightlipped. He then helped himself to a glass of vodka and orange juice from the bar inside the limo and he poured a glass halfway with ginger ale for Lexa. He handed the drink to her and then he took a sip of his screwdriver.

She thanked him for the drink but she appeared uninterested in having it. She then turned and looked outside and she saw the limo driver pacing back and forth and looking at his watch. Since she already knew she had missed her flight and would not be able to catch another one for the evening, she casually turned her attention back to Frank and suggested dinner at her place.

Frank was pleased about the invitation; he would have followed her anywhere so long as he's got a shot at finding out more about what had happened the night of the incident.

"Sure," he said..... I'm OK with your place. I'll take care of the limo driver so he can be on his way. And don't worry about your luggage; I'll see to it the door man get them back upstairs."

Lexa was appeased by Frank's gestures, and she took a sip of the beverage while eyeing him from the corner of her eyes. And in the meantime Frank flung his head back and finished his drink in one gulp.

As soon as they made it to Lexa's condo, she asked Frank if he would be OK with Chinese food. Frank, who was prepared to be agreeable with anything she suggested, quickly said "Chinese sounds divine." She immediately picked up the telephone and placed an order for home delivery.

While they waited for dinner to arrive, Lexa invited Frank to help himself to anything he wanted from her small liquor stash. Frank loosened his tie and with his sleeves still rolled up he strolled over and poured a double scotch.

While this was happening, Lexa left and went inside her bathroom. The bathroom door was left ajar and from there she yelled and told Frank that ice was in a small freezer below, and next to the wet bar.

Her tone sounded even more inviting and Frank took that as a "hopeful" regarding his main objective.

Pale as a ghost, she was, when Frank saw her emerged from the bathroom. She had no makeup on and she had changed and slipped into an off-white maxi sleeveless dress.

She walked passed Frank who was sitting on the sofa with his drink. She went into the kitchen and returned with a tall glass of club soda.

While Frank sipped on his drink, his eyes followed her returning to the living room and getting comfortable. She sat on a green leather club chair which was an accent piece given to her by Barchas, which later became his favorite seat in the house.

The rustic hammerhead detail and overstuffed seating caught Frank's eyes and he really liked the chair primarily because of its manly presence.

"Nice chair, it's quite a conversation piece in this room" Frank remarked.

"Thank you" said Lexa, but in a dry and uninviting tone, which sent Frank wondering if she was having a change of heart about his visit; but that was not the case. She simply found it awkward speaking about the chair and disclosing too much about it, as it was one of her many gifts from Barchas.

So within the same breath of thanking him for the compliment, she moved on with chit chatting as if he had never made any mention of the chair.   That smooth transition, however gave Frank a sense of hope that things were still on the "up -and- up."

"So, what are your thoughts, Frank?   Now that I've told you everything, where do I go from here?" Lexa said:

"Well, for starters. I'm glad you didn't get on that plane. And if you don't mind me asking, where were you planning to go?"

"Well, it's not like I've changed my mind about getting out of Watertown; hopefully, I'll be on a plane by tomorrow morning. I'd like to end up somewhere far away where nobody knows me. But for now I'll be leaving to spend some time with my mother while I sort things through. I just don't know what to do… I'm thinking it's best if I could get them to write me off the set. This baby means everything to me."

Lexa's response did not sit well with Frank. He shuddered to think that she would want to birth the child, given the unfortunate situation. Deep down he was wishing to hear her say she was going to have an abortion.   But he conveniently pushed the idea aside to keep her unperturbed.

"You mean you're planning to give up your career as an actress, after all the hard work you've put in?

"Well let's just say things are a bit premature right now, but I think it's best for me in the long run."

Oh, come on now, Lexa. You can't be serious…not after all those years of the most watched soap opera.

"Yeah, I know what you mean. I've been thinking about that seriously, but my baby takes precedence over everything in my life now; and I mean that from the bottom of my heart.

Lexa's eyes lit up and she gently rubbed her tummy while Frank looked on. Then she continued by saying "Wow, I still can't believe that I'm pregnant, Frank. You have no idea how amazing that sounds to me."

Lexa's eyes widened and she smiled proudly after she expressed her feelings to Frank. A smile followed her comments and Frank looked on unresponsive.

Frank tried not to let any of his feelings show, because he was miserable, confused, and furious at Lexa's for being so ecstatic about having Barchas' baby.

After patiently listening to Lexa, Frank found himself becoming enraged, because in the moment he tried putting himself in Barchas shoes while she talked.   And to him it felt as if he was being told that he had fathered a child with someone with whom he had, had a one –night- stand.

 And knowing Barchas, and how they both thought alike, Frank assumed he knew what had taken place after Lexa landed Barchas with the bad news that night.

His assumption was:

After Barchas got the bad news from Lexa,   he immediately knew that he was in trouble. So, without any further talks about fatherhood, outside of his marriage, Barchas immediately denounced the subject by demanding that she did away with *"it"*....meaning the baby. Then, undoubtedly she fired back and flatly shut him down. *"And that, right there, would be enough to send Barchas over the edge"*... but of course only according to Frank's theory.

With that in mind, Frank felt as if his bits and pieces of information were beginning to fall into place. So with his composure still intact, he answered Lexa on an even keel.

"Oh yes, I can understand how amazing it must be for you, Lexa; my mother always said babies are a blessing. It's a shame I haven't given her a grandchild as yet; I know that would put her over the moon."

Lexa smiled broadly at Frank after his response and he watched her shoulders dropped to a more relaxed position as if finally she had found a friend in him. However, she had nothing to say because she realized that he wasn't done speaking.

"So tell me… how did Barchas handle the big news? I'd asked you about that a while ago, but you didn't answer me."

"A while, ago? I don't remember that." Lexa responded while looking at Frank rather surprised.

"Well, maybe you didn't hear me, but while we were sitting in the limo I did ask." Frank replied in his defense. And he'd hoped that she wasn't trying to avoid the question, but she came forthright with an answer.

"Oh, I see. Well, which married man do you know would be thrilled about finding out that his lover is planning to have his baby?"

"That's a damn good question Lexa. I'm not sure, but I wouldn't be surprised if statistic says one in every five thousand. But let me say this….I'd have trouble believing that Barchas would be one of those men…. Sorry to say."

Oh, no need to apologize. You know him well enough to come up with the right answer. But it doesn't give him the right to mistreat me, regardless.   I'm still in shock about the way Barchas carried on after I told him about our baby."

"Hmm… so what exactly was his reaction?" Frank asked Lexa.

"Well, as you can imagine he was absolutely beside himself, and I clearly identify with that. Even I was in absolute shock after the doctor informed me that I was pregnant; I had to ask him several times if he was certain of this."

"Anyway, after I told him about our baby, he casually walked over to the bar and poured a drink.   I really thought he would have asked me how I felt about the news, before doing any such thing. And, to make matters worse, he simply stood there sipping the drink as if I had not said anything of great importance to him."

Huh, huh, then what happened after that" Frank asked Lexa.

And her response was "Not much, quite frankly. Other than he calmly walked passed me still holding the glass and rubbing his forehead from side to side. I'm telling you Frank, Barchas acted as if the news was nothing major. Like it was nothing! Nothing; just like…ah… one of those easy open and closed cases that occasionally falls in his lap.

"What do you mean by …a closed case?"

"C'mon now, Frank, don't tell me you don't know what I mean by saying that. I mean he already knew what the outcome of the situation was going to be even before discussing it. So in my case he'd already concluded how the situation was going to be handled."

Lexa sighed deeply and looked at Frank while she studied his face. She wondered if he was paying any attention to what she had to say.

Frank then chimed in and said, "Keep talking I'm listening... Tell me what happened next."

"Well, I was soon to find out that Barchas was only interested in finding out where would be the best and the most convenient place for me to go for an abortion. And then it was like... back to business as usual."

"I'm telling you, Frank, I was in utter shock and I was speechless after he said that to me. And, I felt deep rejection.   And, not only that; the way he looked at me when he spoke, was as if killing our baby wasn't worth losing sleep over."

I know that must have been very painful for you, Lexa. But I'm sure he didn't intend to hurt your feelings. His response could be purely out of a state of shock. What you just described to me, is exactly Barchas' way of dealing with certain situation."

"I can appreciate your point Frank, but if you know Barchas as much as you say you do, then you'd know that the man means what he says and says what he means. I don't believe he was into any damn state of shock more than I, when Dr. Pines floored me with the news. And it never crossed my mind that abortion was an option."

"So what did you say to him after all that?"

"Well, I wasn't going to just sit there and let him disregard me like that! I told him repeatedly that he was out of his damn mind if he thought that I'd consider an abortion."

"I see. I know that must have been quite a blow. So what transpired after that?" Frank said

"Well, you're not going to believe what he did after I told him how I felt." Lexa said.

"Go on; what did he do" Frank asked Lexa with high anxiety which made her feel that he was fully engaged in what she had to say. However, he was non-the-less objective all in the same breath.

"Well, *mister high and mighty* had the nerve to grab me, and then he pushed me hard up against the wall, while screaming and yelling at me saying that I was not his wife. I was horrified and I wished if I could have done something to make him feel the hurt that he plunged inside my heart after he said that to me. How dare he, Frank? How, dare he!? Didn't he know that I wasn't his wife for all those years he'd been screwing me! Huh….so, what have you got to say about that!"

Frank was taken suddenly by surprise about the news, and his gut feeling was that Lexa's statement was not exaggerated. He believed her wholeheartedly, but he chose to remain objective in his response.

"What the hell are you saying to me, Lexa? This doesn't sound like the man I know. Are you sure we're talking about the same person?

What's your point, Frank? Do you think that I'm making this up? I still have black and blue marks from the bruises I endured after he slammed me against the wall. Do you need me to take my clothes off so you could be convinced?

Frank hands immediately went up in the air to show Lexa there's no need for her to undress. He had no interest in seeing her undressed under any circumstance.

Oh, no Lexa. Please there's no need for you to even think that way. I believe you. What I'd like to know, however, is, if Barchas had raised his hands and hit you.

No, he never raised his hand and hit me, but it doesn't discount the fact that I was abused. As I've told you previously, he grabbed be by the neck and he pushed me up against the wall, and it left bruises on my back and shoulders! I never dreamed Barchas would lay a hand on me, no matter what.

A tear dropped and Lexa sniffled and looked away in disgust without saying another word. Frank was quick to grab the tissue box and he handed it to her. And while she blew her nose she heard Frank said "Oh, thank God"

Oh, thank God for what, Frank? What do you mean by saying thank God, uh Frank? Lexa blurted.

"I mean I'm relieved to hear that he did not actually raise his hands and hit you, Lexa. If you said he had done that, then things would have been much uglier. But you're right. It doesn't excuse the fact that you were abused. I'm very sorry Lexa, to say the least. I never expected to hear anything of the sort."

Silence followed while Frank watched Lexa reeling a handful of tissue from the box and patted her face. And while the seconds continued to elapse nonproductively, Frank asked:

"So, how did the two of you manage to resolve the evening?"

Lexa's response was:

"Resolve….you say. Let me tell you something, Frank. After he scolded me about not being his wife, rage spewed from my brain. If he had not grabbed me and pushed me aside in the way he did, and then stormed out of here, I swear…..I swear… I would have grabbed my revolver and shoot him. Shoot him until he was dead, Frank. Shoot him until he could no longer make me feel as if I was not worthy enough to birth his child.

"Oh, good God, Lexa, I can't believe my ears" Frank chimed in.

"You better believe your ears Frank. You have no idea how worthless I felt after Barchas said that to me."

Lexa cried piteously for minutes while Frank tried figuring out what next to do. He was undoubtedly stunned by her unexpected reveal. Yet he wondered if there could be more to her story. But even if that was all she had to say, he reckoned it was more than enough for him to make sense out of a very bad situation. And while he remained speechless and watched Lexa crying and trying to pull herself together, she blew her nose again, and she chimed in with a soft attack on Frank's loyalty to Barchas.

"So, now you know, Frank. And, I wouldn't be surprised if you found a way to defend him even after all that I've told you. I know that Barchas is your pride and joy."

'I'm sorry you see it that way Lexa; but right now my focus is only on you. You don't deserve to be in so much pain and I'd like to see you happy and doing well again. I care about you more than you know."

Although Frank's thoughts were still swirling with questions about her previous confessions, he held them back for the moment to address her last comment about his loyalty to Barchas. That thought coming from her, was the very least of his concerns. However, he reckoned she was desperate for answers to help save her shrinking self esteem.

<> <>

But then door bell rang and the conversation was suddenly placed on the back- burner while the Chinese food was being delivered.

Lexa opened the door and Frank was quick to pull out the money to take care of the bill.   While Lexa walked over to the dining table with the bags of food, Frank sidestepped her and went to get another drink. He watched her remove the small packets of condiments and set them aside from the pint size boxes of entrees.

Although Frank's stomach was starting to turn from trying to digest all that Lexa had to say. The aroma of the food spiraled and quickly found its way to a revved up appetite. He immediately joined Lexa at the table, and she gently pushed the containers of food in front of him. As much as he was ready to dig in, he politely asked her what was her fancy...shrimp or pepper steak.   Lexa showed no interest in the food other than two of the eggrolls which she had kept back for herself.

While Frank slouched himself over the table as if he was guarding the food while he ate, Lexa sat erect and was barely picking at the eggrolls. She was more interested in hearing what Frank had to say about her last reveal.

Frank, however, while he ate, wondered inwardly if Lexa had *gone nuts.* His pressing concerns were:

"What would possess her to be OK with having a child with the husband of her very best friend? What would make it OK for her to want to take the risk of the impending dangers ahead, especially at that stage of her life? And where does she come off thinking that running away with the baby would save her from being exposed later on down the road. What, is she…stupid, he thought deeper within himself, or, is she just in plain denial about her situation? And what about Marlene, the friend she claimed that she loved and cared about so much."

While Frank ate and pumped his thoughts for more reasons behind Lexa's motives, he remained clueless, but his appetite remained fully engaged, nonetheless.

As Lexa cleared the table, Frank looked up to her and said:

"You haven't eaten your egg rolls."

She appeared a bit uptight but she sounded quite pleasant when she responded by telling him that she felt full from the glass of club soda.

They left the dining room together and returned to the living room so they could talk some more. And since it was back to business, Frank wasted no time in taking the lead to address her burning desire.

"You know, Lexa, let's be realistic here. According to what the nurses told me, it could take a year or more for Barchas to get back on his feet. But, let's just hope that's a worst case scenario. However, while you are off in some new town, far away from here, I imagine, how do you plan to make it on your own with a child?"

"Frank, what are you talking about? There's more than enough money in the bank for me to provide my child with the best of life. That is something I'm looking forward to, so there's no need for you to be concerned.

Oh, Lexa, the thought of your financials didn't even cross my mind. What I was trying to say is that sooner or later, people are going to recognize you. Don't tell me you've forgotten that you are a celebrity, so quickly. And you know how quickly a person's life can change if they're not careful about where they go and the people they let into their lives.

"So what the hell am I supposed to do, Frank? Run out and have an abortion, and then run to Marlene's side to be her tower of strength as I always have? Huh, Frank… and then what? I'm just to leave well enough alone as if to annul my past? Is this what you're trying to tell me?"

Frank sighed deeply after listening to Lexa spilling her guts, and then his response was:

"I know this may sound horrible, Lexa.   But all things considered I think what you've just said could be the easiest way out for you, and the best solution for everyone involved."

Lexa was not expecting to hear Frank that kind of response from Frank and she was highly pissed off. She raised her right arm with her pointer finger shaking towards him and said:

"Well, I can tell you this much, mister, I will not kill my child even if it is to save my own life. I cannot believe that I'm going to tell you something that I've never even told Marlene. As a matter-of-fact, I've never told it to anyone."

Franks ears perked up even more. And he said to her, "I can't imagine what that could be."

"Well, I had a miscarriage a long, long time ago, and that loss has left me stricken beyond explanation. Anyway, let me stop, as I really don't want to prolong the conversation …I'm sorry…I don't know why I even brought it up. And as you said earlier, "let's be realistic"…. I know you're thinking that I'm a conniving bitch for screwing my best friend's husband… and, what have you. But things aren't always the way they seem, you know. Sometimes people get caught up in situations beyond their control. I don't believe I would have gotten involved with Barchas if things were different." She continued,

"Matter-of-factly, Marlene's breakdown played a major role in all this. As you know I was not always around, but whenever I could, I would spend most of my time with her. However, her abstinence from her husband   kind of put our affair into motion. Needless to say Barchas was very persistent and quite the charmer. But I also saw how the weight of Marlene's condition was driving him to seek comfort outside of their union.   I never thought I could be involved with my best friend's husband this way, but as they say….shit happens, and, I'm sorry to say this, Frank— but I'm so in love with him."

"Wow, sounds like you made a martyr out of yourself, Lexa."

"You could say that again, mister. You've got to believe me when I tell you; I did not want to hurt Marlene. I thought it would only be for a while, but regrettably, it never went that way."

"Anyway, when I heard the dreadful news about Marlene and Barchas, I was flabbergasted. I believe if Barchas was not so mad when he left here to go home, this would not have happened. More than likely, Marlene had a fight with him which could have pissed him off and sent him totally over the edge."

"But why do you suppose she pissed him off Lexa? What would make you assume that?"

"Well, she's under the impression Barchas is having an affair with Blossom Rigby" And they have been arguing about it for a while."

"Oh, for God sake, don't tell me we are back to, Blossom again. And it sounds as if you're of the same opinion as Marlene," Frank said, while throwing his hands in the air to show Lexa how fed up he was about the very mention of Blossom's name.

Lexa appeared shocked, to Frank. The guilt of sleeping with Barchas was gutting her, and she tried shifting her thoughts to blaming Blossom to help ease her pain.

"I don't know what to think at this point, Frank. Maybe that's why he treated me the way he did. I can't help thinking that he could be sleeping with her, especially when I'm not around. The way I see it, is that most husbands are not complete unless they have a mistress, and wives to those men are like, money in the bank ;while mistresses are like, pocket change. But I'll be damned if Barchas thinks of me as some kind of small coin."

Frank was taken aback for a moment after listening to Lexa's story and how she callously referred to Barchas. And, to see her cry so uncontrollably had brought on a great deal of discomfort to him.

He sat quietly and wrestled with his conscience about whether to blame himself for her delusional behavior. He reckoned that he might have been too pushy, given her fragile state of mind. That being considered, Frank decided it was best to get out of there before all was lost.

He suddenly got off the sofa and went over to hug and comfort her and to tell her that he was sorry she had to endure such pain. However, at that point Lexa showed no appreciation for his concerns. She scornfully pushed him away and told him that it was best if he left. He wasn't exactly shocked by her response but he had hoped she would not be so brash. Frank quickly backed way. He then picked up his coat and removed one of his business cards which he left on her coffee table and then he let himself outside her doors.

While Lexa remained smothered in her dilemma that night, Frank spent the night at his condo in Quail Run. His thoughts on his way there were to stay close enough so as to catch up with Lexa the morning after. He imagined that it was not going to be easy to get her to stay in Watertown, but it would make him feel a lot better if they parted ways on more congenial grounds.

As Frank settled in, he unbuttoned his shirt, kicked off his loafers and unbuckled his belt. He strolled over to his stereo and flipped through is LP collection as if he knew exactly what he needed to hear.   And as soon as he found the one by Nat King Cole, he carefully removed it and dropped it on the turntable and then he walked away toward his bar. And while "Mona Lisa" played, he sprawled himself on his chaise while holding a 24 lead crystal tumbler filled with cognac and cream soda.

Deep sighs followed… and with each verse, he'd slowly decompress. He then closed his eyes and lost himself completely into the song as if he was being hypnotized by, Nat.

CHAPTER EIGHT

The morning after, was business as usual at seven fifteen am for Frank. And while he showered and his coffee pot buzzed, Lexa was back at her condo carefully retouching her makeup and outlining her eyes with a black pencil. While she painstakingly applied her mascara she glanced on and off at the clock. Her limo driver was scheduled to pick her up at Eight Thirty a.m.

Marlene, however, during the same hour, was sitting at the edge of her bed and staring into a hand mirror and wondering if her face and neck area would ever go back to the way it used to be. And with every scar she looked at, she despised her husband even more.

The telephone rang and Marlene quickly tossed the mirror aside to answer. It was Frank calling to check up on her.

"Hello, Marlene, It's me, Frank. I know it's a little early, but I wanted to see how things are with you and the kids."

"Well, gee, Frank; thanks for checking up on us. Things are as good as to be expected…considering. I think the medicine is working. I still feel a little groggy but not as sore as I was yesterday when you were here."

"I can hear the difference in your voice, Marlene; pretty soon you'll be back to your old self."

"You think so? I was just wondering if the scars on my face will ever go away."

"I know they will Marlene, and you'll be as flawless as ever in a very short time."

"Thank you, Frank; Thank you, for the vote of confidence," Marlene said, and Frank could tell that she needed to hear someone boosting her self esteem.

"Oh, Marlene, that pretty face of yours isn't going anywhere anytime soon. You are a very beautiful lady and that's never going to change." Frank said.

Anyway my lady, I also wanted you to know that I'm on my way to the hospital to check up on Barchas, and then I'll be spending the rest of the day at the office. Please call if you need me for anything."

Marlene thanked Frank for the call and she hung up. She did not expect to hear Frank complimenting her so candidly, but it was quite a boost to her moral. Frank, on the other hand after telling her that he was going to check upon Barchas, had hoped that she would have had something positive to say. Even if she had asked him to let her know of any changes in her husband's condition, would put her in a much better light, in his mind.

Anyway, Frank grabbed his attaché case thereafter and left his condo. He then drove around to Lexa's place in an attempt to catching up with her. As luck would have it, he was just in time to see her getting inside a limo. He felt disappointed and he pulled up closely to the limo and signaled her to wait, but she instructed the limo driver to keep on going.

Frank was stunned when she looked away from him, and while he remained seated in his car and at a loss for words, he watched Lexa leaving him behind without waving goodbye.

Frank pulled out a cigar, and while he lit up and puffed, he drove away toward the hospital where Barchas was staying.

He was easily recognizable, even from a distance along the lengthy corridor toward the nurses' station. And as Frank continued making his way toward the nurses' station, he was greeted by a broadened smile as he came face to face with a nurse who happened to be walking toward him.

Because she recognized who he was, she suspected that he was there to see Barchas, but she politely asked how she could be of assistance to him. After he told her that he was there to see Mr. Sander, meaning Barchas, her smile vanished when she informed him that Barchas was in the operating room.

A dreadful stillness overshadowed Frank after she landed him with the unexpected news; He immediately assumed the worst. And in a much lower and controlled tone he asked the nurse why Mr. Sander was taken to the operating room. But, so as to politely cut the conversation short and avoid any more queries from Frank, she informed him that it was best if he spoke with the surgeon.

With a stern look and a troubled tone, Frank asked what the name of the surgeon was, and she was proud to assure him that Mr. Sander had the best surgeon in all of Watertown. Frank was not impressed with her vague answers and he dryly asked her if that doctor in question had a name.

"Dr. Wigginton," she replied quickly, while she kept her eyes peering into his.

"Oh, really" said Frank, with an about face while looking at the nurse. And just to be certain of his perception he proceeded by asking her if she was referring to Dr. Jaxon Wigginton, the neurosurgeon.

"Yes sir, that's the one," the nurse replied.

After verifying that it was the "Jax" in question, it was much to Frank's surprise.   He wasted no time digging to see what else he could find out about Jax. The nurse was happy to stay back for a few more minutes to update Frank on Jax's prestigious practice and his unmatched contribution to the community.

Frank was impressed listening to the nurse as she bragged about Jax. He advised her that he would like an opportunity to speak with Dr. Wigginton about Mr. Sander's condition, and he asked her if she knew of his whereabouts in the hospital.

The nurse said to Frank:

"I quite understand your concern sir. The waiting room is just a couple doors down on the left. You can wait there, if you'd like, and I'll try to find him for you."

Frank response to the nurse was:

"Well, thank you, nurse; you've been so kind. But pardon me; I didn't get your name,"

Upon that comment, Frank's eyes changed focus as they rolled down to look at her name badge which was pinned just below her lapel. But after his eyes went a little too far below and landed on her chest. He realized how buxom she was and that was something that uncontrollably bugged his eyes. Though her cleavage was fully covered, the full-bosomed woman left little to the Frank's imagination.

After thinking to himself, "wow"....Frank then looked at her name badge and saw that her name was Milan Dunwoody. Before he could audibly acknowledge her, Milan quickly said "my name is Nurse Dunwoody, sir."

Then in reply, Frank said, "Oh, yes, so I see. That's quite a beautiful name you've got there, Nurse. I'd like to thank you for your time, and I shall be waiting to speak with the good doctor as soon as he's available."

Both parted ways and Frank went to sit in the waiting room. However, while he was walking away from the nurse, he uncontrollably turned his head around to take another look at her. As she walked off in a hurry, as if to make up for lost time, the swing of her hips and the gentle bounce in her rump was quite a head turner for Frank.

Frank was sitting less than fifteen minutes inside the waiting room when he noticed Nurse Dunwoody and Dr. Wigginton entered the room. As soon Dr. Wigginton spotted Frank, he immediately turned to the Nurse and he thanked her for being so helpful and she quietly left the room.

Frank, on the other hand, would not have recognized Jax if he had not walked in with the nurse, but he acted as if he did. He immediately got out of his chair to shake Jax's hand, and to find out about Barchas.

"Good to see you, Doctor. I'm sure Nurse Dunwoody updated you as to why I'm here."

"Yes, I've been updated, and I'm fully aware that you are temporarily standing in for Barchas, while Marlene is recuperating."

'I was shocked to hear that Barchas was in the theatre when I came in this morning, Dr. Wigginton."

"Yes… We found a tumor on his brain and we had to act promptly. I'm happy to inform you that the surgery was quite successful; meaning that the tumor was removed without any damages. However, it's going to take a few weeks before I have the result of the biopsy."

"I must also warn you that he's not out of the woods yet, but I assume you're not too alarmed hearing this."

"I wouldn't say that I am, doctor. But my question is… will Barchas ever get back on his feet again?"

"I can certainly appreciate your concern, Frank. This hospital is outfitted with a great team of doctors and the finest patient care. I assure you that Barchas is in the right place."

"Good, good… I've heard wonderful things about this hospital. So when will I be able to see him?" Frank asked Jax.

"I'd say, check back tomorrow. And…. c'mon on now, man, just call me Jax. So, how is the good lady doing? Feeling better by now, I suppose." Jax asked Frank while smiling.

Frank was taken aback at Jax's question and he turned to Jax and said: "The good lady? I'm not sure I know who that is, Jax"

"I'm talking about Marlene, his wife" Jax replied.

"Oh, yes…sorry man, but that one went right over my head. Matter-of fact I spoke with her earlier this morning and she's starting to sound a lot better. That woman is a fighter and there's no doubt she'll be back to her old self before long.

"Yes, I know what you mean. Anyway, Frank, I've got to run. Here's my card. You can call me anytime."

After Jax handed his business card to Frank, they shook hands and Frank said:

"Look, Jax, I can't begin to tell you how relieved I am, knowing that Barchas is under your care."

"…Glad that I'm here to help. Barchas is a damn good guy if I have to say so myself. I haven't forgotten how hard he'd worked to help save my practice as well as my ass."

Frank then handed one of his business cards to Jax and they parted ways. However, Frank walked away with his eyebrows raised from Jax's last comment.

Frank began racking his brains about what the good doctor could be referring to, when he said Barchas had helped saving his ass and his practice. And then he pondered briefly if Jax could be referring to the time of Shavory's death. He recalled the charges that were placed against Larry Tate for the murder of Shavory Mercantile and how Barchas had worked tirelessly to get an acquittal for him.

Larry Tate who was Marlene's father did get the acquittal which ultimately eliminated Jax as a prime suspect in the murder.

So Frank surmised that could be the only reason for Jax's comment about saving his practice as well as his ass. But even if that weren't the case, he reckoned it was best not to probe any further and to leave *well-enough-alone.*

And, while Jax walked away from Frank he assumed undoubtedly that Frank already knew where his comment was coming from… which essentially left them on the same page.

Jax went to the critical care unit to check upon Barchas, he wondered how Marlene was going to handle the update on her husband's condition. He wondered if Frank even had an inkling of the long road ahead for Barchas to get back on his feet.

Along with his concerns about Frank and the Sanders' family, his thoughts shifted briefly on Chrissy and he became achingly reflective on her.   Despite the unfortunate scarring from their past relationship, Jax, from time to time wished he could have won her back, nonetheless.

Several years have gone by since Chrissy moved away from Gray Banks and changed her name to Gabriella Fairchild.   So, even with Jax's influence ….financial and otherwise… trying to find her without the help of Carolyn and Barchas, who were the only ones aware of her whereabouts, would be a useless endeavor.   Jax would have given damn near anything just to be with Chrissy and her child…..a child he was convinced that he'd fathered with the woman he loved so deeply.

As Jax turned the corner to make it through the CCU entrance, his thoughts of Chrissy were dispelled in a flash and his only focus then rested solely on Barchas.

As he walked towards Barchas' bedside, he saw Nurse Dunwoody standing next to him while recording his vital signs on a clip board.

"How are we doing?" Jax asked Nurse Dunwoody, while he looked at her with a straight face. She replied that Barchas was stable although his temperature reading was a tad elevated. Dr. Jax immediately took the clip board from her and his eyes raced up and down the page. He casually handed the board back, without showing the least bit of concern. But, that was Jax; He was the kind of doctor that was deeply passionate about his profession and his patients, though often times very reserved about his perceptions.

While Jax and the nurse spent time observing Barchas, Frank was already outside of the hospital and heading towards his car in the parking lot.   His next stop from there would be his office; he had spent very little time working since the incident, and he had a lot of catching up to do. However, as he was about the turn the key to unlock his car, along came, Blossom Rigby.

They had not spoken or touched base since their phone conversation the morning after the incident. So running into Blossom definitely behooved him to extend the courtesy of spending a little time with her.

"Good morning, Mr. Roulette," Blossom said, as she approached him quickly. And before Frank could respond likewise, Blossom continued speaking.

"I can't believe my ears, Frank; I'm still in shock!"

As she spoke, her hands were thrown up in the air and she looked quite mystified and barely stopped to take a breath between sentences. She continued with her eyes widened in shock while looking up at Frank.

"We have to be strong for Barchas! God knows how much he's endured since all this craziness and lies took over the city. The city should be sued for spreading rumors! Let me just tell you;   don't think for a minute that I believe Barchas is guilty of laying a hand on his wife; not to mention attempting to kill her. No way… not him!"

Frank appeared stiff while he listened to Blossom defending Barchas. Though he identified with her frustration, and would do anything to help protect Barchas, he wondered if her feelings would remain the same if she saw the damage done to Marlene's face and neck.

So in keeping with that thought, he took the risk of making mention of Marlene, even though he was aware of their estrangement.

"Yes, yes, I know exactly how you feel, Blossom. I haven't had a good night's sleep since this happened, and I will not rest until I get to the bottom of this. However, it's not just Barchas that is going through hell right now.   Let's not forget about his family. They also need our support.

I still don't have all the facts, but Marlene was badly battered and we have to be mindful of that. She and the children are devastated, and I'm deeply concerned about their recovery. Only the Good Lord knows when Barchas will ever be discharged from this hospital."

Frank reached inside his trousers pocket and pulled out a handkerchief and wiped across his brow. He was perspiring heavily and dying to take a smoke.

Blossom, cringed after listening to Frank's comments. She was somewhat at a loss for words after hearing Frank taking up for Marlene. But she rebounded by keeping her concerns strictly on Barchas, and Frank realized that she was not about to care.

"So, how bad is he, Frank? I heard he was unconscious when they brought him in. I'm sorry it has taken this long for me to come to see him. But because of the circumstances, I kind of waited a little for the dust to settle."

"I understand your thinking, Blossom, and that was a wise decision. Anyway he wouldn't have known the difference. What you heard about him being unconscious is true. As a matter of fact, things have gotten a little worse since yesterday, because a tumor was removed from his brain this morning."

Blossom's eyes widened in shock, and she immediately interrupted Frank to show her fright.

"What the hell are you saying, Frank? Did you say a tumor? Or, am I not hearing right?

No, Blossom, you heard right and my response was quite the same as yours…. shocked as hell.   I came in early this morning to check upon him and that was when they landed me with the news."

"Oh, my, God" So what the hell is going to happen to poor Barchas? And were you able to see him, Frank?"

"No, the doctor said it was too soon. But don't worry, I'll be back tomorrow."

"So, according to what you're saying, there's no point in me going inside then… not if I can't see him."

"Yes, you could say that.   But while the doctors are doing their best to get Barchas back on his feet, it would be nice if we could show his family some support. It's the least we can do for him.

Blossom was not expecting to hear Frank asking her to make any kind of contact with Marlene. Matter-of-factly she was surprised that he would expect her entertain the idea of even being polite, to say the least.

Blossom looked away begrudgingly and folded her lips and tried fixing her hair that the wind was teasing out of place. Her attitude showed Frank that mum's- the word when it came to Barchas' wife. She was not someone that she would dare speak her mind about to Frank, knowing the high regards he held for that family.

However, Frank only threw out this comment to Blossom as a measuring stick to get a better feel of her resentment towards Marlene.

Be that as it were, Frank remained quiet to see if his suggestion for sympathy would hit a sensitive nerve inside her.   So he remained quiet and allowed the fleeting seconds to pass in silence, until she was ready to respond.

"Wow, Frank this is very heavy for me.   I know how much you care about them and I can appreciate the thought. And as you know, I will do anything for Barchas. But when it comes to Marlene, I doubt that woman would let me within ten feet of her without calling the police. Frank was soon to realize that both women shared the same level of animosity.

"Has it been that bad between you two?" Frank asked Blossom and looking surprised, but Blossom wasn't sold on his pretense.

"Yes, Frank; and it has been that way for several years. And please… don't stand there and act as if you didn't know. Marlene is not shy about telling everyone how much she detests me." "Anyway, let's just leave that alone; I just don't see how I could find it in my heart to be of any comfort to Marlene, but I wish her a speedy recovery. And, by the way…. she doesn't need me; Lexa will take care of her."

Frank did not find mention made of Lexa, welcoming. He was overly frustrated with the bad blood among all three ladies for inexplicable reasons. So he conveniently looked at his watch and told to her that he had to go, as he was late getting to work.

Blossom thought Frank's excuse was reasonable; and so she smiled and thanked him for staying back to chat with her.

Blossom and Frank parted ways.

CHAPTER NINE

Frank, worked tirelessly at the office to keep things running smoothly, and the rest of his time was shared mostly between Marlene and Barchas. Sometimes, while at the hospital with Barchas, he would spend half his nights praying for a breakthrough. Just to sit and watch him stare aimlessly ahead of himself without acknowledging his presence was gradually tearing him down.

Frank's on and off girlfriend, Jackie Monsoon, along with two other female casual acquaintances left his answering machine jammed with messages about missing him terribly. Although he had planned to go see Barchas after clearing all his messages, he was behooved to telephone Jackie and invite to have dinner with him at "The Vines." Jackie was pleased hearing from Frank and she instantly accepted the offer.

It was six o-clock pm when Frank turned up and rang Jackie's doorbell. She immediately opened the door and when their eyes met, a sense of calmness washed over Frank. They hugged and he told her that she looked fabulous. She smiled at him to show that she was instantly gratified by his compliment.

As they drove along Spinnaker Highway to the "Vines", not much was talked about. However, an occasional glimpse at each other while they listened to the love songs that were being played on the evening radio show was enough to keep them telepathically in tune.

Frank politely pulled out the chair for her to be seated inside the restaurant, her comely face and easy going temperament helped Frank unwind even more. She admired his eyes racing up and down the wine list while she touched her neck and played with her pearl necklace.

Frank was barely through with ordering wine and appetizers when he removed a cigar from his coat and lit up. She smiled and asked how he was doing, but he responded by telling her that he missed her terribly and he apologized for taking so long in returning her phone calls. On that note, Jackie realized that he was not interested in talking about himself which would most likely end up on the subject of Barchas. And probably that was a subject he wanted to avoid… and that was just fine with her.

She sipped on her wine and looked at him with a certain longing that told Frank she was hoping that her evening with him would fall into the night. Anyway in trying to keeping the evening pleasant and cushy she smiled and told him that she understood completely and that there was no need for apologies.

Dinner was lovely, so said Jackie; and Frank agreed by nodding with a full mouth.

As Frank tried finishing up the last bites on his plate, Jackie called for another glass of wine and began speaking to Frank about the ups and downs in her business as a stock broker. Her elevated tone, as she spoke, was signal enough that she had drunk more than enough. However, Frank politely waited for her to finish that last glass of wine and then encouraged her that it was time they went home.

The much needed down time spent with Jackie did wonders for Frank. He had not gone that many weeks without sex, and at one point he'd almost forgotten about it. And that was because of the shock that was thrust upon him due to the ongoing and pressing issues regarding Barchas.

Anyway, while Jackie continued rambling about *stocks and bonds* and laughing her way through, he helped her out of the car and held on to her as they walked towards her house. As soon as they made it inside, he carefully unzipped her dress and allowed her to step out of it. Her dress fell to the floor while she was still wearing her black pumps. Her lacy hot pink bra and matching knickers against her pale white skin, paired well in setting off an amorous glance from Frank. And it was there in the middle of the living room where the foreplay had begun. He plunged his tongue inside her mouth with his eyes closed. She was instantly titillated and she moaned and sucked hard on his tongue. He grabbed her buttocks and pulled her body even closer to himself. And as if she was startled by the tight grasp on her rump, she released her grip on Frank's tongue and giggled while he proceeded to picking her up. She then went quiet and simply closed her eyes while he carried off to bed. And as he laid her down, he looked at her lying almost motionless as if she had carelessly given herself away to him. Frank's arousal heightened as he eagerly unclothed himself. He grabbed her knees and gently parted her legs just enough for him to start unlocking himself inside her.

Jackie's eyes popped wide open with pure pleasure. She gasped and she moaned, she closed her eyes again and she grabbed on to Frank as if she needed his help during her early arrival. But Frank was too busy flexing his butt from an overdue explosion that was coming their way.

However, while Frank made up for lost time on a second round of copulation in bed with Jackie, he struggled deeply with keeping his mind from going astray. As he made love to her, the imagination of nibbling on Nurse Dunwoody's breasts was heavily weighted on his mind while he filled his mouth with those of Jackie's.

Jackie was happy and while she basked in her afterglow, she panted and reminded Frank of his greatness.   She drifted off in deep sleep, and by the strike of dawn, Frank was gone.

< * >

By eight a.m. the morning after, Frank was at his office working and going through several hand- written messages that were left on his desk. While he worked on taking care of business, he came across two messages that were flagged "very important" from Dr. Jax Wigginton. He requesting to have both calls returned as soon as possible.

Frank immediately felt a rush and he wondered if Barchas' condition had worsened.   As he held the note crushed inside his palm, he immediately picked up the telephone and tried calling Jax, but he was not available.

While Frank's head swirled with endless possibilities about speaking with Jax, he managed to regain his composure and he took a break to give Jackie a phone call.   She too was at work, but too busy to for *"morning after chit chats"* even with someone like Frank. However no offense was taken on his part because he understood completely why she had to cut him short.

Frank tried calling Jax again and he was relieved when the receptionist asked him to hold while his call was being transferred.

Jax's voice came off sounding hastened to Frank when he took the call. But as soon as he realized that it was Frank on the other end of the line, his tone took a sudden turn to something a lot more welcoming.

"Hey, Frank! So glad I'm able to catch up you, man... It's about Barchas. I haven't been able to get a hold of Marlene, but I left a message on her machine. Anyway since she hasn't returned the call, I thought I'd give you a holler and have you to come in so we could talk. "

Without a pause Jax looked at his watch while he spoke with Frank, and kept the conversation rolling.

"Can you make it in later today; say… around three, three thirty?

"Oh, sure, Frank replied eagerly."

"…sounds good my man, as soon as you are here, just have them to page me" Jax said.

"Ok, doc, I shall see you then." That was how Frank responded to Jax before hanging up the phone. He then looked at his watch and noticed that he had at least four hours before meeting with Jax…all of which felt like *forever* to him. He started tapping his fingers on his desk with jitters in his feet while he pondered what next to do.

Thereafter, Frank called Marlene simply to touch base and to get a feel of things in general, should in case he had to break news to her about her husband, whether she liked it or not. After all, he reckoned it was full time he told her about the tumor that was removed from his brain.

It was eleven am when Frank telephoned Marlene. He'd caught up with her in just in time when she was desperately seeking someone to talk to. The fact that she and Lexa had not communicated since the incident, and not being able to contact her after several phone calls, was simply driving her nuts.

The telephone rang five times after which the answering machine came on. But Frank felt it was unwise to leave a message. However, just before the hanging up on the answering machine, Marlene was able to quickly pick up to say "hello."

Frank said:

"Hello there my lady, it's me Frank, — just *kinda* touching base in to see what you've been up to lately. I've got a feeling you're doing a lot better; I can hear it in your voice."

"Oh, Frank. My goodness! It's so nice hearing from you. I was just thinking the other day that I haven't heard from you in a while, and I thought to myself I should call to see how you're doing. After all… you're all we've got at this point and I greatly appreciate you."

"Well, as I've told you, Marlene, you're like family to me, and I will be always there for you. So, tell me, how are the kids? Is Monk still at home with you? Or, is he back in college?"

"Oh, well; He's still here.   He's thinking of moving back home to complete his education here."

Marlene cleared her throat and Franked picked up on a slight hesitation in her response. But he remained quiet and allowed her to finish.

Well, Christmas is around the corner so there's no point in him leaving at this time. I don't know what I'd do if he left me now, Frank. I just don't know."

"Huh, huh… I can appreciate your concern. He has grown into a fine young man and I know he'd want to make sure that you're ok before heading back out to college.   And, how's Bethany? I know it's been especially hard for her."

"Well, she's doing a lot better since the last time you were here. I don't know if you knew, but she was one of the contestants in the Miss Watertown pageantry."

No, I didn't know that. Well…that's great news, Marlene! I'm sure she'll do well."

I thought so myself, but she withdrew from the contest because she's embarrassed about putting herself *out there* since the incident and all the hoopla that erupted from it.

Oh gee, poor girl, I'm sorry to hear that she has given up so quickly. I hope she changes her mind and make a go at it. So…have you heard from Lexa?"

"No…not at all. In as much as I'm happy that you called, I had hope it was her calling me back after all the messages that I've left on her answering machine. Normally she'd call to check up on me or to let me know if she's leaving town and I've heard nothing of the sorts. I'm starting to think that something terrible has happened to her. And I've got to let you know, Frank…Oh God… it's driving me over the edge."

Frank cringed from Marlene's response and even more so he felt like a hypocrite by acting as if he knew nothing about Lexa's absenteeism.

"I can't begin to imagine what you're going through. So when was the last time you heard from her?

"I know you're going to find this hard to believe, but we haven't spoken since the day before Barchas and I fought."

Oh, wow! That doesn't sound like her?

As the conversation prolonged, Frank experienced deep discomfort and he wished if he could have told her the truth about Lexa. Having said that, however, he reckoned telling her would send a blow to her psyche which could potentially destroy her. And, added to that, he recalled his promise to Lexa that he would protect her and to never say a word of what she had disclosed to him. So in order to keeping things running smoothly, he had very little to say.

"You're right, that does not sound like the Lexa I know." Marlene said.

I sure hope she'll return your call as soon as possible, Marlene. Try not to wear yourself down too much over this, you've been through enough. Anyway, I'll drop by to see you sometime next week.

Marlene thanked Frank for checking in on her and to lend an ear.

By the time she hung up the phone from speaking with Frank, her heart swelled with anxiety about not hearing from Lexa. She pondered, she wondered, she panicked and frenetically she upped, got dressed and drove directly to Lexa's condo, to which she had a spare key.

She rang the door bell a couple of times and after waiting for a few minutes without any response she proceeded to open the door to Lexa's condo.

Everything seemed to be in place she thought to herself. She looked around some more, checked her closet, but saw no evidence of trouble. She then sat on the sofa with a blank mind as if she was trying to clear her head and to start thinking from a fresh perspective. Then suddenly she looked down on the coffee table and saw a business card. She picked it up and noticed it was Frank's business card. She flipped it over and saw that his home phone number was handwritten there.

Marlene's thoughts went racing. What the hell is going on here, she wondered. As far as she knew, Lexa and Frank didn't communicate. Matter-of-factly she couldn't stand him, Marlene recollected.

Anyway, Marlene found it mind boggling as to why Frank acted as if he had not been in contact with Lexa. After all, she reckoned, they spoke just hours ago and he acted as if he knew nothing about Lexa… not to mention her whereabouts.

"She shook her head in disbelief and mumbled to herself, "something's wrong here, something very, very shady is going on and I would like know what it is."

With nothing coming to mind that would make some sense, she assumed that Lexa might have needed legal advice about something. But she wasn't totally convinced that it was so and that was because of how she felt about Frank. Then she wondered if things had loosened up between them without her being apprised of the situation.

Marlene tucked the business card in her handbag and left Lexa's condo feeling utter confusion and so she drove back home.

As she traveled along Spinnaker Highway, presence of mind told her to change course and swing by Frank's office and poked for some answers. That sinking feeling that there was something shady going on, that she couldn't quite put her finger on was starting to gut her.

She really would have preferred to confront Frank about her hunch, but common sense told her that she was not in a position at the time to cast a cloud on their relationship. So she simply chalked it up to Frank trying to weasel himself into Lexa's bed. And she was convinced that that idea would be definite no, no for Lexa… hence the card left lying on the coffee table.

But where the heck is she? Marlene wondered as she stayed the course and drove back home.

It was three pm and Frank turned up at the hospital and informed the nurses' station of his appointment with Dr. Jax. He was immediately paged but soon found out that he was not yet on site. Frank had no worries because he knew Jax would be there soon. So he left and decided to wait in Barchas' room until the *good* doctor arrived.

As he approached Barchas' room, he saw Nurse Dunwoody standing at his bedside. She was just about to leave and by the time she turned around to walk away they came face to face. Frank's eyes bulged with attraction and he smiled broadly at her. She smiled back at him and said "hello Mr. Roulette."

"Wow, you remembered my name" Frank responded with a broad smile.

And Nurse Dunwoody replied "Yes sir … how could I not. Your name's on everything pertaining to Mr. Sanders, and it's been that way over the past few months.

"So how is he doing today, nurse? Frank asked Ms. Dunwoody." She turned around to look at him and she replied "Mr. Sanders is a miracle…he's coming along very nicely. He's sound asleep right now as you can see, but I'm sure Dr. Jax will update you as soon as he's here; and he's expected any minute now.

She then asked to be excused and she walked away. Frank, who was delighted about seeing her again, couldn't help his eyes from following her as she walked away.

Frank then moved a little closer towards Barchas' bed to take a look. He noticed that the bandage around his head had been removed and he was taken aback by his appearance. Although he found it uncomfortable to look at, he quietly seated himself on the chair inside the room. And without knowing what to assume whether it was a good sign or bad, Frank gazed meditatively at Barchas, with deep sadness. However, while in the same train of thought he recalled Nurse Dunwoody referred to Barchas as a "miracle" and it helped with swinging his focus to a more positive outlook.

Frank heard footsteps and they were none other than those of Dr. Jax, heading towards Barchas' room. Frank immediately got off the chair and walked over to greet him. Both men eyes met in unison as if to say they shared the love of Barchas. They gave a hearty handshake and the vibe between them was powerful and promising.

Thereafter, Frank looked at Jax and before he could get into business as usual, he watched his eyes turned and became fixated on Barchas. Jax could tell that he was deeply concerned about what he saw. So he quickly chimed in and told Frank that seeing Barchas without bandages was a beautiful thing.

Frank was relieved.

Jax then gave a quick glance at Barchas who was still asleep. He then turned to Frank and suggested they continued their meeting in his office where they could speak more at ease. There were fresh brewed coffee, a lunch box and an apple sitting on his desk. Jax pushed the food aside and shuffled a few dockets around while Frank's head swelled with impatience.

"So, what's the verdict, Doc? ... Oh, man, I gotta tell you I was very relieved about what you said about Barchas." Frank said as he seated himself in Jax's office for their meeting.

"Well Frank, first and foremost as you know, the tumor was removed successfully. The result came in a few days ago with even much better news," Jax said while removing his eyeglasses and sitting down to face Frank.

Both men appeared deeply engaged as they expressed their concerns about Barchas' situation.

I'll be damned … that's some good news, man… I'm telling you. And you said you even got something better for me, Doc.?

Oh yes, I'm happy to let you know that the tumor was benign. Oh yes… my brother, that sucker is benign.

Frank felt hopeful after hearing Jax's comment and his heart raced with excitement while Jax continued speaking.

"He's not completely out of the woods yet, but he's steadily improving."

"That's alright… I know it's going to take some time, but you have no idea how great this feels right now. Oh man… that's just awesome. So where do we go from here, what's the next move, Jax?"

"It may be too early to tell, but as he continues to improve, he could experience some cognitive decline."

"Ok. Like what?" Frank asked Jax, with an undertone of anxiety.

Jax responded "Often times memory loss; but to what extent I….I couldn't say at this time.   His fullest recovery depends a great deal on placing him in a rehabilitation institution that provides the most excellent approach to his condition."

"Are you referring to the stroke or the tumor?" Frank asked.

"I'd say both, quite frankly; but recovery from the stroke will be more of a lengthy ordeal. There has been very little limb movement thus far. It's vitally important that he starts therapy as soon as possible; I'd definitely recommend "St. Clements" But of course that's going to be entirely up to you and his wife.

At that point, the weight of the conversation cheated Frank out of his short lived enthusiasm. The thought of getting Marlene's support regarding her husband's recovery seemed so slim at that instance, that he developed a feeling for a drink, or to light up a cigar. But he reckoned he would be way out of line to try acting on his urge while still sitting in Jax's office. So while he twitched unnoticeably for a fix, he said to Jax "Oh, damn, it sounds like my lifelong friend is still in bad shape, Doc. Oh, man I'm at a total loss for words right now—you better believe it. I just don't know what to say! And most importantly what the hell am I suppose to do given the situation I'm caught in."

Jax looked at Frank with a bit of surprise and asked what he meant by saying that. And he was quick to remind Jax that Marlene's greatest joy would be to hear that her husband did not make it out alive. And he went on to inform Jax, that Marlene had no idea that her husband was diagnosed with a brain tumor.

"What! You have got to be kidding!" After that expose, Jax responded with bulging eyes.

And Frank while in a downward spiral for a drink, replied "No, sir, I kid you not. I haven't said a word to Mrs. Sanders about this as yet. I thought it was best to give her a little more time to focus on her own recovery and hopefully she'd come around to deal with reality of the situation."

"Somehow you are going to have to find a way to get her to listen to you, Frank. I'd strongly suggest you drop by the house and have a face to face talk with her." Dr. Jax said.

"That's easier said than done, Jax. The woman is downright adamant about not wanting to discuss her husband's condition.   …Truth –be-told, Jax… I'm not embarrassed to tell you that I'm somewhat afraid of, that face- to- face idea, you suggested."

"And why is that" Jax asked Frank.

"Well, with her on and off episodes of depression, I imagine she could flip and go cuckoo, on me.   And, I'm telling you, man…that would totally complicate things for me, given the situation that I'm dealt with.

Jax's eyebrows rose with curiosity while listening to Frank explained his dilemma. He wasn't completely clear about all that Frank had to say, but he had a haunch that there was much more to the story. However, he wasn't too interested in diminishing his focus on Barchas to that of Marlene's problems. So without any further ado, Jax suggested to Frank that he should take the rest of the day to think about the situation, and then get back with him with his decision.

Frank, on the other hand, wasn't exactly thrilled about the way Jax tried to end their meeting. He assumed that Jax was losing his patience, and also seeing him as being weak under the circumstances. With that said, Frank wasn't   about to let Jax get away with that perception. So, immediately, he tried redeeming himself in his response to Jax.

"Well doc, all things considered, this is what I'm going to do…. I'm going to make an executive decision right now. I'm definitely going along with your suggestion about St. Clements's and I would like to have him transferred there as soon as possible.

Jax was pleased with Frank's response and he was quick to let him know. He immediately rose from his chair, shook his hand and said "You're a good man, Frank. I'll authorize the discharge right away. The administrative department will have some paperwork for you to sign. I usually don't get involved, once the transfer is complete, but you've got my support my brother. You can count on me."

The conversation between Frank and Dr. Jax ended on a high note as both men parted ways. Frank was barely out of the hospital and headed to his car when he reached inside his pocket and pulled out a cigar. And as he continued walking he began to mentally prepare himself for taking full responsibility for Barchas' residency at St. Clements' Rehabilitation Center.

Frank drove off the hospital grounds and was headed back to his office. Anyway, after carefully considering the situation, he reckoned that Jax was right about coming face to face with Marlene and let her know about his decision to transfer Barchas to St. Clements.

He was already speeding on Spinnaker Highway and less than an half an hour away from Marlene's home when he decided to turn around and to pay her the dreaded visit.

It was a few minutes after five- o-clock pm when Frank pulled up in Marlene's driveway. Bethany was first to come out to greet him. She was genuinely pleased to see him when she smiled and said "Uncle Frank, what brought you by? It's so good to see you"

The beautiful young woman along with her enchanting smile was most pleasing to Frank when she addressed him as "Uncle Frank." He embraced her gently and kissed her cheek and told her that she was more beautiful than the last time he saw her. She smiled at him and said "Mom's taking a nap, but that's ok, I'll let her know that you're here."

While Bethany raced upstairs to let her mother know that Frank was downstairs waiting, Allora invited him to wait for Marlene in the living room and she him asked if he would like a drink. Music to his ears; and he quickly said scotch on the rocks.

Within minutes of taking a couple sips of the drink, Bethany went and told Frank that her mother would be down shortly. And so she joined his company and they talked for *a little bit- a- while.*

"So, what have you been up to lately, sweetie? Are you through with Christmas shopping…its only a few weeks away.

"Yes, I know Uncle Frank, but I'm not really in the mood for the holidays. I just wish it would come so I won't have to be bothered with all the excitement."

As Bethany spoke she rubbed both hands together in a nervous gesture and Frank realized that she was hurting a lot more than he'd assumed. So he quickly dropped the conversation to something he thought would be more accommodating but it was nonetheless unnerving.

I was sorely disappointed when I heard that you withdrew from the pageantry. I hope you change your mind and get back in. You are very talented and a beautiful young woman, Beth. And I really think you would win."

"Oh, no Uncle Frank, I really don't want to. Plus it's too late to get back in even if I wanted to"

"Look honey, Uncle Frank has connections…just say the word and I can get you back in if you want. I know you'd win and that would be fantastic."

"Thanks' Uncle Frank, but I really don't want to; maybe next year."

"Then from behind Marlene's voice chimed in and said "may be next year, what. What are you two talking about?"

Frank quickly rose from his chair to greet Marlene while still holding his glass of scotch. He hugged and kissed her while Bethany looked on.

Then Frank said to Marlene "Well I was just telling your beautiful daughter that she should consider getting back into the pageantry, but she turned me down."

Marlene chuckled and said "you're not the only one"

Bethany excused herself and left the room, but in very delightful way as if having Frank around had shot a blast of life throughout the house.

According to Marlene, seeing Frank turned up at her house was like good news as she had wanted to snoop around for answers about himself and Lexa. But the fact that they had spoken earlier that day and he had promised to stop by later on in the week, kind-of made her wondered why the change of plans. However she chose not to remind him that, that was what he had told her.

"Would you like another drink, Frank; your glass looks empty," Marlene said as she seated herself in the sofa facing him.

I would love to, Frank responded.

Thereafter, Marlene got off the sofa and left to fix another drink for Frank. While left alone in the living room, Frank's head swirl on how to accomplish resolve from his pending course of action.

Marlene returned with the drink and while she was handing it to Frank, she casually said to him "it's like you've read my mind; I almost stopped by your office earlier"

Frank responded "Really, that would have been a pleasant surprise. Anything in particular… or were you just in the area?"

"You know, I'm so worried about Lexa that I took upon myself to drive out to her condo to see if something had happened to her"

"Huh, huh, I can understand. So what did you find out?"

"Well, she was nowhere to be found. The one thing out of the ordinary that I found was one of your business cards placed in middle of her coffee table."

Frank remembered clearly that he had placed one of his business cards on the coffee table, when he was there the other day. Anyway, in trying to keep their conversation light, he casually said to Marlene:
"Oh, really; why do you find it out of the ordinary? Oh, wait. Let me answer that one for you. You, know how much that woman cannot stand me. Hmm, I wonder why my business card instead of all the other attorneys in town?"

Marlene was taken aback by Frank's candor, but she wasn't about to appear surprised.

"Yeah…I know exactly what you mean, Frank. But, mind you, I've been going by her condo for years and I don't recall ever seeing your card around. So, after seeing it there, it made me think that this must be something very recent."

"Well, you could be right, and I'm sure she'll tell you all about it after you two are caught up." Frank said.

"I'm sure, but it's not that important to me, Frank. I just want to know where the heck she is."

"OK…I'm sure she's fine but I'll just leave that up to you and her." Frank said.

"Anyway, in as much as I respect your feelings, Marlene, I really thought it's time we sat down and talk about Barchas. I go to see him as often as I can, but it's taking a tremendous toll on me, and I'd really appreciate any support you can provide."

"Look Frank, I've told you time and time again how I feel about that man. He's a pig and I hate him. Do you realize that my husband could have killed me, if Allora weren't around to beat him off me when he tried choking the life out of me?"

"But of course I do, Marlene; there's absolutely no excuse for his actions except for what I've found out after speaking with his doctor, which would explain everything."

"Yeah, what everything, Frank, other than he was a drunken bastard."

"No, Marlene….I wanted to tell you from a while back that they had found a tumor on his brain. I'm sure you'd understand how something like this could alter a person's personality. Maybe if you looked back, there were some subtle changes in his behavior that you couldn't quite understand."

"What are you talking about, Frank?"

"I'm trying to tell you that your husband had been very ill for quite some time.   I'm amazed that he's still alive after all that he'd gone through."

Marlene raised her hand from her lap and rested it on the arm of the sofa.   A frightful look encompassed her face and Frank wondered if what he had to say to her had made a crack into the hard shell that she had become. He remained quiet and waited for her to respond but she said nothing, and within seconds her eyes welled up with tears. She sniffled as if to hold back, but the tears were already streaming down her face.   Although tearful women were always difficult for Frank to handle, watching Marlene sob felt like a major breakthrough for him. He felt assured that she had to have felt some kind of pity towards her husband's demise.

Frank refrained from saying another word while Marlene sank deep in somberness; he thought it was best to wait until she was ready to speak. So he threw his head back and drained the last sip of liquor *down the hatch,* while looking at her.

"Wait a minute, Frank, not so fast," Marlene said as she tried to regain her composure with a fresh presence of mind.

"When you say brain tumor, are you trying to tell me that my husband has brain cancer?" Marlene said.

"No, that's not what I'm saying. I too thought the same when Dr. Wigginton landed me with the news back then.   But thankfully the tumor was removed and it's totally benign. Of course, I only found out about the good news earlier today. But let me just say this to you, Marlene, it doesn't discount the fact that, your husband had been walking around with a tumor on his brain"

"Is there anything else you haven't told me?" Marlene asked Frank dryly and showing no emotion, but Frank surmised she was still hurting, no matter what she tried to do, or however she spoke.

"Well, I'm really glad you asked, Marlene. After talking with his doctor today, he advised that Barchas should be transferred to a rehab facility as soon as possible."

"Uh- huh" Marlene chimed without showing any care.

And Frank continued by explaining that he had made arrangements to have Barchas transferred to St. Clements as soon as the following day. However he impressed upon her that he had only made that decision solely on her longstanding stance regarding the situation. But if she preferred to handle the arrangements, he would be happy step aside.

"St. Clements is the best facility as far as I know; I don't think I could do any better, Frank, Marlene replied and showing a little bit of interest in her body language.
"Well, I'm afraid I can't take credit for making that decision, Marlene; I was only going by Dr. Wigginton's suggestion. I'd be lost without him."

After hearing Frank dropping the name, Dr. Wigginton, her heart skipped a beat.

"Uh-huh. So when you say Dr. Wigginton, are you referring to Jax?"

"But of course, I don't believe there's any other Jax Wigginton around." Jax said.

"Oh my goodness, that's unbelievable. I'm in shock; — this surely brings back a lot of memories…good and bad. Did you know he and my sister was an item fifteen-twenty years ago?"

"But of course, how could I not know. Have you forgotten how hard I worked with Barchas to clear his name? And for that he'd do anything to help get Barchas getting back on his feet."

"Well, I guess you could say he's pretty darn lucky to have both you and Jax in his corner"

Frank couldn't help picking up on Marlene's snide remarks about her husband and his patience was starting to run thin with her.

"Come on now Marlene, I agree that you have every right to your feelings. But, how much longer can you allow yourself to keep punishing your children like this?"

Marlene's eyes widened with anger. ...she was livid by Frank's remarks.

"Excuse me, Frank, I can't believe my ears— what did you just say; and what the hell do you mean by that? I did not do this to myself; and not only that, haven't you noticed what this has done to my children?"

That's my point exactly, Marlene. All I'm saying is, if only you could find it in your heart to accept that your husband who was ailing terribly at time of the incident, your understanding and compassion, would absolutely change the dynamics of your suffering. You'd be amazed by the healing and comfort you could provide for yourself and your children. C'mon now, Marlene, you know Barchas would never lay a hand on you, if he were of sound mind, Frank said.

Frank's reponse to Marlene was more like an outburst. The atmosphere in the room felt thick and heavy. Frank remained quiet and pretended to be cool. Marlene could feel his frustration and she wondered since when he became Lawyer-turned, caregiver, turned, psychotherapist.

Frank kept his composure as being quiet and cool and waited to hear what Marlene had to say to his little spiel.

Marlene suddenly folded her arms and sighed while a multitude of questions flooded her thoughts.

Finally, she decided to break the silence with one of her many questions in mind.

"Oh, wow— you and your infinite wisdom.   While you were speaking, I couldn't help wondering what has gotten in you, Frank; I've never heard you talked like this before? I can certainly appreciate your gesture, but don't expect me to lay down all arms and be the dutiful wife. I guess what I'm trying to say is, my pain is runs deeper that you'd ever understand, and I'm too conflicted to run to my husband's beside and tell him that he's forgiven."

Frank shook his head from side to side while saying, "I hear you, Marlene and you're right in saying, I will never understand the depth of your pain. Quite frankly; no one ever will…not even your children. But with all due respect, it's clear that your children are willing to try help you heal. But first, you must first help them, so they can help you. I know how much you love your children. Please Marlene, think about what I've said and give yourself a break.

Marlene looked at Frank with submission and contriteness. It was as if he wanted her to feel guilty for being upset with her husband. But on the other hand she felt as if he was trying his damndest to just fix her.

"This is just too much for me to handle right now, Frank. I really appreciate your love and support for my family. And I can't thank you enough for being there for us. I must tell you that you've really got me thinking all kind of ways right now. Aunt Carolyn once told me, "A person can never perceive their guilt until they seek forgiveness." "I'm starting to realize I've got some work to do, but all in good time," Marlene said

Frank then raised himself from the sofa while Marlene remained seated. He leaned over and hugged her gently and she simply patted his shoulders with tears in her eyes. Frank responded by letting her know it was too much for him to handle as well, and he apologized for coming down a little heavy on her.

Marlene then looked up at Frank and said "I'll be there tomorrow."

Upon hearing that, Frank straightened his body while standing over Marlene and he quickly asked her "be where tomorrow?"

At St. Clements; I'll be there to pay my husband a visit. Marlene said dryly.

That was the most moving thing Frank had heard from Marlene, and it felt as if a huge weight was lifted off him.

"Oh, thank you, God. Marlene, I can't thank you enough for saying that. Look, If you'd like, I'll pick you up," Frank said, with an eagerness to help keep her to her promise.

No...Frank, I plan to take the children with me, and I'll have Monk to drive. He's still so mad at his father that I'm not sure how he's going to take the idea of going with me. But, we'll see.

"OK...sounds good, Marlene. I have a good feeling about this; Monk is a good kid, I know he'll come through for you."

With everything going so well and a lot better than expected, Frank left Marlene relaxing on her sofa and he drove straight home to do the same.

CHAPTER TEN

Kennedy Wigginton, who was also a doctor, had made reservation for dinner at the Vines, for himself and his father, Dr. Jaxon Wigginton. He was excited about going over a few things with his dad about his wedding plans which was a few months away. But after a long and exhausting day at the hospital, Dr. Jax called his son to take a rain check. However disappointing, Kennedy was quick to encourage his father to take the rest of the night off and get some rest.

Jax, or Dr. Jax, as he's called by many, was less than ten minutes traveling on Spinnaker Highway. He was heading home when suddenly he became distracted by sirens. He immediately checked his rearview mirror and noticed that an ambulance was coming from behind. He quickly pulled off to the soft shoulder and watched the ambulance and a police car zipped by.

Jax assumed that an accident had occurred and he imagined that he was going to be stuck in traffic for while. So he loosened his tie and tried relaxing. Having said that, Jax was feeling even more relieved that he had taken a rain check to meet with his son

It would take some time to clear the area for traffic to proceed. But as soon as he pulled off the soft shoulder to continue driving, he realized that he was much closer to the scene of the accident than he had thought.

He then realized that it was not just another fender bender as he had assumed.

He quickly grabbed his medical bag and exited his white Land Rover and walked up to the scene and identified himself as a medical doctor, to one of the police officers.

One of the officers immediately recognized Dr. Jax and he immediately stepped aside to allow him to get to the spot of where the victim was lying..

"I just checked his vitals, Doc and he's in bad shape" One of the paramedics said to Jax and he tried kneeling down next to the victim.

"This guy's condition is critical and he's losing too much blood. Hurry, hurry…you've got to get him off to the emergency room immediately. But wait…let me do this; this will help stabilize him," Jax said, as he turned his eyes towards his medical bag.   And while the paramedics looked on, Jax immediately gave an injection to the injured male.

Jax immediately backed away and watched as the victim was quickly transferred to the ambulance. And as the sirens sounded off with the fast moving ambulance,   he hoped the victim made it to the hospital before it was too late.

The morning after was business as usual for Frank. He was up early and schlepping around his home while the   coffee pot buzzed with his favorite Columbian brew. He left the kitchen and stepped outside to get the morning newspaper. It was seven o'clock am, and he was very excited about getting to the hospital to finalize procedures regarding Barchas' transfer. He returned and sat at the kitchen table while glancing at the caption in the newspaper "Fiery Crash Left Prominent Businessman Critical" He heard silence…the coffee maker had stopped. He looked up and rolled his eyes towards the toaster, wondering what was taking it so long when suddenly it popped. He then tossed the newspaper aside and went to pour his coffee and butter his toast.

His telephone rang; it was Marlene calling.

"Good morning, Frank. It's Marlene; hope I didn't wake you"

"Oh, no, I was just thinking about you. Is everything ok?" Frank asked Marlene.

"Oh, yes, everything's fine, but after you left last night I've been thinking about what we had talked about."

"Huh-huh, so what's the verdict" Frank asked with a touch of sarcasm and fear of bad news.

"Well, you know…um…I think it's best if I kept the children out of joining me today when I go to visit their dad at St. Clement."

Whatever you're comfortable with, Marlene, will work for me. In that case would you like me to pick you up?

"Yes, Frank. I'd like that very much. Also, instead of just going to St. Clements, I've decided to go with you to the hospital. I really would like to help with finalizing the plans regarding Barchas' transfer to St. Clements."

Those words coming from Marlene was a major breakthrough for Frank; he was excited and relieved all in the same breath. However, he managed to keep his composure neutral while they continued their conversation.

"So, what brought on the change of plans, if you don't mind me asking?" Frank said calmly.

"Not, at all. I had a little chat with the kids last night, and I informed them about their father's condition."

"Huh, huh, and how did they take it?" Frank asked Marlene.

"Well, just like I expected; they were in total shock. And needless to say they are quite upset. Poor Bethany became so distressed that I had to quickly change the idea of taking her along with me to see their dad."

"Oh gee, sorry to hear that; I can't begin to imagine the hell she has been put through. And Monk, how did he handle the news?"

"Well, if you know my son, he never has too much to say, but going by the looks on his face, I could tell he wasn't quite ready, and I know he'd want to support his sister. I hate seeing my children suffer this way, Frank, and I must do whatever it takes to help getting them back on track."

"Well said Marlene and I couldn't agree with you more. I was just about finishing up my breakfast and then I'll be heading over to pick you up, say… around eight-thirty… nine-ish?

"That's fine, I shall see you then. Thank you, so much, Frank; you're a true friend" Marlene said before ending the call.

Frank's mind raced with endless possibilities about seeing the family coming together in support of Barchas' recovery. He welcomed the idea of giving back the power to Marlene in terms of taking over the arduous task of her husband's dilemma.

<> <>

It was nine o'clock am and Dr. Jax was already at the hospital completing a recap of Barchas' file in preparation for his transfer to St. Clements later that day.

"Frank and Marlene had just entered through the hospital doors. She was dressed in a taupe flannel suite, brown leather boots and high fashion sunglasses. She confided in Frank that she was feeling a little nervous, but to him she appeared calm and collected. He tried comforting her by telling her that was to be expected and that he was positive things would change as the day progressed.

They continued walking pass the elevator towards the nursing station when suddenly nurse Dunwoody turned up. Frank was delighted seeing her, and without being able to help himself, his vision dropped helplessly on her bosom. Although her cleavage was fully covered, in his mind's eyes he saw more than enough to excite him. He smiled at her and said "Well, good morning, Nurse."

The Nurse pleasantly smiled while looking up at him and said "Good morning Mr. Roulette, I understand Mr. Sander will be leaving us today"
"That is correct and I'd like you to meet his wife, Mrs. Sander, Frank said"

Marlene politely extended her arm with a forced smile. "It's a pleasure to meet you, Mrs. Sander; your husband is a very remarkable man; I don't remember ever seeing a patient with such resilience, Nurse Dunwoody said to Marlene.

Anyway, with the formalities out of the way, Nurse Dunwoody welcomed them to wait in another waiting room while she sent out a page for Dr. Jax.

Not to Marlene's surprise, she caught Frank eyeing the nurse in a lustful manner. She couldn't help getting a kick out of watching him being the player he's known to be. So in the moment of her nervousness, Frank's favorite pastime helped with lightening her load.

"Nice looking nurse, no wonder you've been spending so much time at the hospital, Marlene said jokingly.

"You're a very perceptive woman Mrs. Sander; I'm glad were on the same page." Frank said with a smirk plastered across his face.

When Frank heard Marlene chuckled at his last comment, he felt hopeful that the old Marlene was definitely coming back.

So, finally Dr. Jax turned up and as usual he greeted Frank with a wide smile. He had no idea Marlene was coming and by no means had he recognized her. Those two had not seen or had been in contact since before the death of her father, Larry Tate. And Jax being so much older and with a grey beard and eyeglasses was easily unrecognizable to her.

Jax looked at Marlene and bowed his head as if to say "howdy," because he wasn't quite certain of whom she was.

"Frank, who immediately picked up on the lapse, turned to Jax and said "I'm happy to have Mrs. Sander join me with regards to her husband's transfer to St. Clements.

"Oh, good heavens; I thought that was you, but I wasn't quite sure. Please accept my apology Marlene; it's been so long…twenty years or more, wouldn't you say."

Jax was quite jovial and friendly towards Marlene; a long way from his standards while working. But seeing her gave him a sense of pleasure even though it wasn't   under the best of circumstance.

Jax, I can't thank you enough for saving my husband's life, I had no idea you were his doctor. Please accept my apology; it's been hellish.

"No need to apologize, Marlene; you have every right to your feeling. The timing for you to come is just perfect and we'll do the best we can to help with your husband's recovery."

Marlene who was still wearing her dark glasses, wept secretly, but the tears overflowed down her cheeks and gave her courage away.

In spite of Marlene's breakdown, both men looked the other way and pulled their chairs closer so they could get down to business.

And in moving forward, Jax said to Marlene, "Well Mrs. Sander I'm sure Frank has updated you about your husband's condition. However, as his doctor, I'd like to go over a few things that Frank and I had previously discussed."

Marlene tried pulling herself together while paying close attention to Dr. Jax as he explained almost verbatim, everything that he had prognosticated to Frank about her husband.

"Do you have any questions" Jax asked Marlene as he prepared to close Barchas' file.

"No, no. I understand and I trust you completely. I'm still at a loss for words and I can't thank you enough for saving my husband's life. Is there anything you'd like me to do, Jax?

"Well, yes. His release package was signed by Frank. But with you in the picture and being his wife, I imagine it would behoove you to take a recap of what Frank had done. If you'd like to make any changes, now is the time. From then on, your signature is required on all of the pages where Frank had previously signed. And after that…he should be on his way."

"Thank you so much, Jax; I'd like to go and see him before he's off, if I may"
"But of course my lady, said Jax."

"Would you like to go alone or would you like me to accompany you," Frank asked Marlene.

"Thank you, Frank, but I'd like to be alone". Marlene replied.

"Very well, I'll wait here for you." Frank said feeling good about the way things were coming together.

As soon as Marlene turned up at her husband's room, she saw Nurse Dunwoody dressing him. She thanked her for being so kind and asked if she could spend a little time alone with her husband. The nurse immediately left the room and within seconds Marlene fell into to chair next to Barchas bed and she was wallowing in tears.

It was like a floodgate of emotion had devoured her. Guilt washed over her, anger beguiled her, good memories taunted her and bad memories gutted her. But most importantly she wanted her husband back. Marlene looked steadfastly in despair. She had no idea what was to be expected and the shock of the visit had her in tailspins beyond explanation.

In sheer pity, she looked at her husband from head to toe. She called his name and he opened his eyes which told her he'd recognized her voice; well… at least that was what she'd believed. She held his hand and massaged his feet but there was not much coming back to her. And that was when it totally came home to her that her husband was lucky to be alive. Anyway she was hopeful that he would continue to improve according to what Jax had told her.

A few minutes later, Nurse Dunwoody returned to the bedroom to inform Marlene that the ambulance was ready to take Mr. Sanders to Clements, and reminded her that she had some paper work to review and sign before they could proceed.

Marlene tried pulling herself together.

As Marlene and Franked walked back to the parking lot, Frank asked her if she'd like to do lunch at Vines before heading over the

St. Clements since they still had a couple hours before Barchas' arrival there. She was in good spirits and she quickly agreed to his suggestion.

But while they waited at the main entrance for the valet to come with their car, a limousine pulled up next to them.

"Thank you, very kindly" said the passenger as she exited the limo. The voice of the woman sounded very familiar; familiar enough to jolt Marlene into an immediate shock. She was afraid to look, but in the same breath she slowly turned her head to see if she was right about her suspicion. And from the corner of her eyes she proved that she was right.

In the moment without having a word to say to Frank, Marlene stood still in awe. Frank noticed an immediate change in her demeanor and he asked her if she was alright.

Under bated breath she said "not now, not at all Frank... I'm in shock"

Frank then turned to look in the same direction as Marlene but he wasn't sure that he was looking at whom he thought it could be.

Then he turned to Marlene and said "Isn't that Mrs. Tate, your mother –in law?

"I think so; I haven't seen her in several years," Marlene replied.

"Oh my God, it is her. What the hell is she doing here so early" Frank exclaimed while Marlene remained speechless.

"Well, aren't you going to say hello? I'm sure she'd like that" Frank continued.

Marlene, still quite pensive said "Not sure if I should, I'm too embarrassed about what took place between me and Barchas. I'm sure her coffee table is filled with every newspaper clippings about us. And quite frankly, our parting weren't under the best of circumstance. You could say I despise her. "

"I'm aware of the situation; but I thought you'd over that by now."

Frank's response was sharp and quite stabbing to Marlene.

Marlene gave Frank an evil eye after his comment; she thought he was being impertinent. But Frank being the closest friend to Barchas, of course, was fully aware of the rift between Carolyn and Marlene after Mr. Tate had passed away.

However, in the spirit of humility, she was able to hide her *thin skin* and she gave in to his suggestion. And, on top of that, she had developed a weird feeling about seeing her there that time of the day.

"OK Frank, I guess you're right; I think I should go over and say hello. But, oh, my God…look at her!"

Frank immediately raised an eye brow and asked Marlene what she meant by that statement and Marlene said "I can't believe that she'd look that old."

By the time Frank and Marlene ended their little talk, Carolyn Tate was halfway inside the hospital lobby carrying a small handbag clutched tightly under her arm.

As Carolyn continued walking through the hospital's main floor, Marlene ran after her saying, "Aunt Carolyn, Aunt Carolyn."

Carolyn, who recognized the voice right away, stopped in surprise and she immediately turned around and looked. On top what was overwhelming her, seeing Marlene turned up in the moment simply took her breath away.

Despite the fact that Carolyn's head spun freakishly from the shock of standing in Marlene's presence, she could not help feeling that a stroke of luck or better yet, a godsend had come her way.

"Aunt Carolyn, how are you, Aunt Carolyn" Marlene said as if she sensed that something had gone awry.

Carolyn, who was obviously shaking, looked at Marlene and she helplessly thrust her head on her shoulders weeping uncontrollably.

"Aunt Carolyn, Aunt Carolyn, what's wrong and why are you crying" Marlene said, while her eyes welled with compassion without knowing what was wrong.

"It's your brother, its Brandon, he was in a terrible accident last night and I just heard the news. I think it's bad, Marlene. Oh, my God, please God, don't take my child away from me, Carolyn said while still resting her head on Marlene's shoulders."

Marlene held her step-mother closely, while she herself was deep in shock about the news. However she tried comforting her step mother by saying "I'm sure Brandon is going to be fine, Aunt Carolyn, thank God he's in the best hospital"

Frank watched curiously from a distance and he wondered what could have been taking place between those two. He then walked up to where both ladies were standing and he cleared his throat. Marlene looked away to face Frank and she whispered to Carolyn "stay here, I'd like to go with you," She then walked over to Frank and said "Oh my God, Frank, something terribly has happened. My brother was in a terrible crash last night and that's why she's here. She's in really bad shape and I just can't leave her alone; not like this.

Oh gee, I'm so sorry to hear this. Do you mind if I go over and say hello. Frank said to Marlene and it showed that he was quite saddened by the news.

"Oh, I don't know if that's such a good idea; she's so devastated. No disrespect, but I'm sure she wouldn't remember you at this point."

"I guess you're right. So, what about, Barchas; you talk as if you'd want me to leave you here with her."

Well, do you mind coming back for me in a couple hours Frank? Or better yet, never mind, I'll call a limo to take me over to St. Clements and we can take it from there, Marlene responded sounding all shook up.

Frank looked at his watch and said to Marlene, "I think I have a better idea"

"And what is that" Marlene asked eagerly.

And Frank responded "OK… so, you go back and spend some time with your stepmother and I'll head over to the hospital cafeteria and grab a bite to eat while I wait for you. Quite frankly, Marlene, I'm not comfortable leaving you here with so much going on."

Another bout of sensitivity washed over Marlene after Frank made that comment. She quickly jumped to assume that he was alluding to her troubled history of mental illness.

"Don't worry, Frank. I'll be just fine.....I promise I won't fall apart on you.

Marlene looked at Frank in admiration of his care and attentiveness. She quickly agreed to his suggestion and she went back to be with Carolyn Tate, one of the most admired women in Watertown.

Frank purchased a newspaper at the News Stand inside the hospital gift store and proceeded to the cafeteria to buy lunch. He presumed that the caption he had glanced at earlier that morning could have been about Brandon Tate, who was Marlene's brother.

With the newspaper tucked under his arm, he looked around for a cozy spot to sit while carrying a tray with an overstuffed corned beef sandwich and a large root beer.

Frank was less than a minute in his chair when suddenly he saw Nurse Dunwoody walked by with lunch. He immediately upped from his chair and walked over to get her attention. She turned to him and she smiled; she kind of had a feeling that he liked her, but she was too shy to be so confident. So she blushed and inwardly and wished that she was right.

"That's one of the many things I like about you, Nurse" Frank said while staring at her with a broad smile.

"And what is that, Mr. Roulette," said the nurse looking up at him smiling and trying to study his face.

"That....right there... is such a beautiful thing about you." Frank said while pointing and shaking his finger towards her face.

"OK" she responded curiously because she was honestly at a loss. However, she kept up with the smiling, but the short suspense was starting to make her feel awkward.

"It's that lovely smile of yours that I'm talking about Nurse Dunwoody. You're always smiling and I'm sure it's one of your many ways of comforting your patients.

"Well, thank you, Sir. That's so kind of you."

Well, I see you're about to have lunch, and I was about to do the same. My dear nurse, I would be honored if you'd join me at my table… I'm sitting right back there."

That was a hair rising moment for Nurse Dunwoody. She never expected to hear something like that coming from Mr. Frank Roulette, one of Watertown's most eligible bachelors.

"She immediately felt a tad bit of nervousness about her, but she didn't hesitate in accepting his invitation.

Frank was glad about the nurse agreeing to join him for lunch. And as they walked back to his table he found another compliment to help keep her engaged.

"You know, Nurse, I can't begin to tell you how much I appreciate all your hard work and dedication toward my good friend, Mr. Sander. I can't thank you enough.

"Well, thank you, sir. But it's just another day in the life of a nurse. However I have to say that Mr. Sander is truly an amazing man; there's no doubt he'll pull through."

"Huh, huh, I can't agree with you more. I've heard some wonderful things about St. Clements." Frank said while pulling out the chair for Nurse Dunwoody to be seated.   She smiled inwardly and she proudly looked around to see if anyone she knew had noticed whose company she was in.

Frank politely asked if there was anything that he could get her. She shook her head to mean no, while looking down at her plate.

Frank was barely two bites into his sandwich when he started with a few subtle probes about the nurse. Twenty minutes later, she looked at her watch and told him that she had run out of time. He asked her for her phone number which she quickly gave, and in return he handed her one of his business cards.

Frank watched the nurse walked away hurriedly and he was pleased about their time spent over lunch. So while he waited for Marlene to turn up, he tried relaxing and thinking about what he had learnt about the nurse.

So, she had just turned forty two…less than a week prior. She had been an employee there for three years, never been married, had no children and was not in a relationship.

Although largely intelligent, after a quick assessment of the nurse, Frank drew conclusion that she was not as worldly or as sophisticated as the other women he'd dated. However he couldn't shake the appealing effect she gave every time they met.

Marlene entered the cafeteria in a tizzy while looking around for Frank. He had not seen her walked in as he was gleaning through the newspaper. However, it didn't take long before she spotted him. She pulled out a chair at his table and sat abruptly as if to show him that she had had enough for the day.

Frank immediately noticed that she was highly stressed, but presence of mind told him to keep his comment to himself. So, he addressed her with in a more positive tone.

"Wow, I never thought you'd be back so quickly; I take it things are not as bad as we thought."

"Well, he's not exactly out of the woods as yet, Frank. He's still in the ICU, but the doctors are very hopeful .

"Well…I'd say that's great news;" Frank said while he switched chairs and sat closer to her.

"I know it's hard to tell, but did you find out about what caused the accident?" Frank queried

"Well, according to Aunt Carolyn, the car spun out of control and hit a guard rail. Thank goodness he didn't hit another vehicle. Who knows…..he could have been speeding, or even drinking, Marlene said, throwing her hands in the air and looking frustrated.

"Poor Mrs. Tate; she must be devastated…I can't begin to imagine what she's going through," Frank responded while showing genuine compassion.

Marlene went on the telling Frank that Brandon's girlfriend had turned up and Carolyn was very relieved seeing her. She too was understandably devastated, but she managed to tell Carolyn that they had gone out to a small dinner party with friends. After he took her home they had a few drinks but he seemed fine when he left. So up until that point, no one knew for sure what had caused the accident.

Frank then asked Marlene if they were back on track regarding their trip to St. Clements.

"But of course, Frank" Marlene responded with much enthusiasm.

"Well, before we do that, I think you should at least try to get a bite to eat. Taking care of business at St. Clements could take several hours and you need your strength. Frank said to Marlene.

Marlene quickly turned down the idea of food, but she nervously unlatched the clutch on her handbag and dug inside for her little pill box. Frank watched her removed a pill and stuck it in her mouth. She tried swallowing the pill with her eyes closed while making a face. And cautiously Frank asked "don't you need some water for that?" She nodded to him while giving him to go ahead to go get her a drink.

Frank left the table and returned with a glass of water. "Thank you, Frank, she said. I'm sorry if I made you uncomfortable….it wasn't that difficult to swallow; but it's just so bitter. This little pill is like a godsend; I don't know what I'd do without them."

Marlene took a few sips of the water and shortly after they left the cafeteria to visit Barchas at St. Clements.

CHAPTER ELEVEN

It was December 7th and for the most part the city was starting to shape up for the Christmas Holidays. The tree lined streets were elegantly decorated with twinkling lights and garlands of various sizes and colors, hence a picturescue commute along the path to St. Clements. Marlene gazed halfheartedly at the falling snowflakes while the Xanax medication helped calmed her to a state of drowsiness.

Meanwhile, thoughts of seeing Nurse Dunwoody sometime soon, had Frank day dreaming as he drove Marlene along Main Street.

"We're almost there," Frank turned to Marlene and said while noticing the flashing amber lights two blocks ahead.

"Uh, huh, I can see that, Marlene said, but that was not entirely true. It was more like a *"wakeup"* call for her. She quickly opened her handbag and removed her lipstick and makeup compact. She flipped the compact open and when she looked into the mirror, she was peeved.

"Good God, look at me! My hair is disheveled and I look like crap. You could've said something to me, Frank. I can't believe you'd let me go in there looking like this." Marlene argued with Frank while patting her face with the powder puff and resetting her lipstick."

And without even looking at her, Frank simply smiled and said, "I don't know what you're talking about Marlene… you're always beautiful to me."

"Oh, stop it already; you're just saying that to make me feel good." Marlene replied brashly.

It was at that point he turned his head to look at her. He smiled and shook his head as he turned his focus back on the street. Then to himself he pondered… *"Women are the strangest creatures; damned if you pay a compliment, damned if you don't."* However in light of the conversation he repeated himself to Marlene to give her the boost that she longed for.

"Well, I'm gonna say it again Marlene, you're always beautiful to me."

She was immensely thrilled by Frank's compliment, but she kept it only to herself. Truth be told, Frank thought she would have responded with a "thank you"… but "mums" was her word. And so she remained staring in the little compact mirror with a blank.

Without staying on the subject Frank quickly changed his point of view and said to Marlene "Up until now, you've been very quiet; you haven't said a word since we left the hospital."

"Marlene replied "I was just thinking the same thing about you; it's not like you to be so quiet"

Frank kept his eyes on the road without responding.

So Marlene continued talking. "I'm just a little exhausted, Frank. After seeing Barchas this morning, it kind of put me in a downward spiral. Honestly to God, I didn't know what to expect but I never imagined it would be so hard. And then, running into Aunt Carolyn after all those years, literally have me floored."

Frank took Marlene's complaints to heart but he found himself at a loss for words in terms of consoling her, because his mind was in and out of sync due to his preoccupation about the nurse.

They had come to a complete stop along the main entrance of the facility when suddenly the valet turned up to assist Marlene out of the car while Frank prepared to hand over the keys.

"Welcome to St. Clements" said the greeter; a woman in her sixties with Della written on her name badge.

Anyway, before Frank could respond, Marlene introduced herself as Mrs. Sander.

The greeter pointed them to the west end of the facility to where they came upon the nurses' station.

She quickly forged ahead of Frank and introduced herself to one of the nurses.

"My name is Mrs. Sander. My husband was transferred here earlier today from Pastor and Finn Memorial Hospital" Marlene continued. And without much ado, Marlene and Frank were given directions to Barchas' suite.

"Oh man, this is a nice place," Frank said as he looked around Barchas' room. And Marlene chimed in by saying "This must be the best room this facility. I don't think they could have topped this one"

Barchas, who was by no means aware of their presence slept peacefully as they looked on. Marlene then removed her coat and washed her hands while Frank looked on. She then stood by her husband's beside and started caressing his face. And with tears in her eyes she tried talking to him.

"Hi sweetie, it's me; I love you and I miss you. I'm praying that God will heal you so that you can be home with me and the kids. Oh honey, I'm so sorry, I've said some horrible things and I'm so sorry."

Marlene wept while Frank stood aside and looked. He imagined that she was in a self-reflective mode and guilt was tearing her down.

Marlene then moved to the foot of the bed and gently rubbed her husband's feet. She felt deep remorse as she recalled the way in which she handled the situation over the previous months.

Then the tears stopped rolling and the few sniffles she had to contend with were quickly remedied by a few Kleenex from Frank. Much to her surprise, Frank pulled her closely to him and embraced her quite with love and tenderness. She was moved by his gesture and she took advantage of his kindness by burrowing her face in his chest and then she let it all out.

And she bawled.

Frank closed his eyes and wrapped his arms tightly around Marlene and tried his damndest to help soothe her, but she kept on crying.

He groped his thoughts for the right words to say, but he was hopeless. Then, out of the clear blue Frank developed an overwhelming urge to kiss Marlene; to kiss her with passion and make her feel loved. His penis thickened almost to a full blown erection. He gently pulled himself back away from her, but just enough to keep her from feeling his bump.

While in the moment, Frank struggled with suppressing his feelings that took him by surprise, and so he remained shocked until Marlene was ready to be done with crying herself to pieces in his arms.

While taking her home that night, Frank had very little to say. He was almost embarrassed for feeling the way he did when Marlene was agonizing about her husband. Though he could not deny that he found her terribly attractive, the thought of being intimate with his best friend's wife had never crossed his mind.….it was definitely not his style.

Having said that, after taking her home that night, Marlene felt an even deeper sense of appreciation for all the support Frank gave during her ordeal.

<> <>

Christmas came and flew by with very little fuss about the season in Marlene's household. She did try to make it a bit more eventful for the children, but they had no interest in her efforts. The strain of their father's absence left little for them to desire from the festivities that they had grown accustomed to. After all, it was their dad who was always responsible for making Christmas the best family-time of their lives.

Bethany complained about the Christmas tree, so Marlene ordered Allora to take it down, Monk whined about the Christmas Carols that he said was giving him a headache, so Marlene agreed not to play them. However, they were in total agreement when Allora offered to bake Monk's favorite apple pie, and Bethany's favorite cheese cake.

Anyway that did not stop Marlene from rocking her brains and going crazy about what she could to do to help erasing the sadness from the long faces of her children.

So, late on Christmas Eve, while they were cooped up inside their bedrooms, Marlene had their gifts delivered.

Monk woke up the next morning and he was overwhelmed with excitement after finding out that his mother had purchased a brand new car for him. Bethany was happy to see her brother so high about his gift, but words could not describe her excitement after ripping the big red bow from the huge box that was sitting on the breakfast table with her name on it.

"A boom box, Mom; you bought me a boom-box? How did you know you? I really like it mom; I really do."

While Bethany admired her gift inside, Monk was outside checking out his new ride amidst the falling snow. He turned and looked towards the kitchen and saw his mother watching him through the window. As soon as their eyes met, he immediately went inside and picked her up; literally picked her up off the floor and kissed his mother's cheeks.

So then with things feeling a lot more comfortable around the house, Marlene left and turned her attention to the basket of mails that was left sitting in the den. They were mostly Christmas cards, three of which came from Carolyn, Lexa and Frank. She anxiously opened the card from Lexa and found there was not enough said to satisfy her longing and curiosity about her disappearance. The caption of the card said:

"Season's Greetings" Then in her own words she penned, "Sorry I had to leave in such an inopportune time. We've got plenty to talk about as soon as I'm back in town. Love Lexa.

Marlene was quite pleased about the lovely Christmas card from her Aunt Carolyn. And after reading it, she wished she had taken the time to send her one. However, suffice it to say, she had never left her out since their reconnection at the hospital and that meant a world to Carolyn.

Marlene carefully displayed the Christmas cards in the middle of the coffee table and then picked up the phone to give Carolyn a call.

As soon as Carolyn was answered the phone, Marlene wasted no time in getting to the point.

"Thank you, Aunt Carolyn for that lovely card. It's like you had Hallmark to specially craft it for me."

"You're quite welcome, dear. I was just thinking about you and the kids. Oh gee, I know it's a bit impromptu, but it would be such a blessing if you could drop by. I would love to see my grandchildren. Oh, Marlene, it's been so long."

Carolyn's plea for company hit a soft chord in Marlene, and goose bumps grew as she listened.

"This is going to be my first Christmas without Brandon being here. Thank God he's doing much better but as you know he still has another week before he's released from the hospital. Please say you'll come, Marlene, I'll have Rosalinda to cook something special."

"Thanks for the invitation, Aunt Carolyn, but first I'll have to check with kids to see if they're up to it. They've been kind of down themselves about their father not being home. Anyway, I'll see what I can do, and I'll get back with you."

Marlene quickly ended the phone call and went looking for Bethany and Monk to tell them about Carolyn's invitation.

Monk was nowhere to be found and neither was his car. She asked Allora for Monk's whereabouts and was soon to be told that he had taken his car for a spin. Marlene then left to go find Bethany. Her boom box was evidently on full blast because the booms filled the void all the way upstairs.

She pushed open her daughter's bedroom door because the hard knockings were unbeknownst to her.

"Mom, you should have knocked" Bethany said in surprise after seeing her mother walked in and caught her dancing half naked while looking at herself in the mirror. She quickly turned the music down and slipped back into her robe.

"Well I'm glad you're enjoying your gift Bethany; was that the new Michael Jackson song everybody's raving about?"

"Uh, huh…you like it Mom?"

"Sure I do, honey. I like all of his songs. Look sweetie, there's something I'd like to talk to you about."

"Mom, what's wrong!" Bethany fired back thinking something bad had happened.

"Oh, no honey, everything's fine. I just got off the phone with Aunt Carolyn, and guess what?"

"What mommy?"

"She has invited us to dinner. So, how would you like spending Christmas at her house?"

Going to Aunt Carolyn's house was the last thing Bethany expected to hear from her mother. She never thought that day would come. After all, she vividly recalled how much her mother had despised her step-mother, and how she openly blamed her for the death of her father. So, with that memory coming back to her, she chose not to let her mother see how excited she was about the idea.

"Oh wow, Mom. I don't know what to say" Bethany, replied with a shrug. And with the same gesture she continued airing her thoughts.

"I haven't seen her Aunt Carolyn since I was little. I think about her all the time and some of the bad stuff that went after grand-daddy died"

That response from Bethany did not sit well with Marlene. She sighed and cringed after listening to her daughter's reflection of the past. One, she herself had struggled with putting behind her.

"Yes, I know what you mean honey, but that was a long time ago. "You know, sweetie" Marlene continued while moving closer to sit next to her daughter and placing her arms around her. "You know what I've learned from this experience… I've learned how to forgive and leave all that stuff behind.

What do you mean, Ma?

"What I'm trying to say, is, holding onto the anger and the pain brought on by someone else only worsens the situation. And bad things can happen to you.

"Uh huh, like what kind of bad things, Ma?"

"Things, like anger, frustration, meanness, and that thump that beats against your heart, every time you see or hear the name of that person that had done something bad to you.

"But how do you forgive someone that did something bad to you, Ma?" I mean something really, really bad.

"Yes sweetie, I see your point and that's exactly how I used to look at it. But if you're able to turn it around and look at it from a different perspective, you can overcome your anger"

"But Mom, I think the tricky part of this, is looking at it from a different perspective."

"Yes, baby, I completely understand, but hear me out."

Marlene then faced Bethany and placed both hands on her shoulders while looking into her eyes with her response.

"Forgiveness is a work in progress and the ultimate destination to an emotional wellbeing. So what I'm trying to say, is, it's not going to be easy to forgive your offender, but it's always worth a try. At the end of the road you are the sole beneficiary of this act." Marlene said.

"Seriously Mom, I just don't get it. It sounds a little complicated and you're starting to sound a little like Grandma Gracie Mae. I used to hear her saying some weird things around the house. But I didn't care because I thought that was how old people are.

You are so right, Bethany. What, I just told you about forgiveness, was what Grandma Gracie taught me, when I was just a young woman around your age. And I too, had no idea what she was talking about. So, don't worry about it honey. Just remember what I've told you on this very important Christmas day... It could come in very handy as you mature."

"And speaking of old people, Beth, you know what else Grandma Gracie taught me?"

No, Mother; I have no idea. But I know you are going to tell me. Bethany snapped.

Marlene then turned to her daughter and said:

"Whether or not you want to hear it, I most certainly am going to say it."

"Aging is nature's way of fading us into something a lot more desirable, than beauty to the inexperienced eyes."

"What? What's that one all about" Bethany asked her mother looking quite puzzled with knitted brows.

"Well I know I may be sounding a little weird. But that's okay; I use to feel the same way about Grandma Gracie whenever she came out saying these things. However, she was a very wise old woman. I haven't quite figured it all out as yet. But the older I get is the more I'm able to make sense of her words. But thank you for having this conversation with me today, Beth. After talking to you, it's clear to me what she was trying to say.

Uh-huh, Bethany replied under her breath disappointingly, because she realized that her mother was struggling for an answer for her. Or, was she?

"Mom, what do you mean by that, I need to know what it means?" Bethany said.

Well, I think what Grandma-Gracie was trying to say is:

Bethany quickly interrupted her mother and said:

"Don't worry mom, I think I got it:"

"Is that so, my dear? Well, why you don't share it with me, Miss Smarty Pants" Marlene chuckled.

"Well, what I think Grandma Gracie meant by that was:

"When you're young, beauty is what you see when you look in the mirror. But after we're old we don't think we're still pretty. But to me, my grandmother was always pretty." Bethany said.

"Hmmm, well that's one way of looking at it. But it doesn't stop there, Beth. What about the rest of her quote? Marlene said.

"I don't know, mother….why don't you should finish it for me." Beth said.

"I imagine she was referring to the wisdom that she gained from her life's experiences, and how it made her the formidable woman she was with such little education. Her depth of knowledge was so was amazing; especially for a woman who had barely finished grade school" Marlene said.

"Hey Mom, that was kind of fun talking about Grandma Gracie, I'm sure you have a lot more stories to share." Bethany said to her mother while showing genuine appreciation for their little talk.

"Of course dear, there's plenty to tell." Her mother replied.

Bethany remained quiet for a while as she was deep in thoughts about going to see Aunt Carolyn.

"What, are you thinking honey" Her mother asked.

Mom, I'm really happy to know that you and Aunt Carolyn are getting along much better now; and I'd really like to go. Bethany said.

"And what about Monk; did you tell him anything about this? Bethany asked her mother while trying to restrain herself from the real excitement of going to meet with family.

"No honey, not, as yet. But I will as soon as soon as he's back. Allora said he took his car out for a spin." Marlene said.

"Well, he better say yes about coming with us, because I would feel a lot better with him being there." Bethany said in an assertive manner.

<> <>

So, with Bethany's music completely turned off, both mother and daughter could hear footsteps climbing the staircase. They assumed it could be none other than Monk. He walked directly to Bethany's room to for look for his mother.

"Well, how do you like your new wheels, son? Marlene asked Monk. But before Monk could get a word in, Bethany chimed in with a smile and said: "

Mom, you shouldn't have to ask….who wouldn't like to get a red mustang for Christmas?   Monk then cleared his throat while smiling broadly and said:

"Mom, you're the best. Oh, yes I've got to let you know I do love my mustang. It was something Dad had promised to get for me, but that wouldn't be until after I've gracuated from   law school. I just can't thank you enough mom; I'll never forget this Christmas day."

"Hey, Monk, Mom's got something to tell you," Bethany chimed in again showing much excitement."

Marlene quickly realized that Bethany was really looking forward to seeing Carolyn. And deep within she hoped Monk would share in her sister's excitement.

Marlene then turned to her son and said:

"Anyway, sweetie, as you know I've been in contact with Aunt Carolyn since your uncle Brandon has been hospitalized.

"Huh-uh" Monk responded looking at his mother curiously while allowing her to finish her statement.

"Well, I just called a while ago to wish her merry Christmas and she was very happy… so happy that she even asked us to join her for dinner."

"Oh wow.' So what did you tell her Mom? Monk asked his mother, wide -eyed.

"I told her I'd get back with her. So what do you think we should do?"

"We should go mom, I feel kind of sorry for her"

"Hmm, hmm, me too" Bethany chimed in.

Carolyn was pleased hearing back from Marlene with a "yes" to her invitation. Rosalinda, the maid was very excited about seeing Marlene and the children after several years. And to top things off, she was especially glad knowing that Allora would be coming. Although they hadn't seen each other since Marlene and Carolyn parted ways, neither Carolyn nor Marlene was aware that the two maids have never lost contact.

With very little time to spare before going to spend Christmas with Aunt Carolyn, Marlene took a few minutes out of her time to call Frank to wish him a merry Christmas. She thanked him for the card he'd sent her and made up an excuse for not sending him one.

Frank was very pleased hearing from Marlene and praised her for taking the steps to spend time with her stepmother. She then asked him how he'd plan to spend his day. And under bated breath his response to her was "alone with a friend."

Right then and there Marlene realized that Frank was not about to disclose or go into any details about his arrangement for Christmas. So after ending the call cordially, she wondered if the friend in question could have been Nurse Dunwoody. That was not the case however; Frank was chilling with Jackie Monsoon.

Marlene remained seated next to the telephone and looking at it while trying to dismiss a slight streak of jealousy that took her by surprise.

However, as beautiful and almost demure as Nurse Dunwoody appeared to be, Marlene felt that she was way out of Frank's league. So she arrogantly tossed her thoughts against the woman as another passing fling for Frank.

CHAPTER TWELVE

Since Carolyn moved away from Blue Field Heights, several years ago, Marlene had never been by seen her new home, neither was she ever invited there.

"Welcome, welcome, everybody," Rosalinda said enthusiastically while stepping aside to allow Marlene and her family inside Carolyn's home. And when Carolyn heard voices, it was like music to her ears. She immediately came forth to greet her long lost family with much gusto and appreciation.

"Oh, Aunt Carolyn your home is gorgeous." Marlene said while her children and Allora looked on.

"Thank you dear" Carolyn said while releasing her hug from Marlene so she could wrap her arms around Bethany and Monk.

Oh, my sweetheart Bethany, you're such a pretty girl…just like your mommy."

"Thank you, Aunt Carolyn; merry Christmas" Bethany said while eyeing Carolyn with much endearment.

She then turned to Monk while smiling and said "I can't believe my eyes." My goodness, Monk, I can barely believe my eyes. If I saw you on the street, I would have passed you without even knowing that you are my grandson. Gee, how time flies."

Monk smiled and said "Merry Christmas Aunt Carolyn; it's great seeing you."

While Carolyn looked up at Monk smiling back at her, she would have loved to tell him how much he resembled his grandfather, but wit and presence of mind told her to keep the moment lighthearted.

Carolyn took Marlene by the hand to show her around the house and the children followed Allora to see Rosalinda in the kitchen.

"Oh wow," Monk said as he entered the kitchen and got a whiff of the old times. The aroma of Rosalinda's cooking gave the kids a throwback to some of the best years of their lives when they used to spend time with their grandfather.

Bethany and Monk left Allora and Rosalinda in the kitchen to roam around the house while looking at photographs hanging on the walls in the living room. It looked almost like a gallery.

Who's that, Bethany asked Aunt Carolyn, while pointing to one of the pictures.

"Oh, that's your uncle and his family, honey."

You, mean, Uncle Brandon?

"No, no, sweetie, that's your uncle Simon, his wife, Leigh, their daughter, Nylah and their son Domain, your cousins."

Monk, who was fixated at a certain picture turned to Carolyn and said, "You don't have to tell me who this is, Aunt Carolyn. I know that's my Uncle Brandon."

A moment of silence quickly ushered its way in after Brandon's name was brought up; all went reflective on his near death experience. But in light of keeping the visit on a brighter side, Carolyn bounced back with a half smile saying "of course that's your uncle Brandon. I'm so glad he's doing so much better and he's expected to be home soon."

Walking through the house with the children had Carolyn acting as if she was a history teacher. After seeing the eagerness in them to learn about their family, she regretted the years lost between them.

Bethany then said "I kind of remember Uncle Simon; he's the pilot, right Aunt Carolyn?"

That's right my love, he's the pilot. Unfortunately he won't be joining us for dinner this year. They will be spending it in England with his in-laws.

Then it was Monk's turn to ask about another family member.

"So, is Miss Cassie still living with you, Aunt Carolyn?"

"Oh, yes she is. I'll take you to see her in a minute. My mother has Alzheimer so she won't remember you kids. But never mind, as soon as you walk in she'll be smiling at you."

Marlene turned and looked at Carolyn in silence. And Carolyn felt her pain; she surmised Marlene felt some degree of guilt about the way she had raised the children to be estranged from their family. And, likewise Carolyn reckoned she could have at least made an attempt to reach out to Marlene especially after hearing about their fight.

Anyway that thought was not a deterrent to making good on Christmas day.

I'd love to see Miss Cassie" Marlene said to Carolyn while showing a genuine longing to seeing the "old witch" as she used to refer to her.
"OK, let's go" Carolyn said while taking Bethany's hand.

"It would be so precious to me, if only I could say, Mom you've got visitors, but there's no point as you'd understand Marlene. My mother has been like this for years and it breaks my heart everyday watching time steal her identity."

While Carolyn spoke, Marlene and her family stood at the bedroom room looking at Miss Cassie sitting on chair while be watched by a nurse sitting next to her.

Marlene poked Monk to get out of her way so she could get through to get closer to Miss Cassie. "Merry Christmas, Miss Cassie." Marlene said while taking her hands and holding them in her claps. Though feint and almost undetected, Marlene sensed a connection between them, while Miss Cassie smiled back at her.

While Carolyn and the children looked on, Marlene stared at Miss Cassie for a few seconds without saying anything. She was quite taken aback by the condition of the old lady whom was once an outstanding pillar in Watertown. With nothing left to say or do, Marlene placed a gentle kiss on Miss Cassie's cheek and backed away to leave the room.

As they walked away from Miss Cassie's room, Marlene enquired about Timothy. Carolyn appeared saddened when she told Marlene that her uncle had passed away two years ago. However, an about face was soon to follow when she bragged about the joy he had brought into their life and the wisdom he had passed on to the family.

Both Monk and Bethany left Marlene and Carolyn to follow their noses back to the kitchen. Allora had whipped up some hot chocolate, while Rosalinda hurried the pots along. And while the kids enjoyed snacking and watching the snow fall, Marlene and her step mother stole some time alone to sit and talk in the drawing room.

"Would you like a drink, Marlene" Carolyn said while turning her eyes on a crystal pitcher filled with apple cider on the sideboard. Marlene accepted and walked over to pour two glasses of the drink.

So as both ladies reclined into the *"hot seat"* so to speak, they looked at each other and sipped on their drink.

Carolyn set off the conversation.

"Oh gee, Marlene. You have two wonderful kids; so well behaved and intelligent.   That Bethany is such a pretty child. Needless to say, Monk is quite handsome. I just can't thank you enough for coming."

Carolyn was dying to tell Marlene that Monk resembled his grandfather, who was her late husband Larry Tate. But she was very guarded about making mention of his name in fear of dredging up the past.

"Marlene responded "I'm the one that should be thanking you for the invite, Aunt Carolyn. The children were miserable and so was I, to tell you the truth. They were missing their dad terribly and I was at my wits end with what to do."

"So tell me, dear. How's your husband doing, really? I must confess when I heard the news on TV, I was deeply saddened. I really wanted to call you.... but, you know....I wasn't sure if it was such a good idea

After Carolyn said that, Marlene experienced an immediate dip in her stomach from being embarrassed. She knew deep down if her step mother had followed through and made that call, more than likely she would have blasted her off the telephone, thinking that she was enemy number one. But little did she know that Carolyn had overcome their strife and held no animosity towards her. For many years she prayed for an intervention to help reuniting the family. But the fear of making things worse had kept her at bay.

However humbling Marlene might have felt after Carolyn's reveal, she came back swinging likewise.

"I appreciate the thought Aunt Carolyn; I was in such a state of disrepair that I don't know how I would have handled hearing from you, given our history over the past. But, you know, Aunt Carolyn, when I saw you at the hospital the other day, something inside of me changed. No matter what the outcome, I knew I had to make the call and made sure that you were ok.

A great comeback for Marlene, Carolyn reckoned, although she felt it was quite benign.

"Well, my dear, I can't thank you enough for finding me. It was like falling from hope and the Good Lord placed you there to catch me."

Carolyn's response filled Marlene with sincerity and hope for a new beginning.

From then on, she moved to telling Carolyn the whole story about what took place between her and Barchas since the night of their quarrel. She confessed how much she had hated her husband and how she wished him to be dead.

Carolyn looked on while Marlene updated her about her life as it were. Marlene praised Frank openly for taking the reins in supporting her husband during his long stay at the hospital and for helping her overcome her anger.

Carolyn watched Marlene sipped on the cider while her demeanor started changing to reflect the pain she tried hard to suppress as she looked back.

"And, if I may be indulged for another few minutes, Aunt Carolyn, I'd like to take our time together as an opportunity to apologize to you. Needless to say I adored my father to a fault, and the way I handled his passing by lashing out on you was completely out of line. You did not deserve to be treated that way…you have been nothing but goodness to me. I really hope you can find it in your heart to forgive me.

Carolyn listened attentively to Marlene

"Oh, Marlene, you have no idea how long I've been praying for this opportunity. I don't want you to think I was without fault in the breakdown of our relationship. There are so many layers to the situation. Anyway, I owe you an apology   after looking back, I found mistakes, after mistakes that were brought on by me. But, I too was ripped wide open and thrown to the onslaught of a grieving widow. I loved your father with every fiber inside of me and the only survival I could grasp onto was the love he'd given to me."

"I would be a hypocrite to say I don't know what you're talking about. I do honey, and I have forgiven both you and myself for our shortcomings. I really hope you can find it in your heart to forgive me."

Both Carolyn and Marlene hugged and vowed to make bygones be bygones, and in moving forward they upped and went to the kitchen to see what's cooking.

Rosalinda and Allora surprised the family with a big festive spread. Miss Cassie was wheeled out to join the rest of the family in the dining room. When everyone was done eating and still sitting at the table, Carolyn smiled while raising her glass and she commented "Isn't Christmas magical? Can anyone else feel the magic? Or, is it just me?"

All smiled and shook their heads in unison that the *magic* was theirs to share.

<> <>

Marlene was anxious to update Frank about her visit with Carolyn and how they've reconciled their differences. But when she tried calling the morning after, his telephone rang without an answer. She was burning with impatience and wished if he would just pick up the phone. So she waited a few minutes and tried calling back when finally his answering machine came on. As soon as she started speaking Frank picked up the phone and said "Hey Marlene, is everything ok" "Marlene quickly heaved a sigh of relief and then tried calming down.

"Am I ever" Marlene said to Frank sounding ecstatic.

"Well, it sounds like you've got some good news….so what's this all about" Frank responded.

"Oh, Frank, I hate to bother you, so if you've got company, I can call back later."

"Oh, come on Marlene. Surely you didn't call sounding worked up just to say you'll call back later. You've got me all worked up now. And I don't handle suspense very well."

"OK, I guess you're right. I just wanted to tell you about my visit with Aunt Carolyn."

"Uh-huh. So, how was it?" Frank asked Marlene while pulling up a chair to listen to her filling his ears with the good news about her visit.

While Frank sat patiently and listened to Marlene reporting how her day went with her stepmother, Jackie Monsoon was left sitting at the breakfast table over juice and coffee that Frank had prepared.

Jackie was starting to feel unwelcomed after sneaking up against the living room wall to eavesdrop on Frank's and Marlene's conversation. She had no idea whom Frank was chatting with but after hearing him say that he would be coming over later to visit, left a bad taste in her mouth. And she was peeved.

Jackie tip toed back to the bedroom and gathered her things to leave. By then, Frank had just ended the call.

"Where you, going and why are you leaving" Frank said to Jackie in surprise.

"I don't know why I put up with you, Frank Roulette! You and all these women! You could have at least showed some respect while I'm here."

"What, what are you talking about? How have I disrespected you?

"I heard you on the phone. You're planning a date with another one of your women. I don't know why I continue to let you using me, Frank. I'm so sick of it!

"Wait a minute, you mean to tell me you were eavesdropping"? Frank retorted.

Jackie's head turned sharply to face Frank's and then in the same manner she looked away. It was not her intention to let him know that she was listening in while he spoke. But her jealousy became unmanageable to where it kicked off the outburst.

"So" Jackie fired back defensively and showing Frank that she was not about to back down.

Frank realized that an even bigger argument was about to ensue, and he was not about to allow that to happen.

He realized that his cavalier lifestyle had frustrated her from time to time. And it was not his intention to make her feel worse. Given their half- assed relationship, Frank did not feel the need to have to explain who he was on the phone with, but he reckoned she deserved the respect.

"Look, I can understand your feeling, and I'm sorry that you're upset. It's really not what you're thinking. So, why don't we go back into the kitchen and finish our breakfast and I'll explain."

"She fired back at him while waving a pointer finger in his face, saying "Oh, no, no, no! No need to explain, Frank; I already know what I heard. I've already overstayed my welcome, so I'll be on my way.

On that note, Frank acquiesced, but without any feeling of great loss. He sat on the sofa and watched her picked up her bags that were already sitting at the front door. She then remembered the Xmas gift he had given her was still left sitting on the coffee table. He watched her turned around and stuffed the gold watch in her purse. And without any further utterances, Jackie slammed the door behind her and drove away.

Jackie cried half way back to her home. She thought Frank would have tried harder to stop her from leaving. And in her opinion, by him trying to get her back into the kitchen so he could fabricate a lie to pacify her was another slap to the face that she would not allow.

Frank calmly stuffed a sofa pillow under his neck and lay peacefully looking up to the ceiling. He reflected on their ups and downs and the few times when he caught Jackie out with other men. She tried her best to make him jealous but not with any great success… hence her understandably frustration with him.

CHAPTER THIRTEEN

While Frank lay pondering what had taken place between him and Jackie, the telephone rang. He imagined it could have been her calling to apologize for her outburst and he was not in the mood to following up with her. He waited for the answering machine to come on to see if he was right about who was calling.

He made a dash to grab the telephone as soon as he realized that it was not Jackie calling….it was Lexa.

"Hi Frank, This is Lexa. I'll try calling back later. Happy Holidays to you"

"Oh shit, how could I let her get away like that? Damn it! Frank reprimanded himself for being so blasé about the call. He wondered what she meant by "later" Is she going to call back later today, later tonight, or sometime tomorrow. He scratched his head and his mind raced as to how to schedule himself around the much anticipated phone call from Lexa. He wondered if she was calling from some faraway place, or from her condo in town.

Lexa, who was dying to speak with Frank, tried calling him back ten minutes later. Without knowing who was calling, Frank picked grabbed the phone by first ring.

"Hello, hello" Frank said, sounding very anxious in his tone.

"Hi Frank; this is Lexa."

"Well, well, well, Lexa, Merry Christmas to you. I just got your message and I was thinking to myself that you could be back in town."

"Merry Christmas to you too, Frank. And yes, I'm back in town. As a matter of fact I got in just a few hours ago"

"Well, that's great news, Lexa! So, how are mother and baby doing?"

Lexa sighed deeply and her voice cracked but she managed to keep her tears at bay and her composure intact while she spoke.

"Oh Frank, I wish I had better news for you. I followed the doctor's orders, and did they have done everything in their powers, but they could not save my baby; they could not save my little "Rose."

"What, little rose are you referring to, I'm not sure I understand" Frank said to Lexa, sounding quite confused. Frank listened to her pause as if she was struggling with the answer. And while he remained quiet and curious about what it could mean, she tearfully said "it was a girl, Frank and I named her, Rose.

"Oh Lexa, I'm so sorry; I didn't realize that was what you were trying to say. Rose, is quite a beautiful name. I'm very sorry for your loss; I know how much you wanted to have a child."

Frank had mixed feelings about his conversation with Lexa. Deep down he felt relieved about what he thought was good news to him. But, at the same time he couldn't help showing some degree of sympathy towards her.

Frank was by no means proud of his private thoughts about Lexa and the baby. But he felt if things had gone otherwise she would most likely wreak havoc in the lives of Barchas and his family.

After Frank told Lexa that "Rose" was quite a beautiful name, she was immediately uplifted by the compliment. That was the first time she was able speak freely and be acknowledged as a mother, by someone.

"Thank you, thank you, so much Frank; you have no idea what this means to me. I had made quite a long list of names for girls and boys which I kept going over, and over, again. But Rose always stood out to me, without even knowing it was going to be a girl."

Frank became uncomfortable with the idea of where the conversation could lead up to. And, he was by no means interested or able to cope with women in distress. And he wondered why she had not sought counseling from a shrink.

Inasmuch as Frank would have preferred to change the subject by steering Lexa on a different path, but her ramblings kept him somewhat engaged.

"So when did this happen? Frank asked Lexa."

"…A month ago. I do not have words to describe my life since then. It's like, like, ugh, it's like waking up day after day in search of my soul. My life is just so baseless at this point." Lexa said.

As Frank listened closely to Lexa's plaintive cry, a sense of compassion took him by surprise. Although she wasn't crying, her explanation of self to him was an outcry for help that far exceeding his capabilities.

Frank said to Lexa:

"I can't begin to imagine the hell you're going through, Lexa; but I know it must be hellish. I wish if I could find the right words to help you recover"

"Thank you Frank. Just to have you listening to me means a lot. You have no idea how much I wanted to call, but I was too embarrassed to take the chance. It didn't take long for me to realize how obnoxious I was to you. But you know, I was really upset and selfish about everything that was taking place in my life; and I took it all out on you. I'm sorry, Frank; please forgive me."

"No need to worry, Lexa. I understand completely what you were going through. I just want you to try and get back on your feet. "

Frank and Lexa ended their call without any mention of Marlene being made. He badly wanted to bring up her name, but he perceived it could add more fury to her fire…given her vulnerable condition. However if he had brought up Marlene's name, Lexa would have been ok with it. She would have welcomed the idea to show Frank that she was hoping to get back into Marlene's good grace. Of course her intention was to never let Marlene find out about her loss. And she'd hope Frank would forever keep his promise about her secret.

Frank left and went to the kitchen to pick on the breakfast that had been sitting there for hours. He poured vodka into the orange juice and munched on the cold sausages and pancakes. He then lit up a cigar and returned to the living room to sit on his big chair so he could think. And while his head swirled with the four women in its forefront, he kept watching the clock to make sure he was on time for his visit with Marlene.

He reflected on his tiff earlier that day with Jackie, and he reckoned it was not worth mulling over especially since he was not guilty of her accusation. Next in mind was Milan Dunwoody, the nurse, whom he had been dreaming of spending time with. So far they had gone to dinner once, and he thoroughly enjoyed her company. But because of her previous plans, she had been gone for a week to spend the holidays with her momma. And then, there's Lexa, the wild card. He realized that she's devious and not very well liked by many. His plan was to keep a close eye on her to make sure she didn't create any roadblock in Marlene's recovery from her painful past. He was pleased that Carolyn was back in her life both as a friend and as a step mother. That Mrs. Tate, he recalled, was a *'sharp shooter'* which undoubtedly has gotten better with age.

Frank hung his head low while looking at the ashtray and outing the cigar from which he'd smoked only half. He then looked up the clock and saw that he still had time to relax or do *whatever,* before going to see Marlene. However, the loneliness was driving him crazy, so he decided to get dressed and to go see her anyway. He assumed turning up a few hours early would not be much of a surprise.

Monk was first to greet Frank as soon as he pulled into the driveway. He immediately turned Frank's attention to his car and asked if he would like a test drive. "Sure" Frank responded with gusto, while walking around the red mustang and enjoying the pride and energy that Monk exuded.

Monk left and returned with the key and immediately handed it over to Frank. Both got in and while Frank drove around the neighborhood Monk bragged about all the cool features inside, but most importantly it was the cassette player that swelled his head the most.

Marlene had just returned from St. Clements after spending a few hours with her husband. She expected Frank would be coming by later that evening. So she went upstairs to relax and watch TV. Her telephone rang and upon answering, her heart raced with relief after hearing Lexa's voice.

"Oh, my God; I can't believe my ears. Lexa, you have no idea how long I've been waiting to hear from you. I was so worried about you that I even went inside your condo to see if something had happened to you. Lexa said:

"Oh my Lord, I didn't realize you'd be so worried about me Marlene, especially with all that hoopla about you and Barchas. Was it really that bad, or was it mostly rumors?"

Marlene said:

"Oh yes, it was that bad and even worse. And, I have to say, if it weren't for Allora, I don't know where I'd be today. My husband choked me half to death, Lexa! "

Lexa said:

"What! You have got to be kidding Marlene. This is unbelievable, I'm so sorry; I didn't realize it was that serious. I was on my way to the airport that same morning when I heard the news. Of course I was quite shocked about it, but I never realized it was that bad. Oh, my God, I'm so sorry about this; I feel guilty. Anyway, I did call to check up on you before boarding the plane. I wanted to let you know I had to get back to work in a rush."

"Marlene was surprised about that response from Lexa. She recalled playing her answering machine several times in hopes that she'd hear from her. And even in her frailty from the abuse she had taken from her husband, she clearly recalled not receiving any messages from Lexa. Marlene became agitated and she fired back at Lexa for verification.

"What message? I never received any message from you."

Lexa said:

"I don't know why you never got my message, Marlene. But with everything that was happening to you all at once, it's understandable you could have missed it."

"Oh- no, Lexa... uh-huh" Marlene said while shaking her head in disbelief. "I know I was a mess back then, Lexa. But I'm quite sure you didn't leave a message on my machine. Maybe, you were the one that was in such a hurry that you thought you'd left a message."

Although Marlene's tone took Lexa by surprise, she tried ignoring her response by laughing and then she tried changing the subject. She realized that if she kept up with the lies she could end up being caught. And up to that point her main objective was to get back on par with her pal.

"Well, you could be right, my dear. That morning in question had me in quite in a tailspin, and quite frankly it stayed that way for all those months while I've been gone. Anyway girlfriend, let's just forget about that, and try moving forward. So what's new; talk to me? Lexa said.

"Well, Merry Christmas to you too girlfriend, and how long will you be staying this time. I hope it will be for a while before you're gone again? Marlene said:

When Marlene extended the greetings to Lexa, it came through with a smile and a lot of warmth. And from that she clearly sensed how badly she was missed.

Well, I'm not going to lie to you; I'm doing a lot better. And it's even better since I'm hearing from you. I'm still surprised you didn't hear more about me and Barchas. It was really bad.

Lexa cleared her throat, followed by a short cough. She was starting to feel nervous and very uncomfortable talking to Marlene about her fight with Barchas, her husband. She assumed she was the main reason why Barchas went and took out his frustration on his wife after telling him about the pregnancy.

"Uh-huh, I do recall hearing something about a fight between you too. But I had to leave in such a hurry that I never got the full gist of it. So, how bad was it; really Marlene?" Lexa said.

"Oh hell yes it was bad, my dear; I almost lost my life"

"Jesus Christ! …Hard to believe. I never thought Barchas was the type."

"Well, you better believe it girlfriend. And, it was all because of some other woman he had been cheating with for some time. Don't tell me you've forgotten our discussion about my suspicions."

"Oh no; I've forgotten at all. So, did you find out if it was Blossom?

…Nope, not really. For a long time I suspected that it was her, but now I'm not so sure.

"Why, what makes you think that?" Lexa asked:

"I don't know. But with everything that has happened since you've been away, it's just a waste of time now to even worry about it." It's just too exhausting to tell you the truth.

That's a good way of looking at it, I think. As long as you're doing ok, is all that matters. So, how was Christmas?"

"Oh wow, Lexa, Christmas was fabulous, Are you ready for this?"

"Go on…I'm all ears, girl."

"I spent Christmas with Aunt Carolyn."

"You mean …the, Mrs. Tate, your stepmother?"

"Uh-huh – you guessed it."

"I find that hard to believe, Marlene. Don't just stop there, fill me in, girlfriend. So, how did that come about?" Lexa asked Marlene after busting out with giggles which was one of her ways handling her stress.

"Long story my dear; it all came about after running into her at the hospital. My brother Brandon was in a terrible car accident and was taken there for treatment. He's lucky to be alive"

"There's so much to talk about.   And since we haven't seen each other in ages, how about lunch at Vines, tomorrow? This way we could sit and relax while we get caught up." Marlene said.

"Lunch sounds wonderful" Lexa said.

As soon as Lexa and Marlene set a time to meet up for lunch at Vines, they ended the call on a high note. Marlene was ecstatic about hearing from her and she couldn't wait to fill Frank's ears with the good news. Frank however, had no intention of letting Marlene know that he had spoken to Lexa long before she did.

Frank slowly pulled up into the driveway with Monk's car. He was glad seeing Monk looking so happy after watching him going through the gloom and doom since the plight of his parents. Frank came out of the car laughing while handing back the keys to Monk and teased him about attracting the prettiest girls in town.

Marlene came downstairs just in time to meet Frank and Monk, who coming inside from the chilly outdoors.

"Well, what have you two been up to?" Marlene said while taking Frank's coat.

"Did you have to ask?" Frank responded while smiling and looking at Marlene.

"It's my son, isn't it Frank? I bet he took you out for a test drive in his new toy" Marlene said while smiling and looking at her son with pride and joy.

Marlene then turned to Frank and said:

"Come on back, Frank. Let's sit in the living room and chat for a while; I've got some more good news to share with you. And, Allora is almost done with fixing dinner, so I hope you can stay back and dine with us."

Frank's mind wandered while he followed behind Marlene to the living room. The words," more good news" as they escaped her mouth had Frank thinking it could have something to do with Lexa. And if that was the case, he decided he would try and stay clear of the conversation by pretending he wasn't aware of her presence in town. He very much hated to deceive Marlene about his connection with Lexa, but that was his way of protecting her for the time being.

Marlene was expecting a response from Frank about staying back for dinner, but he had nothing to say. Dinner sounded great to him, but he was more concerned about what the good news could be.

"Great! I love good news" Frank said to Marlene while sitting down and making himself comfortable on the sofa. "So, talk to me; tell me what's going on." Frank continued while Marlene looked on while thinking that he can be such good company.

"You're not going to believe this, but guess who just called?"

"I can't guess, and I hate suspense, so please come out with it" Frank responded while smiling and enjoying the spark in her eyes.

"Ok…it's about Lexa; she's in town and I've got to tell you Frank— I'm so excited that she's back.

"Well, that is great news, Marlene. Where the heck was she… and did she say why she dropped out of circulation so abruptly?"

"Yeah, she did. It had something to do with her job; she said that she had to drop everything and run. But now that I'm looking back at it, it does seem uncanny that everything happened all at once."

After Marlene said that, Frank watched her brows knit while she turned her head and looked away as if she was wondering if there could be more to Lexa's excuse.

"Well, stranger things have happened" Frank said.

What's that suppose to mean" Marlene asked Frank in a surprised and somewhat of a defensive tone.

Frank immediately backed up by raising his hands to show Marlene that he was on her side.

Oh, Marlene, don't put too much into what I've just said; I only wanted to say that I agree with your way of looking at it. I'm happy she's back and I'm sure you two have a lot of catching up to do.

Then in keeping with Frank's thoughts, Marlene said,

"That's right; and before you know it she'll be gone again. Anyway, we'll be doing lunch at Vines tomorrow and I'm really looking forward to that"

"Frank nodded while looking at Marlene with a straight face because he wasn't comfortable about her meeting up with Lexa— period. Marlene could sense the negative vibe exuding from Frank but she was way off from what he was thinking.

"Why are you looking at me like that? You don't appear to be too thrilled about my friend. But that's ok; I know you two never got along. You'd be surprised how nice a person she is if only you'd give her a chance." Marlene said.

Marlene's comment about Lexa was like water on a duck's back to Frank. However, it was not Frank's intention to dampen Marlene's high expectation of Lexa, so he refrained from voicing his true opinion.

"What can I say, Marlene? You two have been friends for such a long time, that I'm going to have to take your word for it."

Marlene then changed the conversation and began updating Frank about her visit to see Barchas earlier that day. Their conversation ended abruptly after Allora came in and announced that dinner was served. Both Frank and Marlene upped and went to join the kids in the dining room where Bethany was anxiously waiting to greet her Uncle Frank.

<> <> <>

The next day, Lexa showed up at Vines for lunch. She was a few minutes earlier than Marlene, so she picked a table and waited there with anticipation of having a great time. She glanced on and off at the menu while turning her head back and forth to see if Marlene was going to show up. Not long after, she spotted Marlene coming towards her with her broad smile as she usually does. Lexa quickly got up to greet her.

"Oh wow, Marlene, you're looking fabulous" Lexa said while hugging her.

"So do you, my dear… need I say I missed you terribly?" Marlene said while allowing Lexa's embrace to linger a while.

While both ladies picked at their lunches and sipped on ice tea, they spent a long time catching up with each other. Marlene left no stone unturned in updating Lexa about her ordeal and how Frank had supported by her unconditionally.

During their conversation, whenever Barchas' name was brought up, Lexa would find her heart bloating with anger. She felt no remorse towards him even after finding out about his brain tumor. To her, even that could not have caused him to try forcing her to kill their unborn child. However as Marlene continued rambling, Lexa did feel empathy about what she had endured.

So when it came time for Lexa to update Marlene on what had been going on with her back in Movie Land, she had very little to say. Marlene sensed that Lexa was not quite as talkative as her usual self. She imagined that she could be partly responsible for Lexa's evasiveness, because of how she couldn't shut up.

Anyway, the little information that Lexa had to share with Marlene was mostly guarded or fabricated. Aside from deceiving her about having to leave almost overnight when she was attacked by her husband, she went as far as telling her that she had been hospitalized for a while with pneumonia.

However, the truth is Lexa's doctor had put her on total bed rest which lead up to sending her to the hospital to ensure proper treatment to help save her baby.

"You poor girl, pneumonia can be quite debilitating. I'm surprised you didn't come home sooner to get away from the stress of your hectic career." Marlene said while showing genuine concern for Lexa.

A sense of discomfort washed over Lexa while Marlene sympathized with her story. She tried changing the subject to deflect from being cornered should in case Marlene start dwelling on the subject of her illness.   Added to that, the real memory of her hospitalization was making her sick. So she quickly changed the subject.

"Anyway, girl, I'm feeling a lot better now.   So there's not need to worry your gorgeous self over me. As you can see; I'm doing great."

Their waiter turned up smiling and holding a pitcher of lemonade. He enquired if both ladies would like to refill their glasses but they declined.   Marlene then looked at her watch and hinted to Lexa that she should be on her way.   She wanted to leave and spend some time with her husband.   She then asked Lexa if she cared to join her at St. Clements while she paid Barchas a visit.

Lexa was not enthused about the idea of going to St. Clements to see Barchas.   But she felt it was the smart thing to do if she wanted to continue her relationship with Marlene.

The waiter returned and placed the check on the table which was quickly honored by Marlene.

Up until then, Lexa had not responded to Marlene about driving over the Clements.

"What's up, Lexa, you haven't answered me" Marlene said in a much more relaxed tone.

"Oh' gee, I'm sorry. But of course I'm going with you. You shouldn't even have to ask"

As both ladies walked along the corridor to where Barchas' room was located, Marlene was feeling quite relieved and more alive from the venting she had long been waiting for. It was like closure to her to finally having Lexa back in her life.

But to Lexa, each step closer to Barchas room was like another kick I the gut. An immediate rush of her last time with him filled her mind and it left no room for mercy towards what she was about to see.

As soon as both ladies entered Barchas' room, Marlene tossed her handbag on the chair and then washed her hands while Lexa stood aside and looked.

"You can take your coat off and hang it right on that hook over there, if you'd like, Lexa" Marlene said, while she continued washing her hands.

"I think I'll be fine, it feels kind of chilly in here" Lexa replied sounding agitated and with a cold tone in her voice; and Marlene quickly pick up on the change."

"Kind of shocking, eh? I know exactly what you're thinking….I felt the same way when first I saw him at the hospital. Oh, my God, Lexa, it was pretty scary." Marlene said.

Lexa's eyes gave a blank stare on Barchas while listening to Marlene's remarks. Then she said:

"You can say that again, Marlene. Hearing it and seeing it, are two different things, I could never have envisioned seeing him looking like this.

There was no way to be certain, but it appeared as if Barchas had immediately recognized Lexa's voice because his eyes popped wide open as soon as she begun speaking.

"Hi honey, guess who's here? Marlene said with a cheerful voice as she walked over to greet her husband and caress his face as she normally did.

"Oh, wow, look at his eyes; they're so wide and bright today; I think he knows that you're here, Lexa, I think he's happy that you're here."

After Marlene said that, she hoped that Lexa would have looked at her husband in a more promising light. She needed to feel that sense of support coming from her friend.

But Lexa only turned her head and stared back at Barchas with a rather straight face. And while she looked on, she was convinced that Barchas was aware of her presence and wanted her to get away from him. That look, that dreadful, freakish look, was exactly how she remembered him the night of their quarrel when he demanded an abortion for their child.

"What makes you think that, Marlene? I thought you said he's not cognizant of his surroundings." Lexa replied with a shrug and a sharp tone to her utterance.   From that, Marlene reckoned that Lexa could have been in sheer shock of seeing what was left of her husband and so she drew no hard feelings from her response.

"Oh, don't be shy…why don't you come closer and try talking to him, Lexa. I'd like to see how he'd react"

Lexa was not about to take up Marlene on her offer. Her deep seated anger towards Barchas weighed heavy on her mind and having to stand there and watch Marlene hovering over her husband was quite a kick to her gut.

"Oh, Marlene, please forgive me, but this is so overwhelming for me. I don't think I can stay much longer in this room; I never thought it would be so painful to see Barchas in this condition. I'm so sorry; but I must go."

Marlene never expected that reaction from Lexa and she couldn't quite tap into the gist of what she was trying to say. However while she was left to ponder if there was something more to Lexa's behavior, she halfheartedly acquiesced.

"Don't feel bad, Lexa; and there's no need to apologize; I completely understand"

"I know you would, Marlene. You're such a good friend. Call me later if you'd like so we could talk some more."

Lexa turned away and left without another word being said, while Marlene stayed back into stillness of the room and watched her husband closed his eyes.

CHAPTER FOURTEEN

Since then, every day by noontime, Marlene would turn up at St. Clements to spend time with her husband. From time to time, the children would accompany her on the weekends, whereas Frank would go by a few times a week.

While most of the folks in Watertown looked forward to ringing in the New Year with much ado, it came and passed uneventful for Marlene. She spent the night with her children watching TV and enjoying the crackling sounds of fireworks from the neighboring estates in and around town.

Frank, on the other hand, had a heck of a time at the annual Old Court House Dance.

Many, many years ago, the annual old court house dance was "the event" of the season that most people in the community looked forward to attending. However, over time, the tradition started losing its luster to many after it was being supported mostly by geriatrics.

As a long standing pillar of the community, Barchas thought it was his duty to step up and revive the tradition with a new twist. His idea was well received by his colleagues and other government officials in the community, hence the great comeback of the annual event.

Therefore, in keeping Barchas' dream alive, Frank was behooved to continue the tradition in honor of Barchas' accomplishments.

While most of Frank's colleagues and coworkers attended the elegant affair with their spouses and significant others, he turned up alone. However, the night was well spent by him mingling and catching up with old friends that he had not seen for a while.

A slight tap on Frank's shoulder from behind had him turning his head anxiously to see who was trying to get his attention.

"Well, happy New Year, Mr. Roulette…Would you care to join me; I noticed you've been walking around alone. Or, are you waiting for that special someone to arrive?"

When Frank realized that it was Blossom Rigby who was trying to get his attention, his first thought was *"What the hell…say it ain't so because I certainly did not sign up for this kind of drama"*

Frank flashed a big plastic smile at her and said "Oh, wow; is that you, Blossom, looking all spiffy in that gorgeous red gown?

"Sure is, Mr. Roulette; and a happy, happy New Year to you again sir" Blossom said, and immediately Frank could tell that she was a bit tipsy.
"I'm surprised you're here by yourself." Frank said to Blossom while taking a quick sip of his liquor.

"What are you talking about, Frank. I'm always by myself." Blossom replied while looking down at Frank's shoes. And while she kept staring at his shoes, in the same breath she remarked…

"You're looking very handsome tonight; and what are those you're wearing Mr. Roulette— Bruno Magli? Or, should I have known better to assume that I'm right" Blossom asked Frank.

Frank was suddenly jolted by her query, but he kept his cool by smiling and saying "Good eye, for a woman that's always by herself. But, I know that's not quite true my lady. I've seen you quite a few times out there living it up, with some of Watertown's finest."

"Oh, Frank you should know better than that. You, know it's all in the name of business. And, by the way, I'm still waiting to get on your "to do" list, you know. I haven't quite given up on you"

"Knowing Blossom, Frank was not all that surprised at her response, but he was somewhat floored by her boldness."

Then he mumbled to himself *"No, thank you lady, I won't be screwing you, if I had anything to do with it."*

On that note, Frank gave a short chuckle. Then he politely excused himself so he could continue working the crowd just as Barchas would have, had he been there.

Not long after, the formalities, and the meeting and greeting segment of the occasion was winding down and then the lights dimmed. Frank sat back and watched most of the guests scrambling to get in line on the dance floor as soon as the "Electric Slide" music sounded off. And whilst they dipped to the rhythm in unison, he spotted Jackie Monsoon, getting down in full excitement with the blasting sounds.

Seeing Jackie turned up at the Old Court House Dance was quite a shocker for Frank. And so he wondered what she was up to by making her presence known. The fact that an entire week had passed since she wrongfully accused him and stormed out of his home had him believing that she attended the occasion by design.

Frank watched steadfastly as Jackie dipped and swung her hips whilst others continued flocking to the dance floor.   His main objective for keeping his eyes on her however was to see where she would end up sitting once the music was over.   So as the crowd thinned, his eyes followed her to where her supposedly date sat waiting for her.

Frank took a large gulp of his liquor whilst thinking to himself:

"Who the hell is that; do I know this guy? And what the hell does she think she's doing turning up here with some other man?   Oh, I see what's going on here, she's trying to make me jealous, but it's not working"

"Surely Frank tried convincing himself that he was tough enough to resist any blow Jackie was trying to send to his ego. But before long as he kept eyeing her and her date, he could feel the jealousy tapping on his heart.

Although Jackie was never able to get Frank to fall in love with her, she always knew there was something special between them.   However, over the last year or so, she was starting to grow tired of the wishing and the hoping for taking their relationship to the next level.

Frank watched Jackie picked up her purse and began walking as if she was working her way through the crowd towards the other end of the auditorium.   He assumed she was going to the restroom, so he quickly got up and followed behind her.   He was right about her going to the restroom and so he hung around closely to the area.

In less than ten minutes she was out of the bathroom and he spotted her walking towards him.   He made sure his presence was shown by stepping out right in front of her.

She appeared startled seeing him standing there. And a sudden thought that she was being stalked flashed across her mind.

"Oh gee, Frank what you are doing here," Jackie said to him, showing genuine surprise.

"Whatever happened to Happy New Year, Frank; I miss you" Frank said to Jackie quite jokingly, and trying to break the ice. But Jackie was not about to be entertained by him.

"OK, Happy New Year, Frank" Jackie responded with a straight face.
"You're looking beautiful as usual," Frank said, while smiling and trying to make her feel more comfortable. However, Jackie did not find his gesturing appealing, and so she ignored his compliment with silence.
Frank then said:

"Well, I think I should be the one asking you what you're doing here, but I think I already know the answer. You're still upset with me; Aren't you? And this is your way of getting back at me."

"I don't know what you're talking about Frank; you should go back to whomever you're with and stop bothering me." Jackie retorted.

Frank experienced a sudden jab to his ego but he tried taking it with a smile.

"Ha-ha. A, bother, a bother, uh. Is that really how you think of me? Or…could it be that new boyfriend of yours that's making you think like this."

"Look; you can say anything you'd like, Frank; I don't care. And your palavering is not appreciated. I've grown so damn tired of being used by you and it's time for me to cut the cord. Now, if you'll please excuse me…I've got a party to catch."

Frank was left speechless as Jackie stepped aside and walked off to sit with her date. He had never seen that side of Jackie, before. It was like seeing fire from her eyes even in the dimly lit space where they had stood to have words. And the impassioned energy she exuded as she spoke told Frank that she mostly likely had turned the corner as far as their half -assed relationship was concerned.

Frank turned and left to walk back to his table when suddenly Blossom Rigby appeared.

"Is there trouble in paradise, Mr. Roulette?" Blossom asked teasingly, and with a smirk across her face. That was quite an annoyance to Frank and without waiting, he snapped at her by saying, "Not now Blossom… I'm busy."

"I can see that" Blossom said.   "But you shouldn't let her ruin the whole night for you. So, why don't we dance and try having a little fun" she continued while raising her glass to him.

By then Frank was highly pissed at Blossom and he wished if she would stop harassing him. So after her suggestion about having a little fun, he responded:

"May be it's that stuff in your glass that's making you so flighty tonight, Blossom. But you're just too much for me, madam.   I know you mean well, but I'm just not in the mood"

Frank then sidestepped Blossom and continued walking pass his table to the outdoors so he could get a cigar from his car.

By the time Frank was through, lighting up and chilling with his cigar, he had, had enough time to think through his run- in with Jackie. That immediate shock of seeing her was starting to become a blur. And if only he did not have to watch her dancing in the arms of another man, he reckoned he could move on more quickly and fully absolved of any guilt.

So while his head was still full of his decision to finally let Jackie, go, Frank lit up another cigar, and then turned on the engine of his car.

From then on, Frank slowly drove back home.

CHAPTER FIFTEEN

It was January second, and for most people, a new year's resolution would be first and foremost in their minds; and it was no different for Marlene. She woke up that morning and started scoping the yellow pages of the phonebook. She was looking for a contractor to start renovating her art studio. Her vow to complete her life with the passion she so desired to bring out and to share, was long overdue.

While Marlene sat at her desk and compiled a list of companies to call for quotations, Allora walked in with a tray, holding her coffee, juice, English muffin and the morning newspaper. And without acknowledging Allora, she kept her focus uninterrupted.

Marlene was happy finding a contractor that was very familiar with properties in the locale of her soon to be art studio. After scheduling an appointment to meet him there later in that week, the contractor commented that it was about time someone did something to that place.

Marlene then picked up the newspaper while sipping on her coffee. And the headlines caught her full attention. "Watertown Elites Attend Benefit Ball"

Frank could be seen standing at the podium which caused her to assume he was giving a speech. Normally that would have been Barchas, standing there with having a lot to say. But with him out of the picture she could only assume that Frank was doing his best to fill her husband's shoes.

Marlene continued reading the newspaper while trying to wipe away the streaming tears as she reflected in pity about her husband's plight. *"He was such a good leader and he did so much for his community"* Marlene said under bated breath while looking back with pride at the name her husband had made for himself.

Marlene put the newspaper down and she wondered if Frank or anyone had made honorary mention of her husband. So she called Frank. Frank answered the phone sounding half asleep to Marlene.

"Still sleeping?" Marlene asked Frank as soon as he said hello.

"Who's calling?" Frank said, without really knowing who it was.

"Don't tell me you've forgotten what I sound like"

"Oh, Marlene, I'm sorry, I didn't quite catch your voice. What time is it?"

"It's ten-o-clock. I thought you'd be up by now."

"I should be, but I think I drank too much last night."

"Well, I'm sorry to disturb you. If you'd like I can call back later, Frank."

"No worries, tell me what's on your mind" Frank said to Marlene while gathering momentum to pull himself together.

"It's about the dance at the Old Court House last night; I see where you took center stage in this morning's paper. Did you see it?

"Uh-huh, but I will as soon as I get my paper from outside."

"Oh, I forgot that you're still in bed. Anyway the write-up was pretty good; congratulations you guys. Barchas would have been proud reading about this if only there was a way. So, did anyone make mention of him, knowing that that he was the brainchild of this effort?"

"Oh, Marlene, you shouldn't have to even wonder about that. Have you forgotten how much Barchas means to me?"

"I guess you're right; I should never have doubted you; I should have known better. Thank you so much Frank, I'd hate to think that because he's out of sight people might think that he should be out of mind."

Frank easily picked up on Marlene's fear of losing her husband and he completely understood where she was coming from. Neither of them had been saying much about it, but Barchas' progress had been slow and disheartening at times, but they have never expressed their fears.

"I tell you what" Frank said to Marlene as if he had something up his sleeves.

"What" Marlene responded with a lift to her voice and without reservation of whatever Frank would have to say.

"I know it's a spur of the moment thing, but …I like to take you out to dinner later on."

Marlene was elated; it was a great pick me up from the doldrums she was slipping into. However she tried to keep Frank in the *dark* because of her pride.

"You don't have to do that, Frank. You have done enough already."

"Think nothing of it Marlene. You've been put through the ringer far too long. And had it not been for Mrs. Tate, the holidays would have been a total disappointment for you, and you deserve a break. Won't you say yes for this one time?"

Deep sighs followed from Marlene while Frank listened for an answer. "OK, you've convinced me, Frank; I'll be happy to go to dinner with you tonight. So where will you be taking me?" Marlene asked Frank.

"Anywhere you desire, but I'd really like to get out of town and take you to Chateau de Mehr. I heard the food is good and the atmosphere is fabulous this time of year."

"Oh wow! That is... a very nice place. I don't know if Barchas had told you, but we attended an event there many, many years ago. It was something special that my dad had planned there for Chrissy, my long lost sister."

When Frank heard Marlene mentioned her sister's name, he was surprised that her name rolled off her tongue as if she was no longer up in arms about her. But he dared not take the chance by keeping her name alive in their conversation.

As a matter of fact, I do remember Barchas telling me about your dad reserving the place to do something to that effect. But it's been so long that I don't recall all the details.

"Well, I remember it all too well, but it's neither here nor there at this point. So, about what time would you be coming to get me?" Marlene asked Frank with high anxiety.

"How does five —o- clock sound? After all... it's at least a two hour ride"

"Five- o- clock sounds great to me" Marlene said.

"Very well, then I'll call and make reservation for seven" Frank said.

Frank and Marlene ended the call with high expectation for a lovely evening out of town. She immediately woofed down a small piece of the English muffin, and finished the juice in a few gulps.

Then she quickly got dressed and was off to the mall to get something new to wear. Marlene had had never felt so alive in a very long time. And since the quarrel with her husband, that was her first time going to a mall to treat herself.

While Marlene drove along the highway, she called Lexa from her car phone. She would have loved to have her help pick out an outfit and maybe a few more for good measure. But after Lexa answered the phone and found out it was Marlene calling, she immediately complained about having a headache.

Marlene felt disappointed and she tried coaxing Lexa to get her to go with her to the mall despite her complaints, but to no avail. However Lexa tried getting rid of her by saying she would call later as soon as she felt better.

Marlene was not convinced about Lexa's complaints and she tried figuring out what could be putting her in such a foul mood. She found it hard to believe that someone who had experienced a bout with pneumonia could end up being depressed. Every time they talked, Lexa would leave Marlene feeling as if she was being avoided.

In fact, Lexa was suffering from depression, but she wasn't really aware of it. So her indifference towards Marlene wasn't completely out of spite.

Anyway, Marlene was not about to let anything or anyone knock her down in terms of her happy, happy, joy, joy intervention. So she drove directly to her favorite shopping complex and started scouting for something pretty.

So far, she had already blown a couple of hours from stressing to find that special piece of garment without any luck. Things were starting to look futile for Marlene when she decided to hop onto the escalator all the way to the third floor, to check out "First Lady."

"First Lady" was a fine couture Shoppe that was relatively new to the mall. Marlene had only found out about it after she and Lexa had checked it out right after their grand opening, more than a year prior. As soon as she walked in, she had a gut feeling that something special was hanging back there with her name on it…in a manner of speaking.

The mild mannered woman in her sixties that was assigned to help Marlene with finding her outfit, turned out to be genius by Marlene's standards. And by the time she was finished with outfitting her with their latest trends, she ended up spending thousands more than she'd expected.

Marlene, feeling quite satisfied with how her day was going, left the mall and drove directly to St. Clements to spend time with her husband.

"Hi, how are you" Marlene said to the attendant that was sitting inside Barchas' room. "Good day, Mrs. Sander, your husband will be in soon" the attendant replied while finishing up with changing the bed linens. Marlene then went to where she would normally sit, and she reclined her chair and waited comfortably until her husband was brought in.

So after trying to make small talks with her husband and telling him happy New Year, Marlene waited long enough for Barchas to fall asleep.

Mixed feelings developed after she left the room with the intention of joining Frank for dinner later that evening. However, it was not enough to overshadow her plans for doing something fun for a change.

<> <>

Monk was happy to see his mother come home with bags and boxes from the mall. And he was just as happy to help take them upstairs to her bedroom. So on his way upstairs Bethany showed up looking curious.

"What are those, Monk?" Bethany asked her brother.

"They are Mom's; she just came home"

"Mom, went to the mall? I thought she went to spend time with dad"

"Why don't you ask her yourself, Beth? She's in her room." Monk replied to his sister while sounding annoyed.

Bethany then stormed into her mother's bedroom where she saw her unpacking her new finds.

"Mom, you went to the mall without me! You know I need some things, and furthermore, I thought you went to be with dad."

Marlene appeared unmoved by her daughter's outburst, but she responded anyway.

"Yes, I went to the mall. And yes, I was with your dad. Aren't you happy to see your mother treating herself for a change?" Marlene said to her daughter while holding up her favorite piece of garment.

"You like this...I just love the colors" Marlene said to her while eyeing the two-piece multi-colored suede outfit.

"So, mom did you get me anything?" Bethany asked her mother without saying whether or not she liked the outfit.

"No, Bethany I only went to get a few things for myself."

"What is it honey, you don't sound as if you're happy to see your mom doing something fun."

"That's not true, mom. I just wish if you and I would start spending more time together"

Marlene then looked at her daughter through different eyes. Oh baby, you're starting to worry me. What makes you think we aren't spending enough time together?"

"I don't know why I said that, Mom. It's just that I feel so scared sometimes.

"Come on baby, tell you mother what's really on your mind, Marlene said to Bethany while pushing the clothes aside and making room on the bed for them to sit. Then Bethany's eyes welled up as she spoke.

I was thinking that I'll be going away this year to start College and Monk said he thinking of going back Hampton to complete his law degree.

Monk told you that?

I'm sorry mom, he asked me not to tell you. But I couldn't help it.

Oh sweetheart, not to worry, your mother is going to be just fine. Hopefully your dad will be coming home soon. And there's going to be plenty to keep us busy. Anyway, I promise to start spending more quality time with you.

"Bethany hugged her mother while eyeing some of the new clothes lying on the bed. And she wondered where she had bought them."

I kind of like the orange one, mom. Where did you get it?

Well I got them at "First Lady" They have some great looking things.

"No mother, not them; that's an old people store. That store is for ladies like Aunt Carolyn.

Marlene laughed out loud by her daughter's remarks; and she was by no means daunted by them. As a matter of fact she totally enjoyed their little mother and daughter talk.

At that point, Marlene felt it was the right time to let her children know that she would not be having dinner with them later that evening.

After Marlene informed Bethany that she would be going out with Frank for dinner, mixed feelings came about her and she wasn't sure what to make of it.

"Oh, ok. So did you tell Monk, already?" Bethany said to her mother while feeling a bit awkward about the news.

"No. Not yet, but I will when I get back downstairs." Marlene said while walking towards her closet to hang her new outfits. And when she responded to her daughter, she came off sounding nonchalant and carefree of what her daughter might think.

"Are you going out on a date with Uncle Frank, Mom?"

"I wouldn't call it a date, honey; we are just going to have dinner."

Bethany then turned away and started yelling her brother's name. Monk! Monk! Come up stairs!

Monk came running upstairs and asked Bethany why she was calling and making it sound like it was an emergency.

"Mom's going out on date with Uncle Frank, tonight; I think they're planning something special. That's why she went out and bought all those new clothes!"

Monk watched Bethany eyes flared with fury as she expressed concerns about her mother's outing with Frank. However, Monk was not fazed by his sister's excitement. Matter-of-factly, he thought it was cool that his mother was getting out for a change.

"Beth, you're making it sound like Mom's doing something bad; she's only going out to have dinner with Uncle Frank."

Monk then threw his hands in the air, eyes widened and necked longed, as he continued with his response to his sister.

"Bethany, I don't see anything wrong with that. So why are you getting so huffy about it?

"Forget it Monk; just forget it." Bethany fired back at her brother. "You wouldn't understand anyway. You're such a dork."

While the children argued about their mother's plan for the evening, Marlene stood quietly in her bedroom listening. She wasn't surprised by the way the conversation ended. She knew her daughter well enough as a worry wart with a high strung personality. And Monk was always the easygoing, bookworm, but by no means a dork.

"What are you two arguing about" Marlene came out of her bedroom saying to her children while Monk was about to walk away, but then he stayed back to hear his mother out.

"I told Monk about you and Uncle Frank" Bethany said to her mother.

"Uh-huh. So what seems to be the problem Beth; and why do you look so sad? We are only going out to have dinner"

"See, Bethany, I told you." Monk chimed in. "It's not what you're thinking. It's not like a real date; they're just going out."

Bethany remained quiet while staring at Monk and their mother with a feeling of being confused. Marlene smiled and hugged her kids and thanked them for being the best part of her life. Bethany then rolled up a fist threw a friendly thump to her brother's chest which was a good sign to Marlene that her daughter was trying to be more understanding.

<> <>

Allora opened the front door and welcomed Frank inside. His voice carried all the way upstairs to where Bethany and Marlene could hear him saying hi to Allora. Bethany immediately raced downstairs. And as soon as Frank saw her coming he opened up his arms and said "happy new year, sweetheart, did you make a new year's resolution? "No" Bethany said dryly which came off sounding with a tone of sulk to Frank.

"So tell Uncle Frank what's making you so sad;" Frank said to Bethany without any feeling of daunt by her unusual greeting.

Frank's warm and tender response instantly returned Bethany to being her old self.

"I'm not sad, I'm just tired, and I only came down stairs to say hello" Bethany said while allowing Frank to wrap his open arms around her.

By then Marlene was on her way down stairs.

"Oh wow! Take a look at your mother, Beth; see how beautiful she looks" Frank said in amazement of Marlene's transformation. Bethany then released herself from Frank's embrace to look at her mom.

"Uncle Frank is right mom, you do look nice"

Marlene could tell that Bethany was definitely on the mend even if only temporarily, and she reckoned it was time to start keeping a closer eye on her.

Marlene was looking forward to the short getaway and she gave a sigh of relief as she buckled her seat belt while Frank slowly pulled off her property to Chateau de Mehr. She remained quiet while enjoying the music on the cassette tape Frank had selected for the trip.

"Great songs, Frank, I haven't heard music like that in a long time." She almost wanted to say that Barchas used to play those songs, back in the days. Frank turned up the volume a little more and then he started tapping the steering wheel with his fingers as he always does whenever his favorite hits came on.

So while Marlene and Frank were on their way, Bethany and Monk were back at home having supper. The telephone rang and Allora answered. Bethany heard Allora said "She's not home right now, would you like to leave a message?" Bethany's interest immediately piqued as to whom could be calling, so she immediately upped from the dining table and asked Allora who was calling. Allora covered the mouthpiece with her hand and whispered Miss Lexa. Bethany took the phone from Allora so she could speak with Lexa instead.

"Hi, Aunt Lexa; Mom's not here."

"Well Happy New Year to you Beth, how are you? Lexa replied while sounding like her old self.

Thank you, Aunt Lexa. Would you like to leave a message for mom? "Oh no sweetie, I'll give her a call back later. Is she still at the rehab with your dad? Lexa asked Bethany.

"No, she's with Uncle Frank; they went out to dinner."

"Oh, that's nice. So where did they go, Vines?"

"I don't know, she didn't say."

Ha-ha, don't worry about it honey, that's quite all right. Now I know why she wanted me to go with her to the mall with her...I guess she wanted something pretty for the evening.

"I guess so" Bethany said.

Ok, sweetie, you don't have to bother telling mom about me calling. I'll just wait until tomorrow to check up on her.

As soon as Lexa was off the phone with Bethany, her mind went racing and thinking what this could mean. She wondered if her secret was still safe with Frank, she wondered if Marlene was going to tell Frank what she had told her about getting pneumonia, she wondered if Frank had wormed his way into Marlene's bed, since Barchas was out of the picture and she wondered if Marlene had started keeping secrets from her.

Lexa became panicky from the thoughts she had conjured up in her mind. And if they were so, her suspicious mind would like to know. She hastily walked to her closet and threw on some clothes. She then slipped into her high boots, grabbed her purse and jacket and drove herself to Vines.

So, in, she strode, and positioned herself akimbo against the French column. She looked around with quick eye movements and she wondered if she could get away with working her way inside the Vines dining room without being seated. However, that idea flopped, the instant she stepped away from the column and tried getting past the reservationist.

"Oh…I'm sorry, I don't know what came over me. I guess it's because I'm trying to make it quick to the ladies room, but anyway I'm to join Mr. Roulette' Lexa told the reservationist with a believable sense of urgency.

"OK, Madam, you can meet me back at the front desk and I'll take you to his table." The reservationist said to Lexa.

Lexa looked around the area as she pretended to walk to the ladies room. But after not seeing Marlene or Frank, she anxiously approached the reservationist.

"Madam, I don't believe we have a reservation for Mr. Roulette. Could it be under another name?"

"Of course; check to see if it's under Mrs. Sander" Lexa replied while showing confidence

The reservationist eyes raced up and down the page, and told Lexa there was none. However the reservationist suggested that they could be on their way without making reservation and invited Lexa to wait, if she cared to.

Lexa thought that was a great idea and she left to sit at the bar from where she could see most of the patrons coming in. And the fact that she was there first, would make it less awkward for her to approach them.

After three glasses of wine and no Marlene and Frank, Lexa started to feel frustrated with herself. She was certain she would have found them there. And without being able to poke her nose into their business, Lexa became even more intrigued about her assumptions.

Then as if a light bulb went off in her head, she smiled and said to herself "What *the hell was I thinking, I should have known better than that. I should have known Frank would like to keep his relationship with Marlene more private. This is not the place for them to be out on a date.*"

Lexa threw down a handful of money on counter and quickly left Vines. She then drove across town to the Rivers End Restaurant. And without wasting too much time, she told the reservationist she was there to meet Mr. Roulette and Mrs. Sander. Again, she got the same response as she did at Vines…no one there by that name. By then she turned down the offer to wait, should in case they were running late for dinner.

Lexa's frustration deepened from thinking she could have sent herself off on a wild goose chase. She sat inside her car and wondered where else they could have probably gone. But after thinking about the other contenders in the area, she thought it was best to give up on her search and go back home.

So, while Lexa was home and still fuming from her worthless inquiries, Frank and Marlene were just about making it through the entrance of Chateau de Mehr. The lengthy driveway ahead of them was breathtakingly beautiful as they looked ahead at the Chateau.

"Look, Frank, look, how beautiful is that snowy hillside. And, look over there…did you see size of that thing?" Marlene said to Frank.

"Oh, yeah…this place is quite a marvel; I can't wait to see what it's like inside." Frank said.

Finally, they pulled up to the main entrance where the valets were standing in queue.

"Welcome to Chateau de Mehr, Sir" the valet said to Frank as he handed over his car keys.

"Welcome to Chateau de Mehr, Madam" another valet said to Marlene as he opened her side of the car door.

As they walked through the main entrance of the Chateau, Marlene's head raised in awe of what was first to strike her… four marble statues. They were huge and towering above their heads as she moved closer to the niche where they were standing.

Then out came the Greeter to take their coats and to chaperone them to their table.

"So, this is the famous Chateau de Mehr I've been hearing so much about," Frank said as he seated himself across the table to face Marlene. And she responded with a… "huh-uh," while her eyes rolled in admiration of the elegant and well-appointed furniture and fixtures throughout the restaurant. However, Marlene eyes kept going back to her very first fancy. She just wasn't done eyeing the artful display that stole her attention as if a spell was casted upon her. She felt as if that work of art had a special story behind it… one she never thought would have any meaning to her specifically, but then again she reckoned it could have something to do with her calling as an artist.   And so she kept gazing at the display.

Then finally she came back around, after Frank tried breaking the lull between them by letting her know he'd ordered wine for her.

"You know I don't drink; so what was that all about" Marlene asked Frank while smiling at him.

"Well, I had to get your attention somehow; I noticed you've been so enthralled with all this awesomeness that I'm left trying to fend for myself" Frank replied teasingly while smiling at Marlene.

"Ok, I tell you what I'm going to do, Mr. Frank Roulette" Marlene said with a childish giggle; one Frank had never heard coming from her before.

"…And what might that, be, madam?" Frank asked Marlene with a touch of endearment while he was enjoying her company from a different perspective.

"I think I'm going to add a little *something* to my new year's resolution" Marlene said.

"Oh yeah, tell me more, tell me more…my lady" Frank said while still smiling and feeling a bit anxious about what she'd have to say.

"Well, I shall be drinking wine this year and my first glass begins with you" Marlene said while maintaining the same level of perkiness. Frank was not expecting to hear Marlene say that, and he was quite surprised by her reveal. However, he held her decision to start drinking as a sign of high regards towards him which made her even more appealing while he kept his eyes on her.

Although the restaurant was operating at almost half its capacity, it was almost as if Marlene and Frank were alone inside. Neither of them paid any attention the other patrons around. And while the pianist was on the stage playing his heart out, Marlene and Frank had not yet recognized his presence.

"Oh, my god…this is some good steak" Frank said after taking his first bite of his meal.

"No, Frank. I don't think it's as good as my lobster flambé" Marlene chimed in as soon as she was able to swallow her first bite.

"Taste this" Frank said to Marlene, while leaning towards her." He wanted her to try a piece of his steak from his fork. Marlene irresistibly opened her mouth and allowed Frank to feed her. Hmm, "so good" she said, while tilting her head and closing her eyes as the juicy and smoky bit of meat tantalized her taste buds. Marlene then returned the same treatment to Frank with a clump of her lobster flambé and his reaction was nonetheless delightful.

"Wait a minute, I like that song." Marlene said while she tried finishing up her meal.

"What song," Frank asked Marlene while cleaning up his plate.

"I'm talking about the song that's being played by the pianist" Marlene replied.

"Oh geez, I didn't even realize that someone was playing. This place is like a dream and it's hard to keep track of everything around here;

but, yeah, now that I'm paying attention, that song is one of my all time favorites."

Frank then removed the napkin from his lap and dabbed around his mouth while asking Marlene to do the choosing from the dessert menu. And dinner was complete with cappuccino and dark chocolate crepes.

From then on, Frank and Marlene were fully engaged with the all happenings around them.

Frank was pleased about seeing Marlene looking so carefree and relaxed. He thought she deserved so much more than the life that she'd adjusted to and he hoped she would allow him to get away with her again.

"Would you like to dance, my lady. Frank asked Marlene."

"Me? Dance? Oh, no Frank. I haven't danced in so long; I don't believe I'd know what to do if I went out there on the floor."

"Oh, but it's not like that, Marlene. Dancing is not about the way you move on the floor, it's about the way the music moves you. Take a look at all those people out there on the floor. They are all enjoying themselves, wouldn't you agree."

"Huh-huh," Marlene replied.

"Well, if you keep looking you will see that they're all moving in a different direction. But everyone is dancing nonetheless."

Marlene smiled bashfully because she wasn't convinced she should try, and Frank never felt he should have to push her into doing something she wasn't ready for.

Frank then tried changing the subject and asked Marlene "what was her other New Year's resolution, aside from starting to drink wine."

"Well, I don't know if Barchas had told you about the piece of property that I purchased on Gladstone Drive."

"As a matter of fact he did. So, are you planning on moving forward with the studio?" Frank asked her eagerly.

"Yes, and that's my main goal for this year. I've already spoken with a contractor about plans for renovating"

"Glad to hear it, Marlene; it's about time. I can't wait to see all those creative juices you've got bottled up inside, coming to light. If there's anything I can do to help, please Marlene, don't be shy about letting me know." Frank said.

Marlene had only taken two small sips of her wine; she thought to herself that wasn't bad for starters. So after Frank built up her courage so highly, she raised her glass and said "I'll drink to that one, Frank, thank you so much."

Frank looked at his empty glass and said, I'll just raise my glass and pretend there's still some"

"You don't have to do that, here I'll share mine with you, so you can give me a proper thumbs up."

They both smiled and said cheers. Then out of the blue, Marlene turned to Frank and said "I think we should dance to this one. This is something big and it really means a lot to me."

Frank quickly got off his chair and took Marlene's hand and walked her to the dance floor nearby.

By then the pianist had stopped playing and their resident DJ had taken over later into the night.

Percy Sledge's Warm and Tender Love, song sounded off. That song was no stranger to them; they had listened to it being played on Frank's car stereo on their way to the Chateau.

More people started crowding the floor as the DJ continued putting out. The slow riveting love songs came through to Marlene and Frank in such a way that they were almost embarrassed to face each other.

Marlene stood on the floor, stiff as a brick while asking herself "what am I doing here. Have I lost my mind being in the arms of another man?"   And while she was thinking that, she had even more trouble facing Frank, so she kept looking away with racing thoughts about the situation.

Frank remained quiet and deep in thoughts. He too was struggling with his strengthening feelings towards Marlene.

Frank's hand shook uncontrollably with guilt. All of a sudden he started getting flashbacks of his years spent with Barchas and his family. They were a couple he admired greatly, and he never thought he could be looking at his best friend's wife in such a way.   He slowly raised his hand and gently touched her face with a stroke of one finger. She raised her head and looked into his eyes, and very slowly he took her arms and placed them around his waist. Then, he wrapped his arms around her, pulling her closely to him. Marlene closed her eyes and she did exactly what the following song commanded her to do... "Put Your Head on My Shoulders" And while she was doing that, another thought crept up on her saying *"Oh my god, but it feels so good that I can actually feel my heart again."*

While Frank and Marlene stayed on the dance floor arms in arms at Chateau de Mehr, its owner Chrissy, who was Marlene's long lost sister, walked in.

She came through a private entrance in the rear of the chateau. And as she normally does, she went directly upstairs to the skybox and sat in her swivel chair from where she would take a bird's eye view of the area downstairs.

"Nothing unusual, just people dancing and having a good time," Chrissy said to herself while reflecting on the fabulous and talked about "New Year's Eve Ball" her staff had put off the night before.

The DJ had since changed the genre of the music being played to something a lot more upbeat. Chrissy heard clapping and laughing coming from downstairs which was not unusual, but she was always curious to see what was taking place nonetheless. And just as she thought, it was Sir Michael Bromfield and his wife Lady Bromfield who had stolen the show with their version of doing the calypso after the DJ had put "Sparrow" on blast.

So while Chrissy looked down and smiled at seeing the other patrons gathered around the couple and enjoying themselves, she turned to walk away. However, within the same instance she experienced a jolt to her senses; a jolt strong enough to have her thinking the unimaginable. She thought she had seen her sister; or more than likely it was someone with a striking resemblance of her.

Chrissy's, head turned uncontrollably to take a second look, and she was instantly floored and stricken from panic. She longed out her neck while her jaw dropped as she studied the woman's face to see if there could be a mistake. She raised her hand to cover her mouth that was left hanging with awe about the woman's striking resemblance of her sister.

But after seeing Marlene starting to laugh along with the crowd, Chrissy could no longer deny that she was most definitely looking at her sister.

Chrissy's knees buckled as she grabbed onto the chair to help stabilize her balance. The shock of seeing her sister inside her establishment and whom she thought would never find her, sent her scrambling for composure.

And so the once confident woman, Chrissy, who had disappeared and changed her name to Gabriella Fairchild, was starting to feel as if she was double crossed by none other than her stepmother, Carolyn Tate.

Since her disappearance for more than a decade, no one knew of her whereabouts. Well, to let the truth be told, Carolyn and Barchas were the only two people who knew of Chrissy's whereabouts.

Chrissy had gone missing without a trace for several years. And because of the breakdown between her and the family, no one bothered to try finding her. However after her father had passed away, it was Carolyn, her stepmother, who hired Barchas along with private investigators to help find her.

So while the search was still being performed, Carolyn soon found out that Chrissy had changed her name to Gabriella Fairchild. And to be certain of that, Carolyn paid her way onto the doorsteps of Chrissy's Chateau de Mehr. Not only that, Carolyn had paid off Barchas, quite handsomely to never reveal his dealings with her in finding Chrissy.

So, for that reason, Barchas was sworn to secrecy about finding the new Gabriella Fairchild. And, because of the hatred between the two sisters, it was even more reinforcement for Barchas to keep his wife in the dark.

So, in moving forward, all of her three children were raised to believe that their mother's real name was Gabriella Fairchild, and everyone in town addressed her as Ms. Fairchild.

So, while Ms. Fairchild sat speechless in the skybox shaking, she wondered how to approach what seemed to be the worst time of her life, since back in the days at Grey Banks. She immediately called her attorney Chandlon Bow to inform him of what was taking place.

Chandlon was just as surprised hearing that Marlene had turned up at Chateau de Mehr. But he wasn't convinced that Carolyn had anything to do with Marlene's presence at the Chateau. So he tried dissuading her from contacting Carolyn to accuse her of being betrayal without any proof.

"Chandlon then told her to take another look downstairs to see if Marlene was with her husband, which she did. And after looking downstairs again to be certain of who she was looking at, she said to Chandlon:

"No, I haven't seen her husband, but I do see her standing next to a man that appears to be her company. He kind of looks familiar a little bit….. But I don't think I know him."

"What do you mean by kind of looks familiar? Think carefully about this, because it could help us putting the pieces together more quickly. Chandlon said."

"Oh sure, I know that. But I think I made a mistake; I don't think I've seen that guy before."

Then Chandlon said "OK, it's after ten-o-clock… almost eleven. There's nothing I can do this time of night, but I will check into this for you and let you know what I come up with. Just keep an eye on them and let me know tomorrow"

Ms. Fairchild felt slightly better after Chandlon promised to follow up on her hunch. She then got off her chair to take another look and she was just in time to spot her sister and Frank leaving.

'I wonder who that could be, she pondered. And why is she with him and not her husband. If she had come in peace, then most likely would have come with her husband"

Then her thoughts wandered and took a turn assume the worse.

"Oh my God, don't tell me that my sister is out to destroy me, after all that she had put me through."

While Ms. Fairchild was left contemplating what she thought could be disastrous, she hoped and prayed that Chandlon would be able to take care of it.

<> <>

So, while Frank and Marlene waited outside for the valet to return their car, Marlene looked at her watch while smiling and said:

"I don't recall ever being out so late; I surely broke my curfew but it was worth it. I've never had so much fun in ages."

"Hmm, it was magical. So what time is it, anyway?" Frank asked Marlene and she said "its eleven o clock, but as they say, time flies when you're having fun"

Marlene noticed that Frank was a little on the quiet side and she wondered what he could be thinking.

So while he was driving away from Chateau de Mehr, she turned to him and said:

"You must be tired after such a busy week. You were out all night last night at the New Years Eve Dance which I know can be quite a task. And look what you did for me after all that; I just don't know how to thank you."

"Marlene, you don't have to thank me for anything, I'll do anything to see you being so happy. I just have to be careful about the way things are unfolding between us"

"What do you mean by that?" Marlene asked Frank

"What I mean is that I'd hate for you to think that I'm trying to take advantage of you"

"And in what way do you think that could be happening? I'm not going to pretend that I didn't feel something special coming from you tonight; and that feeling still lingers."

"That's exactly what I'm talking about Marlene; the feeling is mutual, and the man that I am would normally act on it. But, I can't'; knowing that you still belong to your husband who's my best friend."

"You don't have to remind me of that, Frank. Just saying that makes me feel guilty enough to be out with you this time of night. We don't have to necessarily act on our feelings at all times, but it doesn't change the fact that we both experienced some special tonight"

"You're a very special lady, Marlene and you deserve the best. You deserve to be happy, you deserve to be loved, and most importantly you deserve to find peace"

Marlene was deeply moved by Frank's comment and her eyes welled with tears of appreciation, but not enough for him to know.

"That was the most beautiful thing anyone had ever said to me Frank; you have no idea how meaningful this is to me. It feels as if you know me more than anyone else."

"Well, I may know a thing or two about you, but I wouldn't dare take it that far; I don't think anyone knows you better than Lexa." Frank said to Marlene, with a chuckle behind his response. But that chuckle was a nervous one because in his hearts of heart he dreaded the thought of her divulging details about their time spent at Chateau de Mehr.

So with Marlene totally in tuned with Frank, she surprised him by saying, "I see where you're going with this one, mister; but you don't have to worry; I don't plan on letting this cat out of the bag."

Frank then busted out laughing with relief and he said to Marlene, "well, I guess I do know you better than anyone else, my lady. I guess you could say I was a little jealous of your girlfriend.

Marlene laughed along with Frank until calm was restored along the way.

Frank and Marlene were on the road for a least an hour with less than another hour to get back home.   Marlene was starting to feel a little tired. She reclined her seat to a more comfortable position while Frank sped along the highway. And from there she closed her eyes whilst enjoying the temporary escape from her life as it was.

Frank, on the other hand found himself reflecting on how he had come to know so much about Marlene and how he'd started seeing her in a different light.

It was through Barchas and the many years spent with the family that made Frank aware of the very longtime Marlene had spent on the sofas of head doctors. From the death of her father, the death of her grandmother and the ongoing insecurities of an adulterous husband was what kept her there.

To know that her best friend Lexa had been deceiving her after all those years, and to unabashedly announced her love for her husband, to him,   raised Frank's ire into feeling that he ought be more protective of her emotions.   He reckoned if Marlene were to ever find out about the adulterous affair between her husband and Lexa, Frank was sure it would undoubtedly destroy her…even more so that what she had gone through with her husband. With that said, Frank was wise enough to never have a bad word to say about Lexa to Marlene.

So as he continued making it back home, every now and then Frank would take a glance at Marlene nodding until she was in complete slumber. And with every look he took she appeared more beautiful and more appealing to him. And so to help with fighting his feelings, Frank uncontrollably stretched his arm across and touched her hair. He then pulled back his hand and waited cautiously.   He tried keeping his eye on the road as the sped along, and from a side eye his heart raced with true passion. And so as to help allay his temptation, he slowly raised his arm again and ran it along her shoulder lightly and then up and down her thigh.

Frank experienced deep satisfaction with the chance he took in getting closer to Marlene.

Soon after, Frank was nudging Marlene to wake up as they were parked in her driveway. "Oh gee, Frank, we are home already" Marlene said while picking up her coat and purse. Frank said "huh-huh…you're home and looking beautiful as ever." He quickly exited the car and went around to help Marlene out and to walk her to her doorstep.

"Would you like to come inside for a nightcap, Frank; or maybe a cup of coffee?" Marlene asked him.

"It sounds tempting, but I think I should be going— and you my dear… need to get some rest."

They both stood looking at each other and Frank was dying to kiss her with every last ounce of passion inside him. But he could not; he just couldn't bypass that little voice in his head that kept telling him, "no."

Marlene saw the look in Frank's eyes when he turned down the offer to come inside and he knew she was sensing his yearning to be with her all night if things were different. However, whilst nothing of the sort seemed possible,   she remained standing in place and waited in case he wanted to change his mind. And like a young girl who had never been kissed before she looked at his lips -- so full and inviting while her lips trembled with anticipation of what they must be like— locked in a kiss.

Marlene immediately caught herself dreaming and in trying to redeem herself as the lady she's known to be, she said to Frank: "Yeah, I guess you're right, I do need to get some rest. It's just that I'm a loss for words about the wonderful time I spent with you, or as you put it…it was magical."

Frank was happy about what Marlene had to say because he was more at a loss for words than her, so he was most grateful when she finally got him off the hook.

CHAPTER SIXTEEN

arlene was slow getting out of bed the next morning. She had no idea she would be so late coming home. So going off the see her husband was much later than usual. However, as soon as she walked inside her husband room, the unexpected, happened. Lexa was waiting there.

Needless to say, Marlene was in utter shock finding her there especially after how she'd acted when she first saw Barchas. So without even saying hello, she asked Lexa what she was doing there.

"What kind of a question is that, Marlene? Am I no longer welcome to visit your husband?"

"Oh stop it now. You should know better than that. I just never expected to see you here, not after   the way you stormed out of here the other day." Marlene said to Lexa.

"Oh, I'd almost forgotten about that. I'm sorry about the way I acted; that was no way to treat a friend."

"No need for apologies Lexa; I know you meant no harm. So have you been waiting long" Marlene said."

"I wouldn't say long, but Since you were out late with Frank last night I imagined you'd be coming in late; if at all. So I thought I could help out by coming in and keeping Barchas' company.

"Well, that's awfully nice of you, Lexa, especially since you haven't been feeling too well lately. But I'd really like to know who told you that I went out for dinner."

"Whom, else my dear; I called you last night and ended up speaking with Bethany.   She told me you were out on a date with Uncle Frank. So, now I know why you went shopping; you wanted to look perfect for the occasion, right?"

Marlene knew Lexa well enough to tell the tone in which she spoke was uninviting, which automatically pushed her on the defensive after Lexa's reveal. She immediately looked at her husband, eyes wide open as if he was fully aware of what that was taking place around him. And going by the way he looked, Marlene assumed that he was quite perturbed and she was not about to be ok with that.

So in an effort to quash the confusion inside Barchas' room, Marlene said:

Lexa! We cannot have this conversation here; I don't think Barchas can handle it.   So why don't we go outside and talk some more; I hear the cafeteria is very nice.

What's wrong with here? I don't mind sitting and spending a little more time with and your husband. I thought he'd be happy knowing that we are here.

"No, not in the way the way we are going about it" Marlene said to Lexa while frustration was starting to develop.

Then Lexa said:

"What do you mean by that? Your husband knows that as friends we talk about everything. So what's causing you to be so uptight, all of a sudden?

Marlene then looked at her husband and she could tell that he was very upset. Although Dr. Jax had warned her that Barchas cognitive health would be compromised, Marlene assumed that he understood most of what was taking place around him.

Marlene then whispered to Lexa:

"I don't like the way Barchas looks, Lexa. I think he's hearing everything and I don't want to upset him.

"Oh, please forgive me, I didn't know that. So I'll just lower my voice." Lexa replied in a whisper.

"Thank you, but there's no need to whisper if we talk about things other than my dinner date with Frank." Marlene said.

"So where did you guys go, Vines? Lexa asked Marlene, loudly. And Marlene's eyes widened with surprise.

"Shhhhh... Lexa! What the hell has gotten in to you; have you lost your mind? I don't understand why you'd want to come here to talk about this around my sick husband. I thought you'd be more mindful of the situation and stop by the house later. Or better yet, I'd love to stop by your place and spend some quality time together."

Lexa was by no means interested in taking up Marlene on the offers of meeting at their homes. So she casually turned her eyes and looked at

Barchas from a distance while saying to Marlene "Why didn't I think of that…it's such a better idea."

Marlene felt relieved about Lexa's response but she wished if she would just leave. And Lexa could feel the tension building while Marlene kept her eyes on her, so the faked a smile and said "Ok, I guess I'll be on my way as I've got some errands to run."

While Lexa hugged Marlene before leaving, Lexa was thinking "mission accomplished." Her deep seated resentment towards Barchas since the night of the incident had left her carrying a grudge for Marlene. And she wanted him to know that his wife, whom he thought was so much better than her as his lover, was no goody two shoes, either.

And what Marlene didn't know also, was that while Lexa was there ahead of her, she stood by Barchas' beside and gave him hell. Everything that was bottled up inside of her came pouring out while Barchas lay helpless and praying that someone would come in and help save him from her wrath.

So Lexa walked away feeling great about her visit to Clements. Owning to the fact that she found an opportunity to get back at Barchas gave her a semi sense of relief. And she imagined it could only get better if she found a way to get back inside his room.

Marlene tried wrapping her head around what could have motivated Lexa to be such a bitch. It was obvious that she wanted to create strife between her and her husband. But for what reason Marlene pondered.

Then her mind raced back to the day she had found Frank's business card left sitting on Lexa's coffee table after she went looking for her. She wondered if she had a secret crush on Frank and became upset after finding out about their dinner date.

And if that was the case, Marlene contemplated why she would chose to act up in the presence of her husband. It was quite obvious Lexa's presence had made Barchas uncomfortable, because she had never seen him cried before.

Marlene was very relieved seeing Lexa go and she promised to get to the bottom of her surprise visit and her weird behavior. She then turned her attention to her husband by calling a nurse to come and check up on him.

Marlene was not surprised hearing the nurse saying that her husband's blood pressure was elevated. But as soon as they had it back to normal, the rest of her time spent with Barchas was as to be expected....peaceful and uneventful.

That peace and quiet time that Marlene was enjoying while visiting her husband provided her enough time to unwind and reminisce about her time spent with Frank.

Frank had just rolled out of bed and wondering how Marlene had spent her night. His night was less than restful because thoughts of himself and Marlene were crowding his mind. He imagined that she could be spending time with her husband which could be the reason she didn't call. Or could it be that she became uncomfortable with the situation they were caught up into while out on their date.

Frank waited anxiously for Marlene to call. Under normal circumstances he would be first to make the call after a night out with a woman, but in this case he found himself timid without a valid explanation.

However, Frank was starting to lose restraints and he built up the courage to make the call after not hearing from Marlene, late into the evening. He knew she had to be home and he wondered if she was ok.

Then the telephone rang and Frank picked it up with high expectation of spending hours on the phone talking with Marlene.

"Well it's about time; I was just about to call, but you beat me to it' Frank said when he answered the phone.

"Hi, this is Woody. I just got back into town and thought I'd call to say hello. Sounds like I caught you at a bad time.

An immediate shift in emotion took Frank by surprise. Hearing from Nurse Woody while craving the voice of Marlene, left him scrambling for composure to handle the nurse's call.

"Well, hello lovely lady, how are you?

"Doing well and glad to be back" Woody replied.

Then Frank said:

"You sound wonderful…sounds like your vacation was thoroughly enjoyed."

"Ha-hah" Woody giggled.   You guessed right, I really had a great time. And what about you…did you have great Christmas?

"As a matter of fact I did; I made the most of it."

'Well, as I said before, it sounds like I caught you at a bad time. So, let me not keep your line engaged for much longer." Woody replied.

Frank chuckled at Woody's response and said:

Oh, my goodness; that was very kind and thoughtful of you. But there's no need for you to be in such a hurry to get off the phone on my behalf. No wonder you're such an awesome nurse, you care so deeply about people.

Woody's heart warmed from Frank's response. She welcomed the idea of him willing to spend more time with her on the phone.

"Well thank you, Mr. Roulette. So any new year's resolution, or is it just me that didn't make one?

Hmmm. Well you know, I haven't been good at keeping those types of promises to myself, so I kind-of not do that sort of thing. Frank replied.

Woody's curiosity heightened and she dug a little to learn any little thing she could about the man she's hoping she could catch.

"I'm the same way too; I stopped doing that a long time ago. But mine were mostly weight related, or taking more vacations, and stuff like that. But I was never able to follow through with the plans. So what were your failed resolutions like?"

"Oh, about the same as yours, along with giving up smoking that I thoroughly enjoy. And, my love of good food isn't going anywhere right now. So what does that tell you?"

"I see. So, did you ever make resolutions about relationships?"

Oh no. That's a very sensitive matter and shouldn't be tossed in the bucket list of New Year's resolutions. People could end up getting hurt and I don't take that very lightly"

Frank paused and waited for a response from the nurse. But after not hearing her saying anything, he jumped back in and said. "And what, about you?"

"Me? Well, I use to do that back in the days, and I always ended up being hurt. So I had to quickly drop that idea like a hot potato. However, speaking of you… dare I say that you most likely have hurt quite a few along those lines, Mr. Roulette?"

"Oh yes I have, but not on the wings of a new year's resolution. It was mostly from not being able to compromise my freedom as a bachelor."

"Ah-hah, oh my Lord, I guess you don't mince your words. So in terms of a meaningful relationship, do you see yourself enjoying it while still being single, or married?"

"That's a tough one for me, Woody. I just don't know. One thing I can tell you though, is that a woman can make a man do things he never dreamed of; but he can't know until he knows."

Woody was starting to feel a slight distance emerging between her and Frank. She paused for a while in hopes that he would try finding out more about her, but she sensed the interest was not really there. However she perceived it was too soon to give up hope, so she decided to stick around for a while.

"Well, I must say this was quite an interesting conversation; I really enjoyed it. I'm certain there's a lot more I can learn from you. Anyway, on a different note, I do have two concert tickets that I received from work last month; they know how much I love going to the Ballet. It would be my greatest joy if you joined me for the occasion."

"Well, well, Nurse Woody, I too am learning quite a bit about you."

"So what's the verdict Mr. attorney, are you going to say yes?"

"Oh, Lord… the ballet, huh? You never struck me as the type"

Nurse Woody chuckled at Frank's response; she was nervous about going to be let down but she tried to stay hopeful.

"Oh, Lord, what? Don't you like the ballet? I think it's so relaxing; it's like being sent off to a musical spa… you'd be amazed.

"Oh gee Woody, you make it sound so tempting but I'm really not a fan of ballet concerts. Please forgive me; I'd hate to ruin your evening by being there."

So…is that a no? Woody asked Frank.

"I don't believe I could stand an entire half an hour of such an event; not to mention two or three. I'm so sorry, Woody, I really am."

On that note Woody ended the conversation feeling let down. She simply told him there's was no need to apologize and that she understood what he was trying to say. Frank remained quiet and allowed her to say goodbye.

As soon as Woody was off the telephone, Frank could not help feeling bad about the way he'd let her down. He wished if he could have made her day a bit more promising, but according to his way of looking at it, it was all for the greater good that she's angry at him for giving her the respect she so deserved.

Frank recognized a huge change within himself. He sat on the sofa and pondered the quick and easy 'in" it would be for him to get Woody out on a rendezvous. He was certain it wouldn't take long before he'd be quenching his thirst from what he recalled of her juicy bosom. But that attraction was no longer there and he hoped she would recognize the change and take the hint that he wasn't that much into her.

Frank then upped from the sofa and he walked over to the liquor trolley and poured a glass of wine while dumping a hearty serving of peanuts in his palms. He threw his head back and washed the down the peanuts with the wine then he attempted to pour another glass with another handful of the nuts; and then the phone rang. He tossed the glass aside and sprang forward to answer.

Hello, hello, Frank said with much urgency in his voice.

Hey, it only me. You sound rushed, are you ok.

"Now, I'm ok. How can I not be, when it's you I'm talking to? I've been waiting for your call all day."

"Well, I've been trying to call you for the last half hour but your line was busy."

"I'm sorry about that, Marlene. I was trying to settle some unfinished business and I didn't realize it would have taken so long."

"Oh. No worries; I understand how hectic things can get sometimes… especially since you've been slacking at the office lately."

"Frank gave a hearty laugh and said "no one has ever called me a slacker, young lady. I guess you're the only one who could get away with saying something like that"

"Marlene's heart raced from the reflection of the time spent with Frank the night before at Chateau de Mehr. She was missing him but terribly and wished if she was close to him.

She then giggled and said "Somehow I get the feeling I can get away with almost anything with you, Frank, and I don't know why."

"Oh, well, let's not worry about things we don't know; let's be realistic about the things we do know. Frank said."

"Like what? Marlene asked Frank while still chuckling.

"Things like you and me, things like me falling in love with you, things like you pretending you haven't noticed, things like, you feeling scared about the two us of together alone, things like, me wishing if I could make it all go away, because I know it's not ok to be this way. Things like that, my dear."

"Frank, Frank, Frank… I don't know what has gotten into you since last night, but I think you should change the subject about these "things" I never thought I'd hear you say these things to me. You have no idea how hard it is for me to listen to you talk this way. Do you realize the seriousness of what you just described to me?"

But of course I do, Marlene; I do. Come on now; are you going to tell me that the thought hasn't crossed your mind?

"I really don't want to talk about this, Frank. This is not good, it's not right and we shouldn't be acting on these instincts."

"That's ok, my dear, you don't have to answer. I already know the truth."

"And what is that truth, Frank?"

"The truth is we are not having this conversation based on our instincts; we are truly acting from the basis of intent."

"OK. So, let's just take your word for it, what are you going to do about it?"

"…Nothing!   There isn't much left for me to do. It is not my intention to pursue you as a lover, Marlene. And I don't expect you to do otherwise."

"What the hell are you talking about Frank? I'm afraid I'm finding your utterances unfathomable…I'm confused here. Will you please explain?"

"I really don't know what the hell has gotten into me, Marlene. But something about you has changed me and I only have eyes for you. I only want to be there for you whenever you need me to. I only want to make you happy for the rest of my life and I only want to love no other woman but you."

"Oh wow, you're certainly off your rockers Frank. And by the way, what about your friend Barchas; have you forgotten about him? Have you forgotten that he's my husband, who happens to be still alive and fighting for his life? And just how do you expect me to feel about you Frank, huh? And why are you trying to make my life more complicated than it already is?"

"Well, I don't want you to be upset about this, Marlene. The last thing I want to hear is that I'm making your life difficult. And by the way, the way I feel about Barchas remains the same, I'll be there to support him in his recovery in any way I can and I mean that wholeheartedly. You've got to understand that this is not something I'm proud of; I still can't believe that this is happening to me. And with much to my chagrin, I swear I can't help falling in love with my best friend's wife."

Marlene was flabbergasted at Frank's response, and at the same time her stomach bloated with butterflies floating halfway up her throat.

Her heart raced with desires of being swept off her feet by Frank. Her hands shook with visions of passionate kisses and romantic splendor in some faraway places where nobody knows their names.

"I just don't know what to say Frank, but I must let you know that I'm still in love with my husband and my commitment as a wife is first and foremost to me."

Frank could hear the cracks and tremors in Marlene's voice when she spoke. His gut feeling was that she wasn't as surprised as she was letting on, but the fact that he came out with it unexpectedly, was what stunned her the most.

"OK, I tell you what…let's not talk about this anymore for the night. I realize that I'd had gone too far already… and I do apologize, but it wasn't my intention to show and disrespect to you and your husband. These unfolding turns of events hit me like a ton of bricks, Marlene. And quite frankly, I just don't know how they came about, but I thought it was time I told you."

"I think you're right Frank; we shouldn't talk about this anymore. The truth be told…I find it very frightening to hear you talking like this. I'm so at a loss for words right now that I think it's best if I hang up the phone. Anyway, I've got to go now as I don't know what to say.

Marlene quickly hung up the telephone and went upstairs to her bedroom. She reeled with frustration from being so terribly attracted to Frank while struggling to stay true to herself as a faithful wife. She tried as best she could not to think about Frank as the night progressed but her effort was to no avail….her head was full of hope and dreams and her heart was bursting with love. She conjured up ways of how they could get away and spend time alone. She wondered if she did it for just one time, it probably wouldn't be regarded as cheating, since her husband was of no use to her. She talked herself into looking at it as a way of maintaining her sanity so she could be around to take care of him.

Frank on the other hand, felt deep discomfort about the way he had expressed himself to Marlene over the phone. He reckoned it would have been a lot more appropriate if he had given the situation a little more time to develop. Also, he wondered if she'd want to turn away from him since she learned the truth about his feelings towards her. And so, as the weeks progressed, Frank wowed not to put any further pressure on her by bringing up the subject.

However, while Frank was being coy and protective of his new found love, Marlene's heart continued to grow fonder with every chance she got to see him.

So as the weeks flew by, Frank kept his promise to behaving himself whenever he was around Marlene. And while he struggled with his keeping his feelings to himself, Marlene did her damndest to suppress her full blown attraction to Frank.

However as the weeks progressed, Marlene started wondering why Frank had not said anything further about his feelings towards her and she wondered if he was having a change of heart. And Frank was hoping Marlene would have had something to say which would give him an opening to pick up from where they had left off. So with no changes on the horizon, the relationship between Marlene and Frank remained status quo.

CHAPTER SEVENTEEN

Two weeks had passed since Marlene and Frank visited the Chateau de Mehr. Ms. Fairchild's attorney had been working diligently to help put her mind at ease, but he'd found nothing to report back to her.

Nights after nights she would sit in her skybox looking down, unflinching, to see if her sister and Frank, who was the man in question, would turn up again. But after not getting anywhere with Chandlon, and losing too much sleep over it, she took it upon herself to call her stepmother.

"Maybe that was a sign from God; maybe He's trying to tell me to listen to Chandlon and give him a little more time" That was what Ms. Fairchild was thinking after hanging up the phone disgustingly when her stepmother's phone rang without an answer. She wondered if she should keep trying until someone picked up or if she should wait and then try back at a later date.

That morning, Ms. Fairchild sat at the edge of her bed deep in thoughts. Her mind raced with endless possibilities as to why, Marlene showed up at her place.

She wondered if perchance "Marlene had come in good faith. But, if that was the case, then who was that man? And, why him, and not her, husband? Could it be that she's divorced and remarry? And if that was the case, why come to her place and not somewhere else?"

Ms. Fairchild closed her eyes and thought more as she dug deep within herself as to all her whys. And then it dawned upon her that she could be on to something.

"Ah, ah…I get it… she consoled herself. Maybe my sister is not aware that I'm the owner of Chateau de Mehr. Never in her wildest dream would my sister imagine that I'd end up at a place like this. Maybe she's thinking that I'm off somewhere as a single mother with a child and living paycheck to paycheck."

And just like a guiding light along the path on which Ms. Fairchild's mind was traveling, she watched her vision explained.

"Oh, my God; I got it; I think I got it! Thank You, Lord…thank You. I thank you for not letting Aunt Carolyn answered the phone. Yes, Lord; it's all coming to me now. Aha. Oh, yes…I'm starting to see the reveal; I'm starting to see that this was all your doing, Lord. And now I'm convinced that my stepmother knows nothing about this.

Ms. Fairchild, while still sitting at the edge of her bed, felt a load lifted off her shoulders. It was her perception that her sister had no inkling of her whereabouts. And, for her to turn up at Chateau de Mehr that night had to be a part of God's plan for her.

So Ms. Fairchild, while fully engaged in her conviction, fell to her knees in prayer. And as she prayed she was tearful and thankful to God that a breakthrough was forthcoming.

<> <>

Chey, who was Shavory's mother, had passed away after the cancer had returned. She died believing that Ms. Fairchild's twins were her biological grandchildren. And Ms. Fairchild still believed that deceiving Chey to think that her children were fathered by her son, Shavory, was what kept her alive and happy over the years. She's convinced Chey would not have lived long enough to find out she had breast cancer, let alone being a survivor for many, many years.

However, the truth be told, Ms. Fairchild felt no pride in giving back to Chey the way she did and the opportunity to being a grandmother which was the most important aspect of her life.

Anyway, the mother and daughter love that Ms. Fairchild and Chey had for each other was far beyond compare. And Ms. Fairchild suffered deeply after losing the one person whom she thought was a godsend to her and her children. She had lost her best friend and no one else mattered to the point of where she had started building walls between the few friends she had made along the way. So with the exception of her three children and her maid, Ms. Fairchild's affection laid dormant towards anyone crossing her path.

Often times she could be found sitting next to the Venetian garden which was located on the west side of the château. That was one of her favorite places when it came time to relax, meditate and watch the sunlight, just before it disappeared behind the mountain peak at six thirty. That was Chey's favorite spot on the compound and Ms. Fairchild's way of keeping her memory alive.

However, Ms. Fairchild soon found out that the walls she had built as her hideaway could no longer provide her a mental safety net of survival. So as time progressed, she was starting to feel trapped. It was as though she had become a prisoner of her past convictions.

The overwhelming fear of her twin sons finding out about their true bloodline was starting to gut her. She shuddered to think of the devastating effect on her children, should in case her secret became exposed. And from time to time she'd look at her boys and hoped she'd pass on just like Chey, without having to face the truth.

Upon those thoughts, Ms. Fairchild felt a sword like sensation slicing though her very core. She realized how much she was just like her father… even to the point of where she'd want to take her own life to escape the shame of deceiving her children.

But unlike her father, Ms. Fairchild was starting to understand that God was always available to take on her worries and help save her from herself. Sometimes in her outcry, she'd struggle for the right words to say when she prayed. Sometimes, she'd even pen them and recite them so she could sound eloquent and worthy in her plea for forgiveness and guidance. But oftentimes on bended knees when she prayed, she would find herself repeating the same sentences.

"Please God, please remember me, I need you in my life; I need you now. Oh, Father God, I confess my sins to you. I've deceived my children; please forgive me, oh father God. I've have deceived the father of my children; please forgive me, oh father God. I have deceived Chey; please forgive me, oh Father God.""And just as I am without a doubt, a sinner unworthy, I beg your pardon as I'm wholly surrendered at your feet."

Oh, heavenly father God, oh, how I've suffered in silence in this lonely and desolate space. Show me the way out of my miseries Holy Father. I feel trapped behind these walls that were once my refuge. Oh, my God, my Holy Father, please hear my cry and break down these walls and set me free. Set me free oh, Heavenly Father…posses my life with peace of mind as I'm dying to breathe a *fresh* air."

So it was there, while sitting on the edge of her bed, where Ms. Fairchild had begun receiving the fruits of her labor. She felt the time spent reading the bible and keeping her promise to God, that she would never again deceive anyone for the benefit of their happiness or hers. Nor, would she turn away from God's promise to her as her redeeming hope.

Ms. Fairchild thereafter picked up the telephone and called Chandlon to advise him to call off the investigation regarding her sister and the man in question…Frank. Chandlon was astonished by her request to drop the investigation and when he asked her why; her response was "Well, Chandlon, my theory is quite simple. I have decided to let the Good Lord take over and handle this for me. You, of all people, know how long I've been praying for God's Favor over my life and I believe this is just the beginning.

"Yes, I can attest to that, but I never expected that you would want to withdraw your investigation so quickly. I think you should give yourself a little more time before calling it quits." Chandlon said.

"As I've told you, Chandlon, I have decided to the let the Good Lord handle it for me. I guess we'll just have to wait and see, as I think this is way bigger than we can imagine. Ms. Fairchild said dryly.

So after listening to her *simple theory* explained, Chandlon was left feeling a little bit conflicted, but he acquiesced nonetheless.

"Whatever you say madam, is good enough for me" Chandlon said, and their conversation ended on that note.

So, Ms. Fairchild, while still being stuck within the confines of her misdeeds, returned to her life as it were…prayerful, steadfast and hopeful.

CHAPTER SEVENTEEN

Meantime back at home with Marlene and her brewing situations, she somewhat managed to keep her growing affection for Frank under wraps, and her renovation project was partly to be blamed. Between time spent with her husband at St. Clements and working alongside with the building contractors, her heart slowed with Frank tucked away inside.

Her art studio was nearing completion and she was extremely ecstatic about this major accomplishment. Although the contractors tried dissuading her from keeping her promise to Mr. Chase, alive, Marlene kept her word by refusing to tear down the old structure. And much to everyone's surprise the old house on top of the hill was starting to take shape and poised to becoming a quaint but very important landmark in the city.

Except for Frank and Lexa, Marlene had not disclosed her plans for the site to anyone. She thought long and hard about informing Carolyn of her plans, but later decided to surprise her after the completion of her project. However Carolyn got wind of what Marlene was up to and she surprised her with a ten thousand check towards the renovation.

Frank watched Marlene changing into what he described as a pioneer woman. He reflected on the years spent being around her and her husband. Time and time again, Barchas complained about his wife's mental breakdown. And, in keeping with Barchas' concerns, Frank could not deny siding with him that she would never be able to stay away from the sofas of psychiatrists. However as time progressed and watching her rebound with gusto and grace, Marlene kept Frank continuously crazy about her.

<> <>

Three months flew by and the treatment Barchas received at the rehab was almost ineffectual. He showed very little neurological improvement and Marlene was starting to feel dismayed.

From time to time she would cry on Frank's shoulders about fear of losing her husband, and sometimes she would cry alone. Frank felt genuine despair towards Barchas condition but his focus was more on keeping Marlene from regressing.

Anyway between planning the grand opening of her art studio, and despite her husband's declining condition, Marlene was able to strike a balance in keeping herself empowered.

<> <>

Winter was barely gone, and while spring was as on the cusp of unveiling the fast approaching blooms with colors too complex to describe, Barchas passed away.

So it would have been a normal routine day for Marlene where she would have spent some time with her husband and then rush off to finalizing the plans for grand opening. However as she was getting dressed early that morning to leave home to be with her husband she heard the doorbell ringing. It was Frank who had stopped by. Marlene wondered what could have caused him to be by that early in the morning.

"Huh, that's unusual" she muttered to herself as she heard Allora allowing Frank inside. She took a final look in the mirror and added a bit more blush to her cheeks before hurrying downstairs to see him.

"Hey there, what brought you by this time of the morning? Is everything okay… you look beat.." Marlene said to Frank while noticing a haggard look about his face.

Frank did not respond and Marlene's curiosity piqued.

"Frank, what is the matter, and why are your eyes were so swollen?"

Frank stood speechless facing Marlene and she watched the tears rolling down his cheeks. She was hapless as to what could have caused him to be at her home so early and devastated.

"Oh, my god; Frank will you please say something….I know it's bad news, but please tell me what it is" Marlene said while holding Frank's hands. But Frank said nothing. Allora came out of the kitchen and watched them still standing in the foyer while Marlene pleaded to Frank for an answer.

So Marlene, while still holding on to Frank urged him to walk with her to the sitting room. He went along with her suggestion while still weeping and then they sat. Allora sneaked up to the side of the room to listen to what could have caused Mr. Roulette to be so upset, and without any more moments lost, he turned to Marlene and said, "I'm so sorry my love, but he's gone."

"What are you talking about, Frank? What you mean by, he's gone? Who's gone Frank? You have got to let me know."

Frank said nothing; he just kept staring at her in hopes that she could read his eyes.

But Allora did not have to look in Frank's eyes to know that he was talking about Barchas; she already knew from the moment he said to Marlene "I'm so sorry my love"

Marlene's heart thumped and raced uncontrollably as she tried confirming what had crossed her mind.

"I think I know what you are trying to tell me Frank, but I will not say it. I need an outright answer from you Frank; I need you to tell me what the hell you're trying to say!

Marlene tried getting up from the sofa and immediately she fell down because her knees buckled from the thought that Frank could be referring to her husband. Frank immediately got up and tried helping her to getting back on the sofa. He then sat next to her, and he placed his hands around her, while rubbing her forearm back and forth.

And, as if he could hardly breathe when he spoke, Frank painstakingly said to Marlene, "It's Barchas; he passed away this morning around three o'clock, the doctor said. I'm so sorry my dear Marlene; I know how much it hurts."

Marlene began screaming and Allora couldn't wait to rush to her side. Frank tried pulling himself together so as to protect Marlene from falling off the chair from shock of the news. But he was barely able to handle himself while holding her throughout her rocking and wailing. Allora then rushed to her side and she tried holding her hands, but Marlene kept pulling them back.

Frank, who was obviously at a loss for words, during the tugging, left the room and wired his way towards the liquor trolley to help himself to a quick fix. He stood next to the liquor trolley, shaken and scared and he gulped a shot of whiskey in one go. He then poured a double and walked back to the room to find Marlene in a more stable condition.

She was sitting next to Allora with her head resting on her shoulder. Frank was relieved and while sipping on his drink he sat quietly on a chair while looking at Marlene from a very special place in his heart. And while he looked on, Allora asked Marlene if she would like her to call her doctor. Marlene shook her head from side to side, meaning no.

Frank then recalled the day at the hospital cafeteria after she had walked in and frantically searched inside her handbag for a little pill. He remembered how quickly it had calmed her after taking it. He then walked over to the sofa where both ladies were sitting and he very softly he said to Marlene

"What about those little pink pills you carry around in your handbag; would you like to try one?"

And without opening her eyes or taking her head of Allora's shoulder, she nodded yes.

Allora knew exactly which pill Frank was referring to and she went in search of Marlene's handbag. And even under the saddest circumstance, Allora couldn't help wondering how come Frank knew so much about Marlene.

"Thank you, Allora, I'm ok now" Marlene said after accepting the glass of water and Xanax medication from Allora.

She looked at Marlene cozying up next to Frank, and she took it as a signal that it was time to leave them alone. A few minutes later, Frank took Marlene by the hand and walked her upstairs to her bedroom. That was the first time he had ever seen inside her and Barcha's bedroom, but by no means had he felt like a stranger there. He helped her getting into bed and he pulled the sheets around her while he sat at the edge of the bed and feeling scared. His greatest fears however came from wondering if this episode of her life would cause the woman that he had grown to love, to fall into the dangers of another mental breakdown.

From that, Frank assumed that his journey ahead could be to be a very long one, but he was fully prepared to stick it out with her.

"What am I going to say to my children, how, how can I let them know that their father is no more. Oh dear Lord, I just don't know what to do, now that he's really gone, Frank." Marlene said with her face buried into the pillow as he looked on."

Silence followed as Frank remained quiet watching Marlene twisting and turning in grief. And then she immediately raised herself out of the bed with an about face as if she was puzzled about something.

Marlene then asked Frank:

"You haven't told me how you got the news before I did. How's that... I don't understand"

"I was right there, Marlene" Frank responded with his voice lowered almost to being inaudible.

"What do you mean you were right there; you said he passed away at about three o'clock this morning." Marlene said.

"Huh-huh, I was very much there, my love. I've been spending most of my nights there with Barchas. Sometimes I'd even fall asleep there until the wee hours of the morning and this was one of them."

"But you have never said anything to me, Frank. I didn't know you were still going to spend time with him."

I understand, but I could never find it in my heart to not go, Marlene. Anyway, last night in question, Barchas was awake when I got there. And as usual I try talking with him about what's taking place in office....you know....just little things that I thought he'd like to hear.

So he fell asleep as he usually does and I fell asleep in the chair. When I finally woke up, it was four thirty. I went over to check on him and to let him know that I was leaving. But something about the way he looked, struck a chord in me…he just didn't look himself. So I touched him…you know… I picked up his hand, and it was ice cold. God damn it, Marlene, I froze in a way I can't explain."

Marlene clutched on to the sheet while listening to Frank explain and she used it to wipe the streaming tears along her face.

"Huh-huh, so what happened after that" Marlene asked Frank."

"So, I immediately called the nurse.

"But, how did my husband die, Frank. Did they not tell you?"

"No, but I'm sure we'll will find out. Marlene, I begged them not to contact you by phone. I knew how painful this was going to be, so I wanted to be there for you when you got the news."

"So, what do I do now, Frank, now that he's gone. I'm so confused and shocked; I just don't know where to begin."

"That's understandable, Marlene, but as you know…I'll always be available to help in any which way I can. Just tell me what you need me to do."

"I think I should call Aunt Carolyn; she of all people will know how to handle these situations"

"I couldn't agree more" Frank replied sounding a bit more relaxed.

<> <>

By nightfall, the news about Barchas' death was broadcasted throughout country. The morning newspapers were captioned with his name followed by stories about his life and his flawless dedication to his calling as District Attorney.

The shocking news rocked the hearts of Watertown and everyone grieved the loss of another longstanding pillar of the community.

So while this turn of event was taking place, Dr. Jax was vacationing in New York and getting suited in tux to attend his son's wedding the following day. However, upon his return, he dropped everything in support of Marlene's and Frank's endeavors with completing the final arrangements for a proper funeral.

Ms. Fairchild who was watching evening news as she usually does was floored while learning about the passing of her brother-in-law, Barchas Sander. As she listened she covered her mouth in awe when she saw his picture flashed across the TV screen. Mr. Sander is survived by his wife Mrs. Marlene Sander, his son Monk and daughter Bethany.

Some of the best years of her life were shared with Barchas and her sister and she felt deep regrets about his passing.

She immediately picked up the telephone and gave Chandlon a telephone call

That night after hearing the news about Barchas, Ms. Fairchild wondered what is must be like for her sister losing her husband, and the devastating impact to their children. She wondered if it was best to come out of hiding and show her support. But given the deceptive life she had been living for all those many years, she reckoned it would be unwise to change course.

She twisted and turned in bed from wondering what would happen to her children if she should die and leave them behind to a life without a single family member to call on. The very thought of realizing the devastating effect to her children if they were left behind under such circumstance was chilling.

Finally, she threw caution to wind and decided to attend Barchas' funeral. She figured a funeral of that size where more than a thousand mourners was to be expected, it would be very unlikely anyone would recognize her there.

Then she began asking herself:

"What would be the purpose of attending the funeral if not for the benefit of my sister? She's the main one I'm trying to reconcile with."

"At best, this is my opportunity to start taking charge of my life and try working things out my way."

"I know she blamed me for my death of our father which is totally ridiculous. We both have played the blame game long enough and I'm going to do my damndest to put an end to this."

While Ms. Fairchild kept tossing and turning in bed about her thoughts as they developed, a streak of panic emerged and shot down her confidence. By daybreak she came to the realization that she really didn't have the guts to show her face to the family she had left behind.

A week later, all eight hundred and fifty seats were filled at the "Watertown Methodist Church," where Barchas' body took center stage for viewing and last respect. The front pew that was reserved for family was where Marlene, Monk, Bethany, Carolyn, Brandon, Simon, and his wife Leigh, could be seen woeful and quiet. And directly behind them, were Frank, Allora, Lexa, Dr. Jax, Jeptha and a few others that were considered close friends of the family.

Soon after, Bishop Dawes appeared and the choir rose and sang "His Eyes on The Sparrow."

Then a reading from Psalm 139, verses 1 thru10, was delivered by Mrs. Maggie Cuthbert, a prominent member of the Church and the wife of the pianist.

1. O Lord, you have searched me and known me.

2. You know when I sit down and when I rise up;
    You discern my thoughts from far away.

3. You search out my path and my lying down;
    And are acquainted with all my ways.

4. Even before a word is on my tongue,
    O Lord, You know it completely.

5. You hem me in, behind and before.
    And lay Your hand upon me.

6. Such knowledge is too wonderful for me;
    It is so high that I cannot attain it.

7. Where can I go from Your spirit?
    Or where can I flee from Your presence?

8. If I ascend to heaven, You are there;
    If I make my bed in Sheol, You are there.

9. If I take the wings of the morning,
    And settle at the farthest limits of the sea,

10. Even there, Your hand shall lead me,
    And Your right hand shall hold me fast.

<>

Thereafter, The Reverend Lennox Swallow delivered the Homily, followed by another hymnal from the Choir.

There were several names listed on the program next to "Remembrances," and Frank was one of them. However, when it came time for him take the stand and read what he had carefully penned about his *'brother'* it was all for naught.

Frank's heart raced uncontrollably, his palms became sweaty and his strength failed him and he fell to his knees. Jeptha Stoddard, a colleague of himself and Barchas, was quick to assist Frank with getting back on his feet while he wept openly with the crowd of people looking on. Frank tried pulling himself together and he made another attempt to read his script, but he was still too broken to utter even the first word.

So, Brandon Tate, who was still recuperating from his near death experience walked up to Frank and took the five pages document from his hand. And with Frank still standing next to him, Brandon eloquently delivered the bone-chilling and absorbing portrait about a friendship of two men and a "vow" to be his brother's keeper

Frank then shook Brandon's hands to show appreciation for his kindness.

And so in moving forward, and as things continued winding down, there was only one item left on the program before leaving for the graveside …a hymnal, by the choir "Swing Low, Sweet Chariot, Coming for to carry me home"

And while everyone remained quiet and deep in reflection about Barchas, and deep in their own way of grieving as they listened to the choir, the unimaginable occurred. A veiled woman emerged from the rear of the building and walked all the way up to the podium to join the choir. In as much as they were startled by this unknown person turning up, and much to the shock of Reverend Swallow, they kept on singing. And when the woman opened her mouth and lifted her voice in unison, the lead singer quickly handed her the microphone and backed away. Then the choir stopped singing and the stage was hers.

The angelic and melodious voice of the woman drew gasps from the crowd. And she had the pianist working at his full potential; from his bopping head, rocking shoulders and all it took to keep up with her. Her astounding rendition of the song warmed the hearts and soul of the saddened as they rose to their feet and hummed along with her.

Marlene kept looking at the woman and wondered who it could be. Carolyn turned to Marlene and asked if she knew who it was, but Marlene had no idea. Frank, by then, had regained his composure. And as he watched the woman who was still being disguised during her performance, he developed a notion of who it could be. But he reckoned he could be so farfetched about his idea that he chose to keep it only to himself. However, Frank was not wrong in thinking that it was Blossom Rigby on the stage. Although he had never heard her sung or had any idea that she could, there was something special about her that kept him thinking that she was the one.

As Blossom handed back the microphone to the choir member that was standing behind her, the crowd of people applauded her as she stepped off the stage. Lexa, who was also clapping, turned to Frank and asked if he had any idea of who she was. But without looking at her, Frank simply shook his side from side to side. She then nudged him with her elbow and in a low voice she commented:

"Sounds like she was in love with him; any fool could tell"

Frank was quite annoyed at Lexa, and under bated breath he responded "not now, Lexa; for the love of God, show some respect. Lexa's eyes were filled with contempt as they followed Blossom Rigby walking along the aisle to where she was seated. She then elbowed Frank again and without looking at her, he snapped by saying "what!" And she asked Frank "Why the hell is she hiding behind that black veil; she shouldn't have come if she didn't want anyone to know about them."

Lexa's comment disgusted Frank and his response to her showed likewise:

"The man is dead, Lexa! What more do you want? I thought you'd be happy that he's finally in heaven with Rose"

Lexa was shocked at Frank's response. His quick thinking told him by making mention of "Rose" could be an effective way of getting her to shut up; but that was somewhat of a flawed attempt. But on the other hand it did work out, because her response to Frank was:

"Don't you dare, Frank! That man went to hell. And my little Rose doesn't need him in heaven; my little Rose is in the arms of Jesus. So please leave my baby out of this. You hear me!"

Frank said nothing and he tried ignoring her in a form of acquiescing. However he concluded that she was still a basket case and she could be very dangerous if not kept at arm's length.

On that note, Lexa turned away and she started sobbing which lead others to believe that she was mourning the loss of Barchas along with the others who were still teary eyed.

Soon after, Frank, Jeptha, Dr. Jax, Simon, and two other attorneys from Frank's office, presented themselves as the pallbearers for taking the casket out to the hearse.

Marlene and her children remained very quiet during the entire event. Carolyn, Brandon and Leigh, followed behind them as they were escorted out of the church to the Limo that was waiting behind the hearse.

The crowd scattered thereafter; some waiting in queue to join the procession onward to the burial while others left to be elsewhere.

CHAPTER EIGHTEEN

While inside the church, Ms. Fairchild sat quietly in the middle row. Her thick sunglasses and wig sufficed in maintaining her confidence that she would remain unrecognizable. Along with that; she reckoned "out of sight-out of mind" would help in keeping her inconspicuous. And for the most part she kept her head hung low while reading the program and looking at several photographs of Barchas.

Although it was on such a sad occasion, Ms. Fairchild was proud taking the first steps towards what she saw as the beginning of a family reunion and her day of atonement.   However, she was by no means convinced that it was going to be easy; but deep within she felt that being there was the beginning of the end of her fractured life.

And when her eyes landed on Jax as he walked by with the other pallbearers, it tore her up inside and her conscience tugged hard on her heartstrings.

Ms. Fairchild suffered great pain from her guilty conscience about the way she lied to her sons which lead them to believe that they were fatherless. Time and time again her sons would look at old photographs of Shavory who they believe was their father. Those old photographs of course were gathered and put together in a photo album by their grandmother Chey. And while Chey was alive she would spend hours telling the children great stories about their father from the time he just a little boy.

The haunting memories of Chey making sure her beloved grandsons knew as much as she could about the family before she died came back to Ms. Fairchild as a knife in her back. She realized that she was betrayed by her own convictions. What she thought was the right thing to do in giving Chey something to live for after losing her son Shavory, turned out to be the thorn in the crown she was left with…..Chateau de Mehr.

While Ms. Fairchild remained seated and quivering from the onslaught of her pass, she saw Marlene and the rest of family coming down the aisle. She quickly turned her face to the other side of the church, but they had passed her by without even turning their heads in her direction.

Soon after they were gone and as the crowd continued thinning, Ms. Fairchild forged ahead and went directly to her limo.

"Where to, Madam" the limo driver asked Ms. Fairchild

"Back to the Chateau" she replied. She thought she would have be able to pull it off by attending the burial, but after what she experienced inside the church, she reckoned she could easily blow her cover by just passing out at the site.

Ms. Fairchild quickly removed her wig and sunglasses and tried relaxing with a glass of club soda. And then her mind went in motion about fixing her life as it were. At first she thought about the enormous wealth she was left with. It was the kind of money she never dreamt of having, and quite frankly it had crossed her mind that she'd be willing to lose it all to her children as a down payment towards the justice they deserve….the truth.

Anyway, having said all that, Ms. Fairchild started brainstorming of ways she could try and fix her fractured life. She imagined herself turning up at Marlene's doorstep with her story and to beg forgiveness. She then changed her mind and thought about writing a letter to Carolyn, her step mother whom she assumed would be a lot more reasonable and forgiving.

"But what would I say to her, if I did sit down to write that letter" Ms. Fairchild asked herself.

"This is really about my sons. So maybe I should be more concerned about contacting Jax and let him know the truth. I hardly think he'd forgive me for what I did, but undoubtedly he'd be pleased knowing that he was right all along about being the father." Ms. Fairchild continued wrestling with her thoughts as the limo driver picked up speed towards taking her back home.

But nothing she thought about thus far felt as if she would be on the right path to success. Deep within she never felt as if she had the confidence to ever face her sister knowing that she had blamed her for the death of their father. And as for Aunt Carolyn…a force to reckon with, Ms Fairchild assumed she could only get better with age and it would be unwise to start out on the wrong foot with her.

Then her last resort came to mind…Chandlon Bow. Ms. Fairchild dreaded the idea of him finding out about what she had done. Knowing that he was the Shavory's best friend, attorney and fiduciary, Ms. Fairchild imagined that he'd most likely drop her as his most important client after finding out about her secret. Since she acquired "Chateau de Mehr," it was Chandlon who had been handling her financial and personal affairs. He's responsible for getting her name changed from Christina Tate to Ms. Gabriella Fairchild. And after Chey passed away, he was even more protective of her wellbeing. And to her children,

Chandlon was the only man around that could be looked upon as family.

But Chandlon was not her type, and even on her loneliest nights and her down and out moments when Chandlon would stick it out with her, she found no interest in his advances romantically. Finally after several years, Chandlon met his soul mate, Selah, whom he married and was enjoying a beautiful life with.

Anyway, the next morning under the dawn of a new light, Ms. Fairchild went outside and sat amidst the overgrown shrubbery where the iconic elegance of the property stood tall. She'd past through the night taunted by guilt every time she closed her eyes to sleep. And with her heart full and running over with pain, she fearlessly contacted Chandlon and told him to meet her there. She was holding the diary she'd written and placed in hiding many, many years ago.

The diary she had kept during the time of her transformation, the one she promised never to bring to light as long as she was alive, was the same diary she exhumed. It was bur ied beneath the wooden floor inside her bedroom at the foot of her bed.

"Oh, gee, I was thinking to myself on my way over here that something big is going on with you. I sure hope its good news. You and I have never met outside here before. So what's the story?" Chandlon said as he walked up the Ms. Fairchild sitting and hold the bag with the diary.

"Good morning Chandlon, have a seat; I've got something very important to share with you" Ms. Fairchild replied without her usual smiley face.

Chandlon sat and placed his briefcase on the grass next to his feet while keeping his eyes fixated on Ms. Chandlon. Something told him it was not going to be good news as he'd hoped for.

"Oh, oh; I'm not so sure I want to hear what it its….sounds like all hell is about to break loose. Anyway, I'm all ears" Chandlon said.

Ms. Fairchild raised her hand and scratched the top her head while thinking and bracing herself for the "bust-out."

"Now Chandlon, what I'm about to say to you is the truth and nothing but the truth. So I hope to God that after this meeting is over, you don't have to doubt me in any way, shape, or form in moving forward. And if you chose not to believe in me after all is said and done here, I promise not to fault you in any way."

Chandlon had never been engaged in any meeting, business or personal where Ms. Fairchild had to deliver, anytime of disclaimer before speaking her mind. And he immediately came to his own conclusion.
"Oh gee, this sounds like a well thought out project that you've working on. I reckon I'm about to take on the case of a lifetime, but I'm as ready as I'm ever going to be. So will you please tell me what this is all about?"

The looks on Chandlon's face changed to a more serious side and his tone matched just as well.

Ms. Fairchild took a deep sigh while holding on to the bag containing the diary that was sitting on her lap.

Chandlon gave her a curious eye while looking at her gripping tightly to the bag.

"What's that on your lap?" Chandlon asked Ms. Fairchild in a soft but businesslike tone.

"Well, sir, what I have here on my lap is the beginning of my journey to Chateau de Mehr. My fear is that I may have come to the end of my road after you've read this diary. I never thought I'd live to see the day that I share this diary with anyone. It was meant for my children after I was deceased. But my life as it is now, Chandlon, is worthless and without favor. So please take this and promise me you will read it carefully.

"Good God; Gabby; this is more serious than I thought. Yes, I promise I will read your diary but not without you telling me what it's about." Chandlon said.

"Well, as you can see it's clearly titled "Diary to My Children" Ms. Fairchild replied.

Chandlon then said:

"So, I think it's best to let it remain that way and let them be the first to read it as it was intended."

I can't blame you for that response, Chandlon. But as you can see, I've changed my mind. Ms. Fairchild said.

Come on now, Ms. Fairchild, you've got to tell me in your own words what that book is all about. Chandlon said.

Ms. Fairchild took the diary from Chandlon and placed in inside the bag. She then turned her body to face him directly and then she began speaking.

"Well this all started with a lie and it ended with lies on top of lies. And this is the story of my life." That was how Ms. Fairchild began her *"tell all"* story to Chandlon Bow, her attorney, whom she trusted with her life.

Ms. Fairchild was less than three minutes into her story which took her back to her childhood years after the death of her mother, when Chandlon interrupted her with a change of heart.

"Wait a minute, Gabriella" as he addressed her most times. "I'm sorry… I had no idea you were going as far back as to your childhood. So on second thought, I'll be happy to take the diary go through it with a fine tooth come, I promise.

Ms. Fairchild was relieved by Chandlon's idea of taking the book, but it was not her intention for him to leave the premises with it.

"At all cost, Chandlon, you have to remain here while reading this diary. In as must as I trust you, I cannot allow you to leave with it. When you are through reading, I'm sure you'll understand why I'm taking this stance.

"Very well, Madam…you are the boss." Chandlon replied.

Ms. Fairchild carefully removed the diary again from the bag and placed it in Chandlon's hands and she developed a sinking feeling that after all was said and done, Chandlon wouldn't want to touch her with a ten foot pole. But she was prepared for whatever came her way.

Both Chandlon and Ms. Fairchild walked back to the main house and she invited him to use her office for the day into the night or however long it would take him to read the book in its entirety.

Four hours later, into reading the diary he was getting bored and had no interest in learning about her teenage crush on Shavory. And reading about Shavory who was his best friend conjured up the pain the suffered after his tragic death.

Anyway, it was way past lunchtime and Chandlon was famished. He left the diary locked away in the office and walked across the compound to have lunch. There, he saw Ms. Fairchild speaking with her food and beverage manager. When she saw Chandlon coming in, she panicked and abruptly left the manager and rushed towards Chandlon saying what have you done with the book, don't tell me you're through. Chandlon who had not yet picked up on anything earth shattering in the book, smiled at Ms. Fairchild and said. "Don't worry about the book; I left it on your desk. I only took a break to grab a bite to eat.

So, what do you think, She asked him and impatiently waited for a response.

We'll its very interesting, but I'm not too far into it. I'm sure there are going to be things that will keep me on the edge of the chair but I'm not there yet. Anyway the sooner I get something to eat is the sooner I'll get back to the book.

"Oh sorry, I should have known better" Ms. Fairchild said. She then returned to the Manager and requested her to bring lunch to Mr. Bow.

Ms. Fairchild reckoned that Chandlon had not yet touched on the pages in the book where she expected him to be blown away. She reckoned he was taking his time as he said that he would.

And so she tried relaxing and thinking of ways protect her children after the expose finally makes landfall. She left and went upstairs to the skybox which is more like the nerve center for her troubled life.

And that was where she chose to spend the rest of day and night while waiting to hear from Chandlon.

It wasn't until after eight o'clock that night when Ms. Fairchild heard footsteps coming upstairs towards her skybox. She knew it had to be Chandlon as no one else was allowed to enter that space. Her heart raced with the expectation of him coming down on her with the axe. And within the next few seconds of him entering the room she made a final plea asking God not to let him turn away from her. She'd be ok with his vengeance, or any which way he chose to handle the matter, as long as he never turned his back on her.

She sat in her comfy chair and waited for the door to be pushed in followed by the screechy sound from its rusty hinge. Cold sweats flooded her palms and her heart raced and thumped hard against her chest plate.

"Well are you going to say something, or are you just going to stand there and finish killing me with that deadly look on your face" Ms. Fairchild said to Chandlon who was standing next her chair while being speechless and holding the diary.

"Please Chandlon, say something….anything! Please." Ms. Fairchild appeared desperate and while looking up at Chandlon as he watched the tears rolled from her eyes."

Chandlon then gently handed the diary back to Ms. Fairchild and without a single utterance he turned and closed the door behind and tried walking away.

Ms. Fairchild immediately upped from her chair and ran after Chandlon while screaming and grabbing his hand in an effort to get him to go back inside the sky box. Chandlon stopped and closed his eyes in disgust and he did not want to look at her.

"Chandlon, please I beg of you…don't go. You can't just walk away like this. I trusted you with my life and I still do. I'm begging you to please don't leave; come back inside the box and tell me what you're thinking."

Chandlon then opened his eyes and turned around to look at Ms. Fairchild and he pushed her away from him which immediately released her grip from his hand. Ms. Fairchild then covered her face with her hands and began weeping in front of Chandlon, or so she thought. Because after she opened her eyes he was already half way down stairs.

She quickly returned to the sky box and picked up the diary. She held it close to her chest and she bawled filling the room with bellows from the pit of her belly. A few minutes elapsed with Ms. Fairchild pouring her guts out regrettably about sharing her secret with Chandlon. She assumed it was huge mistake and she wondered what he was going to do with what he had learnt about her. Anyway by midnight she was totally exhausted and at a loss for words, or answers pertaining to what the outcome of her children's future would be….which all she cared about at that point.

The morning after, Ms. Fairchild returned the diary beneath the wooden slat at the foot of her bed where she had kept it for thirteen years. She then slipped into her robe and walked into the kitchen to join her children and Dorchas, who were at the table having breakfast that Saturday morning.

Dorchas, who was no longer considered the maid, but more like family, looked at Ms. Fairchild and commented "You, look like you nevva get much sleep last night Ms. G. You want a likkle coffee?"

"No, but I I'll take some of your herbal tea and a piece of toast."Ms. Fairchild responded.

So while Dorchas was off fixing the tea for Ms. Fairchild, she looked at the boys with an eyeful of fear and despair.

Christian, who was the spitting image of his father Jax, looked at his mom and said "Mom, what's wrong; it seems that you were crying.

"No sweetie, I wasn't crying; your mommy's eyes are just sore." Ms. Fairchild replied.

Chateau, who was picking at her pancakes, and watching cartoons from the dining table, turned and looked at her mother after overhearing their conversation. And she too noticed that her mother's eyes were terribly swollen.

"But Mommy, what make your eyes so sore and so sad?"

Chateau melted her mother's heart with her concerns and she wished if her daughter had not seen her in that state. She immediately stretched out her arms and said:

"Come here baby. Your mommy is going to be just fine; you just wait and see. As soon as Dorchas fixes my herbal tea it will clear everything up." She responded to her daughter while hugging her and kissing her on the cheeks.

Christopher on the other hand sat quietly at the table without having anything to say, but he never took his eyes off his mother which lead her to believe that he suspected that she was not being truthful to them.
"Are you ok, Christopher?"

"Huh-huh"

"Is that all you've to say to your mother?

"Huh-huh"

"Christopher….what is the matter dear; you don't sound as if you're ok. And you haven't touched your breakfast"

"I'm fine mommy; I'm just not hungry."

Ms. Fairchild became very concerned about Christopher's attitude and she turned to Christian and said:

"Christian, what is wrong with your brother; tell me why he's in such a bad mood.

"I don't know; he only told me that he heard sounds in your bedroom as if you were crying" Christian responded to his mother.

"I told you not to say anything, Christian! You promised you wouldn't say anything to Mom!" Christopher retorted while being ignored by his brother.

Ms. Fairchild quickly rushed to the other side of the table where Christopher was sitting and she apologized for causing him to be upset. And in keeping with being truthful, she confessed that she was crying.

All three of her kids turned to her and asked why she was crying, and again in keeping with the truth, she told them she was crying because of a huge mistake she had made concerning Uncle Chandlon.

"Oh, don't worry Mom; Uncle Chandlon isn't upset with you. As soon as he comes back around, everything is going to be fine" Christian said in trying to console his mother. Christopher and Chateau seemed ok with what Christian had to say and things were back to normal once more.

<>< >

Two days later, Ms. Fairchild was at her wits end from not hearing from Chandlon. She tried telling herself it was not in her best interest to call him, but she was burning with anxiety from what he could be thinking about her.

By then it was Tuesday morning and she was dressed and ready to visit him at his office which was halfway across town. Surely, Chandlon was not expecting to see her turn up. In the thirteen years he had spent being her attorney, she had only showed up twice or thrice at his office. Since then, as his most important client, all her needs were met by him coming out to see her at Chateau de Mehr.

Chandlon had not been himself since his last visit with Ms. Fairchild, or Gabriella, as he preferred to call her. What he walked away with after reading the diary that day, left him riddled with rage and puzzled with questions about the woman he thought he knew well enough to be trustworthy and best suited to becoming his wife. And upon until he found out so much more about her, he'd always felt that Selah was second best after Gabriella's continuous rejections.

Chandlon sat idly at his desk that Tuesday morning, preoccupied with his recollection of Ms. Fairchild's diary and contemplating severing their relationship, both personal and professional.

And while he twiddled his thumbs with his eyes closed and rocking back and forth in his chair, Ms. Fairchild entered the room and made a slight knock on his door. His eyes popped open as he tried steadying himself in the chair.

Upon seeing her, his heart swelled and was heavy with animosity towards her. And to let his feeling show, Chandlon did not mince his words while she stood facing him.

"Well, this is quite a rare initiative for you to be coming out here. And furthermore I don't recall scheduling an appointment for us to meet. But who am I kidding; the great witch of Chateau de Mehr has arrived and she's the boss."

Ms. Fairchild watched Chandlon's eyes casting downward as if they were heavy with scorn. She kept her eyes on him while she remained quiet. He then looked towards her and called her a witch.

Ms Fairchild was not at all surprised by Chandlon's attack. Going there to try meeting with him without prior notice, had mentally prepared her for his affront.

"Oh, Chandlon, I did not mean to upset you to such an extent. Had I known it would turn out like this; most likely I would have changed my mind about sharing my horrible life with you. But you are the only friend I have left in this world and I don't want to lose you. Can't you find it in your heart to understand my plight? After all, I'm doing everything in my power to rectify the situation simply for the sake of my children. Please Chandlon, as my friend and confidant I need you to help me through this."

"Well are you going to stand there all day and preach to me? Why not pull up a chair and tell me how you think I can help you recover.

Ms. Fairchild quickly plopped herself on a chair and threw down her handbag on Chandlon's desk.

"As my attorney, I'm seeking your expertise regarding this matter, but clearly you're not interested.

"Well as your attorney, I can only advise you on legal issues. I think you should try finding the father of your boys and letting him know the truth. Of course finding him shouldn't be a problem since he's still working at the hospital; not to mention you saw him a week and a half ago at your brother-in-law's funeral."

"Yes, I'm already aware of all of that. However, my fear is there could be legal ramifications after the truth is revealed, and I'm going to need protection for my boys. I really thought I could count on you."

Up to that point, Chandlon still had mixed feeling about Ms. Fairchild, and he remained quiet as he was waiting to hear what else she'd have to say. Her eyes started welling up and soon after she broke down in tears and started spilling her guts to Chandlon.

"I know you must be thinking that I'm a wicked woman, or a bitch as you put it. But that's okay— you have no idea how badly I wanted to tell Chey the truth. But After all that poor woman had gone through after losing her only son, and the guilt that I was paralyzed with at the time, I really thought giving her my children was all I could do to help breathe some life back into her. You have got to believe that I truly had no idea that things would ever turn out the way they did."

"The horror I was plagued with at the time of losing Shavory, way surpassed what I thought could be damaging and unconscionable to my unborn children, to say the least."

"And, it wasn't too long after Chey was gone and out of harm's way, that I started thinking about my children and their future. I'd hate for them to find out about this as men; they are going to be fourteen soon and I've got to make sure they are aware of their true identity before it's too late".

Chandlon sat unmoved by Ms. Fairchild's confession and as much as she tried getting him to understand her point of view he showed no compassion towards her. It appeared that he was more fixated on the idea that Ms. Fairchild had ulterior motives about his Shavory's wealth.

Chandlon then responded to Ms. Fairchild:

"So, you are going to just sit there and tell me that you had no idea that Shavory…the so call love of your life, had returned to Watertown as a wealthy man? C'mon now Gabriella…the man is dead and gone; theres no need to keep up the charade.   Do you really expect me to believe all that innocence you've portrayed so eloquently in your diary where you said couldn't care less about the damage over financial gains?"

Charade! Is that what you this is, Chandlon; a charade?   Look…. my future and the future of my children are at stake here… I do not have time charades. I'm done! Done with the lying…I want to come clean and I'm doing the best I can, but you are not helping!

I understand that's what you are trying to do, Gabriella, I guess you could say that I never realized you had it in you to look at what you have done to your children and all that you have gained from it.

Ms. Fairchild was appalled at her attorney's comments; she never expected that he would be so brutal.

What the hell are you talking about, Chandlon? I'd never even had sex with the man….not since I was in my teen. Did you not read my book?

Yes, I've read your book! And I have seen the bottom of your heart, I have seen the core of your soul and I know now you are a woman that I dare not touch with a ten foot pole. Much to my chagrin I never thought you could have me fooled for those many years, Gabriella!

Feeling stung by his open revolt, Ms. Fairchild realized that despite her efforts to mend fences with her attorney, he continued to being a formidable foe.

She felt like firing back at him, but she reckoned acting on a spur of the moment could ultimately leave her at a disadvantage. So she went with her gut instincts and tried to bring him back around.

Look Chandlon, you said something earlier about contacting Jax who is the father of my children. I realize I made a terrible mistake by bringing you into all this mess, and for that, I'm sorry. So…, I'll tell you what I am going to do…."

Ms. Fairchild appeared pensive and mysterious while expressing her thoughts and looking down at the floor and it shook Chandlon's confidence as her attorney. After reading her book and finding out so much about her, he reckoned that she could be quite devious and the bovine stare in her eyes when she spoke had him straightening up in his chair.

"Go on; I'm listening. So what are you thinking of doing?" Chandlon asked her.

"Well, as you've suggested, Mr. Bow, I should go out and start finding the father of my children. Quite frankly, I couldn't agree with you more. But since I obviously don't have the nerve to go out on that limb without the support of my attorney, I guess I'll just have to find one who will be interested in the job.   I'm confident I'll be able to buy his loyalty and get things done in a timely manner" Ms. Fairchild said in a cool and confident tone.

She then retrieved her handbag from his desk and she calmly walked out of her attorney's office without him trying to stop her. But deep inside, her about face, had him unnerved, and he began thinking that maybe she was being truthful and was not holding anything back. He reckoned his tactic had pushed her way too far and he was not about to lose his largest paycheck in the business.

Chandlon then tried running after Ms. Fairchild in an attempt to get her to go back inside his office. She was just about entering her car when she heard his voice hollering from a short distance behind. She refused to look back and she continued ignoring him. By the time she was inside her car he'd caught up with her. He quickly apologized and begged her to go back inside his office.

Ms. Fairchild was relieved that Chandlon came running after her and she hoped that he would try and overcome his disappointment in her.

Ms. Fairchild then came out of her car and walked back with Chandlon to his office. And while she walked back with him she said:

"I hope you are not asking me to go back to your office so you can ridicule me some more"

"I don't know what come over me, Gabriella. But I've haven't been myself since I put your diary down. As your attorney, I have no right to treat you the way I did…and I'm sorry. Let's get back inside and see if we can start things from a fresh perspective."

"Forget about being my attorney, Chandlon; you are my best friend!"

Chandlon's reply was:

<u>Absolutely!</u> And that was the problem. You see my dear, I have to be your attorney first in this situation, and I must be more careful and try keeping my emotions out of the way, Gabriella.

"What emotions are you talking about, Chandlon?"

Chandlon had nothing to say to Gabriella, but it soon became obvious what he wanted to say, because of how he was looking at her, that only she would understand.

She was not all interested in his sexual attraction toward her, and so as to swing his thoughts back around to her desires, she blurted:

"You've got to be crazy…Don't tell me we are back to that again. As badly as I'd do anything to make sure that my children get the truth that they justly deserve, going to bed with you isn't going to be an option of making things easier for me."

Chandlon remained quiet while he opened the door so she could enter his office. Again, she plopped her handbag on his desk and began discussing their plan of action for preparing her twin sons to meeting their father.

CHAPTER NINETEEN

Three months had passed since Marlene had been widowed. Her children have been in counseling and have been recovering surprisingly well. Although Frank was still in mourning, he tried his best in fostering their concerns. However, Marlene showed no real interest in his efforts and it didn't take him long to realize that Marlene preferred if he was out of the picture.

Frank tried respecting Marlene's wishes; but staying away from her was just as devastating as mourning the loss of Barchas. And going by the relationship they've developed, he found it unfathomable that she couldn't care less about his feelings.

So with Frank being kept in the dark and not being able to keep an eye on Marlene, he relied heavily on Allora to keep him abreast of how things were coming along within the household.

Marlene's plight of returning to her life as she knew it was almost futile. She had no idea what it was going to feel like after burying her husband. Yes, while he was at St. Clements and showing no real signs of recovery, Marlene from time to time imagined that she would be able to deal with the loss, should in case her husband didn't make it. She was certain Frank would never let her down and would be her main source of comfort whenever called upon.

However, Marlene soon found out that without being able to see pass her perception, things could change quickly and pitch her hard against the unexpected and the unknown.

She had no idea that after he was gone, she was going to be left with emptiness inside her; an empty space that no other love from a different heart could fill. She never thought about the chill that cramped her bones whenever she's called a widow and not a wife. She had no inkling that after he was gone she would find herself waking up in the middle of the night and start talking to him as if he were still there lying next to her.

And although it never really happened while her husband was alive, everything she touched, tasted, smelled, hated, loved, and dreamed of, reminded her of him. And the more distracted she became with her reflections, was the more she'd find herself crumbling with despair.

<> <>

Carolyn had spent several weeks telephoning Marlene just so she could stay in contact with her and to see how she was doing. But with each attempt, Allora would let her know that Marlene was either sleeping or busy. So finally Carolyn decided to turn up at her doors without any notice.

Marlene could hear the doorbell from upstairs, but she assumed it was Frank stopping by. And she was prepped to tell him that she wasn't feeling well and not up to company. But after she recognized the voice to be Carolyn's, Marlene's thinking cap immediately went off. Surely it was too late to tell Allora what to say to her, to cancel the visit. So without a fighting chance, Marlene slipped out of her pajamas and into something a little more inviting before going down stairs to greet and welcome her stepmother.

"Hi, Aunt Carolyn, I thought I heard your voice."

Allora remained unmoved as Marlene came closer to greet Carolyn. And before Carolyn responded to Marlene's welcome she turned and thanked Allora for letting her inside. However, Allora was more interested in hanging around to be inquisitive. All three ladies stood quietly until Allora finally got the message that she should be on her way. She desperately wanted to get as much information about those two, so she could report back to Frank when he checked in with her later that evening.

Before Allora was completely out of the way, she heard Marlene inviting Carolyn to join her in the living room.

Marlene watched Carolyn slowly lowered herself on the sofa and tried placing one of the cushions against her backside.

Marlene waited as she watched Carolyn twisting for comfort while she spoke:

"Well honey, I'm very sorry for the unannounced visit, but after trying to get a hold of you for so long, and not hearing back, I decided to take the chance and come." Carolyn said as soon as she sat down.

"Well, I thank you for thinking of me, Aunt Carolyn, but I'm doing ok....just a little tired."

"Huh-huh, I quite understand dear. But I'm not going to beat around the bush. I know what you're doing...and what you're doing is okay...but sometimes, you need people to help take the edge off. As you may recall, Marlene, after your father passed away, I was in such turmoil that it took several months before I was able to turn up at the office. And you, of all people know that I couldn't care less if the entire company went under. The only thing I could think about was, if *my husband is never ever coming back, then what is the point?* The built up anger had me wreathing in pain for so long, that I never thought it would change. But had it not been for your grandmother, I don't know if I'd ever be able to work my way through it."

Marlene sat quietly while listening to Carolyn while the tears streamed down her face. And as she tried brushing away her eye waters, she softly asked her stepmother to explain what her grandmother had done.

"Well, she walked into my room late one evening while I was smothered in tears, and she sat at the foot of my bed. She started rubbing my feet and I looked at her and saw nothing short of love and courage. And with my feet still inside her palms, she said, "Larry was my son and I miss him more than words can describe. Sadly for all of us he's gone, but we are still here and life goes on. Carolyn, I did not come inside your bedroom to lecture you on how you should feel, but I sure would like to pray with you and ask the good Lord to see you through this chapter of your life story."

Marlene then chimed in and said: "And I know my grandmother; once she starts praying, not even Jesus can get a word in."

"That is so true....we all know how she loved to pray. But in this case, she only wanted to me repeat the twenty third Psalms. I must confess, Marlene I never felt up to it, but she made me get out of bed and we both fell to our knees and prayed the twenty third Palms. Since then it has become my go to prayer every morning I wake up and every night before I *go to* bed. And in between I prayed and prayed until I was able to pray my way of that dreadful place."

Carolyn eyes welled with tears while she remained peaceful and calm and looking at Marlene. And then she said:

"My dear, Marlene, I am no Gracie Mae, but I'm not going to sit back and allow you throw away the rest of your life on mourning. There's neither victory nor closure from mourning; its value is useless in terms of changing the outcome of our loss. So why should you be dragged down another degree, every day— knowing that you're only going to wake up to the status quo? Please take my advice and start occupying your life with prayer. If you don't know what to say and where to start, do what I did and let the twenty third Psalms become your song, the music to your ears and your longest waltz with life."

Carolyn was quiet sure if Marlene was paying attention to what she had to say, but all that changed after Marlene said:

"I think I'm going to have to find my bible, I think I have one somewhere around the house. It's been such a long time, Aunt Carolyn, since I've read my bible that I think it's easier to go out and buy one."

"You don't have to dear, I brought one for you. Carolyn said to Marlene as she carefully removed the bible from her handbag. Here; this is my gift to you, this in my handbook for spiritual healing."

"Thank you, Aunt Carolyn. I shall cherish this bible it will never leave my nightstand."

After Marlene said that, Carolyn noticed her eyes lit up as if something had come to mind. So after she said nothing, Carolyn said: "What is it dear, it seems as if you have something to say."

"It's nothing really, Aunt Carolyn. I was only reflecting on Grandma Gracie and the many markings in her bible; I was just wondering where it ended up after she passed away.

And without thinking about the consequences, Carolyn quickly replied to Marlene's curiosity about Gracie Mae's bible.

"Oh, honey you don't have worry about that bible; I had given it to your sister, and I'm sure she's still treasuring it"

So, before the words completely rolled off Carolyn's tongue, Marlene eyes and ears lit up.

"You, said what…Aunt Carolyn? Did you say you gave my Grandmother's bible to my sister? I don't understand how you could have done that?

It was at that time Carolyn realized that she had flubbed and her long last and best kept secret was about to unfold.

Carolyn appeared shaken while Marlene looked on and waited for an answer. And while Carolyn waited with bated breath before saying another word, Marlene remained speechless while watching her stepmother struggling for a good comeback.

"Look dear, I've said too much already; that was a slip of the tongue and I should know better not to bring up your sister. I don't know what come over me."

But Aunt Carolyn, this is very important to me and I'm baffled as to how you could have given the bible to Chrissy. How could that have happened knowing that daddy passed away long after she had disappeared… matter-of-factly, three years, at least? So what am I missing here, Aunt Carolyn, could you please explain?

After watching Marlene going through the motions, Carolyn reckoned there was no way she could skirt around the question. And most importantly, she didn't want to jeopardize the new found bond they were starting to build after those many years of silence between them.

Carolyn then turned to Marlene and said:

All right, I'll explain. You deserve to know the truth. And she's been gone for so long; I hardly think it's going to make a difference at this point."

Carolyn had Marlene's full attention and she was starting to look like her old self; it was like she'd forgotten about the doldrums of lying around in her room day after day in tears.

"Go on Aunt Carolyn; you've got me all worked up and I can't wait to hear this" Marlene said.

"Well, after your father and grandmother were gone, I took it upon myself to find your sister. Although she was the one that deserted us without a trace, I felt the need to try and locate her. First of all, I wanted to let her know that her father had passed away, and to turn over the property to her. Of course, it was after you made it clear you wanted to no part of the house.

"Huh-huh" Marlene said calmly but her heart was racing while she kept her eyes on Carolyn.

"Anyway, without knowing what to do and where to start, I met with Barchas and told him about my plans."

Huh-huh" Marlene said while still being engrossed.

"But we soon found out that your sister was nowhere around; and would require a lot more intelligence to locate her. After finding out about the will, I wanted to get her side of the story and most importantly I wanted her to make sure she knew the property was vacant and all hers.

"OK, so what happened….did you really find her?" Marlene said.

"Let me tell you, it was not an easy task, but yes we did after three years of digging.

"Unbelievable! This is unbelievable. You mean to tell me Barchas did all this and never said a word to me?

"Well dear, after finding Chrissy, and did what I needed to do, I walked away and never looked back. It was her wish to stay lost and I promised to honor that. And about Barchas not telling you about it, we agreed that it was best not to apprise you of what I had asked him to do. And that was primarily because of the way you felt about her"

Marlene was starting to appear uncomfortable during her stepmother's reveal; and Carolyn could pick up on the change in her. It was so much so that Carolyn wondered if she was embarrassed about the way she had treated her sister in past which was part of the reason she had distanced herself from the family. However, Carolyn thought it was best not to prolong the conversation on top on what she was going through. And quite frankly Carolyn found no pleasure in rehashing the thirteen years of dirt that basically destroyed the family.

Carolyn then sighed and took a few deep breaths. She appeared tired and worn out from the visit. Marlene asked if she'd like another cup of tea and she gladly accepted. Carolyn looked at her watch and said: "If you don't mind dear, I'm feeling a little hungry and I've got to take my medication. I must go now and we can finish our little talk some other time, if you care to."

Oh, no, no, Aunt Carolyn, please don't leave. I do care, and I would really like to hear more about this.   If you'll excuse me while I go find Allora and get her to fix a quick lunch for you, I'll be right back.

Marlene sprang off the sofa with gusto and swiftly headed to the kitchen to find Allora. And within minutes she was back inside the living room with a cup of tea for Carolyn.

"I'm still in shock, Aunt Carolyn…I can't believe my ears. Marlene said to Carolyn while sitting back down on the sofa.

Carolyn then sipped on the tea and said:

"Well, dear, are you sure you want to go through with this; that was such a long time ago."

And Marlene responded:

To be honest, I no longer carry any ill feelings towards my sister, Aunt Carolyn.   I sometimes wonder about her and kids, and I not ashamed to tell you that I miss my sister a great deal and I love her with all my heart. But with her being gone without a single trace, I reckoned that we both lost out one of life's greatest opportunities.

How so, dear? Carolyn asked and Marlene tried to explain.

"Well, after my near death experience with Barchas, I found myself looking at life differently. And it shouldn't have to take my husband beating me so I could start appreciating the value of family. Anyway, when all was said and done I'd hit rock bottom and I had to rise on my own, eating a lot of humble pies."

Oh dear, I have eaten quite a bit of those too; but that's all part of life, Carolyn said, followed by a slight chuckle.

On that note, Allora entered the room with drinks, sandwiches and sliced fruits on a tray. Marlene quickly pushed aside the crystal centerpiece with flowers that was crowding the coffee table, to make room for the tray.

"Anyway dear as you were saying, Carolyn said to Marlene while picking up a sandwich."

"Oh, Aunt Carolyn, there's so much to say. But to put it all in a nutshell, I have learned the benefit of forgiveness. And if I had only one wish before I die, it would be an opportunity to apologize to my sister, and to beg her forgiveness."

"I'm very proud of you, Marlene. God knows you have come a long way and there's no doubt you'll be able to move on and find happiness again."

"Thank you. So would be so kind and tell me the whereabouts of my sister is, Aunt Carolyn. I often times wonder what her life must be like being single with two kids and limited income.

Carolyn eyes popped, as she was swallowing the last piece of fruit. Marlene thought she was choking on the fruit, but that was not the case. She was only shocked at her remark about Chrissy being poor.

"Well, at the time of my visit, ten years ago, she was doing exceptionally well and I doubt that has changed given the size of her estate" Carolyn said in a cool and calm manner.

"Ok…go on, Aunt Carolyn. You said she's living on an estate.

"Oh, yes I did; and a pretty one too."

"Oh wow, but how did she manage to do that?"

"That's the *million- dollar* question my dear; I have no idea. From what I recall, Barchas had only found out that she was the new owner of the place, but he didn't quite get to the bottom of how that came to be. So after walking away from that visit I'd washed my hands from the whole experience and left it all behind."

Marlene's head swirled with curiosity. She was still vague about the fullness of her sister's lifestyle.

"So where is this place you're referring to," Marlene asked her stepmother.

Oh, by the way, listen to this. I almost forgot to let you know that she had a name change. That was the main reason why it took us three years and three hundred thousand dollars to find her.

"What! A named change; are you sure about this, Aunt Carolyn?"

"Huh-huh and I'm pretty darn sure of it dear."

So what was that all about name change, what is the name of my sister, I knew she was crazy, but God…a name change? I can't believe this.
"Gabriella Fairchild"

Who's that? What do you mean by that?

"That, my dear, is the name of your sister; that name has been etched in my mind for years and I have never repeated to anyone including Brandon.'

"Ok, so now you've got me all riled up Aunt Carolyn. So you are telling me that my sister has moved away, has had a name change so where is this estate that you're telling me about?"

Well, I'm sure you recall the big party your dad and I had put off for her in East Watertown. I can't think of the name right now, but it had the word chateau in it.

Yes, I know exactly what you're talking about, Aunt Carolyn; I was just there a few months ago; it's called Chateau de Mehr.

The shocking news as it rolled off Marlene's lips, had Carolyn floored, speechless and dumbfounded all at once. She gasped and raised her hand to cover her mouth while it every bit of willpower to keep her from passing out.

Soon after, Carolyn was a pale as a ghost.

"What's the matter Aunt Carolyn, are you ok...you look as if your about to pass out." Marlene said showing deep concerns.

Carolyn then removed her hand and told Marlene that it was no biggie. She then removed her pillbox from the handbag and swallowed three tablets with the last drop of tea left in her cup.

Marlene wondered inwardly the reasons for her medication, but with her head spinning with the news about her sister, she said nothing. Her main focus was to get to the bottom of what else she hadn't heard.

However Carolyn made a point of explaining the reason for the three pills.

I should have taken my medication from earlier this morning, but sometimes I forget. She then opened the pillbox to get Marlene's attention:

"This one is for my heart, this is for my blood pressure and this *little guy* is for my memory. I don't think my doctor knows what he's talking about, but he said I have a touch of the Alzheimer's."

"Are you feeling any better, Aunt Carolyn?" Marlene asked her stepmother.

"Oh yes dear… a whole lot better. So where were we?" Carolyn said.

"You'd mentioned something about the Chateau de Mehr, but you didn't finish telling me why you brought it up.

"That's right, and you said something about being there a few months ago."

"Right…I was there with a friend during the New Year festivities and it was a beautiful experience.

"I couldn't agree with you more. Even though my visit was only for a short while, just driving up to the main entrance and casting my eyes to the mountaintop was breathtaking beautiful"

Marlene sensed that Carolyn was not forthcoming and she was at a lost as to where the conversation was headed.

"So, Aunt Carolyn, let's try and get back to my sister…you still haven't told me where she's living. I'm starting to think that you're holding back. In as much as I would love to find my sister you don't have to worry about me showing up at her door step. I promise I wouldn't betray her trust in you."

'Thank you dear, but I think it's already too late; you have already turned up at your sisters doorsteps.   And who knows….I wouldn't be surprised knowing she had seen you.'

Marlene was starting to become impatient with her stepmother's winding and condescending conversations. She wasn't able to make sense of what she was trying to say.

But how could I have turned up at my sister's doorsteps, Aunt Carolyn when I've never been to her house? I just don't understand and I'm so puzzled...you've got to help me out.

All right...I thought by now you would have figured it out, but I guess I should just spit it out.

"Please do, Aunt Carolyn–I just can't take it anymore."

"Well, it goes like this. Your sister, Ms. Gabriella Fairchild is the owner and operator of the Chateau de Mehr. And that's what I meant by saying you were just at her doorsteps a few months ago."

Carolyn stopped speaking and waited for a response from Marlene. But there was dead silence in the room. Marlene's jaw dropped and her shoulders slouched while her eyes rolled and fell into a deep stare across the floor.

Never in her wildest dreams could she ever imagine hearing that her sister was the owner of the Chateau de Mehr. But the thought of her being there with Frank was the most gut wrenching episode of the drama as it played out in her head.

"You're awfully quiet" Carolyn said to Marlene in trying to get her to comeback around.

Say what? What did you say Aunt Carolyn?

"I said you're awfully quiet"

"I heard that, but that's not what I'm talking about, Aunt Carolyn. Did you just say that Chrissy is the owner of Chateau de Mehr?"

"Yes… except that her name is now Gabriella Fairchild….not Chrissy."

Carolyn's manner of speaking was very slow and deliberate, and to Marlene if felt like her stepmother had pushed a knife into her and was slowly turning it with every word she said.

Marlene then rose from the sofa and placed her hands on top of her head as if she was trying to keep it from exploding.   Carolyn sat speechless while looking up at her pacing back and forth saying "Oh my God, how could this be, I sure hope to God she didn't see me there…I couldn't stand the embarrassment of knowing she did."

Carolyn then looked at her watch and quickly rose from the chair.

"Leaving already, Aunt Carolyn?" Marlene asked her stepmother and she responded:

"Yes dear, it was quite a visit and I thoroughly enjoyed it. Thank you for having me, but I must be on my way." Carolyn then turned her eyes to the bible that was left sitting on the lamp table, next to the sofa. She then turned her attention to Marlene and said, "Promise me you will do as I ask. Start praying – the sooner the better."

As soon as Carolyn and her chauffeur drove off her property, Marlene was on the phone calling Frank. It was after three pm and she called his office first, but he was not available. She then called his home but there was no answer. However she left an urgent message on his voicemail.

"Hey, Frank, it's Marlene. I need you to get over here as quickly as possible; something just came up and we've got to talk."

Marlene then walked across the hall to where Barchas' wine stash was located and she poured a tall glass of Merlot without knowing what it tasted like. And while her nerves rattled and her hand shook from being at her wits end, she quickly spat out the very first sip the moment it wet her palate.

"Allora! Allora! Marlene yelled"

Allora came running towards her saying "yes ma'am, I coming."

"Take this glass of wine and put some sugar in it... lots of sugar." Marlene said to Allora, sounding rather crass. However, Allora took her behavior as a good sign that her boss was on the mend. And since burying her husband, that was the longest she had spent out of bed and being up and about her home.

Marlene returned to the living room and plopped herself on the sofa while pulling a throw across her mid section. She took a tiny sip of the wine and placed it next to the bible on the lamp table. From then on, an instant replay of the time spent with Carolyn came rushing back with a surreal effect to it.

"This can't be happening" Marlene kept telling herself. "Aunt Carolyn must be going off her rockers. No wonder her doctor put her on that memory medication" she reckoned. But after long deliberations about Carolyn's story being made up, Marlene decided to it was best to put her assumptions on hold until Frank got there.

Those two, meaning Marlene and Frank, had not seen each other in more than two weeks, and Frank was starting to grow sick and tired of the space Marlene had placed between them. So after he got home later that evening and cleared her message from his answering machine, he was thrilled about the opportunity to spend a little time with her. On his way there he stopped and picked up a huge bunch of flowers for her. And as he tried making up for lost time, Frank sped along with his head swirling with possibilities of what could be making her so panicked. And to him he assumed it could be nothing more than another setback with her contractor and her soon to be complete art studio.

Marlene heard the roaring of an engine pulling up next to her garage and she could tell Frank was on his way in. She walked briskly through the kitchen to meet him. And when she saw him exiting the car with the large bunch of flowers, a beautiful smile came through and it warmed Frank's heart seeing her that way.

"Oh wow, Frank, you are such a charmer; come on in." Marlene said while taking the flowers from Frank to get a whiff of the roses. She carefully placed the flowers on the kitchen counter for Allora to do the rest after she returned from picking up Bethany from the library.

As they walked back to the living room, Frank look at the woman who he had been craving to spend the rest of his life with.

And he said to her

"You look beautiful; that smile you just flashed me back there, transformed you so beautifully that you've got me thinking I may have to buy you a whole flower shop." A slight chuckle ensued between them and Frank was glad he could get another smile out of her.

Then a lull came through and Frank took the lead by asking Marlene "So what's up, your voicemail had me racing to get to you"

"Oh my God, Frank I thought you were never going to ask. Sit down, sit down; I'm about to blow your mind."

"Go on baby, I'm all ears" Frank replied eagerly while looking at her and admiring every inch of her appearance.

About twenty minutes later, or thereabout, Frank was fully updated on all the happenings that had Marlene all fired up about her long lost sister.

Frank was most certainly flabbergasted about what he had learned about Ms. Fairchild. But, the mere thought about the value of the Chateau, and what it would take the average person to acquire it, was mind boggling to say the least. So to make sense of the whole scenario as it unfolded, Frank simply chalked it up as being impossible and that Carolyn was going bonkers.

Frank then said to Marlene:

"Oh wow that is some story. I still don't know what to make of it, Marlene, it all sound so surreal."

Marlene's eyes popped and she threw her hands in the air and said: "My thinking exactly, but there has to be some way for me to find out"

"Huh-huh...But I thought you said you promised Mrs. Tate you weren't going to try and find your sister."

"I know, but its killing me Frank. Quite frankly, Aunt Carolyn's memory is on the decline; I found out she's taking medicine for Alzheimer. But something else is telling me there's an element of truth to what she said; but I'm just not able to figure it out."

"So what would you like to do...I'm on board; you know I'll do anything to keep your mind at ease." Frank said.

Marlene turned and looked at Frank feeling assured that he's got her back.

"Thank you for saying that Frank, it means a lot to me. However I have no idea how to make any sense of this, but I'm sure you do."

Listen sweetheart, just give me a few days, and I'll see what I can do for you. It's as simple as finding out who is the true owner of the Chateau, which, in fact, could be a Ms. Fairchild as you said. The challenging part is finding out if that name really belongs to your sister, Chrissy.

Then Frank's eyes popped and his mouth opened as if an idea was about to fall out.

"What now; and why the peculiar looks about your face" Marlene said.

"Well, I got an idea" Frank said while still being focused on putting this thoughts together.

"OK, so let's hear it" Marlene chimed in.

"Well, why don't I just go back out there and see if your sister is anywhere around. She hardly knew me anyway; I doubt she'd recognize me. Let's face it… nothing Mrs. Tate has told you, so far, is being supported by evidence or fact. So theoretically this is just a shot in the dark."

"Marlene sprung off the sofa and she became livid. Frank watched her eyes widened while throwing her hands in the air with an awkward stance»

"Frank, are you crazy! You can't do that…no, no, no, not happening" Marlene retorted."

Frank was unmoved by Marlene's response. Matter-of-fact he was enjoying that flighty side of her and was glad something else came along to take her mind off Barchas if even short lived.

So Frank said:

"Why, what's wrong with my idea? I think it's the easiest and fastest way to find out if there's any truth to all this. Who knows....maybe she did work there under an assumed name thirteen years ago."

Frank then folded his arms and thrust his back deeper into the sofa with his legs spread apart as if to show Marlene... *case closed.* Silence followed and Marlene reckoned he could be right.

"Well, I guess you know what you're doing, Frank. I shouldn't have to question anything you put your mind to. You're the best... and that's why I lo"

Marlene caught herself and stopped herself immediately from finishing the sentence.

Frank's heart raced with gladness and he couldn't help laughing while looking at her with steadfast eyes and saying "What were you going to say...you need to finish that sentence. I really need to hear it"

By this time Marlene was sitting back on the sofa with her eyes casting to the floor. She felt shy and she realized she was a dead giveaway.... about telling Frank that she loved him.

An unexpected innocence encompassed her face and it pushed Frank into a state of lush erotica. He then painfully rose from the sofa and made two or three steps to where she was sitting. He took her hands and pulled her up closely to him. Marlene said nothing, but she was shaking like a leaf....a feeling that shook her sensuality to the core.

By then she was in his total embrace with his tongue plunged deep inside her mouth. Frank moved his hands from side to side around her buttocks; stroke the back of her neck with his strong... yet soft and long fingers. And with every gentle touch he gave, was the stronger and faster her heart would race.

Frank then pulled himself back to look at Marlene and he saw that her eyes were closed. He then cupped her face inside his palms while staring at her with a heart full of love. Marlene then opened her eyes to look at him but she was too overwhelmed to lend a simple stare. And effortlessly, her eyelids dropped into place while she moaned and groaned from the ecstasy that subdued her.

"He began kissing her again, but this time all around her face, neck and ear. She heard him sigh and she wondered why, but then again, she told herself, it could be nothing less than love.

Seconds later, Frank sighed again and started whispering in her ears. "Marry me Marlene; tell me yes you will. Marry me and let me stay with you forever; tell me yes, my love…say you will be mine"

More caresses and smooches followed.

As Marlene stood speechless from Frank's proposal, passion rained inside her with every stroke and licking he gave across her face. He then fondled her breasts while working his aim towards her nipples that were peaked and full. By then her limbs became weakened and her knees started to buckle. Frank grabbed her with a firm hold and laid her gently down on the sofa; and the raining passion inside her soon came gushing like a severed gum tree.

"Whoa…Oh dear me, Frank I don't know how you do it, but what you did to me was genius," Marlene said while smiling and trying to catch her breath.

Frank was just as breathless as Marlene, but he tried responding to her comment.

"Oh my darling, words cannot describe what I experienced with you. But for now, let's just say you were simply amazing and I'm delirious with joy."

Frank, while still holding Marlene closely to him, rolled away from the sofa and they both landed on the carpet with Marlene lying on top of him. He kept looking inside her eyes until she closed them and started kissing about his face and sucking on his lips. She then whispered, I'd love to be your wife and I want you to stay with me for the rest of my life."

Frank immediately gave a sigh of relief with a "whew" He then hugged her tightly to his chest and thanked her over and over again for the "yes"

"If there was a way for you see how good it feels inside; knowing that I lived to see the day I found a wife…the woman of my dreams, my soul mate and my joy, you'd probably pass out from the view." Frank said.

Marlene giggled and strummed his lips with her tiny fingers and he kissed her again and again.

Anyway, with marriage on both the minds of Marlene and Frank, they promised to keep the news quiet to give Marlene a little time to thaw from the shock of everything that was happening to her all at once.

By the following day, Frank was hot on the trail of finding out more about the "Ms. Fairchild story" Although he wasn't expecting anything positive from the lengthy research, Frank wasted no time in putting a private detective on the case.

However, his theory was as good as obliterated as soon as he showed Marlene pictures of the owner of Chateau de Mehr. Those pictures of course, were taken by his private investigators.

"Jesus Christ, Frank. That is her! That's my sister! This is incredible…I can't believe my eyes!"

That was Marlene's reaction after seeing a few of the photographs. And there were many more for her to look at. And with everyone she saw it sent shock waves up and down her spine.

So while still holding the package of photographs, Marlene asked Frank how he got the pictures so quickly. Frank explained that he had taken her advice by staying away from the Chateau and had hired a private detective to work on his behalf.

"So what do we do now Frank? For starters we know that she works there." Marlene said.

"Not only that, we also know that your sister goes by the name of Ms. Fairchild, which means she could be in fact the owner of the Chateau de Mehr. But let's not get ahead of ourselves here…I'm still working on it." Frank replied.

Frank then looked at Marlene and she appeared confused and stunned while looking over and over at the pictures. She then turned to Frank and said, "Well, maybe I'm the one going off my rocker and not Aunt Carolyn; so far her story is starting to pan out."

Frank then glared at her with a smile and said…just give me another week, honey, and I promise to have it all figured out for you.

It took far more than another week before Frank was able to figure out that Ms. Fairchild was the sole owner of Chateau de Mehr.

Although Frank was able to discover that Shavory Mercantile was the previous owner of the Chateau, which was another mind blowing piece of information for Marlene, finding out how Ms. Fairchild acquired the property after his death was not likely in the forecast. And Marlene was left dissatisfied with the outcome of the investigation.

However as time progressed, Frank was able to piece together that Shavory's mother had lived there with Ms. Fairchild until her death. And according to Frank's theory, where there was no proof of purchase made by Ms. Fairchild, the property was most likely gifted to her for some reason or another.

However, Marlene found Frank's theory to be farfetched. But in the spirit of moving forward with her life as he had suggested, she acquiesced to make peace abide.

So, except for the mysterious news about Ms. Fairchild, Marlene was getting her life back on track with Frank as her crutch. The idea of getting married and completing her art studio was more than enough to stave off her doldrums.

Everything turned out exactly as she had imagined. And except for the old oak tree that Barchas was taken in by, Marlene had the property cleared of all its bushes, leaving herself exposed to the wide open lake. And while standing close to the edge of the lake and staring peacefully at its vastness, she heard a splash and a whoosh; a whoosh that drew a pleasing sound from three fish frolicking in her backyard. So after standing there watching and imagining a bright future and the joy it would bring, Marlene reckoned her first inspiration painting would be "Three fish airborne on a lake."

CHAPTER TWENTY

Meanwhile back at Chateau de Mehr, Ms. Fairchild and her attorney spent weeks in deliberation about her true confession by way of her tell all diaries. And after careful consideration she finally agreed to throw *caution to the wind* and let Chandlon meet with Jax.

So an appointment had been scheduled to meet Jax at his office without him being apprised of what it would entail.

On the morning of the appointment, Jax's looked at his watch with high anxiety because of time constraints. He reckoned he would only have twenty five to thirty minutes to spend on whatever this Lawyer; Mr. Bow's concerns were about. And from then on, he would be spending the rest of his time at the hospital.

Chandlon turned up a little later than expected. He had brought with him Ms. Fairchild's diary and a photo album containing pictures of their sons, Christopher and Christian.

Within minutes, Nyomah, Jax's secretary, came knocking on his door to inform him about Mr. Bow's presence.

"Send him in" Jax said anxiously.

"Good morning, Mr. Bow. Welcome and please…have a seat" Jax said in a fresh and inviting tone.

Chandlon, without knowing what to expect, felt a sudden shift and was eased by Jax's calming presence and cool overture. He quickly extended his arm to meet Jax's that was already out and waiting to be shook.

"Well, good morning, Dr. Wigginton; I most certainly appreciate your kindness, I realize you're a very busy man, and there's hardly any excuse for my tardiness." Chandlon replied:

"Very well my good man. So, tell me…what is the purpose of your visit? Jax asked:

That pointed question from Jax to Chandlon came to him with an unexpected jab to his nerves. By no means had he ever had to deal with anything of this nature, and it never occurred to him that he would be the one in the hot seat.

"Well, sir, as you know, I am an attorney. My practice is in the Eastside of Watertown, and I'm here to represent my client, Ms. Gabriella Fairchild."

That name did not ring a bell to Jax. However he immediately straightened himself in his chair and said "never heard that name before, but go on"

"Yes, I know it would come as a surprise to you, Dr. Wigginton; and rightly so. But Ms. Fairchild was in fact Christina Tate … aka Chrissy. Quite frankly, I was the one who had handled the name change for her thirteen years ago"

All that Chandlon had said so far was mind blowing to Jax, but it was the mere mention of the name "Chrissy," that sent his heart pumping out of whack and he was stunned beyond belief.

"Tell me this is a joke. This can't be happening. Why on God's green earth Chrissy would do such a thing?" Jax responded.

"Well, for various reasons, Dr. Wigginton." Chandlon said.

"I can only imagine…and I can't wait to hear them." Jax responded dryly.

Chandlon's response to Jax was:

Well you see, after she had her babies, things changed very quickly; so quickly, that she had to pack her bags and moved away from Grey Banks without leaving a trace."

When Chandlon mentioned the word babies, Jax experienced deep stress. All along he had felt that the child Chrissy was carrying belonged to him. However, he remained quiet to hear out Chandlon and what else he had to say.

"So, where has she been living and whatever happened to that baby of hers?"

"Well, sir, I'm glad you asked, because that is the main reason why I'm here."

Jax remained quiet and watched while Chandlon removed the photo album his briefcase.

"What I'm about to show you, are pictures of two boys, who Ms. Fairchild claimed you fathered almost fifteen years ago; they will be turning fourteen in a month."

Jax hands shook with anxiety from all aspects of his thoughts as Chandlon released the photo album into his hand. And without having a word to say, he opened the album and began looking.

Newborn photographs were placed on the first page. And Jax spent several seconds in dead silence staring at the pictures as neither of them was speaking.   He then flipped to the second page where the boys were three months old. Then there were pictures of when they were one year old, at which things started to change.

Chandlon sat quietly and motionless with his eyes fixated on every move Jax was making during the slide show, if you will.

Jax's deep dark skin that glows even in the dead of midnight was starting to change right before Chandlon's eyes. He appeared drained and ashy. His jaw line sagged from a long deep sigh that he drew from holding his breath too long; and his forehead crinkled….all making way for the tears he could no longer fight back. By the time Jax was on the last page of the album where the boys were thirteen, he was grossly inflicted and despaired.

"Are you alright Dr. Wigginton? If you'd like I'd be happy to get you a glass of water" Chandlon said while sounding genuinely compassionate.

Jax said nothing, but he acknowledged Chandlon's offer by nodding his head as a sign that he was going to be ok.

Soon after, Jax closed the photo album and returned it to Chandlon. Chandlon wondered what Jax could be thinking while taking back the album and locking it away inside his attaché case. He then looked up at Jax and searched his eyes for answers. Jax lips shook and Chandlon was relieved when the eerie silence was finally broken by Jax's outburst.

"Those are my children, my children!   I have seen enough and I don't need to be convinced in any way, shape or form that those boys are mine. My blood, my eyes, my lips, my ears...god damn it! And, that was my fourteen years of life that was taken away from me undeservingly!"

"I don't know how much she's told you, but let me tell you… I loved that woman with every fiber of my being. And even after she dumped me for that guy…..I can't think of his name right now, my affection towards her had not changed."

"That guy, meaning Shavory Mercantile" Chandlon chimed in to help Jax out in completing his statement. However, Jax was not keen in being reminded of Shavory's name. Frankly, he was more comfortable with referring to Shavory as 'that guy" Anyway he politely accepted the help and continued with spilling his guts.

"So anyway, after I found out that she was pregnant, I had a gut feeling that she was carrying my baby. I begged her, time and time again to give our relationship another chance, but it was too late, man. It was too damn late. This Shavory guy was murdered from which I was ostracized and almost lost my practice…mind you. And I had nothing to do with it!"

And as you may already know, the rest is history. That woman hated my guts. Anyway, as time progressed, I started to believing and accepting that she was right all along when she told me that I wasn't the father of her child. Somehow she's got me fooled; I never saw her as the type that would be sleeping with both of us at the same time."

Jax stopped speaking as if to gather his thoughts and keep them from straying too far into the past. He then threw his hands in the air with fingers spread apart while Chandlon looked on.

"So now what, what is she up to this time. She robbed both my children and I of the best years of our lives. She robbed them of their once in a lifetime opportunity to create their best memories as little boys; they're half way through puberty for god sakes! And pretty soon, I'll be sixty years of age. What the hell was she thinking concealing the truth from me?" Jax yelled.

Jax hands came down slamming the desk in fury as he spoke while Chandlon looked on.

Silence fell and chilled the four corners of the room. Chandlon felt the urge to respond, but after watching Jax's eyes, cocked towards the floor, presence of mind told him that he was still on the hunt for answers. However, his self reflective mode was ineffectual in terms of finding answers.

Jax began shaking his head from side to side and feeling deeply perplexed. He then turned his attention to Chandlon and said:

"Something isn't matching up; this is quite an enigma. So would you be kind enough to tell me what it is that she wants; is it money, or is she in some kind of trouble. What would push her to get an attorney to do something like this?"

Chandlon then lowered his voice even more in his response to Jax: "I can appreciate the question Dr. Wigginton. But as her attorney, I've been handling all her affairs over the past thirteen years. However, had I not been her attorney for those many years I doubt I'd be interested in taking on this task. Quite frankly you've handled the news much better than I had anticipated, and I'll like to thank you for making my job so much easier."

Chandlon then retrieved the diary from his attaché case and while still holding on to it, he said to Jax:

"Well sir, what you've learned from me a little while ago, was just the beginning."

"Is that so?"Jax replied frantically.

"I'm afraid so.   You see Doctor, Chrissy, as you know her, had been dealt some unfavorable hands in the past. And her way of coping and creating life skills has transformed her into the woman she is today. Anyway, throughout her journey, Ms. Fairchild as she's known to by many has documented her life story. I have read it and it is her wish for you to read it. I'm sure you'll find all the answers you're looking for. So, would you be interested in what she has to say?"

Jax became all riled up again saying, "This is getting crazier and crazier as we speak. I know something fishy is going on here, but I just can't put my finger on it. Jax then paused and looked away in disgust. He then turned and looked at Chandlon and in a more subdued tone he said "I guess it wouldn't hurt; what have I got lose?
Chandlon said:

"I agree; that's a very good question. And I can certainly appreciate the way you're looking at it"

Jax said:

Well, if reading this so called memoir of this *Fairchild* person is going to help shed some light on how and when I'll get a chance to meet my children, then of course …I'd definitely be interested in taking a look at it."

Chandlon then handed the diary to Jax and asked him to keep the information confidential so as to protect the welfare of his sons. Jax concurred with a nod and a handshake after which Chandlon picked up his belongings and showed himself out.

That was the first time Jax had ever sat down with anyone and expressed his feelings about Chrissy since their fifteen year break-up. In retrospect, he never thought it could happen given the fact that time had healed his wound….or so he thought. But holding the diary with the anticipation of reading every word, dealt him a throwback as fresh as the last time he'd set eyes on her.

Jax carefully locked away the diary in his desk drawer and tried making up for lost time as he hurried along to the hospital. However, the overwhelming toll from his meeting with Chandlon left him grappling for focus and concentration. So he called and made arrangements for another doctor to cover for him.

Jax returned to his office and retrieved the diary from his desk drawer and he began reading.

CHAPTER TWENTY ONE

Meanwhile back at the Chateau De Mehr, Ms. Fairchild sat waiting on pins and needles to hear from her attorney about the outcome of his meeting with Jax. But soon after she was relieved seeing him turned up so she could exhale.

"Longest day of my life" Ms. Fairchild said to Chandlon as he pulled out a chair to join her at her table.

"Well it's three o'clock, and I'm starving….I should order something before I pass out on you" Chandlon said without paying any attention to the anxiety Ms. Fairchild was experiencing.

"Well, are you going to tell me about your appointment with Jax? Or, are you going to let me suffer and wait until you're done feeding your face? Ms. Fairchild said.

"Well, I've got good news and bad news, my dear. So which would you like first? Chandlon inquired of Ms. Fairchild.

For god sakes, Chandlon…don't put me through this! I want it all…I don't care how you bring it…just start talking, please. You can start with the bad news

"Oh well, that Dr. Jax is quite a man, I like him."

OK, Mr. Attorney, I'm not paying you to like, Jax; I wish if you would get off your high horse and quit all this foolery. This is my life and my children's life you're playing with." Ms. Fairchild retorted.

"OK, all right, Madam Fairchild...I thought you'd know me well enough to tell that you're still in good hands with Jax. It was quite a shock after he found out that I was there to represent you."

"Huh-huh and what happened after you showed him the photos?"

Oh, my God;that tore him up completely. He wept like a baby seeing the boys and he knew first hand they were his; he didn't even flinch about being their father. Matter-of-factly he said the moment he found out that you were pregnant, he had no doubts he was going to be a dad."

"That's true. So what else did he say? I already know that he hates my guts, but that's ok, I deserve it and that would come as no surprise."

Chandlon acted as if he did not hear all the negatives Ms. Fairchild had to say about herself and he responded to her question as he so pleased.

"Well, the man is very anxious to meet his children. And he'd like to know why it has taken so long for you to come forward. That was just one of the umpteen questions he had, but I tried holding back as much as I could."

"Why did you do that?" Ms. Fairchild asked Chandlon with a straight face as if to show him she was disappointed in his response.

Chandlon fired back at her saying:

"For obvious reasons my dear; the whole idea as we discussed is to get Dr. Jax to read your diary. Have you forgotten about that?"

"No, I haven't forgotten about that, Chandlon….how could I? And, how could you be so nonchalant about this. You do know how important this is to me. Anyway in moving forward what was his reaction after you landed him with the news? Ms. Fairchild asked:

"Shocked, upset and quite hopeful he'll find the answers to all his questions. And most importantly he'd like to know how soon he'll get a chance to meet his sons."

"So, you're saying Jax is ok with reading the dairy?" Ms. Fairchild said:

"Yes, Madam… that is what I'm saying" Chandlon replied.

A slight sense of relief came over Ms. Fairchild and Chandlon noticed the difference when she spoke thereafter.

"But it all sounds like it was good news to me Chandlon. So what do you think is going to happen?"

"I think we should just wait and see. It could go either way after he's through reading the diary. Of course I'm just using myself as an example."

"So what's the bad news?"

"I thought you said you wanted the bad news first, Ms. Fairchild"

"Huh-huh, and I'm still waiting;

"All right I guess I'm going to have to repeat myself: that Dr. Jax is quite a man, I like him."

"That's the bad news, seriously?"

"Yep…not very often you'll hear me say I like a guy; especially one that is still in love with you."

Ms. Fairchild heart skipped a beat and she broke out in hives after hearing Chandlon telling her he believed Jax still had feeling for her, let alone being in love. Over the years her heart grew so much fonder of him. But if for nothing…she always hoped for an opportunity to beg his forgiveness to help give her closure from her devious past.

"Oh, wow Chandlon, look at my arms….you gave me Goosebumps; I can't believe my ears."

"You better believe, it my dear; that man is going to die loving you… you take it from me as a man that only wants the best for you."

Ms. Fairchild was overcome with a sigh of relief, confusion, fear and humility all bundled in the one knot around her heart. Tears flowed while she got off her chair to hug Chandlon for a while.

"You are a great guy; I don't know what I'd do without you in my life. I can't thank you enough for putting up with me over all those years. Thank you, thank you, Chandlon, and as you said…we'll just have to wait and see."

"Chandlon kissed her on the cheek and said, "You are going to be just fine.….just continue praying and believing in yourself.

CHAPTER TWENTY TWO

By midnight Jax had completed reading Ms. Fairchild's diary. He was devastated learning the truth about her life both as a child and how it unfolded into womanhood. And after being in a relationship with her for more than three years, it bothered him that she didn't trust him enough to share her past.

In retrospect her sporadic behavior back then, spoke volume to Jax in terms of the premature and acrimonious ending of their relationship. Almost everything she did, Jax reckoned, was done out of fear of losing because she was never able to hold on to anything or anyone she loved.

The loss of her mother, the loss of her first born by way of an abortion after which she lost Shavory to another woman, played a huge impact in her life. And just when she thought her dad had had her "back" in terms of her dead mothers will, along came, Carolyn. And the beautiful life she had been dreaming about was inevitably a nightmare in the making.

Jax spent several hours into the night, picking apart word by word, everything Chrissy had written about their relationship. He realized she had loved him even more than he had imagined, but the fear of it not working out, was what kept her gun-shy about his marriage proposal.

However, be that as it were, Jax also realized that after Shavory showed up in her life after those many years, his presence took her by a pleasant surprise and she fell for it, simply because she wasn't done loving him.

And without any further deliberation, Jax closed the diary and carefully replaced it inside his drawer.

So instead of dwelling from the context of his viewpoint and the painful ordeals he had endured prior to reading her memoir, Jax was able to forgive Chrissy from looking at the makeup of her character and he found no deterrent from the complexities of her personality.

However, the exuberance was far too overwhelming for Jax to withstand. He was about going out of his mind thinking and wondering how soon before he met his sons and fill his eyes with the woman of his dreams.

The morning after…barely six-o-clock, Jax broke his promise about keeping the information private. He could no longer withhold it all to himself so he picked up the telephone and called his son, Kennedy.

Kennedy was by no means unaccustomed to getting phone calls six o-clock in the mornings. But after hearing his dad's voice coming through that early, had him thinking something had gone dreadfully wrong.

"Dad, what's wrong?" Kennedy asked his father while sounding panicky and rushed.

"Calm down, son; your daddy is just fine. I've got a bit of news that I couldn't wait to share with you because it all feels so surreal."

"Oh wow, this must be something huge for you to call me this time of the morning. I don't believe you've even done that before."

"Well, it's something big for me. Guess what?

"I don't know Dad, I can't guess; just tell me what it is."

"Well, you remember, Chrissy?
"Of course I do, Dad. I remember her very well. What about her; don't tell me she's returned back to earth"

After that response from Kennedy, it immediately put a damper on his father's enthusiasm to share the "joyous occasion."

"Well son, since you put it that way, I guess I can go along with it. But what really happened was that I met with her attorney yesterday"

Kennedy immediately drew an indifference towards his father and he wondered if perchance he had missed out on something important.

"OK, Dad, you have got to help me understand what exactly you're trying to say. So, are we talking about Chrissy, that same woman that has caused nothing but trouble while you two were together?'

"Huh-huh, that's her. She's the same one"

"Dad, that was fifteen years ago… do you realize that? And the fact that she arranged to have you speak with some kind of attorney on her behalf…. doesn't that seem strange to you?"

"Yes, Kennedy; but, the thing is, you, don't understand there's so much going on here. If you'll give me a chance to explain, maybe you won't think that your old man has lost his mind. "

"Dad, seriously, and that's why you're calling me at this time of the morning to tell me about a woman that dumped you over fifteen years ago?

"You could say that" Jax replied while sounding rather smug.

Dad, even though I was still a little boy when it happened, I haven't forgotten what she had put you through."

"Look son, I realize that you are upset. But I really would like sharing more about this with you.   I'm off for the most part of the morning, so if you can spare an hour or so, maybe we could meet for breakfast. This is important."

"Well, if you say so dad. So where would you like to meet?"

"I don't care…anywhere….McDonalds. I believe there's one around the corner from your hospital"

"Works for me" Kennedy said while letting his dad hear the skepticism in his voice.

An hour later, Jax and his son Kennedy, were sitting inside the restaurant speaking man to man, each with a cup of coffee before them.

Kennedy was by no means convinced that his father had fathered children with Chrissy. And the fact that she tried contacting him through the help of an attorney, had Kennedy thinking that Chrissy was on the prowl for financial gains.

That whole spiel about Chrissy being Ms. Fairchild and the wealthy owner of "Chateau de Mehr" went over Kennedy's head like a dodged bullet. Quite frankly he simply refused to waste his time thinking about such fallacy.

However, Kennedy tried hearing out the rest of the story while watching his father's face changing from time to time according to how the story was unfolding.   But the animation on his face about being the father of Chrissy's twin sons, had Kennedy reeked with digust.

He then turned to his dad and said:

"Dad, don't you think it's best to wait and see those boys first before buying into all this. I mean….I kind-of understand that you feel this way about her, but she's been gone for fifteen years, Dad. And, she did say, time and time again, you were not the father of her child. Didn't she Dad?

"Yes, son; you're absolutely right about that." Jax said.

"And now, fifteen years later, this woman that you haven't even spoken to as of yet is claiming that you are in fact the father of her children."

"Again, Kennedy I couldn't agree with your reasoning more. But son, there's so much more going on here that apparently I am not able to fully express."

"Come on now dad. You, of all persons are always capable of expressing yourself eloquently. You're just being modest by doubting yourself"

"Your pride in me son, is appreciated.   But I need you to give me some advice regarding response to this matter. It means a lot to me"

Kennedy looked into his dad's eyes and saw how much it meant to him talking about Chrissy. A quick flashback of the good times his father had shared with Chrissy softened his heart enough to wanting to help.

"I don't know what to tell you dad, other than to write her a letter."

"A letter, son, you think a letter is appropriate?"

"I think so, dad. Just go home and write a letter telling her exactly what you feel. Then we'll play it by air and see what happens next."

Jax took his son's advice and returned home with his head full of all the things he'd like to say to Chrissy, but he tried keeping it a minimal.

"Dearest Chrissy,

As I write this letter, I'm still asking myself if this is really happening. Thank you, so much, for putting an end to the turmoil I endured. The mystery surrounding your disappearance has been horrific, to say the least.

After meeting with Mr. Bow and hearing that I am the father of your twin sons, Christian and Christopher, words cannot describe the joy it has brought to my life. I can't wait to meet them and to let them know how much I love them. The mere thought of this gives me the closure I thought I'd never have.

However, I realize it is going to be quite a challenge for you to let them know firsthand that they in fact have a daddy that is alive and well.

Undoubtedly, I am confident you will find a way to break the news to them in such a way that their faith in you will remain unbroken. However, as their father, I'd be honored to help reshaping their lives into becoming successful young men.

I have read your memoir and I was deeply moved by your reveal. Your courage to share your innermost life experiences with me has humbled me in a very special way; thank you.

The raw portrait of your journey left you with a considerable amount of fear and hopelessness. And as I continued turning the pages I clearly identified how you came to be.

Even as a doctor, I must say there's no prescription for human healing without pain, humility and acceptance of failure. It was quite moving on how you've managed to transform yourself by the renewing of your mind. Congratulations!

I'm convinced that you are a changed woman, and my heart goes out to you.

There's so much I'd like to say to you, Chrissy; but in a word "love" conquers all.

Warm regards,
Jax"

So, with the letter off and on its way to Ms. Fairchild, Jax tried to be patient, and life to him thereafter was back to business as usual.

CHAPTER TWENTY THREE

The completion of Marlene's Art Studio was quite a success. But with only a few pieces taken from her home and staged on a few easels inside the studio, she took Frank's advice to postpone the grand opening until after she was able to add a few more pieces to her collection.

Anyway after telling Carolyn about the completion of her project, both she and Brandon were not interested in waiting for grand opening to see what the place looked like.   And she was only too proud to allow coming and taking a look at what she had accomplished.

Carolyn was very pleased with the calm and soothing effect from moving around the quaint studio.   To her it felt like a place of refuge and the perfect sight for sore eyes.   Brandon was blown away by the breathtaking view of the huge lake and immediately, he suggested a boat would be nice to have back there.

After Brandon mentioned the word "boat" it occurred to Marlene that her dead husband's boat was left at the dock and unattended for more than a year.

"Oh, my goodness," she turned to Brandon and said. You are not going to believe this Brandon, but if you didn't mention something

About putting a boat on the lake, I would never have remembered anything about Uncle Barchas boat.

Oh my word, I have got to do something about it. I don't know what to do, quite frankly, Brandon! Marlene complained.

"Well, maybe you should just let it stay there in case Monk and Bethany would like to go sailing sometime." Brandon replied.

Oh, no, not Monk; he hates sailing just like his mother. Bethany…. maybe, but I doubt she'd want to be bothered by that. But, I'll ask her anyway." Marlene said.

So, what about you, Sis? Don't you like sailing?

"Me? Oh, no. I, doubt I've gone out on that thing four times since he'd bought it. Maybe you should take it and make good use of it." Marlene said.

"We'll see, can't have too many boats…I guess. I'll be happy to go with you, sis, to check up on it."

"That sounds like a plan, baby brother. I am free tomorrow if you are"

"Sure thing; so I guess I'll meet you there around noon."

"Oh, no, sis; I'll pick you up, and we'll go together." Brandon said.

Not long after, Brandon and his mother, Carolyn, left the studio while Marlene stayed back adding more adornments to the walls.

Later that night, Frank stopped by Marlene's home on his way from work. Ever since their first sexual encounter, they have been inseparable. And when Frank was not at home with her, she was at home with him.

They were madly in love with each other and could be seen all over town arms in arms.

Marlene could hear Frank's footstep coming upstairs. She was happy to see him walked in.

"Hello my love, I missed you terribly" Frank said to Marlene while walking over to kiss her.

"So how was your day" Marlene said helping him to loosening his tie. She then unbuttoned his shirt and burrowed her face between his pecks with her eyes closed."

"Don't remember how my day went, but my evening is going pretty darn good, Frank replied."

"Hmmm…honey you smell so good, even after a hard day's work." Marlene said.

She then sighed and kissed him gently followed by saying, "It's so nice having you coming home to me.

Later, they went downstairs and shared a glass of wine and chit chatted for while until she finally came around to telling Frank that she and Brandon had made plans for doing something about Barchas' boat that had been left unattended at the Dry Dock Marine for almost two years.

Although she trusted Brandon's input wholeheartedly, Marlene would have been more comfortable having Frank with her at the dock. However due his heavy work load, Frank apologized for not being able to make the trip with them.

By noontime the next day, Brandon and Marlene were on their way to check on the boat. During the same timeframe, Frank, while being at work recalled a few conversations with Barchas where he had mentioned being out on the water with Lexa.

Frank panicked from assuming Marlene could run into a few surprises while inspecting the boat.

And if his gut feeling served him right, Frank imagined Marlene would assume that as her husband's best friend, he was most likely aware of his affair with Lexa or some other woman to say the least.

If that exposé ever did happen, Frank reckoned his relationship with Marlene could suffer a tremendous blow; let alone their plans on getting married.   Given her personality and her fragility Frank was convinced Marlene would have lost faith in him forever.

And while his mind was racing about losing Marlene, Frank dropped everything at the office and decided to take the trip to meet up with Brandon and Marlene where the yacht was docked.

Frank tried calling Marlene on her car phone to let her know he was on his way to join her, but it was too late. By the time he arrived at "Naked Rock" which was the name of the dock site, Marlene and Brandon could be seen walking back to their car. He tried honking his horn to get their attention. Brandon turned and looked into the direction of honking horn and recognized Frank's car. He waved at Frank and immediately he apprised his sister of the surprise visit.

Brandon was relieved seeing Frank turned up. He welcomed the idea of having someone else other than himself to help calm her down from the shock of finding a weekend bag filled with toiletries, handcuffs, thongs, stilettos and several pairs of colorful stockings.

"What are you doing out here?" Marlene asked Frank. Her attitude and tone along with the question, had Frank thinking it was a foregone conclusion his worst nightmare was about to blow up in his face.

However, he showed no sign of insecurity as he approached her with a kiss.

Much to his surprise, Frank expected a cold shoulder from Marlene when he tried kissing her on the lips. But she received him quite well as if she was glad he came.

'Why the long face my darling; you don't sound too thrilled about coming out to Naked Rock" Frank replied.

"I'm sorry, I didn't mean to be rude, but I just got the biggest shock of my life." Marlene said.

"Oh, honey, no offense taken. But what could be making you so upset?" Frank asked.

"Never mind, I'm too embarrassed to talk about it. Frank."

"Well, has it got anything to do with me?" Frank asked Marlene with a racing heart.

"You… I don't think so. Well I'd hope not" Marlene said.

"Come on honey, you have got to do better than this. What do you mean by saying you'd hope that I had nothing to do with it?"

"Marlene refused to answer Frank's question, so he turned to Brandon and said "Do you know anything about this, Brandon; I can see something is really making her mad."

"That, she is. But I'm sure she'll explain once she's gotten the chance to calm down." Brandon said, after which Marlene chimed in.

"Well, if you must know Frank, I discovered some horrible things about my dead husband. I do not wish to speak about it right now, as I need some time to think."

Frank appeared shocked at what Marlene said, but that shock was just an act of innocence to help keep him out of harm's way.

"Oh wow" Frank replied while staring at Marlene with his eyes widened. "I can hardly wait to hear what this is all about."

Frank noticed that Brandon was becoming more and more uncomfortable with the situation, and he presumed it would help feel a lot better being let go. He then turned to Brandon and offered to take Marlene back home.   And Brandon was very relieved to turn over his sister to Frank.

"So what brought you by; I thought you said your work load would not allow you to come out with me to Naked Rock" Marlene said to Frank as they drove off the parking lot.

"Yes, I know honey, but after getting into the office, I realized I could have made the time for you. So I tried calling on your car phone to let you know that I had changed my mind, but of course you were already gone with Brandon."

"Well, that was very nice of you" Marlene turned to Frank and said with an about face which gave Frank a boost of confidence.

"Well, you look a lot better now, honey. You had me thinking that you were upset about seeing me turned up at the dock." Frank said.

"Oh, for goodness sakes, Frank; I don't believe I'd live to see the day when I don't want to see you turn up in my life; I love you." Marlene said.

"I know you do honey, and I feel the same way about you. But when you are upset and I'm not able to help, it puts me in an uncomfortable position."

"All right, I know you're dying to find out what was making me so mad. But the more I think about it is the more I realize there's no point in bringing that mess into our relationship…I just want to leave the past in the past. I've been through enough already, and it's my turn to be happy. "

Frank was taken aback by Marlene's response. Deep down he knew what she was alluding to, and much to his relief, he felt no need to press her on it. Matter-of-factly he found another level of respect towards the woman she had become, and he was even more grateful having her being madly in love with him.

Frank then turned and looked at Marlene while saying:

"As you wish, my darling; anything you want is my command."

<><>

Frank had been pushing for a an early wedding date, but Marlene thought rushing it would not allow enough time to give her the kind of wedding day she was dreaming of. Frank however, was of the opinion that if they hired enough people in the business, there was nothing to prevent them from tying the knot much sooner.

Frank was by no means as well off as Barchas, and that was because of the head start he had acquired simply from being Marlene's husband. Added to that, after Larry Tate's death, Carolyn had paid off Barchas quite handsomely for keeping his mouth shut about their investigation in finding Ms. Fairchild.

Anyway…having said that… Frank was not at all strapped for cash. He was financially stable enough to provide his "soon to be wife" with the same lavish lifestyle she had been accustomed to. And without knowing how long before she would have liked to set their wedding date, Frank had forged ahead with purchasing a ring for Marlene.

Anyway after much back and forth, they finally agreed to a mid fall wedding, on a Sunday, sometime in October.

Weeks later,   the invitations were out… all sixty five of them; except the one for Carolyn Tate, which was hand delivered by Marlene. As soon as Carolyn found out about the wedding, she made it clear she wanted to foot the bill, but Frank graciously denied the offer. He made it clear to Marlene that he preferred to be solely responsible for their "big day"

CHAPTER TWENTY FOUR

At last the wait was over! The letter Jax had sent to Ms. Fairchild had finally arrived and she was quite confounded after receiving it. Holding the letter in her hands sent her heart racing with suspicions of "bad news."

The letter left Ms. Fairchild simply stunned and at a loss for words, after reading it. She had presumed that after Jax was through reading her memoir, he would've diagnosed her as a mentally deranged woman who could not be trusted. She reckoned he would be thanking his lucky stars she'd dumped him before it was too late.

But after reading the letter time and time again, it was her thanking her lucky stars that Jax was able to see the *rainbow beyond her clouds.*

She immediately called Chandlon to inform him about the good news and to get his advice about taking the next steps with regards to her greatest fear that was still waiting to be addressed.

Her first thought was to have Chandlon present whenever she found the courage to let her sons know the truth about their father.

"You are not going to believe what just happened" Ms Fairchild said to Chandlon as soon as he picked up the phone.

"You sound rushed; tell me what just happened" Chandlon replied. "I just received a letter from Jax and I'd like to read it to you"

Chandlon was very surprised hearing that Jax had contacted Ms. Fairchild without going through him first. However, he tried to keep an open mind.

"Well, I'll be damned; I thought he'd be contacting me first. I guess he couldn't wait to tell you what's on his mind." Chandlon said and then he chuckled.

"I guess you're right, but I really would like to start reading this letter" Ms. Fairchild said with eagerness in her voice.

"Go on; I'm all ears" Chandlon said.

As soon as Ms. Fairchild got through reading the letter to Chandlon, she asked his opinion.

And Chandlon's response was:

"Well, I'm not very surprised that he'd respond that way; Gabriella. Quite frankly the guy is truly remarkable.....I told you that already. And as he clearly articulated in that letter he's ready and willing to help you break the news to the boys."

"So what do you think we should do at this point, Chandlon? I'm really scared about approaching the boys with news; this is no small thing for me as you know." Ms. Fairchild replied.

Chandlon said:

"Yes, I understand. This is huge and we have to be very careful about making the right approach. They are at an age where things could go either way"

"What do you mean by that, Chandlon? You're making me even more scared with that remark."Ms. Fairchild said grimly.

Chandlon said:

"Look Gabby, we've got to be realistic here. And before we start mapping out our strategy, we have to prepare ourselves for the worse."

"So what do you mean by that; what do presume the worse could be?" Ms. Fairchild asked Chandlon in a sharp tone.

Chandlon said:

"Well, I mean the easy way out is to assume the boys would understand what you were going through at the time when you made the decision to deceive their father. And once they've gotten over the shock of it, it would be great if they could find it in their hearts to forgive you. However, the worst case scenario is they could flip out on you and things could go haywire."

Ms. Fairchild, while clearing her throat before responding to Chandlon, said:

"That thought has never left my mind, Chandlon; but I owe it to my sons to let them know the truth…come hell or high water. I pray every day for God's guidance through this. But, you know…. sometimes it's so hard to stay focus on "faith" under such duress.

"Well you can't stop praying now, Gabriella, especially when we are so close to coming out with the truth. And the more I think about it, is the more I know I can only help you from a distance. I hate to come off sounding harsh, but I'm definitely not the right person for the job; I'm a lawyer. I think you should be seeking council from a psychologist"

So what are you trying to say Chandlon? Are you backing out on me? Because if you are, I don't know what the hell I'm going to do; I need you now more than ever" She retorted.

Chandlon easily picked up on the panic and frustration is Ms. Fairchild's voice, especially in her last few words. Added to that, her open candor left him feeling uptight with empathy towards her. However, the more he thought about it, was the more he realized her situation was more than he could handle, but as her friend, he was prepared to keep forging ahead in spite of his limitation.

So in his response, Chandlon said to Ms. Fairchild:

"Gabby, let's not get ahead of ourselves here. I understand your fears but I need some time to think this through. There's no quick fix to this thing; we're talking about two little boys who could be damaged for the rest of their lives. And as I've suggested, I really think you should be getting help from a psychologist on how to approach this matter."

And Ms. Fairchild replied:

"OK, Chandlon, you're right I shouldn't be so demanding; but my nerves are spiraling out of control."

Deep sighs followed as if she was trying to catch her breath while thinking of what next to say.

"Anyway, let's say I'm going along with your suggestion about seeking outside help for the boys, do you know of anyone I may be interested in seeing?" Ms. Fairchild asked Chandlon.

"I might. But let me think about it some more and I'll get back with you on that tomorrow. I'll check with the medical complex next door to my office. I heard they have a great team of medical professionals working out of there." Chandlon said.

"...Sounds good to me." Ms. Fairchild said, and their phone conversation was completed at that point.

Ms. Fairchild and her attorney completed their phone conversation in hopes of a better tomorrow.

Anyway, unbeknownst to Chandlon and Ms. Fairchild, their phone conversation had a third party listener. And what they thought would remain their secret was no longer going to be the case.

Dorchas, Ms. Fairchild's housekeeper, spent the entire fifteen minutes eavesdropping on their conversation. And as soon as they were done speaking, Dorchas quickly hung up and raced to her bed room in utter shock. She suffered deep distress from learning that the woman who she had grown to love and adore had deceived her children since birth. She tried long and hard to make sense of what could have pushed her into doing something so horrific, but nothing could change her mind about her stance.

So without hearing the full story about Ms. Fairchild, Dorchas threw herself across her bed deep in thought:

"Oh, my God, this is unbelievable! How could she do such a thing to her children? After they found out their mother is liar, I'm sure they're going to hate her for the rest of her life, and she deserves it. And to think what she did to poor Miss Chey, she must be rolling over in her grave. That poor woman died thinking her so called daughter was a saint; far from it! That witch had me fooled but she won't get away with it. You just wait and see."

Ms. Fairchild left the privacy of her bedroom and went to kitchen to get a drink. She looked around and noticed Dorchas was not around. But as usual she assumed she was taking a break in her bedroom watching her favorite soap opera. And while sitting at the table in the breakfast nook, she saw her daughter Chateau walked in.

"Hi Mom" Chateau said while smiling at her mom and dropping her book bag to the floor so she could go over and kiss her mother."

"Hi princess, Ms. Fairchild said while pushing her face forward and pouting her lips to receive the tender kiss from her little girl."

"Come on sit on my lap and tell mommy all about school."

"Mom, I'm too big to sit on your lap….I'm nine."

"You are never too old to sit on my lap, Chateau. C'mon put your little butt here and tell me all about school."

Ms. Fairchild spent a few minutes chit chatting with her daughter and was thankful she was not a part of the pending quagmire that could destroy her and the entire family. Chateau was fully aware that she was an adoptee but she never felt indifferent around her siblings; they were inseparable.

Anyway, moments later, while Chateau and Ms. Fairchild were still spending time together, they heard Christian and Christopher walked in.

Hi Mom, Christian said: while dropping his book bag on the floor and approached her with pouting lips….a kiss followed with his mother saying "muah."

"Hi Mom" Christopher said, while dropping his book bag on the floor and approached her with pouting lips… a kiss followed with his mother saying "muah."

And with a little peck on the cheek from her twins, her stomach churned with fear. However she did her best to keep things looking normal by saying:

"Now boys, how many times do I and Dorchas have to tell you not to leave your book bags on the floor? C'mon boys, pick those up and put them away; and get your sister's as well."

Christopher the feisty one, immediately turned to his mother and said "Why does she always get away with everything; why can't she get her bag herself?"

Little Chateau jumped off her mother's lap and responded to Christopher while pointing to herself braggingly, and she said to him "Because I am a princess!"

Deep within Ms. Fairchild reckoned Christopher was the one to watch…he would be first to turn against her and most likely unforgiving. She watched her boys walked away with their book bags while Chateau followed behind them. And while alone still sitting at the table, she reflected on the phone conversation with Chandlon.

The fear of losing her children deepened and she began contemplating the idea that she should be first in seeking the help of a psychologist.

Later on, Dorchas emerged from her bedroom. She entered the kitchen looking sad and not her usual cheerful self.

Ms. Fairchild tried brushing her feelings aside to address the looks on Dorchas:

"Why the long face; your soap opera didn't end well again?"

"Couldn't be better, Ma'am; It was really interesting. I can't wait to see what's going to happen to Jack tomorrow.

Ms. Fairchild wasn't convinced that all was well with Dorchas, because her tone was dry and her body language was peculiar. Anyway, Ms. Fairchild chose not to dwell on Dorchas because she had a lot more important things to be concerned with.

She then left the kitchen and went upstairs to check on her children and to spend some quality time with them.

By the following day, Chandlon went by the Chateau to check upon Ms. Fairchild. Their last phone conversation left him pitying her from what he had perceived "a looming disaster" So he reckoned stopping by to have lunch with her and to chit chat about whatever came to mind would somewhat lighten her load.

She had barely touched the chicken salad but the diet cola was down to half. She gently pushed the flan across the table because she noticed Chandlon had been eyeing it since he cleaned up everything that was on his plate.

The intensity of her gaze seemed arresting with her head tilted towards the floor. Chandlon, while enjoying what he considered was the perfect ending to his lunch, turned his attention to her and said "penny for your thoughts, Gabriella; I can see you are way out there."

"You can say that again; I hardly got any sleep last night, but it was worth it." Miss Fairchild responded.

"I didn't think you would, but what were you doing up all night… reading that letter from Jax over and over again."

"No Chandlon, I spent the entire night praying and begging the Good Lord for grace and mercy through this new phase of my life."

"Well, I thought I'd stop by to let you know I followed through with helping to find a therapist for the boys, and I did find one."

Ms. Fairchild was pleasantly uplifted with Chandlon's answer and she smiled at him while saying:

"Well that was fast, Chandlon; I'm impressed.   So… tell me more. Is he someone from around these parts?"

"Well, actually it's a female, and her name is Dr. Aneecia Fleur. I'm told she's quite good and she's not too far away; she's in the complex close to my office."

"Fleur; what is she…French? Miss Fairchild asked Chandlon with her body bracing backwards and her chest puffed up with widened eyes.

"I don't know, Gabriella, but if it matters to you, I could find out. Chandlon fired back at Ms. Fairchild while thinking she was being petty.

"…Didn't mean to ruffle your feathers, Mr. Bow. …not that it mattered, I was just curious." Ms. Fairchild replied while Chandlon watched her normal composure came back into view.

So a week later without Ms. Fairchild knowing what to expect, she found herself sitting face to face with Dr. Aneecia Fleur and talking about her fears and her cares.

Dr. Fleur was in fact a French woman who was raised in England by adoptive parents. However, with her lineage tracing back to Haiti, she was never successful in her attempts with making connection with her bloodline.

The therapy sessions with Dr. Fleur and Ms. Fairchild continued for a month. She had started to see progress in Ms. Fairchild and she thought it was time for her to bring in the children including her daughter Chateau.

However, Ms. Fairchild's progress began backsliding in the presence of her children. And Dr. Fleur had to quickly split the sessions between mother and children.

By the time another month came to pass, Dr. Fleur and Ms. Fairchild found themselves developing a friendship outside of their professional relationship. Both ladies did not have many friends, but from the onset of their meeting something special clicked between them.

Anyway in keeping with their objectives, Dr. Fleur experienced great challenges in maintaining peace and harmony inside Ms. Fairchild's home. It was at that pivotal time when the boys were coming to the realization that they in fact were not fatherless, and that their father's name was Dr. Jaxon Wigginton and not Shavory Mercantile as they were raised to believe.

Dr. Fleur in some small way was able to keep them stabilized from the shock of the news. And their anticipation of meeting their real father was making great progress.

However, the whole dynamic surrounding the wellbeing of the boys took a drastic turn after they realized their Grandma Chey was neither their grandmother nor a relative in any way. This revelation took place one evening after they came home from therapy with Dr. Fleur.

In fact, before the boys left that evening Dr. Fleur had picked up a deeper level of resentment the boys had displayed towards their mother. But having said that, she wasn't that fazed by their reaction because she reckoned she would take care of that in a timely manner.

However their love for their so called "grandmother" ran much deeper than their therapist had assumed. And after the boys spoke amongst themselves while putting *two and two together*, it was clear their grandmother died without ever knowing the truth about their relationship. And this reveal unfolded, grew their anger to an unspeakable dimension.

So before going to bed that night, the twins decided to take matters into their own hands by running away from home as soon as they figured out a way to make it happen.

The next morning the twins emptied their piggy banks and dumped the monies inside their book bags. And one morning after their chauffeur dropped them off at school; they skipped classes and boarded a bus en-route to West Watertown, where they were told their father resided.

Two hours later, the bus made a "pit stop" and like majority of the passengers, the boys got off to relieve themselves. Another couple of hours later, the bus had come to its final destination where everyone came off but the twins.

The bus conductor who had been eyeing them since they came onboard, went over and said "This is it young man, you're at the last stop in West Watertown."

Christopher immediately looked at Christian as if to say "What do we do now" But Christian only looked back at his brother as if to say "What do want me to say"

The boys appeared dumbstruck while staring at the conductor as they searched for an answer.

"Come on, Christopher; let's go" Christian said to his brother with a courageous tone to his response.

So with their book bags in tow, they upped and began walking towards the exit door of the bus.

The bus conductor immediately assumed the boys could be runaways. He immediately approached the bus driver with his suspicions.

"Hold on a minute there young man" The bus driver said to Christian and Christopher as they attempted to walk off the bus.

They stopped and looked at both men without a verbal response, but their body language showed they were frightful.

"Where are you two heading; do you live in these parts?" The bus driver asked.

Christopher immediately looked at Christian, while he kept his eyes fixated on the bus driver.

"Yes sir, we live in these parts" Christian replied.

"Whereabouts?" the bus driver asked.

"In these parts, sir" Christian responded.

"Hmmm" said the bus driver while scratching his head and thinking what to do next; he was convinced they were runaways.

"Come on, Christopher, let's go" Christian said while they proceeded to get off the bus.

The bus driver, while straightening his cap on his head and staring down at Christian, said

"Not so fast, young man; you aren't going anywhere until you tell me how you two plan to get home from here."

Neither of the boys responded and a brief pause followed his inquisition. A fearless look from Christian filled the bus driver's eyes and he immediately switched his focus to Christopher while saying "Well, why don't you tell me where you live, since your brother doesn't seem to know."

And without skipping a beat, Christopher blurted out to the bus driver:

"Chateau de Mehr, sir, is where we live."

"Shut up, Christopher!" Christian blurted to his brother.

"Don't tell me to shut up! You shut up!" Christopher fired back at his brother while the bus driver looked on.

The bus driver appeared puzzled by the name 'Chateau de Mehr'. He turned his head away and he tried searching his thoughts to see if that name ring a bell, but he only drew a blank.

And while Christian looked on in shock about his brother's telling, the bus driver said to Christopher:

"So, tell me young man; tell me a little bit more about this place called Chateau de Mehr, because I've never heard that name before. Or, is this some imaginary place you're talking about?"

Christopher noticed the impatience on the face of the bus driver while his brows knitted and his cheeks reddened.

"No Sir; it's not an imaginary name… its back East. But me and my brother only came out here to spend the weekend with our dad. And he's coming to pick us up" Christopher replied.

The bus driver was immediately taken aback by Christopher's response. His tone, paired with his humble disposition, left the driver believing every word.   So, he patted the boys on their shoulders and said: "OK boys, run along… you don't want to keep your dad waiting."

As the boys walked away, they kept looking over their shoulders to make sure they were not being followed by the driver. And even long after they have cleared the area, their minds were still clouded with paranoia.

Soon after, the boys were in the heart of downtown with a much better sense of security. And as they walked along the busy streets, they came upon a small café where they stopped for hamburgers and cola.

<>< >

So while the twins were at the café enjoying their meal, their mother was back at home deep in turbulent times.

It was nearing nightfall and many, many hours since Christopher and Christian were gone missing.   Miss Fairchild immediately called

Chandlon and Dr. Fleur to inform them of the news and shortly after they turned up at the Chateau to show support.   And with the advice of Dr. Fleur, Ms. Fairchild agreed to call the police.

However, without knowing the extent of her sons' animosity towards her, Ms. Fairchild was at a disadvantage in terms of giving the police any information leading up to their disappearance. So with not much to go on, Ms. Fairchild agreed to let the two police officers search their bedrooms.

Everything appeared neat and in order as the policemen walked around the bedroom. They looked under the beds and inside the closets. They shuffled things around and inside their chest of drawers and found nothing out of the ordinary. Then the piggy bank finally caught the attention of one of the officers, because it was left lying on its side.   The officer immediately picked it up and found no reason to shake it because he also noticed it was opened and empty.

Ms. Fairchild was immediately taken by surprise seeing the policeman holding the empty piggybank.

"This thing was full; both of them! As a matter of fact, less than a week ago I'd stuffed them with more money.

And while she reeled with confusion the officer looked around some more until they found the other piggy bank in the laundry basket… penniless.

"I'm speechless; I don't know what to say. There has to be an explanation for this. Are you guys thinking what I'm thinking?" Ms. Fairchild turned to Chandlon and Dr. Fleur and said.

Dr. Fleur responded immediately and said "Now Gabriella, let's not think the worse here; I know they have never done this before, but maybe they goofed off with their friends and are just out having fun."

Chandlon looked at Dr. Fleur and found her speculation farfetched.

"That could be the case, and I hope to God you're right" Chandlon said, while he was thinking the boys had run away from home.

The policemen then came over to Ms. Fairchild and asked her to give a brief description of what the boys were wearing.

The dreadful sounding request from the officers sent her heart racing uncontrollably. Her lips shook with trying to respond to their requirements.

Chandlon saw the distress that was taking over her already shaken composure and he tried helping out by pointing the officers to the boys' pictures hanging on a wall inside their bedroom.

The officers then turned their attention to Ms. Fairchild for a response.

"Blue blazer, khaki pants and brown shoes." She replied.

"Other than their attire, is there anything specific about them that you'd like us to know, Ms. Fairchild" Asked one of the officers.

"No sir, other than they're about five-five in height."

Ms. Fairchild then asked:

"What do you think officer? Do you think they were kidnapped?"

All, including Dr. Fleur and Chandlon looked at her in surprise about her question, but they remained quiet.

And with a raised eyebrow one of the officers turned and said:

"What behooves you think your sons may have been abducted Ms. Fairchild?" Is there something you're not telling us?"

"Oh, no-no; I'm just scared, that's all…I honestly don't know why I said that" Ms. Fairchild replied.

However, her response to the officers left them a sinking feeling there could be more to her story.

So one of the officers tried to see what else he could get out of her.

"Are you sure about this, Ms. Fairchild? And what about their father; is he around?"

Chandlon immediately looked at her as well as Dr. Fleur and they waited with bated breath to hear what her response was going to be.

And with tearful eyes, she looked at the officers and said:

"Father; what father are you talking about? Their father is dead, sir. He died long before they were born. All I ask of you is to please help me find my sons"

"Oh, well I'm sorry to hear that ma'am. Anyway there isn't much left back here for us to do so we must be on our way.

"So what's the next move, officer? Chandlon asked

"Well, with this report, my department will be moving as quickly as possible to issue a bulletin regarding the disappearance of Christopher and Christian Mercantile. We do have their photographs here and you can rest assure we are doing the best we can to bring your sons back home."

As soon as the policemen were out of range, Ms. Fairchild turned to Chandlon and Dr. Fleur saying:

"Look guys, I'm sorry, but I couldn't tell those cops that Jax is the father of my boys. The first thing they would want to do is drag him into all this confusion and make matters worse for all of us."

"No need to apologize, Gabriella; I clearly understand your plight." Dr. Fleur said in trying to comfort her as they walked away deep in fear about the safety of the boys.

As soon as they were downstairs, Dorchas and Chateau could be seen sitting on the sofa waiting anxiously to hear what was going on. Chateau immediately ran to her mother's side while saying "mommy, I scared"

Then as they all sat around and waited for their prayers to be answered; Ms. Fairchild got an idea.

She turned to Chandlon and asked what he thought about her calling Jax to inform him of what was taking place, but Chandlon was stumped by her question.

"I really don't know what you tell you, Gabriella; I think you should be asking Dr. Fleur for advice in this case." Chandlon then took a deep sigh, shrugged his shoulders and then he continued speaking. "Oh wow…this is huge. It's been so many years…at least fifteen that you too haven't communicated, not to mention you haven't yet responded to his letter. Quite frankly Gabriella, I wouldn't be surprised he's wondering if you even got his letter."

As soon as Chandlon ended his comment, Ms. Fairchild immediately turned her attention Dr. Fleur for answers.

"It may not be such a bad idea to give him a heads up now that he's fully aware that he's their father. However it could be a bit premature trying to involve him in something we aren't sure about. So why don't we give it a little more time should in case the boys are out, just playing hooky"

Ms. Fairchild found no comfort in what Dr. Fleur and Chandlon had to say.

"So what am I suppose to do; just sit here with my hands folded in my lap and do nothing? What if my children were abducted?

"Abducted; you said the same thing to the policemen earlier on, Gabriella. What made you think that could be the case, and who do you think would do such a thing? Chandlon said.

"Who else, guys? What if Jax is behind this?

"You can't be serious, Gabriella; I think you're way off" Chandlon said.

"Well, I'm sorry… but it's the only thing that makes sense to me." Ms. Chandlon said.

Then all of a sudden, all eyes turned to Dorchas while she sat at the kitchen table and chimed in her unsolicited opinion.

"Ms. G, I have a feeling de boys dem run-way; dats what I tink, Miss G."

"Whatever gave you that idea, Dorchas? What did they say to you? Ms. Fairchild asked Dorchas with much urgency in her voice.

And Dorchas said:

"They really didn't seh anyting to me, you know ma'am. But I ova-heard dem saying someting about finding dere dad"

"Oh, really, and when was this? Ms. Fairchild asked her while the others looked on.

"Just the odder, ma'am while they were at the dinner table."

"And why didn't you say something to me, Dorchas, didn't you think it was important to let me know this?"

"No Miss G. I didn't tink it was important because I know dat dem fauder dead. So what's the pint baddering you head bout a dead man?"

Dorchas' tone to Ms. Fairchild felt as if she was being ridiculed for being a liar. But she quickly chalked it up to her guilty conscience; because she had no idea Dorchas was aware of the truth.

"So, what else did you hear them say, Dorchas?" Ms. Fairchild asked Dorchas.

"Just dat, ma'am…nottin else." Dorchas replied.

Dorchas' intervention left the atmosphere in the room with a cold and exacerbating feel to it. However, Chandlon and Dr. Fleur were able to draw a sense of relief after listening to her spelling it out to Ms. Fairchild for them.

So without giving Ms. Fairchild too much time to think about what Dorchas had to say, Chandlon immediately chimed in to say:

"Well we don't know if that's the case, but let's just assume that her theory is right. I think we should call the police and apprise them of this information. I think it would help in getting the boys back home much sooner."

Ms. Fairchild's heart trembled with disappointed and anger towards herself for the outcome of her sons' disappearance.

"I think they hate me, Chandlon; I think they're never coming back. Look what I've done to my children…..they are ruined for life."

Dr. Fleur then turned to Ms. Fairchild saying:

"Oh, Gabriella, I know it's hard, but let's trying focusing on bringing the boys home as Chandlon suggested. Once they're home and safe we can get to the bottom of things later on."

Ms. Fairchild then leaned herself forward with her face almost touching her lap and she began crying while Chandlon moved to making the call to the police.

CHAPTER TWENTY FIVE

Meanwhile, back West in the city of Watertown, Christopher and Christian had left the street side café and have been wandering around town aimlessly. Christopher started complaining about being tired and looked to his brother for advice as regarding the next plan of action.

Christian ignored his brother's complaint but he was quick in reminding him brother about what Dr. Fleur had told them about their father, that he's a doctor working at a hospital there.

"Uh-huh, I haven't forgotten. I remember everything she said; and Mom too. I don't think I ever want to see my mother again; I think she's a witch." Christopher said.

"I feel the same way brother; I hate her. How could she do this to us?" Christian responded.

As the boys wandered along Brock Street, Christian looked up and noticed a hospital sign a few blocks over, when a light bulb went off in his head.

"Hey Christopher, look at that hospital sign over there. That could be the hospital where our dad works. Why don't we go over there and see if we could find him."

"But we don't know him, Christian. And he may think we are bad boys for running away from home." Christopher replied shyly.

"But I thought that was why we came out here in the beginning; it was your idea at first." Christian said to his brother with a feeling of being let down.

A feeling of guilt came over Christopher after his brother's response and he quickly regained some courage, going forward.

"Okay Christian, let's do it. But first let's make a plan about what we should say to him before we go inside there." Christopher replied.

"Okay, so what do you think we should say?" Christian asked his brother.

"I don't know, let's just think of something." Christopher said.

"Yeah, I think that's a good idea, brother. Let's do it" Christian replied sounding all pumped up and ready to go.

As nightfall set- in, Christopher and Christian entered through the doors of Watertown Hospital while their mother feared the worse back at home. News of their disappearance was scheduled to make headline at ten o'clock.

"Good evening, Ma'am" Christopher said to the front desk clerk as they walked up closer to the desk.

"Well, good evening; and what brought you two young men by this time of the evening." The clerk said while smiling.

And with a straight face, Christian replied:

"We're here to see Dr. Wigginton"

"Alright, let me see if he's here, and I'll be happy to page him for you." The clerk said.

Panic set in as soon as the boys heard the clerk placing the request for Dr. Wigginton to come to forth.

And while they were still standing in her presence, her telephone rang.

"No Doctor I didn't get their names, please hold on they are right here, I'll be happy to get their names for you." The nurse said.

"And before she could ask their names they both came out with their names at the same time. She smiled and reported the names to Dr. Wigginton who already overheard their responses.

"I don't know anyone with those names, but tell them I'll be down shortly." Dr. Wigginton replied without being too concerned by the visit.

Moments later, Dr. Wigginton emerged from the elevator and saw the twins sitting close by. He immediately walked over to them and said you must be Christopher and Christian, I hear you're here to see me."

The boys quickly rose to their feet deep in shock while looking at each other and being speechless.

"Is everything alright, I don't believe we've met; so which one of you is Christopher?"

Christopher, while still being speechless only pointed to himself and then the good doctor's eyes rolled to Christian saying, so you must be Christian.

So tell me, what brought you by and why do you need to see me, is everything ok? And why are the two of you looking so scared?

I'm so sorry sir, I think we've made mistake.

"Mistake…. What kind of mistake? I thought you told the lady at the desk you came to see me.   Isn't that correct?"

"Yes, sir, but we are trying to find our father, and I don't believe you're him." Christian said.

"Well, you've got that right; I couldn't be your father. You two look like twins. And how old are you by the way?

"Fourteen" they replied in unison.

Kennedy took a closer look at the boys and his heart skipped a beat while he tried catching his breath for composure. It didn't take him long to recall vaguely the conversation he had with his father, a few months prior. He wondered to himself if the boys he was looking at, could in fact be his brothers. Of course the striking resemblance to his father was more than he could handle; but he was not about to be led away by his suspicions. It was all too eerie and too farfetched to believe.

So, who brought you here? Kennedy asked the boys.

We took the bus from back east and we started walking around until we found the hospital.

And who is your mother, is she outside. Or did you come out here by yourself?

No, sir our mother is not outside. Her name is Gabriella Fairchild and she doesn't know we are here.

Kennedy was expecting to hear the boys say their mother's name was Christina Tate or Chrissy as she was called by many, including his dad. So after hearing the name Gabriella Fairchild, he quickly concluded a big mix-up was taking place. Anyway with not much left to go on, Kennedy asked the boys if they knew the first name of their dad. Christian was quick in telling Kennedy that his dad's first name was "Jaxon." He also went as far as asking Kennedy if he knew anyone by that name but Kennedy refused to respond.

Kennedy was flabbergasted. He tried as best he could to hold himself together, just as hard as he tried making sense of the story as it unfolded. And from there he started thinking the boys could be runaways. Deep down he wished if he could put them back on a bus and pretend nothing had happened. He had no desire to drag his father into what was taking place. He thought it would be too much for him to handle and his professional career could be at risk.

Kennedy, while being ravaged with anxiety about what to do, said to the boys:

"OK guys, you stay right here, and let me see if I can find him for you."

He went back upstairs to his office where he could find privacy to inform his dad about what he thought was a nightmare.

Jax was already home and relaxing with a drink while browsing through his mails in hopes a letter from Chrissy would finally turn up. He heard the telephone ringing but his mellow mood gave him no impetus to pick up. The answering machine came on and after hearing Kennedy's voice saying "Dad, it's important; pick up the phone" he upped from his chaise and grabbed the phone.

So while Kennedy carefully landed his father with the news about the boys, the boys were downstairs getting restless and confused about the way things were going.

After careful consideration, Christian told his brother it was a mistake going to the hospital as it was obvious that Dr. Wigginton was not their father. So they saw no need hanging about especially since it was getting dark outside.

"What should we do now, Christian?" Christopher asked his brother with a mind full of disillusionment.

"Let's get out of here "Christian snapped.

"And go where" Christopher asked his brother in a disappointing tone.

"I don't know Christopher! Christian retorted, while his brother gave him an evil eye.

"C'mon, let's go; we'll think of something later." Christian said while Christopher picked up his book bag and followed behind his brother.

The boys were less than five minutes away from the hospital compound when Kennedy came out of the elevator looking rather frantic. His eyes went straight into the direction of where he had left the boys sitting; but of course they were gone.

He threw his hands in the air while turning to Miss Johnson, the front desk clerk, for help in finding the boys.

"I don't know where they went, doctor; I left them sitting over there just five minutes ago and they seemed fine to me." Miss Johnson said to Kennedy.

So while all this was taking place, Jax was wiring his way to the hospital to finally meet his sons. His car phone rang; it was Kennedy calling to inform him that his supposedly sons were nowhere to be found. Jax panicked, he sped even more while still talking to Kennedy.

"You can't be serious son; where did they go and what did you say to them? Jax said to Kennedy.

"Dad, what do you mean by that? I just told you I left them sitting in the waiting area and I specifically told them not to leave; so what more could I have done?

"You've done plenty by contacting me, son. You can't imagine the shock I'm in since we last spoke. Anyway, if they came all this way to find me, I don't think they'd be gone for long. I'm sure they will come back."

So with another twenty minutes or so to spare until Jax made it to the hospital, Kennedy kept up his search without creating a scene.

In the meantime, the police department in the area was already on the beat in search of the boys. And, the newscasters at WPBX were carefully updating their story to read that Christian and Christopher Mercantile were runaways.

Jax pulled up at the hospital and as soon as he walked in, he ran into his son Kennedy who appeared frustrated. He then threw his hands in the air saying:

"Nothing; I've looked everywhere. They're gone dad; quiet possibly they went back home.

Jax shook his head while saying to Kennedy "No son, I think they are still around. You stay here and I'll drive around the city to see if they're anywhere around."

It was already night-time and Main Street was bustling with town folks in and out of the little shops and cafes. Jax slowly drove around the city with his eyes peeled for the two young boys he had never seen before. But in his heart, he's praying to find them.

So after going around in circles without any sign of luck, Jax parked his car and began walking along the streets. After, walking pass Mr. Shorty's Ice Creamery, presence of mind turned him back around and he went inside. And without too much effort in rolling eyes his eyes around the small parlor, he soon spotted two boys sitting and licking on their cones.   He was immediately floored, he felt his heart raced and thumped against his chest. He stood still and speechless with unblinking eyes until finally one of the boys' eyes met with his. But the boys were too engrossed into their enjoyment to even imagine that the man they just looked at could have been their father.

So while still in the moment of fright, Jax pondered deeply and he said to himself:

"It has got to be them. God damn; I already see myself in them."

Jax's began walking towards the boys and with each short step he made his heart raced even faster.   And with only a few more steps away from their table, he found the tightening inside his chest left him gasping for air. He exhaled slowly with pouted lips as if to buy a little more time for composure.

And while the boys sat quietly licking on their cones totally oblivious to the man standing almost next to them, Jax took his final steps and one of the most defining moments in his life towards coming face to face with his sons

The boys looked up at Jax and he rolled his eyes to look at Christian and he said:

"Christopher"

After hearing their father's voice for the first time, the boys were immediately taken by surprise. It was as if they knew they would find him, but most definitely not inside "Mr. Shorty's."

Moments of disbelief lingered while father and sons were under the spell of fate and silence.

Then Christopher said:

"Dad"

Jax said nothing, but his eyes rolled to look at Christian. Then Christian said:

"Dad; are you our dad?"

"Yes, my sons; I am your dad, I am your father and I have loved you long before you came into the world. I can't believe you came all this way to find me. It means so much to me"

Jax eyes welled and tears covered his face while his sons broke down in his arms.   He immediately pulled out a chair and joined them at the table as they all tried regaining composure. But he couldn't stop looking at the boys while shaking his heads and saying "I'm in shock; I can't believe this is really happening to me.

"We've never stopped thinking about you, even though we thought you were dead. And after we found out that you're alive, we just couldn't wait any longer to see you." Christian said.

Christian's comment pierced their father's heart, but however excruciating, he had to put his feelings aside and try to be strong.

However Jax pressing concern could not be held back much longer, so he asked the boys how they made it to West Watertown. They hesitated to answer; it didn't take long for Jax to realize that they boys had run away from home.

Christian's comment pierced their father's heart, but however excruciating, he had to put his feelings aside in recognition of what their mother was going through. He was convinced she had no idea of her sons' whereabouts.

"So, Christian and Christopher, I've been looking around, but I haven't seen your mother anywhere around. What exactly do you mean by saying you couldn't wait to see me?" Jax asked the boys while looking around nervously for their mother.

"She's home" Christopher replied.

"Oh, I see. So, tell me how you made it into town from all that way" Jax said.

"We took the bus, Dad. After we got dropped off at school we left and took the bus. We've been planning this for weeks." Christian said while Jax bask in the warmth of being addressed as "dad"

But with time of the essence, Jax tried taking full control on Chrissy's behalf by eliminating the mind games.

"Look son, I can't you enough for putting an end to my worries; I will never forget this day. And I'm sure you feel the same. And from this day forward we will never be apart. However we have to call your mother to let her know that you guys are safe and sound. I think we have put her through enough."

Christian looked at his brother and he did likewise. And from that Jax realized they did not exactly share his concern.

But in order to solidify his stance for saving Chrissy from anymore heartache, Jax said to the boys "So which do you prefer....that I make the phone call, or one of you?"

The boys remained stubborn by not responding.

"That's quite all right sons, I understand. I'm quite sure you're thinking that you're in big trouble. But things could get ugly if your mother called the police and report that her sons are missing. And you guys must be scared. But we can work through it; at least were together now and that's the most important thing."

Christopher was first in calling a truce by saying to his dad "Ok, I'll call mommy"

Jax looked at Christian and he surmised the hostility towards their mother ran much deeper than that of his brother.

"Well, that is great news; I'm so glad we all agree to make these steps together. So why do we leave to where we can find a phone; I'm sure there's one somewhere around. Or, we could use the one inside my car." Jax said.

Within minutes Jax and his sons were on their way towards joining him inside his car to make the phone call to Chrissy.

As Jax begun dialing the phone numbers while Christopher called them out to him, his hands shook and his emotions roared like a fast approaching tornado. The bitter –sweet memories, the scandals and the devastation he was left with after their miserable breakup came hurling back at him like debris from the storm.

But by the time the telephone picked up on the third ring, her voice came through like a ray of sunshine and he was instantly stilled and under her spell again.

So, after Jax was through listening to Ms. Fairchild's answering machine, he turned to his sons and said "The answering machine came on, son; I think one of you should leave a message letting her of your whereabouts."

But I don't know what to say to her dad, I don't want to make her mad. Christopher said.

"And, what about you, Christian, this is extremely urgent; you've got to let you mother know that you are with me and not in any danger."

After Jax said that, their ten second window of opportunity to leave a brief message elapsed by the "beeping sound."

Matter-of-factly Ms. Fairchild was rushing to grab the telephone before it went to voicemail. But after missing the call by a smidgen, she stood by and waited for the caller to leave a message. Although a formal message was not being recorded at the time, she clearly overheard the conversation between Jax and their children.

Hearing Jax's voice and trying to piece together what was taking place all in the same breath threw Ms. Fairchild in a state of trauma and without being able to respond in any way, shape or form.

However, as the seconds flew by, Ms. Fairchild tried pulling herself together in coming to terms with *facing the music* that she had been avoiding--- far too long.

Ms. Fairchild immediately called for back-up; she needed the help of Chandlon and Dr. Fleur should in case Jax called back. They could hear her calling from inside her bedroom where the answering machine was placed. They rushed to her side and asked if that was the police calling. She did not respond right away and they imagined the worse.

"Gabriella, what was that all about…please say something….tell me they found the boys" Dr. Fleur said while holding her.

Chandlon, who thought it was bad news coming, panicked and waited to hear what Ms. Fairchild was going to say without him asking her anything.

"You are not going to believe this" Ms Fairchild said.

"Believe what, Gabriella; please say something" Chandlon chimed in.

"You are not going to believe who just called" Ms. Fairchild said:

"Was it the boys or was it the police…it's hard for us to guess" Dr. Fleur said sounding very conflicted and anxious.

"That was Jax"

Chandlon looked at Dr. Fleur and Dr. Fleur did likewise, when both of them looked at Ms. Fairchild and blurted out "Jax?"

Ms. Fairchild nodded her head with tears dripping from her eyes. She appeared very frightened as were Chandlon and Dr. Fleur with their jaws dropped from what they thought was a bombshell.

And with tremors in her voice Ms. Fairchild said:

"Yes, that was him and he has the boys with him"

Deep sighs emerged from Dr. Fleur as she struggled with her thoughts about things went. She wondered if perchance she was too lax during her sessions with boys. And if it could be the reason they took matters into their own hands. Anyway by the time the thought was fully developed in her mind, she quickly squashed it by telling herself she handled the case as best she could.

Chandlon, while still trying to emerge from under the *smoke* cleared his throat and said grimly,

"He's going to have to answer to me; he's going have to explain how he got those boys to be in his keep. God damn, I'm in shock Gabriella."

Everyone remained quiet as they looked on Chandlon all riled up in blaming Jax for the boys' disappearance.

"Look…I even liked the guy; and for him to do something like this is beyond me. I promise you Gabriella I will get to the bottom of this" Chandlon continued… all of which meant little if any at all to Ms. Fairchild.

Dr. Fleur did not share Chandlon's views in anyway and very calmly she said:

"Look guys, before we get ahead of ourselves; let's look on the bright side. Clearly we're on a path to recovery; at least we know the boys are safe. It's almost nine o'clock and pretty soon the news will be taking the city by storm. Let's call the police to let them know what has transpired."

Ms. Fairchild immediately picked up the phone and called the police to inform them of the news. And by the time the call ended, the telephone rang and it was Jax calling back in hopes to speak with Chrissy.

"Hello" Ms. Fairchild said as she picked up the phone while Chandlon and Dr. Fleur looked on.

"Hello, is this Chrissy; excuse me I meant to ask for Ms. Fairchild" Jax said in his deep baritone voice.

Hearing Jax's voice and him calling her Chrissy, sent shivers down her spine. That was a de ja vue moment for her but in the most delightful way.

"Yes, it is. Is this Jax?"

"Yes, it's me."

"Oh my God, Jax; I can't thank you enough for calling. I'm so sorry, I'm so sorry, Jax. It was not my intention for things to go the way they did; please accept my apology. After I overheard you and the boys talking while the answering machine was still running, I was in such a state of shock that I could not respond. Oh my God, Jax you have no idea how relieved I am, knowing that they are alive and well. You have got to believe that I was doing everything in my powers to prepare them for a proper introduction, but obviously it didn't work out. I'm so very sorry about this, Jax; I really am."

"Ahh, Jax thought to himself. She hasn't changed one bit. She's as crazy as the first time we met."

And Jax's response to Ms. Fairchild was:

"I'm just as surprised as you are; I still don't know where to begin with all this, Ms. Fairchild. I just hope and pray you didn't assume I had anything to do with their disappearance."

Ms. Fairchild eyes rolled with evil as she turned and looked at Chandlon while responding to Jax.

"Oh Jax, for heaven's sake…that thought had never crossed my mind. I take full responsibility for my sons' disappearance. I should have been paying closer attention to their movements and quite frankly I've dropped the ball.

Jax said:

It's so wonderful hearing from you, Ms. Fairchild.

May I congratulate you on raising two awesome young men? I do realize their action has caused you much grief and disappointment. But, you know….even under such dreadful circumstance; your hard work speaks volume nonetheless."

Ms. Fairchild was moved by Jax's high regards. To her it felt as if he was ready to let bygones be bygones without allowing her to grovel for atonement. But anyway, without belaboring her point of view, she coyly asked him to let her speak with her sons.

Inasmuch as she would have loved to scold her sons about their disappearing act and the agony she was put through, Ms. Fairchild was able to restrain herself to the point of where she found herself apologizing for being a failure, and she begged them to come home.

Without any input or interference from their father, Christopher and Christian showed reluctance about returning home to their mother. Their desire to spend more time with their father left their mother utterly heartbroken.   It broke her heart from fear that she could eventually lose her children. However having said that, another side of her was grateful that her burden was finally being lifted knowing that the truth, that deep dark secret she carried with shame and guilt had finally come to light.   And she was no longer faced with the trepidation of bringing her sons face to face with their father.

As soon as she was through speaking with the boys, Ms. Fairchild asked Christian to give the phone back to Jax.

And their conversation started with her saying to Jax:

"Well, I'm sure you overheard the whole conversation between me and your sons. As you can tell both of them are against coming home."

"Huh-huh" Jax said, while being careful about not taking any sides.

Ms. Fairchild immediately picked up on Jax's reluctance to have a say into the matter. So she tried keeping him on the phone as long as he'd oblige her the time.

"Oh well; I'm certainly at a loss for words. And with everything happening so fast, my head is spinning out of control. I can't help thinking that my sons hate me, Jax. And, I also believe what they did today was purely out of spite. Anyway Jax, I'm sure you can appreciate that they should be home with me until we have sat down and come to some amicable arrangements" Ms. Fairchild said.

"Oh, yes. Sure, sure, I totally agree with you. Just let me know how you'd like to go about this and it's done." Jax said.

After much back and forth, Chrissy decided it was best if she went to pick up the boys. And not long after their phone conversation was ended, Ms. Fairchild was dressed and on her to West Watertown to meet with Jax so she could get her sons back.

After all that the boys had gone through to find him; it pained Jax to see his long lost sons cringed with anger about leaving him. However, another side of Jax was bursting with joy and his heart grew lovely thoughts about seeing Chrissy again.

So while Ms. Fairchild was on her way, Jax drove the boys to his home where they would wait until their mother arrived somewhere around midnight.

"You guys must be tired; you've been going all day…and with not much to eat I suppose" Jax said to his sons as they looked around his living room with roving eyes.

The boys remained quiet deep in distress about seeing their mother. They were disappointed their father took their mother's side about them going back home until proper arrangements were agreed upon.

Well, if you'd like we can order pizza or Chinese; your mom won't be here for another few hours. So what will it be?" Jax asked his sons in hopes that he'd help clear the air and keep their minds off their worries.

"I'll have pizza" Christopher said. "Me too" Christian followed suit, both with long faces.

While they waited for the food to be delivered, Jax invited his sons to take a look around his home. Although it was dark outside, the boys asked if they could see the back yard. Jax was happy to turn the lights on and he immediately unlocked the huge double French doors that opened up to the back porch.

"No pool?" Christopher blurted as he looked around. Jax remained unresponsive while being taken aback by his son's unexpected observation.

"That's ok Christopher; we don't have to have a pool." Christian said as if to show they'll settle for nothing as long they had the luxury of their father. Jax was moved beyond measure listening to the boys, and his eyes welled from pride and joy.

Soon after, they were back inside and eating pizza. Dinner was especially memorable because of the interesting exchange of conversation. The boys asked their dad what it was like being a doctor, what it was like raising their brother Kennedy without his mother around, if he knew how to play chess, if he had a maid and if he knew how to play football.

What an eventful time of his life, Jax was having while being in the company of his sons? Since Kennedy left, his home was like a desolate place where he'd learned to make peace with life as it were.

As the limo turned into Jax's driveway, Ms. Fairchild's heart raced with anxiety about seeing Jax. After the way the treated him in the past, she wasn't convinced he would look at her through rose- colored glasses.

However, as her chauffeur Lloyden, slowed the limo in preparation for parking, she quickly removed her compact and patted her face with powder and then rolled her lip gloss nervously and swiftly across her lips.

Jax and the boys saw the bright lights coming through the front window from outside. Their eyes widened--- each with their own fear about how things could turn out for them.

Christian immediately turned his father and said:

"Dad, Dad I really don't want to go, please talk to her and see if we could spend the rest of the weekend with you."

"I'll do the best I can, son" Jax responded while his heart shivered with possible confliction from their mother.

"Dad, I'll ask mom if you could come home with us for the weekend; there's plenty of room for you to stay." Christopher said with much urgency to his voice.

"Let's just be calm son, I promise you I'll do the best I can. Your mother loves you and she only wants the best for you" Jax said.

"But dad, you are the best for us; how could our own mother do this to us." Christopher replied angrily.

Then the door bell rang. And as Jax walked towards opening the door he somehow managed to dissolve his children's concern to give importance to his. He wondered if perchance the distance and the years between himself and Chrissy would have made him more of an eyeful for her.

Jax opened his front door and saw Ms. Fairchild. He broke a wide and friendly smile.

"Oh, wow, I can't believe my eyes; I can't believe you're actually standing in front of me" Jax said as he stepped aside to allow Chrissy inside.

Jax's eyes uncontrollably followed Chrissy as she entered the room. And without knowing what to expect after almost fifteen years, he found her as enchanting as ever. And her "oh so familiar scent" as she stood up close and personal to him, evoked sweet remembrances of her lush sensuality.

A nervous sigh came from Ms. Fairchild as she scrambled for the appropriate opening to say to Jax.

"Well, well, good to see you Jax; where do we start? Chrissy said while smiling and shaking her head in disbelief that she was actually standing inside his home.

Jax smiled back at her and said "I think we off to a great start"

"I still can't believe things turned out the way they did. I never expected the boys could do anything of the sort." Chrissy said while turning her head in the direction of where the boys were sitting on the sofa.

"There's so much to talk about, Jax, in terms of the boys. But it's obvious the timing is inopportune.

"I can appreciate that, especially after what you've been put through" Jax said while looking at the boys.

Chrissy then looked at her watch and said," its way past midnight and you must be tired; I know how hard you work."

"True…but I've spent the last fifteen years of my life waiting for this one dream to come through. And when I least expect it; my whole life fell into place. So, my dear I couldn't give more importance to what's taking place right now." Jax said.

"Oh, Jax, words cannot describe the burden that's been lifted off me. For years I've prayed and prayed asking God's forgiveness for what I had done. Look what I did to my own children, look what I have done to my life."

Ms. Fairchild broke down in tears and the boys immediately ran to her side. Christopher removed her handbag and hung it on the coat rack next to the front door while Christian held her hand. Christopher then took her by the other hand while Jax stood aside and looked.

And she cried even harder, yelping and wailing in the arms of her sons.

"Oh my God, Oh dear God, please forgive me! Oh my children, oh Jax, please forgive me; I'm so sorry for what I've put you through. Please, please forgive me."

The boys cried along with their mother and they too apologized for running away and scaring her half to pieces.

Jax then stepped a little closer as if to take matters into his own hands. And with his eyes also dripping wet he corralled everyone into his arms and they all wept together.

Moments of silence followed while the family stood still in reflection of their individual journey that brought them from a state of calamity to a place of tender redemption.

Soon after they separated and sat in the sofa. Ms. Fairchild looked around amid the dimly lit room. Everything remained the same as the last night she'd spent with Jax. Jax watched her eyes roved around the room and he swung his hands backwards to rest the back of his tilted head.

Jax immediately assumed her roving eyes were criticizing the dated looks of his house; when in fact, those eyes were taking her back to a very special and endearing time of her life; a time when Jax was all about her. And she wondered if someday her heart would allow her to feel quite the same.

So in keeping with his assumptions, Jax smiled at her and in an apologetic tone he said:

"Yes, Chrissy, I know. I have been thinking about fixing this place up for ages; but I just never got around to doing it. If I only knew something like this was going to happen, I would have made a few changes. And, I would have most definitely installed a pool." Jax said while looking at Christopher and smiling.

And without knowing where life would take them after that night, Ms. Fairchild smiled back at Jax and told him there was no need for apologies because she was only reminiscing on the good time they've had together there. Jax's heart swelled with tenderness and pleasantries t from Chrissy's response and he remained calm while admiring her timeless beauty.

A deep sigh came from Chrissy while she flexed her wrist to look at her watch. Then she said:

"Well boys, we have got to be on our way now. There's so much to talk about, Jax; but as you can see it's almost two am which means we won't be home until around five"

Jax, who was not in favor of seeing them go so quickly turned to Chrissy and said:

"After such a hectic and nerve racking day, I know you must be bushed. You're welcome to spend the rest of the night Chrissy; there's plenty of room.

Christian's ears immediately stood on ends after hearing his dad referring to his mother as "Chrissy" and he chimed in after his father's invitation by saying:

"Dad, why do you call my mom, Chrissy; is that a special name you used to call her?"

Christopher chimed in thereafter to echo his brother's observation:

"Yeah, why is that dad? I've never heard anyone called her that name before."

Jax's and Chrissy's eyes met as if to say "Oh God; here we go again" And so she turned to her sons and replied:

"No son, Chrissy, isn't a special name your dad gave to me. It's a little complicated, but I promise I'll explain everything to you as soon as soon as things have calmed down."

Jax then pulled Chrissy inside one of the bedrooms for a quick chat away from the boys.

"As you can see they are still very confused. I should have known better to address you as Ms. Fairchild; forgive me. But with everything happening so fast, it's hard to keep up with the name change."

"There's no need to apologize, Jax; I understand.   Quite honestly it sounded very strange when you called me Chrissy, out there. No one has called me by that name in fifteen years; but it's not your fault. As you can see I've totally screwed up and made a mess of their lives including yours." Ms. Fairchild said.

"Oh, sweetheart, I wish if you'd stop beating up on yourself like this. After reading your diary time and time again, it helped me a great deal in understanding more of you. Your choices and your decisions are justifiable in my opinion.   You've been through enough already and it's time for you to forgive yourself and let life take its course." Jax responded.

"I think I have Jax, but there's still that little part of me that keeps tugging against my heart. I'm sorry but I keep asking myself if you've truly forgiven me.

Jax immediately pointed to himself with raised eyebrows from Chrissy's surprising question, and he wondered if she'd heard a word he'd said.

"Me? Is that what your worries are all about?"

Ms. Fairchild's eyes brimmed with tears, while looking at him and nodding her head as sign of "yes."

Jax pitied her for still being victimized from her guilt because of the way she'd treat him in the past. And he wished if he knew the magic words to say to her to help liberate her from he thought was a "useless emotion."

He then pulled Ms. Fairchild closely to him and wrapped his arms around her so he could speak softly and tenderly to her; it was almost as if he was whispering.

"There's nothing left to forgive my darling; I love you more than life itself and I don't want you to change."

A strong sense of relief developed inside Chrissy while still being held in Jax's embrace. And she gently raised her hands and hugged him just as closely. Jax felt the warmth and tenderness that was starting to build inside him; a feeling that only she could exude to complete him.

Chrissy then rested her head on Jax's shoulders and he badly wanted to kiss her to say the least, but he felt it was best to show restraints from his urge.

Chrissy then raised her head off his shoulders saying;

"I think we should be on our way Jax; its way past two- o-clock." Jax was disappointed but he kept his calm.

They both walked back to the living room where they found the boys fast asleep on the sofa; and Jax loved every moment of what was taking place. He broke a wide smile, threw his hands in the air and said to Chrissy:

"See what I'm talking about; that's a sign from God that you should stay. You can take any room you want, and I'll be happy staying out here with my sons.   Oh man, it all feels so good that I wish this day never ends." Jax said.

After listening to Jax's comment, Chrissy found herself in an awkward position in that she wasn't quite comfortable spending the rest of the night there.   However, on the other hand she felt a pressing obligation to Jax in terms of the boys spending more time with him.

I guess you're right Jax; I know the boys will be thrilled after they found out they actually spent the night with their father. Ms. Fairchild said.

But instead of taking Jax's suggestion about resting in one of the bedrooms, Ms. Fairchild slowly slouched herself on the sofa next to Christopher's feet. A single glance from her sliced through Jax amorously as he watched her kicked off her pumps and wiggled her toes as a form of unwinding.

"I think I'll be fine right here, Jax; this is quite comfortable" Miss Fairchild said to Jax, while yawning and twisting back and forth to find a cozier spot on the old leather sectional. And with every move she made it felt to Jax as if she was deliberately taunting him with her sexy long legs.

By then Jax was on the verge of going over to touch her, but he tried holding back. "After all….the boys were still in their midst, and who's to tell they wouldn't wake up" Jax pondered.

"God damn Chrissy, you're as beautiful as the first time we met; Woman; you haven't changed a bit"

Chrissy responded to Jax in the form of a smile. And while the lull developed he broke it and said to her:

"You do look a little tired, so why don't I take those pretty little feet in my hands and rub them for you."

Again Chrissy glanced at him and gave a chuckle. She looked away while pulling up her feet from off the floor to fold them on the sofa. Jax kept his eyes on her awaiting permission to rub her feet.

"My feet are fine Jax; you're too kind.   Maybe some other time, but not tonight, thanks."

Jax then went over to cozy up next to her and he began whispering in her ears while gliding his fingers tenderly along her side-swept bangs.

Chrissy felt thrills racing down her spine from the gentle motion of Jax's hand alongside her forehead. She closed her eyes and listened closely to his whispering gestures.

"So, tell me Ms. Fairchild….when was the last time you've had your feet rubbed?"

"Hmmm…let me think. At least fifteen years ago" Chrissy responded in slow motion with her eyes closed while allowing Jax to enjoy his moment with her.

"And when was the last time your beautiful lips got sucked on?" Jax asked her while throwing his head backwards with his eyes closed from his rising titillations.

"Hmmm… At least fifteen years ago" she responded under bated breath.

Jax smiled to himself.

He then worked his hand alongside her face and played a little with her earlobe, he stroked his fingers softly and tenderly down her neckline until his hand was inside her cleavage. And there he cupped her breast inside his palm and began fondling her nipples. Suddenly her nipples plumped and bounced against his palm and it pitched him into a state of intense ecstasy.

Then he whispered:

"And how about these….. Don't answer that; let me guess…. They haven't been licked in fifteen years.

"Huh-huh" Chrissy muffled from the "oh too familiar touches "that lay dormant inside her for fifteen years.

Jax began breathing in short gasps as he was barely able to keep up with the foreplays he gave to Chrissy.   And as he continued working his way back to her, her jaw dropped halfway to exhale and to allow the "moaning"--- a much familiar sound to let him know she was restless and ready to be taken down *memory lane.*

Jax then took her by the hand and helped her up from the sofa and they quickly went to his bedroom.

First, he held her closely to himself and he they kissed wildly. Still shaking from the overwhelming erotica between them she began unbuttoning his shirt while he slipped off his moccasins. He unzipped her dress, she unzipped his pants–when suddenly he backed away and ---when suddenly he backed away and said "wait."

And in an impatient tone she muttered:

"Oh my… Why?"

"I forgot to lock the door" he replied achingly.

She quickly slipped off her bra while he locked the bedroom door. She hit the sack, and then he came back and peeled off his brief. He tossed it aside, removed her undies and did with it likewise. He climbed into bed and wrapped himself all around her.

He then sunk his nostril into her skin and inhaled deeply the essence of her warmth.

"You're so beautiful; and I love you, and I want you back" He whispered.

For the umpteenth time Chrissy recalled Jax telling her how much he loved her. But hearing him saying it again that night triggered an even deeper level of respect that she had developed for him after receiving his letter.

And like a thief in the night, Jax stole Chrissy's heart and she fell in love with him.

"I love you too, Jax. You're a good man, you've made me the luckiest woman alive and I want you back." Chrissy responded with tears pooling from her eyes.

Jax never expected to hear Chrissy say those words and he was dumfounded by her response. Her reveal instantly switched his erection into a meltdown mode, and his *"humpty dumpty"* had a great fall.

Jax immediately sprang and sat up in bed with his eyes glued to Chrissy.

"Do you really mean that, my love?" Jax asked Chrissy.

"With all my heart Jaxon Wiggington; with all my heart" Chrissy said.

She then turned and faced Jax and she began caressing his face. She then burrowed her face into his big, broad chest-plate and swiped her tongue across his pecks. Jax then ran his hands slowly through her hair while his toes curled from the much desired affection Chrissy gave.

Jax said to Chrissy "I love you and let us never be apart"

And without saying another word, Jax laid back down on the bed and Chrissy went on top of him and filled her mouth with his lips and he was thrilled beyond words. Soon after Jax was all fired up and ready to unleash his sexual prowess to Chrissy's delight. And when he was done pleasing her, he locked her into his warm embrace while the blissful hours between them lingered long after they were both asleep.

Christopher and Christian had no idea their mother and father had slept together in the same bed. But they were quite happy waking up the next morning in their father's house and seeing their mother around. She was still dressed as the way she'd turned up and without a hair out of place.

However after seeing their parents sitting at the dining table over coffee, their gut feelings told them something special was taking place, and it made them feel at ease.

And as the boys moved back and forth from room to room and checking things out, their mother said:

"Well boys, I hate to be the bearer of bad news, but we've got to be on our way now."

"Why, so early Mom?" Christian asked his mother.

She then looked at Jax while smiling and said:

"Well, your father has several patients at the hospital to care for and he needs some time to himself to catch upon his rest. But don't worry you'll be back before long.

Jax's chest puffed up with joy and pride listening to Chrissy. And while he stood aside and watched them picked up their book bags to leave with their mother, he was deliriously in love with that new chapter of his life unfolding.

Anyway, as Ms. Fairchild and her boys relaxed in the back of their limo while Lloyden whist them home, she tried explaining as best she could, her life, and how she transitioned from being Chrissy to Ms. Fairchild.

As soon as Chrissy and her sons pulled out of Jax's driveway, he immediately contacted Kennedy to update him on the happenings since his brothers' bombshell appearance at the hospital, the night before.

Kennedy's idea of being a big brother to his father's twins felt surreal to him. However, after meeting them there was no question boys were undoubtedly his brothers: Kennedy thought to himself. And that was because of their striking resemblances to their father, especially Christian. But with everything happening so quickly and the likely changes in his father's life, Kennedy took a dim view in light of his father's excitement.

However, Jax was not about to let Kennedy's *words to the wise* intervention slow down or shake his confidence about winning Chrissy back.

Anyway, as soon as Jax was off the telephone from speaking with Kennedy, he turned his attention to finish sorting through his mails. With not much left to go through, Jax came upon a letter from Marlene.

Needless to say Jax was shocked receiving a letter from Marlene. That had never happened before. However, because of his dedicated service to Barchas up until his death, Jax quickly assumed Marlene had sent him a "Thank You Card."

However, that was not the case, or even close to it. He was flabbergasted after realizing it was an invitation for two, to Marlene's and Frank's wedding.

Jax thought inwardly while still holding and admiring the delicately embossed card with gold lettering:

"Oh my, imagine that; Frank and Marlene tying the knot. Well, I'll be damned; Mr. Roulette sure didn't waste any time in making his moves on the good lady. He's certainly his brother's keeper.

And while smiling to himself about Marlene and Frank tying the knot, Jax began daydreaming how perfect his day spent at their wedding would be if only Chrissy and their sons could attend. And while still holding on to the invitation he half-heartedly rsvp the invitation for "one" and left it sitting on the couch.

CHAPTER TWENTY SIX:

In less than a week Jax was on his way to Chateau de Mehr to visit Chrissy and the boys. They were missing each other terribly and they were miserable being apart.

Dorchas answered the doorbell and allowed Jax inside. As soon he came through the foyer, he saw Ms. Fairchild standing with her hands clasp. She was wearing a red sleeveless low cut maxi dress. He thought she looked beautiful. He smiled at her and she felt special. Then he heard footsteps coming in their direction. And from the corner of his eyes he could see Chateau running towards her mother's side where she stopped and stood shyly.   And without any further acknowledgement of Ms. Fairchild's voluptuous yet demure appearance, He stopped in the middle of the room and said:

 "Well, you must be Chateau." Jax was smiling broadly while speaking to her and quite frankly he thought she was even more stunning than her mother had described.

Chateau pulled a little closer to her mother while staring at Jax. She then began biting her nail while Chrissy waited for her to respond to Jax.

"Well honey, aren't you going to say something; take your hand from your mouth and say something" Chrissy said to Chateau.

She immediately removed her hand from her mouth and said:

"Yes sir"

"Well, I'm pleased to meet you Chateau. You're the most beautiful girl on the planet; did you know that" Jax said while laughing with a wide grin.

"Huh-huh" Chateau said with a straight face. But Jax was not very surprised by her shyness because of how Chrissy had described her in her diary.

Jax then walked over next to Chrissy and he looked at Chateau. He then picked up the pint- size little girl off the floor unexpectedly. And as he picked her up he said:

"Come here beautiful; give your daddy a hug"

The overwhelming task listening to Christian and Christopher speaking about their father and making plans of going back to spend time with him, was simply tearing Chateau apart. And the burden that was lifted off her shoulders after hearing Jax introducing himself as her daddy, simply took her breath away. She was astounded beyond words and all she could do while her little heart pumped with glee, was to hug on tightly to him.

Jax then put Chateau down and he hugged and kissed Chrissy while saying:

I certainly needed that, thank you"

"For what," Chrissy asked Jax

"For giving me a daughter; she's beautiful and you couldn't make me any happier" Jax said.

Of all the surprises Jax had given to Chrissy, what he had done for Chateau at that moment was confirmation she had been totally redeemed through God's grace and mercy, according to her reckoning.

Chateau then ran off to find her brothers to inform them of the great news. Chrissy then took Jax by the hand and began showing him around. Soon after, the boys showed up with Chateau, and Jax picked her up again. And as they walked along the beautiful garden paths of Chateau de Mehr, the children and their parents had begun experiencing a lovelier time of their lives.

Later than night over dinner for two, Jax broke the news to Chrissy about Marlene's wedding which was less than month away. She was quite surprised hearing that her sister would be tying the knot so quickly after her husband's death. But on the other hand, she vividly recalled her sister as the type who hated the single life.

"Get out…you've got to be kidding?" Chrissy blurted to Jax.

"Oh no my love… and guess who your new brother-in law is going to be" Jax said teasingly.

"Surely you don't expect me to know that…have you forgotten I'd fallen off the face of the earth for fifteen years. Chrissy said to Jax while laughing.

Jax felt thrills seeing Chrissy laughing, and while he was admiring her beautiful smile, he said:

"Well, your, soon to be brother-in-law is Frank Roulette, You remember him; don't you"

"Huh-huh" Chrissy said while nodding her head.

Anyway, after Jax had disclosed the news about Marlene, Chrissy was soon behooved to come clean and let Jax know about her disguised visit to Barchas' funeral.

It felt surreal to Jax, hearing Chrissy talked about the most unexpected story. However he tried to make light of the situation as she continued confessing.

"Did you actually see me in the crowd?" Jax asked her.

She then busted out laughing and saying "Did I! Of course I did; I was right. And let me tell you…I was as nervous as a hooker in church. I was wearing a big ole wig and some ugly sunglasses. Oh, my God, Jax I was literally shaking and then I began asking myself:

"How could you be so stupid…what were you thinking."

"Huh-uh… and then what happened next? Jax asked her laughingly"

Chrissy said:

"All I could think of doing was to pray. I kept saying to myself: "Oh sweet Jesus …please dear Lord, don't let anyone recognize me, 'because I would surely die a horrible death up in here."

Without responding Jax remained completely entertained while looking at Chrissy.

She then looked at Jax and said:

"I haven't forgotten that look in your eyes, Jax; I know what you're thinking. You can call me crazy all you want, but I just couldn't help it; I had to be there." She said while throwing her hands in the air.

Jax was awestruck about Chrissy's reveal. However, because of her unchanged gesticulations and sometimes giddy behavior that he loved so much when she spoke, it was more of a heartwarming escapade than a bombshell for Jax.

However, having said that, Chrissy continued with telling Jax more of her reveals. And an even deeper level of hilarity kicked off between them, after she told Jax about the frightful night when she saw Marlene and Frank dancing inside her ballroom.

Again, Jax was flabbergasted listening to Chrissy making him the happiest he has ever been in decades.

And so, as the night progressed with things winding down, Jax reached across the table and took Chrissy's hands into his, and he squeezed them gently. She watched a pensive look developed across his face and she wondered if she had said too much in too little time.

"Is everything all right Jax; you look tired." she said while he was still holding on to her.

"Are you kidding me; tired...with you sitting right next to me? Oh no my darling; nothing could be further from the truth."

"So why the long face; I know something's on your mind." Chrissy said.

"You're on my mind. I'm dying to ask you to marry me, but I don't know if I should.

Chrissy was instantly silenced and quite frankly befuddled by Jax's response.

"Should I? Answer me my love and tell me what you think" Jax said.

Chrissy remained speechless while staring steadfastly at Jax. He felt her palms shaking inside his and he picked them up and kissed them.

Moments passed without a sound or movement coming from her; she was still stunned. Tears began streaming down her face and she became choked up while Jax waited with a doubtful heart.

Then a little while later she cleared her throat to give him her response with her twist to the unusual marriage proposal.

"Well, Jax, I think you should follow your heart and ask me to marry you and then see what I would say"

Jax felt panic, his head raised, his chest tightened and water sprung inside his mouth; but he faced the fear of rejection, nonetheless.

"Well, I'm about to ask you to marry me, as you can tell" Jax said to Chrissy with tremors in his voice.

Goosebumps grew all over Chrissy and she sniffled while her lips parted with tremors from trying to respond. And in a soft and humble-like tone she looked at Jax and said:

"Well, I think I'm about to say yes"

"So, my darling, is that a yes" Jax asked her and she said: "Yes, yes… it's a yes. It is a yes"

Tears flowed from Jax's eyes as they looked at each from other across the table. Jax was dying to pick her up from around the table and kiss her. But with many of her employees moving back and forth serving her patrons, they left and went outside to take a walk along her favorite part of the gardens. And as they strolled along the pungent gardenia pathway, they'd stop every now and then to hug and kiss, to cry and laugh and to hug and kiss again and again.

Then finally they came upon a garden bench, where they sat to talk and share more of their feelings.

Jax said to Chrissy:

You are the love of my life. You've given me three beautiful children. And above all, you've given yourself to me….how great and complete my life has become all because of you, my love.

Chrissy was deeply touched by Jax's comment. She then took his hands in hers and said:

"What I feel for you is beyond comprehension; it's beyond me. I know I'd put you through some challenging times, but you never gave up on me… that's so amazing.

"Everything about you Chrissy is amazing." Jax said.

"Since our reunion less than a week ago, I haven't stopped thinking how our lives could have fallen into place so quickly. My God, Jax it's been fifteen years since we haven't been in contact!" Chrissy blurted.

"That may be true honey, but even though you were out of sight you were never out of my mind" Jax chimed in.

"Well, I must confess the same hasn't been the case with me, but that was way back then, when I was being deceived by my mistakes. Anyway, as time progressed, I was able to look back and reexamine my perceptions and awareness according my actions. And little by little through prayer and devotion I was able to understand how toxic my life had become.

"Sweetheart, I am a woman of faith now; a product of God's grace and mercy. And, before I let you put that ring on my finger, I have got to let you know where I'm coming from."

"I was put through the fire for years, and after due process my life has been transformed, refined and reshaped to fit all our needs and all our desires unconditionally. All those things I had to go through to be deserving of a man like you. So what does that tell you?"

While Chrissy poured her heart out to Jax, he sat patiently in awe while she spoke. And after she was through he said:

"That's so profound my darling; you talk as if your soul was borrowed from women of centuries ago. I could sit here all night and just listen to you. You've brought nothing but to peace and harmony to my life.

Chrissy smiled and said:

"Well, don't we have a wedding to plan; or, are we going to sit here all night being googly-eyed over one another"

Jax laughed out loud and said: "just name the place and time, my darling and I'll say, I do"

And without any hesitation Chrissy chimed in saying:

"Well, what better place than here, Jax? It's just so beautiful; wouldn't you agree?"

"I agree… the sooner the better. Why don't you get the kids and lets drive back home with me. My good friend who's also my golfing buddy owns a jewelry store downtown. I think he's the best man for the job.

"Oh my Lord, Jax…I see you're not wasting anytime in making me Mrs. Wiggington. Oh, my Lord…hold on, baby, let me pinch myself…. It all feels so surreal:" Chrissy said laughingly.

And to that Jax said

Why should I waste anymore time? You should have been my wife a long time ago baby. So, how do you feel about getting the kids and let us all drive back out west. I know they'll love it; and we'll break the news to them once we're home.

"Once we're home" Those three words, "once we're home" took Chrissy by great surprise and she pondered deeply on them. Then an unexpected pang hit her chest as she turned and glanced at her vast estate amid the misty moonlight. And not just the vastness and the magnificence, but her self- taught entrepreneurial skills that have brought her millions after Chey's death. And she wondered briefly to herself... "Where is home"

Jax immediately picked up on the lapse in their communication and he wondered if he was being too pushy. So in order to keep her from feeling pressured, he smiled and said to her: "Look baby, I don't have to be a doctor to have *patience,* you know. If things are moving a little too fast for you, I can wait."

Chrissy burst out laughing while saying: Oh, no, no, no; it's nothing like that honey. You're so crazy…I've forgotten how funny you are.

By early next morning, Jax and Chrissy came up with a date for their wedding. And with everything already in place at the Chateau de Mehr, they presumed it wouldn't take much to pull off their dream wedding… given their short guest list.

Jax then stepped away and went inside his car to call Kennedy to tell him the good news.

"Are you sure about this, Dad? You've only seen her once in fifteen years. And after turning up with two kids, you've decided to get married? "

"Yes son; unequivocally yes. And it's not only two kids; actually there are three---a little girl name Chateau who's nine years old. I can't say I don't appreciate your concerns, son; I do. But I've got to follow my heart, and all I ask of you is your blessings."

Kennedy was livid; and he said to his dad:

"What little girl are you talking about Dad? Have you lost your mind; a little girl? You've never made any mention of a little girl before. Dad, for God's sakes, please tell me what is going on."

Jax said:

Come on now Kennedy; give your old man some credit. You make it sound as if I've gone off the deep end. This little girl, Chateau who happens to be an adoptee stole my heart the minute I set eyes on her. And no, I haven't lost my mind. As soon as I marry Chrissy, she's going to become my daughter. And as I have asked you before, all I need are your blessings.

Kennedy paused and waited a few seconds before responding to his father. He reckoned he'd lost the fight.

Well, Dad, it sounds as if your mind is made up. You're my dad and I love you. All I've ever wanted is for you to be happy and in love. And if marrying Chrissy is your heart's desire, then dad, you've got my blessings. Congratulations.

Jax felt great relief and he smiled while responding to his son:

Thank you son; I always knew I could depend on you; I couldn't be happier. He then left the car and went back inside to join Chrissy and the kids for breakfast.

As soon as Dorchas was through serving breakfast, Chrissy, Jax and the children were on their way back to Jax's house. And as soon as they made it home and were settled in, Jax began flipping through the yellow pages of the phone book. He was looking for the top notch "RoRo Jewelers" which was where his son Kennedy had purchased his wife's ring. And with time of the essence according to their early wedding plans, Chrissy then took the phone book from Jax and began thumbing through the pages for the famous "Madame Toussan" Her wish was to get an early appointment for consultation regarding her wedding gown. Although she didn't get an appointment to meet with the Madam, she was able to get in that same day, nonetheless.

Admittedly, Jax would have preferred if he could have dragged Chrissy with him to "RoRo" to help with choosing her ring. However, after much back and forth, Chrissy convinced him that her ring of his choosing only was what would make it extra special. Added to that, she was more interested in keeping her appointment with Madame Toussan which was within the same timeframe as Jax's.

So with a little time left to spare before their appointments, Jax and Chrissy sat down with the children to tell them about their wedding plans.

To say the children jumped for joy after being told they were going to be a family, paled in comparison to their actual response, but they were jumping and rejoicing with all their might.

Soon after, Jax and Chrissy were off on their separate ways to jump start their wedding plans. Chrissy was accompanied by Chateau, while Christopher and Christian were excited after being told they would be helping with choosing their mother's wedding ring.

Chrissy turned up a little ahead of her scheduled appointment at "Madame Toussan" Bridal Gallery" only to be told her consultant was not yet in the facility.

"May I look around in the meanwhile?" Chrissy asked the Front Desk Clerk.
"Yes ma'am, with pleasure," said the clerk, while pointing her along the aisle where some of the gowns were displayed on mannequins no larger than a size six.

Chateau, while holding on to her mother's hand, her eyes wandered widely on the bedazzled little girl dresses displayed next to the larger ones.

"Mommy, I want that one, and you should pick that one for yourself" Chateau said, while pointing to one of the dresses that struck her fancy"

"Well, that's quite a pretty dress, honey. If you really like that one, then I think we should get it. But let's look around a little more and see what else they've got for mommy" Chrissy said.

And while they strolled along the marble pathway, Chrissy kept her eyes peeled for the wedding dress of her dreams… a simple, but elegant A-line chiffon with beaded waist. But up to that point, nothing of the sort was to be seen, but she kept walking and dreaming nonetheless.

So, almost immediately around the corner where Chrissy and Chateau would have come to the end of the walkway, Marlene and her daughter Bethany could be seen walking along the same walkway, but from the opposite direction, where both sisters would have come face to face, moments later.

Then the unimaginable happened…..Chrissy and Marlene, finally came face to face after fifteen years of estrangement due to irreconcilable differences.

No one spoke; they were too petrified from the shock of being caught up in the moment.

Bethany, who had not seen her aunt since she was five years old, had no idea that she was actually looking at her. So without any idea of what was taking place during the perfect stillness of silence that had fallen upon them, Bethany tried making sense of the situation.

"Who is this, Mom? And why are you two looking at if you've seen a ghost?" Bethany said.

Marlene then said:

"Say hello to your Aunt Chrissy, Bethany"

Bethany eyes widened and she quickly placed her hand over her mouth while saying:

Oh my God; is this really Aunt Chrissy, Mom?"

"Yes, she is" Marlene said.

Deep down Bethany would have wanted to hug and kiss her aunt because of the distant but pleasant memories she still recalled. However, she was more concerned about not upsetting her mother by showing any great joy about seeing her aunt. And that was because of the years of unpleasant and ugly things she had heard her mother said about her sister. So based on that, Bethany smiled and said:

"I had no idea that was you, Aunt Chrissy; it's been so long. It's so good to see you"

Based on Bethany's half ass response, Christy reckoned the kid was caught between a rock and a hard place and she did not fault her niece for being so stiff.

So immediately after, Chrissy became tearful from the years of pain she carried knowing that Marlene had blamed her for driving their father to his death. Quite frankly she would have loved to take her sister in her arms and just hold her, but she was scared of getting pushed away. And that was something she did not want Chateau to witness.

Marlene, on the other hand wondered if it would be okay to hug her sister and never let her go, but she was afraid of getting rejected by her sister in front of her daughter.

Chateau, who was quite oblivious to the emotional breakdown that was taking place between her mother and the woman whom she thought, was a stranger, turned to mother and said:

"Mom, Mom, look at that dress over there; I think you should pick that one; it's really, really pretty.

"We'll take a look later, honey, but right now I'm a little busy." Chrissy said.

Marlene then looked at Chateau and said:

"Your daughter"

"huh-uh" Chrissy replied with a racing heart."

"She's beautiful" Marlene said

"So are you" Chrissy said.

Soon after, the tears began tumbling down Marlene's face and shattered the *"glass- wall"* between them.

Chrissy leaned in and took her sister into her embrace and they both cried while holding on to each other. With nothing else to do, Bethany and Chateau held on to their parents and cried along with them.

Not long afterwards, they separated themselves and Marlene said to her Chrissy, it's been so long and there's so much to say, that I don't know where to begin.

I understand exactly where you're coming from my sister. We've put each other and ourselves through enough already. So why don't we make it easy on ourselves and begin with "love." Chrissy said.

Marlene instantly grew Goosebumps, followed by tears welling up inside her eyes. She then turned to her sister and said"

"You're amazing; I needed to hear that; thank you, thank you, my sister"

"I'm still in shock, but in a good way. You have no idea how long I've been praying to for God to bring us back together, Marlene. I wanted to have you back in my life so bad, that when I prayed at times I could taste the joy of you rising up inside my spirit. I'm speaking about those good old days, when it was just the two of us and the loving feeling we shared. You're so right my sister, there's a lot to talk about, but all I can say right now is thank you God for giving my sister back to me." Chrissy said:

All I can say is ditto…I'm glad you're able to speak for the both of us…because other than those few words….I'm speechless, I'm speechless beyond words. Marlene said.

Then both sisters went quiet again and shook their heads from side to side in disbelief. They really could not believe the chasm has been lifted and a path to redemption was being paved literally before their eyes.

Chrissy then took Chateau by the hand and said:

"Honey, I want you to meet my sister, who's your Auntie Marlene."

"Hi Auntie Marlene" Chateau said.

And before Marlene could respond to Chateau's greeting, Bethany chimed with a question to her Aunt Chrissy as if she was reading her mother's mind.

"So Aunt Chrissy what are you doing here"

Chrissy gave a broad smile and said just shopping. She then turned her attention to Marlene while saying:

"So I hear you're getting married, congratulations"

Marlene was surprised by Chrissy's comment.

Oh wow; news does travel fast. So how did you find that out? Marlene asked:

"I only found out yesterday, from Jax. He told me he received an invitation from you."

Marlene was shocked hearing Chrissy talked about Jax as if they were still friends.

"Jax; you, and Jax are still in contact? Marlene asked Chrissy and looking rather surprised.

"Huh-uh, and that's why I'm here." Chrissy said while laughing which told Marlene there was a lot more to bumping into her at "Madam Toussan"

What do you mean….explain? Marlene said, while sounding rather confused about Chrissy's response. But that was only for a few seconds more, because Chateau chimed in and fixed the problem right away.

"My mom and my dad are getting married Auntie Marlene, and we came all the way to look for a wedding dress for her and for me. Chateau said.

Marlene stood in shock with her eyes unblinking and bugged from what she considered a bombshell. Chrissy was a little surprised herself at Chateau for being such a blabber mouth. But it was the excitement of becoming Jax's daughter and then a bridesmaid, on top of being out shopping for a dress…all in less than a day that had her little heart overflowed.

So, after that mouthful from Chateau, Marlene said:

Did I hear her correctly? Are you really getting married, Chrissy?

Chrissy nodded her head in a motion to mean yes.

Oh my God! I'm so happy for you; this is great news. So who's the lucky guy? Marlene asked Chrissy:

"Who, else could it be my dear, sister? Who else would put up with me and want to make me his wife? You shouldn't even have to guess. Chrissy said while laughing.

And with a puzzled look on her face while laughing as well, Marlene said:

Come on now Chrissy, you've got to help me out. Truthfully I'd have to say Jax, but I hardly think that would be so, seen that it's Chateau's dad that you're marrying.

Well, you guessed it…Jax and I will be getting married in two months.

"Marlene then looked at Chateau and said to herself, this child looks nothing like neither mother nor father. I really don't understand what she's saying but I'll just go along with it anyways…I'm just so totally lost".

Then Marlene turned to Chrissy and said, that is such great news, and we have a lot of catching up to do. So how are the twins, they must be way up in their teens now. I'd love to meet my nephews.

You will; their just out shopping with their dad, but I'll make sure they get a chance to meet you before we get back home. We live in the east end you see. Chrissy said.

After Chrissy's response, Marlene's thoughts raced back to the information she'd gathered from Frank and Aunt Carolyn and she wondered how much of it was true. But she dared not make mention of anything.

Marlene then smiled and said: "I don't know about you, Chrissy. But truthfully I'm so confused right now… that it could take quite some time for everything to sink in."

But she couldn't help asking her sister if she'd heard that Barchas had passed away. And after Chrissy told her yes, Marlene wondered how much more she knew about her.

Anyway, so as to keep things on a much happier note Marlene said to Chrissy:

"One thing I must ask of you, Chrissy, is for you and the rest of family to attend my wedding. Nothing would make my day more complete if you could find it in your heart to be there,

Chrissy was thrilled about the invitation and she gladly accepted.

"And from my heart to yours, my wedding day wouldn't be the same without you and your family there." Chrissy said.

Oh for heaven's sake, Sis; I wouldn't miss it for the world. We had planned a two week honeymoon in Monaco, but we'll cut it short to be back in time for your wedding. Marlene said:

"Well, I just came out of the final fitting of my gown. Would you like to see it?" Marlene asked Chrissy.

"But of course– you know I'd never say no to that, and I hope you're not planning on leaving just yet. I'm going to need your expertise in finding my wedding dress."

Also I'm depending on you, Bethany, to help your cousin find the perfect bridesmaid dress.   Chrissy said.

Don't worry, the consultants here are the best in the region. People come from all over the world to shop here I'm sure you're going to be happy as I am, when they are done with you and little Miss Chateau. I'm still in shock that you have three children; what a gift…I've got two nephews and a niece." Marlene said with a smile.

Chrissy wanted to tell Marlene that Chateau was adopted, but she chose not to stay quiet with for the time being. And to Marlene's comment she said:

"We have so much catching up to do; Lord knows when we'll find time for that."

"I know what you mean sis, but it feels so good knowing that we are together again that all you'd to do is talk.

So tell me about your soon to be husband; do I know him? Or is he someone you've met not so long ago? Chrissy asked Marlene as they walked back to where her dress was left hanging. And that was when the real *"labrish"* kicked off, with Marlene telling Chrissy about Frank and how they ended up being lovers.

Not long into their conversation, Chrissy's designer turned up and squashed their lollygagging with her no nonsense business acumen.

That being said, Chrissy was glad to have Marlene's help along with her designer during the painstaking three hours in finding the perfect wedding dress and one for Chateau.

As soon as they left Madame Toussaint's Bridal Gallery, Marlene took great pride in telling Chrissy about her Art Studio, which was located within a few miles of Madame Toussaint's.

Since the completion of her art studio, only Carolyn, Brandon and Frank have had the pleasure of seeing what it looked like inside. And she vowed not to let anyone else see her work until after grand opening.

Anyway with this unexpected gusher of excitement from being back in her sister's good graces, Marlene quickly seized the opportunity to show Chrissy what she had accomplished on her own.

Seeing the quaint little house on the hill as Marlene drove up the steep pathway to her studio, solidified Chrissy's assumption about her sister. It was more than enough to prove her sister had come down from her high horse in many ways.

"This is quite charming Marlene; how did you manage to find this place….it's more me than you. Back in the days you'd hardly want to drive down Gladstone Street" Chrissy said while her eyes roved from side to side.

"You're right about that, but that was a long time ago when I was the old Marlene. It's unbelievable how far I've come from being that person. And I must say it all happened after I had lost everything."

"Everything, what do you mean by everything?" Chrissy turned to her and said.

Marlene pulled up closely to the front porch and parked. Bethany and Chateau quickly got out of the car and they began walking around to the back of the house so she could see the lake that Bethany had told her about.

Marlene rolled down the window on her side of the car and rested her hand on the steering wheel. Chrissy looked at her sister grimly from the sadness that stole the charm from her countenance.

"Well, my dear sister, I didn't realize how much I was living in the shadows of my father until after he was gone. I had loved him to the moon and back; and you knew it.

Chrissy began rolling down her side of the window to get a breath of fresh air. The very mention of their father caused her heart to palpitate because she assumed Marlene was going to confess that she had blamed her for their father's suicide.

"Huh-huh, I know" Chrissy said shyly.

"Well after daddy passed away, he took with him the biggest part of me.

"Oh wow, sis. What do you mean by that? "Chrissy asked with a racing heart.

"Well, for starters, he took my confidence with him, and after that my life went to pieces. Anyway over time I was able to recover, so much so that I had the guts to prove to Barchas I could accomplish something on my own.

"I'm proud of you Marlene; I can see you've come a long way after all that you've been through. I'm happy for you sis. Chrissy said.

It then occurred to Marlene that she could have said too much in the little time she had spent with her sister. So she quickly changed the subject and said:

"Oh my Lord, I'm sorry sis, that's not why I brought you here. I don't know what came over me to be overloading you with my gripes. I guess I'm so excited about seeing that I just can't help myself."

Chrissy shrugged her shoulders and said "I think we're doing just fine, we shouldn't have to apologize for being sisters, and doing what sisters do best.

Marlene smiled and she turned to look at Chrissy with much endearment.

"I guess you're right sis. And I know there's plenty left for us to talk about, and you haven't said a word yet. But let's promise we won't talk about this kind of stuff until we're old ladies with nothing better to do. Marlene said while still eyeing her sister.

Chrissy was relieved by Marlene's idea of putting their past on hold as she wasn't quite ready to start spilling her guts to her sister.

Soon after, they were inside Marlene's art gallery. And without saying a word, Marlene waited to see what Chrissy's reactions would be like.

Going by the mesmerized look on Chrissy's face, Marlene drew some comfort thinking that her sister approved of her work. However it would have meant so much more to her if she had used the time to verbalize her thoughts.

So with nothing being said, Marlene chose to break the ice by saying:

"So what do you think, sis? These two pieces are my latest; I was inspired to do this one after seeing two fish airborne on the lake outback."

Chrissy remained spellbound as she rolled her eyes on the various paintings. Marlene then pointed to another piece with Chrissy's eyes following her direction.

"And that one above the fireplace is my recollection of Dr.Fiji's chaise; the likes of which my ass will never go back to, especially with you back in my life."

Marlene felt relief after Chrissy broke her silence and asked her who Dr. Fiji was.

"He was my psychiatrist for many, many years." Marlene replied while looking at her sister for a reaction. But Chrissy was unmoved by Marlene's response, because she had already assumed that to be the case.

Chrissy finally turned and gave Marlene her full attention while speaking:

Oh my God, Marlene, your gallery is unbelievable! Each one pulls you in with their intense vibrancy and depth; it's magical. Your paintings are so amazing that it's hard not to be seduced by its unexpected surrealism; I have to say I'm in love.

Oh wow, Chrissy; that's the highest compliment I've ever received from anyone. Thank you.
Marlene said.

"Since you were little, I've always known you'd be good as a painter; but this is no longer a hobby for you my dear; this is your calling... your ultimate gift from God. And as soon as your gallery is open for business you'll have the best of the best vying for your talent." Chrissy said.

Chrissy then moved a little closer to the painting, with the two fish airborne on the lake. And as she leaned in with her eyes peeled on the tiniest details, she thought to herself she should own it.

"How much is this one; I think its calling my name; I should have it" Chrissy said.

Marlene became uncomfortable with Chrissy's question about the price of the painting. Although she had not forgotten what she had learnt from Aunt Carolyn and Frank about her sister being the supposedly "wealthy Ms. Fairchild" her unassuming behavior helped confirmed her doubts about her sister being the owner of Chateau de Mehr.

However, because of the proof of evidence Frank had provided her during his investigation, Marlene was still of the opinion there was some kind of connection between her sister and Chateau de Mehr.

Anyway, with things going as well as they were, Marlene was mindful about putting her sister into an uncomfortable situation by revealing the high ticket price of her artwork.

"You haven't answered me sis. Or you haven't yet decided on the price?" Chrissy said.

"Oh, I'm sorry sis; I didn't realize what you were saying. Yes you're right, I haven't decided on a price as yet. But as soon as I do, you'll be the first to know" Marlene said.

But Chrissy wasn't sold on Marlene's response so she pressed on.

"I really love this piece sis; don't tell me you haven't got an idea of what you'd want for it" Chrissy said.

After paying careful attention to her manner of speaking, Marlene realized that her sister was not about to back down, so she cautiously acquiesced.

"Well, I was thinking along the lines of forty to twenty thousand dollars. But I wouldn't charge you that much. I'll accept whatever you can afford. Marlene said.

Chrissy immediately removed her check book from her handbag and wrote a check for Twenty Thousand dollars without allowing any time for a haggling from her sister. And as she handed the check to Marlene, she said:

"We'll just leave it there until after you've had your grand opening sis; I'm sure you'd like others to see this masterpiece along with the rest of your exhibits.

Marlene was enormously befuddled by her sister's endorsement of her lifelong dream. It was so much so, that she was moved to go back on her promise to wait until they were old ladies to talk about their past. Added to that, she wondered if she was in fact looking at the well to do Ms. Fairchild.

So while still holding on to the Twenty Thousand dollar check, she reckoned the only way to find out more about her sister was to start digging.

"I don't know what to say, Chrissy; I'm in complete shock. Look at me; I'm shaking. After everything that I've put you through, it turns out you're the first one to forgive. I know you said let's keep the past in the past, but I can't live with myself if I didn't tell you how sorry I am for turning my back on you, when you needed me the most; I haven't forgotten.

Chrissy smiled at her sister and said:

"I thought we had fixed all that, back at Madame Toussaint's; I was no angel either so don't feel bad"

"With everything going so well, I'd hate for us to part this evening without me telling you something that's been heavy on my mind. I promise you sis… the rest can remain until we're in our rocking chairs with nothing better to do." Marlene said with a smile emerging from the long face she grew"

"So what could be so bothersome that couldn't wait?" Chrissy said.

"Well I don't know how to say this…but I guess I'll just come right out with it, and hope you don't hate me after I'm done" Marlene said while Chrissy looked on unfazed by her sister's jitters.

Marlene exhaled audibly as if to relieve her guts from the tangled nerves

"Well, not so long ago; News Years Day, to be exact, Frank and I had dinner at the Chateau de Mehr. We had a fabulous time and the place is simply breathtaking. And by the way, let me tell you, since daddy gave you that party there that was my first time going back."

Hmm-hmm: Chrissy chimed in.

"Anyway, just a few months ago I heard that's where you have been living there ever since you'd moved away from Grey Banks. Needless to say I was flabbergasted by the news; and wondered what could have behooved you to give up everything including your career to be there."

Again Chrissy smiled. And, as if all that Marlene had told her went unregistered, she said:

"How is she, by the way?"

Marlene knitted her eyebrows from being taken aback by Chrissy's question.

"What she; I'm not clear on what you're asking sis" Marlene said while appearing lost.

"I'm talking about Aunt Carolyn. There's no need for us beating around the bush; she's only person who could have given you that precise information. And Lord knows what else she told you.

After thinking about Chrissy's response, Marlene realized she had no room for mind games with her sister; so she poignantly surrendered her strategy. She then began shaking her head from side to side while smiling and saying:

"Sister, sister, sister; you're so good. I'd forgotten how savvy you are; I can see that you haven't lost that powerful sixth sense of yours. Marlene said.

"I guess you could say that" Chrissy replied with a slight smirk on her face while zoning in on Marlene's response which she thought was condescending. Anyway the "million dollar question" that was foremost in Marlene's mind finally came out.

So, are you in fact the "Ms. Fairchild" that I've heard so much about?" Marlene asked.

Chrissy gave a deep sigh; she was relieved Marlene asked so she could get it over with.

Chrissy began bopping her head in a motion to mean yes followed by saying to Marlene:

"Matter-of-factly, I am. My name is Gabriella Fairchild. No one has called me Chrissy in fifteen years.

"Which in fact means that you are the owner of Chateau de Mehr?" Marlene said with a hint of drawback in her tone.

"Yes, you heard right" Chrissy replied with unwavering confidence.

At that point Marlene became stricken from a hair-raising experience that took her by surprise. And the only thing she that came to her mind was "How the hell did she do that." Her eyes popped and her mind raced back to what Frank had told her upon the completion of his investigation. She then raised her hand while still holding on to the check and she covered her mouth that was heavy with awe.

Silence followed with both ladies staring at each other; one, out in left field, while the other relaxed with her home run.

"Oh my wonderland; I don't know what to say; I'm in shock." Marlene muffled.

Then out of the clear blue Marlene's reaction apparently hit a funny bone inside Chrissy, and she busted out laughing while staring steadfastly at her.

Marlene immediately felt as if she was being laughed at and she became uptight.

"Is this a joke… because if it is, I'm starting to feel like an idiot? You've got to let me know what is so funny." Marlene said with a hint of agitation.

But Chrissy kept laughing and laughing until tears dribbled down her cheeks. Marlene became confused, upset and quite out of sorts about her sister's laughing.

I'm sorry sis, I couldn't help it. Chrissy said.

Couldn't help what? Marlene asked while throwing her hands in the air and looking frustrated.

"Let me tell you, let me tell you…Oh my God this is so funny…too funny." Chrissy said.

Marlene's confusion about her sister's unexplained bout of laughing deepened to the point of utter discomfort. Anyway, after a few more cackles, Chrissy tried pulling herself together to explain her reason for being so joyful.

"That New Years Eve night when you came to Chateau de Mehr; I saw you. I had just entered the building and as usual I'd check out the scene to see how things are going. And then it was like all hell broke loose inside of me, when I saw you out on the dance floor rocking the night away with Frank.

You what! Stop lying; you're driving me crazy! Marlene said frantically.

Chrissy smiled at her antics and said:

"Nope…no lying here sis; you had on an orange dress; a beautiful outfit I might add.

Oh my God, that is so true. So what did you do?

"What did I do? Ha; you don't want to know. Girl, I was so shocked and frozen into time, that if I had gotten cut with a knife, there wouldn't be a drop of blood to be found. It was that bad."

And you sat there and watched us all night?

All night…I just couldn't look away. And that's why I began laughing because I clearly remember that night. And if you had seen the look on my face, and how I was cowering from God knows what; there's no doubt you'd be laughing just as bad or even worse.   Quite frankly I thought Aunt Carolyn was behind it; and I was at my wits end. I've had sleepless nights over this; I thought it must have been a set up….I must confess.

"That's insane….too funny" Marlene said followed by busting out laughing. Both ladies laughed so hard that the girls who were in the basement chilling, heard the ruckus coming from upstairs.

Bethany and Chateau immediately ran upstairs to see what their mothers were up to.

"Mom, what's going on?" Bethany asked.

 Marlene shrugged her shoulders without paying too much attention to Bethany.

"Nothing dear; we're just two idiots coming out of a serious meltdown and we love it."

That afternoon was the most memorable Chrissy and Marlene has had in decades. Even when times were good between them, they had never experienced such great joy.

CHAPTER TWENTY SEVEN

Well, it's about time; I was starting to think you were having trouble finding your dress at Madam Toussaint's." Jax said to Chrissy as she and Chateau entered through the living room of his house.

"Oh, let me tell you… the most unbelievable thing happened to me today." Chrissy said while tossing her handbag on the sofa where she went and sat next to Jax.

"Well, is it about the dress; I want to hear all about it" Jax said to Chrissy, half heartedly with his main interest on Chateau. And before Chrissy could get into her bombshell spiel, Jax cut her off and said to Chateau "Come her little darling, give your daddy a hug and let me know if you picked the most beautiful dress in the whole store."

Chateau's heart raced with joy and she smiled openly to her new found dad. However as the idea of having a daddy was still sinking in, she stood shy aside and began biting her nails. Jax then upped from the sofa and he scooped up her tiny and skinny mini body off the floor in a playful manner. She laughed out loudly with Chrissy looking on and feeling blessed to have found her soul mate.

And before putting her down, Jax asked Chateau what color her dress was and she said "pink"

"Oh wow, I love pink. Well, did you pick it all by yourself?" Jax asked her:

"No, my cousin helped me to pick it out"

Jax was instantly taken aback by his daughter's response. He quickly put her down while rolling his eyes to Chrissy and then back at Chateau.

"Your cousin; who's your cousin" Jax asked her

"Bethany" Chateau said.

Bethany's name went right over Jax's head; he was by no means cognizant of her because of the number of years lost between them.

He then turned to Chateau and said:

"I'm at a total loss honey; you've got to help me out. Who is Bethany? Is she someone you met at the store today?

"Huh-huh;" Chateau replied while biting her nails again and trying to make sense of her father's ignorance. Chrissy then chimed in and said "Ok pumpkin, go find your brothers and tell them about the fun time you had today with your cousin."

"What is she talking about? Going by the looks on your face I can that I'm the only one who doesn't know Bethany." Jax said.

Chrissy then kissed Jax while smiling and she said to him: "Well Bethany is not an imaginary person….she's actually her cousin who happens to be Marlene's daughter."

"Say that again" Jax said

"You heard me, "

"Come on, baby; give it to me straight. Tell me again very slowly what you're trying to say to me"

"I just did, honey. I ran into my sister today at Madame Toussaint's, and I was just as blown away. Never in a million years had I thought something like this would happen....but it did."

Jax returned to sitting on the sofa feeling stunned and anxious to hear what took place during Marlene's and Chrissy's run-in.

Not long after Chrissy began entertaining Jax with the lowdown of finding her sister at Chateau de Mehr, Christopher and Christian stormed into the room with Chateau behind them. They were anxious to know more about their auntie and cousin.

With things coming so fast at Chrissy, she felt overwhelmed with the little time left to spend with Jax. Anyway to help address the boys anxiety about meeting the rest of their family, Jax suggested dinner at the Vines with the idea of inviting Marlene and her family.

Chrissy who knew nothing about the Vines, took Jax's idea and she immediately called to invite Marlene and her family to join them for dinner at the Vines.

Marlene's heartfelt excitement and utter love towards her sister behooved her to share the good news with her Aunt Carolyn. So instead of going straight home as planned, she drove directly to Carolyn's home with the news.

So when Chrissy called Marlene's home about her invitation, it was Allora who had answered the phone. And after being told that, "Mrs. Sander was not home" Chrissy's response was "Thank you, I'll call back later."

It was almost sundown when Marlene and Bethany finally came home.

"What a day, what a marvelous day; wasn't it honey?" Marlene said to Bethany as they pulled inside the garage.

"It sure was Mom, I think it was the best day of your life, mom; I've never seen you happier" Bethany said.

As soon as Marlene made it inside the house, she went straight inside her den and kicked off her pumps to start getting cozy in her chaise. And without a minute longer to spare, Bethany raced upstairs to her bedroom and she locked the door. As much as she enjoyed meeting her long lost Auntie and being head over heels about her cousin Chateau, she just couldn't keep her mind off a boy name, "Joop." So with all the excitement that was taking place, deep down she was anxious about her mother taking care of business so she could get back home. She then pushed the button on her boom box and turned the dial to her favorite music station. And from then on she sprawled herself across her bed while talking *"sweet nothings"* with her secret love, Joop, whom her mother knew nothing about.

Anyway, as clock work would have it, Allora poured a glass of sweet red wine and brought it in to Marlene as she tried to unwind.

"What time would you like dinner served Ma'am," Allora asked Marlene as she handed her the glass of wine.

"I'm not sure, Allora. What did you prepare?"

"Beef pot roast with oyster sauce, some mash potatoes, creamed spinach and salad"

"Hmmm, Frank's favorite" Marlene said as she sipped on the wine.

"Well, did anyone call for me today while I was out?" Marlene asked.

"Oh, yes ma'am; I almost forgot. It was a lady, but she didn't leave a message."

"Well, did she leave her name?" Marlene asked.

"No ma'am, but I'm almost sure is Miss Lexa" Allora replied

Marlene quickly put the drink down on the lamp table and straightened herself in chair out of frustration. But she kept her cool.

"Are you sure about this, Allora? And what makes you think it was her?" Marlene asked.

"I'm not sure Ma'am but her voice sounded just like Miss Lexa, that's why I say that. Anyway she said she would call back" Allora replied.

"Thank you, Allora; Lets hold off on dinner until later" Marlene said to Allora as she left the room.

The idea of reconnecting with Lexa wasn't such a bad one, Marlene reckoned. And she sat quietly and pondered what it would be like hearing from Lexa:

"If that was really her calling, then maybe she has finally come to her senses and is ready to apologize so we can clear the air and move on. I haven't forgotten her caring and patience towards me when I had no one else to turn to, including my husband. It would be great hearing from her. She's so awesome. Oh, man…it would be just fabulous to sit and play catch up about everything in our lives. After all, she was my best friend."

While Marlene sat in reflection of Lexa and their years of friendship, she was hopeful Allora was right in assuming that she was the woman in question that had called to speak with her. So she sat patiently while sipping on the wine in hopes that she'd call back.

Anyway, that being said, Chrissy kept calling back to speak with Marlene, as she had promised that she would. But due to Bethany's long winded conversation on the telephone with her "first crush" the line remained busy upwards of two hours.

Marlene soon grew tired of the anticipation for Lexa to call back. So to help her pass the time she picked up the phone to call Frank who had been out with Monk and his golf club buddies all day. She wanted to know what time they would be coming home mostly because she was dying to fill their ears with *labrish* about running into the elusive Ms. Gabriella Fairchild.

Bethany heard a click and presence of mind told it could be her mother attempting to use the phone. So she said to Joop, "gotta go" and she immediately hung up on him before her mother was able to hear any of their conversation.

Anyway, after two attempts without any answer from Frank, Marlene assumed they most likely are still having fun with friends.

With that in mind, she went and told Allora to fix supper for just herself and Bethany. And as soon as she entered the kitchen the telephone rang; it was Chrissy making one last try to get a hold of her sister.

"Oh, my dear sister, thank goodness you're there; I almost gave up trying." Chrissy said to Marlene as she tried making sense of her comment."

"So glad you called, I was just thinking about the great time we had; and I'm missing you already" Marlene said.

"…Which is the reason why I've been trying to call you. The boys are insisting that they meet you and their cousins before heading back home tomorrow. I know it's kind of late notice and with nightfall setting in, you guys mostly like ate already." Chrissy said.

"I would most definitely love to meet my nephews. So what did you have in mind?" Marlene replied.

"Well…how about dinner at the Vines…it would do us a world of favor if you all could make it." Chrissy said.

"Oh gee, Chrissy, there's nothing I'd like better than to spend more time with you, but Frank and Monk aren't home as yet. Anyway, we haven't had supper as yet, so I think it would be fabulous if you Jax and the boys could join us here for dinner. I'm sure by then Frank and Monk would be home."

Oh, sis, that's so kind of you, but I hate to put you on the spot like that on such short notice.

"No, no, not to worry; there's nothing I'd like more. Allora has a way of making things happen even on a short notice, so she'll be able to pull it off. So is that a yes?" Marlene said with high anticipation Chrissy would give in.

Chrissy gladly took up Marlene on her offer and shortly after they were on their way. Marlene then called Brandon to update him of the good news about his long lost sister and her family coming to her house for dinner.

It had been many, many years since Marlene and her children have had such great fun at their home. That was the first and finest get together she has had in fifteen years. And with such good news in the making, Brandon went and got his mother to take the ride with him; he couldn't stand to keep her out of what he thought was a healing opportunity for his fractured family.

So with time of the essence, Marlene and Bethany tried stepping in to help Allora with getting things organized. And things only got better after Monk and Frank walked in and heard the good news.

However, before Marlene was able to fill them in about her all her surprises of the day, Chrissy and her family turned up. Monk quickly opened the door and Chrissy fell into his wide opened arms.

"Oh, my God, Monk; look at you! So tall and handsome; I never would have recognized you on the street. This is just so wonderful; I can't believe I'm here. Chrissy blurted."

Marlene heard her sister's voice at the front and she came out to greet her. Chrissy then released herself from Monk's embrace so she could introduce her children. Then Frank came out behind Marlene, followed by Bethany.

"Come on over here, boys; I want you to meet your Aunt Marlene and your cousins" Chirssy said with heartfelt pride.

The boys were delirious with glee; they almost didn't know what to do with themselves. Again the doorbell rang, and Frank quickly opened it.

A loud scream followed after Chrissy looked around and saw Carolyn.

Aunt Carolyn, Aunt Carolyn, they didn't tell me you were coming. Oh my God, I'm in shock, this is so beautiful. Thank you sis, I know you did this for me. Chrissy turned to Marlene and said.

"Don't thank me, dear. I had nothing to with it. I'm just as surprised as you are." Marlene said.

"Then Brandon who was still standing next to the door cleared his throat as if he was still waiting for his special welcome from his sister"

"Chrissy then busted out laughing and saying, "You did this for me; I should have known. Oh my brother, it's so good seeing you: I never thought the day would come when I'd see you again. Oh wow, this is so amazing.

After all the handshakes and hugging and kissing followed by a few teardrops here and there, everyone walked back and filled the house with a joyful noise. And after their celebratory dinner, Chrissy soon became a dartboard from having many questions about her disappearance being poked at her in many different ways.

Surely for Chrissy, there was no easy way of making it simple for them to understand her complexities back then. Even though they all made it seem their concerns were out of love, it was more of a disturbing echo for Chrissy reflecting on her past. Matter-of-factly, Chrissy would have been okay with the drill, but only if it were on her terms. She thought it was too soon to start telling her whole story as she was more interested in the reunion.

Be that as it were, Chrissy poignantly expressed her gratitude for having her family back and how much it meant knowing that her children could have a place in their lives. And with regards to their curiosities she promised to let everyone be apprised of her journey from Christina Tate to that of Ms. Gabriella Fairchild, by way of her diary.

So with that being said, all were in favor of letting Chrissy off the hook, and Marlene's wedding which was only a few weeks away became the main topic for discussion the rest of the night.

CHAPTER TWENTY EIGHT

The palatial "Bradfordt Colony Mansion" was where Frank's and Marlene's wedding took place. The historic and beautiful site was where Watertown's inner city elites – like the Tate's, Cromwell's and Okumba's, would oftentimes drop in for an exclusive affair such as this.

The striking tall moss-draped trees served as the backdrop for the garden wedding. The expansive curvature of the old oaks, posed their leafy branches as a botanical head-dress above the massive all white tent.

And as far as the eye could see from the ground up to the ceiling, was a creative display of orchids, hydrangeas, ferns and baby's breath, floated on tulle. However, the focal point of the room was a five piece Grecian column display with floral sprays throughout.

There were ushers everywhere--- always smiling and ready to pin buttoners on the gentlemen's lapels and put corsages on the wrists of the ladies as they walked in.

From the moment the Limo pulled up with Frank, the swift moving videographers and photographers, swarmed around the vehicle with hopes of catching the very first detail of his appearance. And before his feet had even touched the ground, they had captured the tiniest stitches and every other detail of his pricey and glossy black shoes.

This all-time debonair and well polished gentleman stepped out of the limo dressed in a black tuxedo, white shirt and black bowtie. His shiny diamond cufflinks were gifted to him from Carolyn Tate. And his sophisticated charm was completed with a small yellow rose boutonniere pinned on his lapel.

As Frank entered the covered tent where a few guests were already in place, he walked right up to the focal point of the room to await his bride to be. And not too far away from where he was standing, were the pianist and a harpist playing parts of what sounded like "You Raise Me Up."

Meanwhile inside the Bradfordt Mansion, where Marlene was getting dressed, she had the help of three assistants, and Chrissy as her confidante. Her elegant ivory colored bridal gown was tailored with embroidered beading on its trumpet high neck; and the cathedral train had satin and lace florets tacked throughout.

Her something "old" was Carolyn Tate's bridal gloves, her something "borrowed" was one of Miss Cassie's diamond bracelets, and her something "blue" was a lacy blue satin teddy lingerie with matching garter, from Chrissy.

Inside another room was where Bethany and Chateau could be found pacing back and forth on the hardwood floor. They were exquisitely dressed and anxious to get out so they could see what was taking place outside.

Then it was time, and just as Marlene was about to emerged from the ornately decorated boudoir. Chrissy walked up from behind and tried holding her back. Marlene appeared panicked as she turned to face her sister.

"It's my makeup isn't it? Too much rouge, you think?" Marlene said tremulously.

"You are flawless…simply stunning. I just wanted to tell you how much I love you and to thank you for letting me back into your life.

"I love you too, sis. But say no more…as I'm starting to get the shakes and I don't want my make up to start running." Marlene said while touching her sister's face endearingly.

Marlene was then on her way out with a small bouquet of calla lilies in one hand while clinging tightly to the arm of Mr. Sander, Frank's dad.

Soon after, the musical interlude stopped and the much anticipated tune 'Here Comes the Bride" sounded off. Everyone rose to their feet as they watched the bride and her entourage strolled in. Chateau lead the way by throwing handfuls of pink, and red rose petals along the floating white carpet.

Frank was moved to tears after seeing his bride to be coming in and looking steadfastly ahead. And as she continued marching down the aisle to meet him, he tried fighting back the tears. He was doing his damndest to push Barchas out of his mind and to keep his focus on every step Marlene was making as she got closer to him.

As memories of Barchas continued tugging at Frank's heart, he felt justified in giving prominence over his main attraction, so as to engage one of Barchas' longstanding jokes with him:

"Hey man, when are you going to put a ring on one of those ladies' finger? And how much longer do I have to wait to get a niece or nephew to call me Uncle B?"

Frank would say:

"Can't you see I'm still waiting for you to pick the right one for me bro? If I can trust you with my life, then finding a wife for me shouldn't be so hard."

And Barchas' response was always the same:

"Only the best for you my brother; that's all I want for you."

And they would always laugh about it, most likely over drinks.

As Frank watched Marlene coming closer and closer to him, he drew a long deep breath and said to himself:

"I never thought it was going to be this way my friend; but you've kept your promise and gave me the best, and I couldn't be more thankful."

And with eyes of cheers and a smiley face, Frank adored every inch of Marlene as she smiled and took her place next to him.

Also standing next to Frank was his best man Jeptha Stoddard and Monk as the ring bearer. Alongside Marlene were Carolyn as Mother of the Bride and Bethany as her bridesmaid.

The front row seats were occupied with, Simon and his wife Leigh, Jax, his sons Christian and Christopher, his soon to be wife Ms. Fairchild and their daughter Chateau.

Bishop Timmins, who was a close friend of Carolyn Tate's, performed the wedding ceremony. The order of the ceremony was comprised largely of traditional formalities. However after a few punctuations of secular readings and comments, the outcome of the ceremony was an eruption of good-humored pleasantries.

The reception dinner was more of a semi-formal style. The high class caterers from out of town offered an elaborate display of heavy hors-d'oeuvres followed by a wide range of classic dishes.

And before long, the ivory and gold fondant cake with intricate lace detail was unveiled. The three tiered stacked masterpiece quickly disappeared after everyone asked for seconds. And as Carolyn ate her piece, she wasn't shy about taking credit for the moist delicious cake, which was a recipe passed on from both her mothers.

As the reception dinner came to a close, Mr. and Mrs. Sander took center stage with their first dance.

"It's a good thing you've been teaching me a few of your moves, honey; otherwise I'd be shuffling on the floor as if I had two left feet" Marlene said to her husband as they danced.

From then on, the dance floor came alive with their guests sharing the dance floor and dancing the night away.

CHAPTER TWENTY NINE

Oh my God, Jax; wasn't that a beautiful wedding? I haven't danced like that in years." Chrissy said to Jax as they left the wedding to get back home.

"Yeah baby; it was a beautiful wedding. It wouldn't mean the same to me without you and the kids there with me. I'm so thankful things worked out the way they did. And, you my lady, danced as if you've been practicing all week for the occasion. I see you've still got your moves.

Chrissy laughed and said:

"But of course my darling; and there's plenty more where those came from."

So where did you say they're going on their honeymoon? Jax asked Chrissy

"Monaco. But Marlene promised to cut their trip short to be back for our wedding." Chrissy said.

"I'd like that very much" Jax said while the limo pulled into his driveway.

By early next morning, Jax was on his way to work while Chrissy and the children slept. Later that day, Chrissy called her stepmother, just to see if she was up to a visit from her. Carolyn was delighted about the call. Having Chrissy spend time alone with her, was a much needed form of closure she felt she needed. And since Chrissy's return to the city, some unresolved issues kept taunting her under the quiet.

Rosalinda's heart flowed with joy seeing Chrissy entering Carolyn's home. Over time, she was able to gather enough information mostly from eavesdropping, to assume she would never see Chrissy again.

"Oh, Miss Chrissy, Miss Chrissy, it's so good to see you, I miss you so much. Oh, Miss Chrissy you are still so very pretty; no change, no change at all." Rosalinda said to Chrissy while she was still standing inside the foyer.

"Thank you, Rosalinda, I miss you too; Aunt Carolyn is blessed to have you. Chrissy said, while smiling at Rosalinda and giving her a hug.

Thank you Miss Chrissy; I love Mrs. Tate very much' she's so good to me." Rosalinda replied.

These are my children, Rosalinda; Christian, Christopher and Chateau. Chrissy said while pointing out the children as she called their names.

Carolyn heard the meeting and greeting and in the foyer and she quickly came out to meet Chrissy and the children.

"Oh, my darling I can't tell you how much this means to me; I've been praying to the Good Lord to smile on my family and make us whole again. Come in, come on in honey, let's sit down and allow life to happen." Aunt Carolyn said, while being tucked away in Chrissy's embrace."

Chrissy then released herself from Carolyn and she immediately started hugging the kids who were standing next to their mother.

Carolyn continued talking:

"Come on darling; let me show you around the house. As you can see it's not very big, but it's more than I need."

"So, how is Miss Cassie, Aunt Carolyn; is she ok?" Chrissy asked as they walked through the living room behind Carolyn.

"Oh' honey, she's bad…really bad. She doesn't know anyone… Alzheimer. I was going to take you and the kids to the family room so we could sit a while. But since you asked, I'll just take you to see mother: Carolyn said grimly.

Needless to say the kids had a dreadful shock after seeing the old woman propped up in bed between crisp white sheets just barely below her bosom. She was covered in frailty with vacant eyes. Her gaping mouth and vapor-thin lips had Chrissy speechless as she recalled the once gritty and outspoken woman of years gone by. Her thinning hair, stark-white and short, were pressed against her scalp. And to Chrissy it was an unfavorable reminder of the short pixie cuts she'd donned for years.

Chateau grabbed on to her mother's hand while Christopher and Christian looked on.

"What's her name Mommy" Christian asked his mother.

"Her name is Miss Cassie, son. She's Aunt Carolyn's mother"

"Which means, she's my great grand-mother" Christian said.

"Yes, honey, you're right; she's your great grandmother"

"That's so cool, Mom; I'm glad I got a chance to meet her.

Christopher then turned to Carolyn and asked: "How old is she, Aunt Carolyn?

"She's almost a hundred years old, dear"

"…A hundred!" Chateau blurted with her eyes widened and her hand thrown in the air.

"Be quiet Chateau," Christian said and he went on to ask:

"Do you think she knows we're here, Aunt Carolyn?"

"Let's hope that she does, sweetheart; that would be such a wonderful thing"

"Chrissy remained quiet as she was tearing up from memories flooding back at her from her final days spent with Chey and how she died in her arms.

Aside from the usual hint of lavender permeating the air in Miss Cassie's room, Carolyn sensed a sudden change in the atmosphere. And after looking at all the grim faces, she reckoned Chrissy and the kids had seen more than enough.

"Come on you guys, let's go; I'd like to show you some pictures of the family." Carolyn said.

Chateau was first to pull away from her mother and she bolted right past her brothers to wait outside of Cassie's bedroom. Soon after they all went into the den to hang out with Carolyn. She took great pride in showing the kids several family photo albums which she called her prized possessions.

The children felt right at home being with their grandmother. And that was a realization Chrissy could not deny especially after watching Chateau drawing closer to Carolyn and placing her hands in her lap.

Carolyn then raised her head with her nose turned up, and she blurted:

"Hmm, what is that I smell?"

The boys who were so engrossed into the pictures had to stop to tune in with Carolyn. But Chateau didn't skip a beat.

"Yeah, cookies" Chateau shouted while grinning with her eyes widened and throwing her hands in the air.

"Oh yeah" Christopher said while Christian chimed in and wondered where the kitchen was. Carolyn smiled and said:
"Go on, follow your noses and Rosalinda will take care of you"

So, with the kids out of their hair, Carolyn and Chrissy had some quality time spent between them.

"Thank you, Aunt Carolyn, for having me; I should have done this a long time ago. More and more, I realize the damage done to my children by keeping them away from their roots"

"You're doing just fine honey; as you can see we are all on a path to recovery. And to be considered a part of your roots gives me a healing touch that I haven't felt since the last time your father held my hands. Thank you; thank you. He must be here with us and I feel so good." Carolyn said.

Chrissy's mind then raced to Timothy, but she was afraid to ask; she assumed the worse after not seeing or hearing mention made of him.

With that in mind Chrissy was starting to get too emotional from the reflections brought on by Carolyn and she tried to stay strong by hiding from them. So she turned her head and looked around and said:

Have I told you how beautiful your home is, Aunt Carolyn?

"No honey. But that's quite all right; sooner or later, I know you would. I haven't forgotten how kind you are." Carolyn said.

"Speaking of "home" Aunt Carolyn as you may recall I was very stubborn and adamant about not wanting to have anything to do with the house at Bluefield Heights" Chrissy said.

"Huh-huh, I remember it well; and I must let you know I was heartbroken. And if I heard you correctly, I believe you said the house at Bluefield Heights.

"Huh-huh, that's what I said" Chrissy replied wondering what was her point.

"But you see honey; you refer to it as "the house," when in fact it is "your" house." Carolyn said.

Chrissy quickly acquiesced. She reckoned after all Carolyn had gone through to return what she thought was rightfully hers, the least she could do was to be more agreeable and show a higher level of appreciation.

Chrissy then said:

I'm sorry Aunt Carolyn, you're right. With everything happening so fast I guessed it hasn't sunken in quite fully. Anyway, since my reconnection with Jax, which I never thought could ever happen, I find myself thinking a lot about my home here."

Carolyn said:

Well, I'm glad to hear you say that dear. Why don't you drive by some time and see what's going on with it. Last time Brandon went by was more than three-four years ago, and he told me it looked like a forest back there. Matter-of-fact, the house can no longer be seen from off the street.

Chrissy said:

Oh wow; I can only imagine. Anyway Aunt Carolyn, as I've told you, I just can't get it off my mind. So I thought you'd be the best person to help me with ideas of could be done with it.

Oh, my dear, there's so much you could do. But why beat up yourself over it. Quite simple, nothing would make happier than to see you living in that house. You've spent most of your life fighting for it; and you got it. So why slam the door on the elephant's tail? The minute you unlock that door is the minute you'll discover that last little piece of you that was still missing."

After carefully listening to Carolyn, Chrissy paused for a few seconds to think about what she had said. A deeper feeling of profound veneration towards Carolyn developed because of how Chrissy was moved by her comment. And with heartfelt appreciation she rose from the chair and hugged her stepmother while saying:

"Thank you, Aunt Carolyn; you're so amazing. I know I was right when I told myself only you could set me straight. I promise to take your advice and get that tail of mine unlocked" Chrissy said jokingly to Carolyn while she was still in her embrace.

Carolyn laughed out loudly, and then she said: Come on honey, let's go and find out what Rosalinda is doing with my grandchildren; it feels so good hearing them moving around the house.

So, after a fabulous rest of the afternoon with Carolyn, Chrissy left with feeling of great accomplishment and a lot to think about. Although she was committed to bring about change to her home in Bluefield Heights, she was more focused on her wedding day which was less than a month away.

CHAPTER THIRTY

As Chrissy and Jax prepared for a beautiful life together their bond grew stronger, and stronger with every waking moment they shared. But every time the subject of where they would call home came up, Jax, and Chrissy too, would find themselves twiddling their thumbs.

With three children and a wife, Jax reckoned it would take a large chunk of money to renovate and make his home a comparable option to bring to the table. That being said, nothing would make him prouder than taking on the challenge of creating such great dream for his family.

In as much as the massive beauty of the Chateau de Mehr had kept Jax in unending awe every time he was there, he had never felt complete about calling it home. However, he was prepared to do whatever it took to make his family happy if it did come down to the wire that, that was where they ought to be.

And then there was one. Despite Chrissy's busy schedule with her wedding at hand, she rounded up the family and drove out to see her house at Bluefield Heights. Except for the thick tall brush and tall trees with limbs spanning out of bounds, there was no sign of the house from off the street. Jax suggested they parked on the side of the road and chanced walking in.

Although Carolyn had warned Chrissy that the house could be in a state of disrepair, she was by no means prepared for what she was about to see.

"Oh- my- God," she blurted with her hands over her mouth.

"Yes, baby it's pretty bad" Jax said, while rolling his eyes all the way up to the roof.

"Christopher get back over here, I don't want you going in there!" Chrissy cautioned as the boy attempted to move closer to the house.

"This is unbelievable, Jax, it seemed as if this placed had been vandalized from the minute it became vacant." Chrissy said grimly.

"Well, you've been talking about it, and it's good that you came and saw what's left of it." Jax said.

They stuck together and kept walking around the property until they bumped into the cashew apple tree which was Chrissy's favorite place to sit with her grandmother for mentoring. She paused and looked up and sure enough there were bright yellow cashew apples hanging and begging to be picked. She said nothing because she was starting to break from the precious memories spent there with her Gracie Mae.

"Daddy, there's bugs on my shoes and pants and they're biting me." Chateau whined as she held on to her dad's hand and kept stomping her feet.

"Those are not bugs sweetheart; they are called burrs."

"What's that" she said annoyingly.

As Jax searched his thoughts for an answer for Chateau, Chrissy chimed in and said "They're tiny little seeds with prickles on them, honey."

"Ouch, that hurt! I don't like it here; it's kind of spooky." Chateau snapped.

"Stop being such a big baby, Chateau; we're going to be leaving soon" Christopher fired back at his sister while they kept walking.

Finally they came around to the back of the house where the stable could be seen clearly at the far end of the property.

"What's that little house over there?" Chateau asked while pointing to the stable.

"Yeah dad, what is that?" Christopher asked.

"I believe that was a stable, son" Jax said while eyeing Chrissy for confirmation.

Chrissy did not respond because she was more caught up into the moment that was causing her heart to pound with heightened force against her chest.

Walking up and seeing the stable sent shockwaves through Chrissy. She stood still with her eyes fixed on the stable until she was overpowered by her imagination. And in the moment she imagined seeing her father going in with the intention of taking his life.

She wondered what it must have felt like to him while sitting on the cusp of his deadly abyss.   She pondered hard and deep about the fact that she was foremost in his mind before ending his life.

Was he at peace within himself, or was he angry within himself; she pondered. She imagined he was crying or quite possible fresh out of tears. Did he take a shower, shaved and sat on the john that day? Or was he just plain out of sorts and being a drunk.

And as her imagination stretched, her psyche held her captive until it was all over. She immediately closed her eyes and covered her ears as if it were a sudden reflex from the imaginary sounding "pow!" after her dad pulled the fatal trigger.

That was a head-raising moment for Chrissy as she experienced an unexplainable anguish.

So while Chrissy stood speechless and was only staring in one direction, Jax's eyes roved from side to side while taking in the unbelievable condition of the place. From the humongous hole in the ground which used to be a pool, to the roofless stable that Chrissy couldn't take her eyes off, Jax only had one thing to say:

"I can't believe my eyes"

Jax became concerned after not getting a response from Chrissy. He turned to take a closer look at her and noticed that she was looking dazed.

"Sweetheart, are you okay; you look a little uncomfortable" Jax said to Chrissy.

And without her having anything to say, she turned and burrowed her face on his chest and then she began to sob.

It didn't take much more than that for Jax to put two and two together to figure out what was making her so upset.

And while the kids looked on dumbfounded, Jax said to them while he massaged their mother's back:

Don't worry, your mother is going to be fine....just give her a few more minutes to come around. She's a little upset because she misses her grandmother. Truth be told, Jax only used Gracie Mae as a scapegoat for Chrissy's woes. He perceived bringing her dad more into the picture would only deepen her pain.

Jax then said to Chrissy:

"Look baby, I think this is too much for you; I think we should leave and do this another time. And furthermore the kids are getting restless"
But Chrissy wasn't quite ready to leave. She tried pulling herself together and continued walking until they were in front of the house again. She went up to the front door and peered through the shattered glass windows. And as her eyes rolled around she recalled her time there as a life of splendor with her sister and grandmother, long before her father had met Carolyn.

Jax walked up closely behind her and placed his arms around her waist to take a peek as well. And while their eyes rolled up and down and back and forth of the once stately mansion, Jax turned to Chrissy and said:

"You know, honey, this old house could be our home. I can't explain this feeling that came over me, but it feels like this is where our hearts belong."

Chrissy immediately turned to face Jax with tear- filled eyes. She was deeply moved from what he had said and she thanked him. She then went on to telling him that despite the sadness she portrayed, there was tugging on her heart telling her that was where her destiny would take root.

He then kissed her gently on the cheek as seal of confirmation. And then he whispered in her ear: The first thing I'll do is tear down those four walls left standing, so you'll never have to see that stable again."

Granted, it was a bit chilly outside; Chrissy, Jax and the kids left the and drove straight to "Mr. Shorty's" for ice cream as a form of cooling off from their little outing to Bluefield Heights.

At first the kids were a little skeptical after being told that someday the family would be moving to Bluefield Heights, to call home. However, they've been so excited about having both parents in their lives, as well as other family members around, that any old place would do as long as they were together.

Chrissy changed Carolyn's life in a very special way. She was relieved, elated and ecstatic after Chrissy informed her of her decision to move back to Bluefield Heights. She was quick to offer any help needed to make the transition faster. Although it was unlikely, she would call on her stepmother for any kind of help, Chrissy thanked her for the offer; moving forward.

Carolyn and Chrissy chatted a while longer; mostly about her health issues and her fear of ending up like her mother. Chrissy had no idea that Carolyn was diagnosed with early stage dementia, and she never suspected anything of the sort, because their conversations together gave no hint.

Chrissy's reply to Carolyn was:

"Oh gee, I'm sorry to hear Aunt Carolyn; I never would have thought"

"Well, thanks dear. Sometimes I'm just a mess; I don't know if I'm going or coming. So, let's talk about something different; you don't need to hear me rambling about my condition. Anyway dear, have you made up your mind about what you're going to do with your house?

"House" Chrissy said while feeling as if she was thrown off course.

"Huh-huh

Which one? Are you taking about Chateau de Mehr, Aunt Carolyn? Chrissy said with a bit of hesitation to her tone.

"No dear; I'm talking about your house at Bluefield Heights. Have you forgotten already what you and I had talked about?"

"I'm sorry Aunt Carolyn, but with the wedding just around the corner, things are a little crazy for me right now."

That's quite all right dear, I understand.   But while you were here the other day, you promised you'd go by and take a look at it. I must warn you however, what Brandon had told me after he drove by there a few years ago." Carolyn said.

After listening to Carolyn, Chrissy wasn't quite sure on how to respond to her stepmother without sounding conflicted.

"I'd love to hear what Brandon had told you, Aunt Carolyn" Chrissy said.

"He said the property was dilapidated and needed immediate attention." Carolyn replied quickly.

"Well, I wouldn't doubt it, Aunt Carolyn. After all it's been left unattended for almost fifteen years." Chrissy said while choosing her response cautiously.

So without belaboring the topic, Chrissy thanked Carolyn for updating her and she tried changing the subject.

"You know Aunt Carolyn; I've been meaning to ask about Timothy. Is he doing alright, I haven't heard much said about him?"

"Oh, good Lord… poor Uncle Timmy. I had to put him in a nursing home, because it was just too much for me keeping him here. He hasn't changed a bit, he stays busy preaching to the folks around him and he prays for anyone he can lay his hands on.   Luckily for him his head still works.   Carolyn said grimly.

"Well, I'm glad I asked Aunt Carolyn; that's great news hearing that Uncle Timmy is still hanging in there and doing the Lord's work. Anyway, as always, it was great chatting with you. I must be on my way now Aunt Carolyn and I look forward to having you at my wedding.

Their phone conversation ended thereafter leaving Carolyn glad she had heard from Chrissy. However, Chrissy walked away feeling a little glum about the looming fate of her stepmother.

CHAPTER THIRTY ONE

As the days flew by and drew their wedding day closer, Chrissy and Jax had less than twenty four hours before they are a couple.

As part of the arrangements, Chrissy made it clear to all of her designers, planners and coordinators for her wedding, that she wanted nothing less than perfection at all costs.

A gazebo was installed on her favorite side of the widespread reserve. It was soon to be transformed to look like a chapel for the ceremonial proceedings. Not far from there, the iconic mountain side with its glistening waters was in clear view. This feature served as the main backdrop to the chapel that was adequately sized to accommodate their small gathering of thirty.

The focal point of the chapel was a tall arch draped with white toile that was exquisitely decorated with tropical palms leaves, beautiful flowers and large faux pearls cascading to the ground. This was flanked by gold tone pedestals with white birdcages for doves to come later.

The three rows of chairs were covered in all white satin with goldthread embroidered tiebacks.

Meanwhile, back inside the Chateau de Mehr, the master banquet hall was reorganized and perfectly staged to deliver the opulence according to Ms. Fairchild's expectations.

The linens on the dining tables were gold tone and shimmery and the centerpieces were gilded candelabras with ivory colored roses and peach colored peonies artfully placed around the bases. And the oversize gold-patina chairs that were placed around the tables left the outcome of the room with a look of Victorian grandeur.

On the morning of the wedding, Kennedy and his wife turned up early.

"Holy smokes" He exclaimed. "This is the coolest place ever! Look babe; is that the top of a mountain I'm looking on?" Kennedy said excitingly as he pulled into the driveway of the Chateau de Mehr.

"Holy smokes alright" His wife said under bated breath while her eyes rolled to look at the top of the mountain Kennedy that got Kennedy so worked up.

Are you sure we're at the right place, honey? She asked Kennedy cautiously.

"Well, it said it said right there on those big iron gates; Chateau de Mehr. So, we've got to be in the right place." Kennedy said.

"Huh-huh: Okay, which means this must be the venue for the wedding; not where she lives" she replied.

"You could be right about that, Mrs. Tate. I guess the only way to find out is to go inside and find out what's going on back there" Kennedy said to his wife while squeezing her hand inside his palm.

Jax was proud and overjoyed seeing his son and daughter in law turning up in support of his decision to marry Chrissy. Although Chrissy tried getting him to warm up to her over a few phone calls, she could sense that he remained apprehensive about his father's future with her. That being said, Chrissy reckoned her past had left a lot to be desired, so she held no grudges about her future step-son.

Jax immediately walked up to the car and greeted his son and daughter in law with gusto. And with a huge smile across his face he had them to follow him along the pathway to the main house.

"So what do you think of the place son; isn't it marvelous? " Jax said to Kennedy as they continued walking.

"I'm speechless, Dad. I never expected to run into anything like this, to tell you the truth."

"Oh yes, son; this place is something else." Jax said proudly as if he had lived there all his life.

"So where are you taking us now Dad? I thought we were supposed to be meeting you at Chrissy's house?

"This is where she lives son, and the wedding will be taking place on the same compound." Jax said.

Kennedy and his wife remained speechless as they continued walking behind their dad.

"Huh-huh; hard to believe, doesn't it?" Jax said.

Kennedy and XXXXX kept walking and listening to what Jax had to say without responding.

He then looked at Kennedy and said:

"I know exactly what you're thinking son; but sooner or later you'll find out." Jax said.

"What am I thinking Dad?" Kennedy asked his father.

"…What most people would think; they'd want to know how the heck she ended up at a place like this to call home." Jax said laughingly, while Kennedy gave in with a nod and patting his dad on the shoulder.

By the time Kennedy and Leigh made it inside the main house to be wowed by Chrissy's elegant interiors, she was standing in the foyer and ready to welcome them inside her humble abode, as she called it.

Kennedy proudly introduced his wife to Chrissy. And without giving her to chance to say "Hi, nice meeting you" to his wife, he moved to tell her that she had not changed since the last time he saw her, in terms of her timeless beauty. He continued talking and then he complimented her on her beautiful home, and thanked her for making his dad the happiest man in the world.

Chrissy felt great relief, seeing Kennedy standing there with his wife.

She smiled at Kennedy and thanked him for coming and for being his dad's best man. She then hugged Leigh and said:

I've heard such great things about you Leigh; I'm so glad we've finally met. Jax talked so much

With hardly much time left for Chrissy to play the perfect hostess, her hair-stylist turned up and she had to be excused, leaving her guests to make themselves at home.

Since Marlene's return from her honeymoon, she had not been able to catch up with her sister to update her on how their trip went. Anyway, while she hovered over her sister as she was getting dressed she surprised her with a blue teddy, as her something blue for the occasion.

Chrissy smiled after she noticed Marlene twirling the skimpy little piece of undergarment on her pointer finger, while rocking her hips from side to side with her eyes closed.

"You naughty girl, is there something you're trying to tell me" Chrissy stopped to ask her sister while still smiling.

"Oh-my-god, Sis; you shouldn't have to ask. My husband went crazy the instant I stepped out of my gown and flashed him with the unexpected look. Since then I bought a few more of these little babies to keep him chasing me around the room."

Marlene then handed her the lingerie and said:

"So here, I want you to put this on and see what tricks old Jax could pull out of his birthday suit for you."

Chrissy busted out laughing while wiggling her butt to fit into the delicately trimmed lingerie without tearing it.

Chrissy then turned to look into the mirror to see how she looked. She thought she looked sexy from the front because of the perfect fit for her cleavage. And while still eyeing herself in the mirror with her sister looking on, she turned to look at her backside.

Chrissy eyes, popped while looking at her sister and she said:

"So where's the rest of it; I don't see anything!"

Marlene tried containing herself from laughing. She immediately covered her mouth and said:

"Oops; I'd forgotten about that big butt of yours, sis. Don't ask me how, but as soon as you put it on, the rest of it just disappeared. But don't worry it's in there somewhere. Marlene said while still being amused at her sister's expense.

Chrissy didn't appear to be satisfied with her looks. She made a deep sigh while staring at herself in the mirror. And then she said:

"Damn sis, don't you think I'm too old for this? Women my age don't wear these things; I might as well be naked; Jax will be just as crazy seeing me without any frills.

"No sis, you don't want to do that; you need these. Trust me…if it's even for the sake of your cleavage, you've got to do this. Furthermore, where else are you going to find something blue when you're about to be married in less than an hour." Marlene cautioned."

"Well, I guess you're right; so let's continue with getting the show on the road then" Chrissy said while feeling upbeat and happy at the mere thought of having her sister around.

It was five o-clock pm and things were finally shaping up for Chrissy and Jax to tie the knot. The red carpet was rolled out and the doves put in their cages. Minister Billings was already there and waiting to perform the wedding ceremonies. The clarinet player kept Minister Billings entertained with his fingerings as there was no one else around to show off his skills to.

However, not much longer into the soulful musical escapade, Minister Billings and the Clarinet Player became distracted by the guests being ushered inside the chapel.

Carolyn was having a good day from all the compliments she'd received about her stunning appearance. She stood out quite elegantly in her extraordinary wide rim hat that was embellished with an onyx, crystals and pearl vintage hatpin. Her flesh colored silk gown; just a tad lighter than her skin, matched perfectly with her scarf that was draped loosely around her shoulders.

Carolyn looked around and thought everything was perfect. And before taking her seat, she went over and shook the hand of the pastor and introduced herself as mother of the bride. She then stepped away and kept looking around with bits and pieces of old memories emerging inside her. And with much clarity she was able to recapture the first time when she'd met Larry, the lawn- man, who later turned out to be her husband and the one true love of her life. And oh, she loved him so. So much so, that even in his death she'd want the best for his daughters. And even when things looked like they'd never be the same again between them, she never gave up and she never stopped praying. And for her to end up being recognized as the matriarch of the family, it gave chills to her bones and water to her eyes.

Carolyn then took to her seat and tried as best she could to recall more of her exquisitely- beautiful life with Larry. And despite her struggles with putting things into their proper perspectives, she was grateful and humble enough to accept Marlene and Chrissy as her ultimate recovery. She mumbled "Thank You Father God for being so good to me. The life I've dreamed of has finally come home to me."

Soon after a horse drawn carriage pulled up next to the chapel with Chrissy sitting beautifully posed inside. The driver of the carriage was Chandlon Bow. The clarinet player began playing "Here Comes the Bride" and everyone looked around and saw that she was there.

Amid the group of photographers wiring their way around Chrissy as Chandlon helped her off the carriage, Frank stood patiently waiting so she could take a hold of his arm and be escorted inside.

Beneath the amber sky, a cool evening breeze blustered off the mountain side as Chrissy walked gingerly towards the chapel. Gusts of whistling wind encircled the hem of her dress and flipped its way above her thighs to where her naked buttocks were instantly exposed. Gasps and giggles followed from the unexpected mooning…but she was too thrilled about marrying Jax, to care how high her dress could fly.

Jax's hands twitched with anticipation; he wondered how long before the nuptials are read. He was dying to hear the pastor say "you may kiss your bride," so that he could take her in his arms and seal his fate with hers.

And as she moved closer to taking her last step before she's standing next to him, his lips dribbled with desire and hers parted with a smile, and she was as beautiful as Jax could have never imagined.

"You are the most beautiful woman in the world; I feel like the luckiest man alive to have you standing next to me" Jax whispered to Chrissy, and she only smiled broader at his response.

As all eyes became fixated on Chrissy and Jax, Minister Billings got the attention of the room by starting off with "Dearly Beloved" And it remained that way until he was through delivering his commencement speech.

And when it came time for the exchange of vows and rings, Jax carefully repeated after Minister Billings while slipping on a single diamond band on his bride's finger.

Chrissy's eyes welled up as she turned to Marlene to get her handwritten vow. She then placed her hand in Jax's palm as she began to read.

My Dearest Jax,

"The evidence is clear your love for me is a true reflection of God's Grace inside you. Being with you has opened my mind to a love I could not forsake. I'm abundantly blessed to become your wife.

Every time I look into your eyes, I see the person I could become--- a woman more deserving of you. Every time you touch me, my spirit soars and set my heart upon a throne that only God could understand, and every time I think about you, all my secret hopes come through.

I prayed for forgiveness and God sent you, I prayed for happiness and God sent you. You're the perfect gift to my life; you're my heaven sent.

Baby, you're the greatest outcome of my life, and with pride and gratitude, I receive your undying love. I promise to love you, to honor you and to carry you in my spirit until I draw my last breath.

I love you.

The room became at a standstill hearing Chrissy read her vows to Jax. Jax was barely able to keep a calm composure as he was caught up in her words, and the thrills they gave. And with tearful eyes she gently slid the simple gold band on Jax's finger.

They were then pronounced husband and wife. Minister Billings smiled while raising his voice to say: You may kiss your bride.

Jax then looked at his wife with a sigh of satisfaction and a heart of jubilation. She waited as he looked at her. She then smiled and he gently wrapped his arms around her and kissed her while the guests cheered.

Soon after, Minister Billings chimed in with his closing remarks followed a few last words that sent shivers through Chrissy and Jax:

"Ladies and gentlemen, I now present to you Dr. and Mrs. Wigginton"

More cheers followed while Jax hugged and kissed his bride. Soon after, they left to get back on the carriage that was waiting to take them around the beautiful landscapes. Following behind them were a few other carriages with family members who were part of the picture taking event.

Meanwhile back inside the Chateau de Mehr, the Maitre d, hostesses and escorts were anxiously waiting to meet and greet the rest of the family and guests as they entered through the banquet hall.

The venue dazzled; and it was a true reflection of Chrissy's eclectic and sophisticated taste. From the luminous crystal chandeliers, the ornate tapestry walls, the lighted carpet runners to the flickering tea lights, their eyes gleamed with enchantment as they followed behind their escorts to their designated tables.

The Master of Ceremony with microphone in hand, the pianist with twiddling fingers and the videographer, quickly positioned themselves as soon as they heard the bride and groom were about to enter.

Soon after Dr. and Mrs. Wigginton showed up and was greeted by a room full of cheering friends and family.

The Master of Ceremony graciously took control of the overzealous gathering; some of whom were still giggling about Mrs. Wigginton's naked derriere, while others pondered amongst themselves how she acquired her sizeable fortune.

Soon after, all heads were bowed in honor of the wedding prayer that was about to be recited by Minister Billings. That motion was followed by the introduction of family members who were mostly part of the wedding party.

Not only was the dinner menu extravagant; it was also scrumptiously decadent. From the finest caviar salads, red curry lamb, to the apple-beet cake with raspberry crème frosting, the guests were more than wowed with every bite they had.

Soon after, the Emcee took center stage again to announce it was time for the toasts. The bartenders and servers moved promptly with bringing out the best of the best bottles of wines for the occasion.

Wineglasses began clinking, toast after toast; and Jax and Chrissy never grew tired of kissing each other clink after clink.

Anyway with things going so well and quite frankly better than expected for Carolyn, she was behooved to make a toast which turned out to be more of a speech.

"Not only did I get my daughter back; she also gave me a son-in-law" Carolyn said, and crowd cheered after the commencement of her toast and some even laughed. Carolyn broke a faint smile, but it was obvious she wanted to continue with her toast, simply before she loses her train of thought.

"Jax, I can't thank you enough for going above and beyond, and obviously quite out of your way to stay in love with my daughter, over the years. I can't honestly say I remember how long it's been since you were first introduced to me, but I've never forgotten that special fondness about you and how it grew over the years.

"Chrissy, there's no doubt that long after this day, your beautiful wedding day, the love you've expressed in your vow will remain the standard by which you live. It's a great honor to be a part of such a monumental milestone in your life. But, as the woman of faith that you are, I know you will continue to put God first in your lives. I love you with all my heart. I wish you love, peace and joy always; congratulation!" Carolyn said.

As Carolyn walked away to get back to her seat the guests raised their glasses and applauded her. More toasts continued from other friends and family members as the evening began winding down with the cutting of the cake.

Soon after, Dr. and Mrs. Wigginton were asked to take center stage to perform their first dance as a couple.

"I'm so proud to be your husband; you've made me the happiest man alive" Jax whispered in Chrissy's ear as he tightened his embrace around her while they waltz.

"And you've made me the happiest woman alive; I love you more than I can say. But right now I'm just itching to get out of these clothes" Chrissy responded to her husband.

Jax got a kick out of his wife's response. He smiled at her and said: "Oh baby, I like the sound of that. Just hold on a little bit longer darling, and I'll take care of all that itching before the night is through"

Chrissy kept smiling at her husband as they continued dancing alone on the floor. However, the friction from the ill-fitting thong between her butts, kept her itching with every move.

Then the tone of the music switched and they were immediately joined by their guests crowding around them with dancing feet and smiles. And as they looked around and saw how beautifully things turned out, Jax turned to Chrissy and said:

"This is the best wedding I've ever attended, and luck would have it turned out to be ours."

So while Jax and Chrissy were having a good time, both Marlene and Frank were also out on the dance floor shaking their backsides to the music. However, Carolyn who loved to dance was not quite ready to start shaking-a-leg. And after watching every one going back and forth to the bar, she unwittingly went up and asked for a drink. The Maitre d showed her their best wine selection, but she was only interested in getting a drink of cognac. That being said, "Cognac" was one of her dead husband's favorite night caps.

The bartender, said to her:

"As you wish, Ma'am" and he poured the drink.

Carolyn looked at him and said:

"Oh dear, I think I'd like a little more, please."

"As you wish Ma'am" the bartender said with a smile while pouring.

Carolyn tasted the drink and handed it back to the bartender, and then she said:

"A little more ice please, and just a drop more of your ginger ale"

Carolyn looked around and reckoned the coast was clear since the others were on the dance floor. She quickly went back to her table and poured the liquor in her wine glass that was left sitting there empty.

She took a moment and stared at the liquor while thinking about Larry. And as if nothing really mattered since he's been gone, she threw caution to the wind and said:

"This one is for you, my love; it won't be long before we're together again. Cheers."

She slowly picked up the drink and took a few big sips. She replaced the glass and sighed deeply while her shoulders dropped in relaxation.

Carolyn felt joyful in the moment. Quite frankly, she hadn't given any thought about the "PAA" and the ramifications if she were to be caught drinking in public. To her defense, however, sometimes she's not cognizant of her role as, president of the prestigious organization.

With that said, she perceived her actions as being a glorious time of her life. Soon after, Marlene and Frank returned to their table to take a rest.

"Oh, Aunt Carolyn, I can see you haven't finished your champagne" Marlene said to her.

"I know dear, but don't worry, I get to it. The night is still young."

Frank chuckled at Carolyn's response and he wondered if she was all there. He then leaned over the Marlene and said:

"I don't think you should encourage her to drink anymore of that wine; she already sounds a bit off to me."

"Her glass is barely half, Frank. She seems fine to me. Come on, let's get back out there and dance some more." Marlene said to her husband.

Carolyn welcomed the idea of being left undisturbed. She began shaking her head from side to side as her way of enjoying the music while she drank.

As the party continued rocking, Brandon looked over and saw that his mother was sitting alone at her table. He went over to check upon her and realized that she was not quite her old self.

"Mom, are you okay, you look a little tired."

"What makes you think that son? How can I be tired when I'm not working? I'm just sitting here having a good time"

Brandon was surprised by his mother's slurred speech and droopy eyes.

"Mom, Mom, what's the matter with you, I can see that you're not feeling well." Brandon said.

"Don't be silly, son; I couldn't be feeling any better. Get back over there and dance some more; your mother will be just fine." Carolyn said.

Brandon was left at a loss for words, because he was certain of his mother's stance against drinking. Quite frankly he was right about his conviction, but without giving it a second thought, his mother ended up breaking her own rule.

"Never mind, Mother, I'll get back to dancing later; I'm more concerned about the way you're acting. Have you been drinking?"

"Who…. Me! What a foolish thing to say. You, know how I feel about that." Carolyn quipped.

Brandon turned and looked at the half empty wine glass on table and he picked it up and took a whiff. He immediately realized his mother had drunk something much, much stronger than wine.

"Mom, you've been drinking, haven't you?"

"Son, I don't like your tone; I wish if you would just let me be. I'm feeling a little tired and all I'm endeavoring to do is relax." Carolyn said.

"Okay, you've said enough. I don't know what came over you, Mom." but it's time for you to get out of here before things get worse." Brandon said.

He looked around to see if anyone was looking in their direction. But after taking a quick scan around the room, he assumed everyone was too busy dancing and having a good time to notice anything different about his mother. He quickly picked up his mother's purse from off the table, and he gently straightened her scarf around her shoulders and straightened her hat while she sat stoically through his hovering. By then her head bopped, and her half-opened eyes finally closed.

Again, Brandon looked around before trying to shake his mother.

"Mom, Mom, wake up; we're ready to leave." Brandon said anxiously.

She slowly opened one eye and tried raising her head. Brandon shook her a little harder while saying: "Come on mother; it's time to take you home"

Finally, Carolyn showed signs of cooperation.

"I think you're right son; I do feel a little exhausted" Carolyn said without realizing that she was inebriated.   However, she tried getting out of the chair with the help of her son, but she was too wobbly to stand on her own.

By then Simon was on his way to the bar to get another drink when he noticed his brother trying to help their mother out of her chair. His eyebrows rose from the unexpected view as he walked over towards them.

"What's up; is Mom okay" Simon asked Brandon.

"Not really…I don't know what got into her, but she's drunk" Brandon said.

Simon was not expecting that kind of response from Brandon….and far from it.

"What are you talking about; Mom doesn't drink. Maybe something else is going on with her Brandon. You know that is something mom would never do" Simon said.

"I know what you mean, but not tonight, bro; I, think I'm right about this. Let's not spend too much time talking about it here. We need to get her out of here before anyone else sees her like this. Can you imagine the fiasco this would bring to our lives if one of those photographers got a snap of this?   And, the negative effect it would have on the "Foundation?" Brandon replied.

Of course, the foundation Brandon was referring to, "People against Alcoholism" was created after Simon's mother, Sue, was killed by a drunk driver. They have thousands of members and are well respected for their contribution in the area. And through her work and dedication to helping victims of alcoholism, she has made millions of dollars from supporters near and far.

Simon feverishly picked up the glass of cognac off the table and returned it to the bar.

He then returned to Brandon and said:

"Come on Bro; let's get the hell out of here. You, sit next to Mom and try to make things looking normal, while I go outside and get Lennox to bring the limo around.

Marlene and Frank turned up at their table just in time to see Brandon holding on to his mother.

"What's the matter with Aunt Carolyn, and why are you holding on to her as if she's not feeling well?" Marlene questioned Brandon.

"I think she's had too much to eat; mom tends to forget she has sensitive a stomach. I really think she got carried away eating something spicy. But how could you blame her when everything was so good."

Don't worry Sis; Mom will be just fine.

"I couldn't agree with you more, Brandon. But as you know, she sat next to me; and all she had was a little bit of the duck a l'orange with some pumpkin bread" Marlene said.

"Trust me, Marlene, Mom will be just fine. Simon left to get Lennox to bring the limo around so I can get her home to sleep it off." Brandon said.

"I think it's more like she had too much to drink" Frank said under his breath.

Marlene went over and took Carolyn's hand and said: "Aunt Carolyn, how do you feel; would you like some hot tea"

"Oh no, Sweetie; I'm so full, I couldn't take a message." Carolyn said with a raspy voice.

Soon after, Simon came back and told Brandon their limo was waiting at the front door. So while Simon stayed back with his wife Leigh, Brandon and his mother left the function without drawing any further attention to their little mishap.

Frank stayed back while Marlene walked with Brandon and Carolyn to see them off in their limo. And as they walked away; Frank smiled to himself and said:

"There goes Miss Cassie; as drunk as a skunk."

CHAPTER THIRTY TWO

By the next morning, news about Dr. and Mrs. Wigginton's wedding made front page in the Sunday Newspaper. But by then they and their children were boarding the "Queen Mary" on a three week European cruise.

Thankfully Brandon and Simon were relieved their lives as it were, remained uninterrupted by their mother's lack of judgment.

However, the well-respected and beloved Dr. Wigginton, took most the hospital staff by a huge surprise after learning about his high profile wedding. The shock of the news left many of his staff digging around for information about this woman called Gabriella and how she was able to catch the good doctor.

While at sea, Jax and his family tightened their bond both as doting parents and grateful children of a life neither could have ever imagined. The unusual honeymoon arrangement was even more memorable having their children share in their joy of marriage.

Upon their return, Jax wasted no time in seeking out architects, building contractors and designers to start renovation on the house at Bluefield Heights.

The unexpected challenges during the planning stage at Bluefield Heights, kept Jax and Chrissy hard at work in trying to determine what was best for their new home. However, after much deliberation, they both agreed it was best to demolish the great old house and make a fresh start.

Except for the cashew apple tree and a few of the old oaks, nothing was left behind to identify with the past.

In less than a year, their newly constructed mansion was complete and Jax and his family couldn't be excited about moving in.

The established neighborhood of very large estate homes had not seen anything to the likes of Jax's and Chrissy's new home. The stately mansion...though true to its name, is the kind of home where family and friends could come feel right at home. From the tiniest detail inside every room to the meandering garden paths on the outside, nothing went overlooked in terms of perfection.

For Chrissy, life in her new home brought perfect peace from being able to giving her children the truth they deserved and liberating herself from years of being imprisoned as Gabriella.

In terms of her relationship with her husband, she never thought that thing called "love" could ever find her heart again. But when she least expected it, her heart was able to find love and brought it back to her. From the love of her children, her husband and everyone in her family, she'd found love; and it was love made well.

A few years later, Jax retired from his practice to enjoy every minute of his beautiful life with his beautiful wife and kids.

Chrissy sold Chateau de Mehr for an undisclosed amount of millions.

Christian and Christopher went off to college; the likes of which has kept their sister Chateau pining over them.

However, to help with her painful void, her parents surprised her with two dogs instead of one. And her life was twice as nice having her pets to keep her company, and for being her parents pride and joy.

The Tates, the Wiggintons and the Roulettes all turned out to be one big happy family. And their lives together created a love, made well.

Muah!

BACK MATTER/BLURB

Barchas' best friend and colleague, Frank Roulette, had just poured his morning coffee and stepped outside his front doors to pick up the morning paper.

Words, could not describe the looks on his face when the saw the headline on the front page of the newspaper.

He took another sip of the coffee and hurried towards the den where his collection of cigars was stored. His hands shook while he anxiously poked one in his mouth and tried lighting it up. He then sat down and sucked deeply on the cigar as if he needed that fix to help him with digesting the news about Barchas and Marlene.